MW01230342

A KNIGHT'S JOURNEY!

by

Dean O'Quinn

DORRANCE
PUBLISHING CO
EST. 1920
PITTSBURGH, PENNSYLVANIA 15238

The contents of this work, including, but not limited to, the accuracy of events, people, and places depicted; opinions expressed; permission to use previously published materials included; and any advice given or actions advocated are solely the responsibility of the author, who assumes all liability for said work and indemnifies the publisher against any claims stemming from publication of the work.

Dorrance Publishing Co
585 Alpha Drive
Suite 103
Pittsburgh, PA 15238
Visit our website at www.dorrancebookstore.com

ISBN: 979-8-88729-154-3
eISBN: 979-8-88729-654-8

DEDICATIONS AND HONORS OF PEOPLE BEHIND THE STORY:

This book is dedicated to the many people who have post-traumatic stress disorder (PTSD), panic attacks, mental disorders, head and brain injuries, Dementia and Alzheimer's Diseases. This is also dedicated to the families of the loved ones that these horrible disorders affect as they are hugely impacted as well. My mother and father both recently passed away from dementia. I miss them very much and think proudly of them every day. My mother did not know her father as he was killed seventeen days before she was born, and she did not know anything about her mother's side of the family either. I did extensive research into this side of our family history, and it is because of her rich heritage and the stories involved in her family history that I developed some of the historical characters in this story. This novel is dedicated to my Mother & Father and the families that they came from. I also want this novel to be dedicated to my good friends Ryan Pachek and Max McGrann. This is also dedicated with all my heart to the very kind nurses, physical therapists, occupational therapists and vocal therapists who helped me to be able to walk and to have a voice again.

I wrote this novel while being under the care of all these wonderful people. I had several different injuries that I was recovering from and without these individuals to assist me, I could never have accomplished writing a novel. I spent one year in a nursing home/recovery center and one year in hospital and therapists' waiting rooms. I wrote two novels during this time period and showed the progress in my health through my writing. I had lost my voice and my walking ability, and these angels let me find them again. I started to write as a form of escapism and started my own therapy to keep my mind sharp and strengthen a surgically replaced shoulder. I truly believe writing saved my life during this period.

As I mentioned, this is the second novel that I wrote. My first novel is titled "The Soldiers Who Ate Rattlesnakes". It shows the beginning of my journey of using writing as a form of therapy and shows the progression of my abilities from the start of my injuries. I am the first to admit that it was not written perfectly and shows the many errors that I created in trying to become healthier and stronger. However, I fell in love with the characters and the story that I created. I didn't write it to become a successful author, I wrote it to improve my health. I am very proud what I created and overcame to make this a possibility. I am going to release a "revised issue" of this first novel to make it more reader friendly and have it become a more professional product. However, the therapy version of the novel is going to be printed in a limited edition and will mainly be available in a limited supply. This book is the second story that I created during this time. This novel once again shows how much stronger my writing ability has become and I am once again incredibly proud of that fact.

I want others to feel that way, so this is now becoming a therapy program that I am creating called "The Write Therapy". I can attest that this program works in overcoming PTSD, mental problems, and anxiety issues, skull fractures and head injuries. If I can accomplish this, anyone can as well. I am still dealing with these issues, but I find writing as a way of fighting through issues and never giving up. This is my own story. Create your own and find inspiration and confidence in doing so. Always keep fighting to get better.

Prologue

If a person has never had a panic attack themselves, then that person will have no idea what one of these horrible attacks feels like. As I have found, these people should not give their opinions or act as if they have any knowledge on the issue. A person can read extensively on the issue and can listen to other people's experiences on the problem, but they can never truly understand the thoughts and the feelings that go through a person's mind and body. An average person may have a panic attack once or twice in their entire lifetime.

Now, imagine having those same feelings and thoughts every day of the week while having the fight of your life on your hands in order to get through them. The best way that I have found to describe the feelings associated with PTSD and panic disorders is to imagine a person standing on the peak of a snowy mountain. That person then rolls a snowball down the side of the mountain. As the snowball gains speed, it grows bigger and bigger as it descends the glacial peak. This is how the thoughts of a victim of these horrible mental diseases behave.

Any negative thought at all starts as a small snowflake and ends up growing into a huge, worrisome avalanche of a problem for the person that is being inflicted. Eventually, the snowball, as well as the fear and panic associated with it, are now getting out of control.

These "out of control" feelings are both severely difficult in order to stop or even slow down at this time, and many times an ambulance has got to be called. These people often think that they are having a heart attack or massive stroke. These are the thoughts that the victims of these mental disorders fear the most.

This is what it is like to live a life with PTSD (Post Traumatic Stress Disorder) and panic disorder. In my opinion, it is time that a truly brave literary hero emerges that has these intense issues. The people with these disorders are all truly honorable and strong, but they just don't feel that way.

The problem used to be called shell shock or battle fatigue in the military, but the time and mentality of the problems have changed since then. A good historical example of the problem is that of General George S. Patton during World War II.

General Patton was visiting troops in the field hospital tents of Sicily, and there was one soldier that could only cry. He could not salute the general, stand up, or even speak to General Patton. He could only sit there and cry. Now, the General nor the doctors did not know what was causing these mental disorders as it was in the 1940s. They only knew that it occurred to a person after several series of battles or even one bout of intense fighting.

Now this was extremely upsetting for General Patton, as he didn't understand the problem and only saw cowardice from the man. Many have heard of this story happening once, but truthfully, it happened twice, within a week's timeframe. He was so angry, that he slapped each man with his glove in order to make them respect his authority and show the bravery of the other soldiers. However, each man was so mentally damaged by the carnage that surrounded them that they could not even explain the problem to the General or to any of their doctors.

Patton was reprimanded by future President, Dwight D. Eisenhower, and he was pulled out of the command of his troops. The General was aghast that he would lose his command over these actions, and he tried to temper the situation by putting out an apology. To the General's credit, this apology was not ordered by any of his superior officers, and it was his own idea. He apologized to not only the two men that he had slapped, but also to the entire American regiment for how he had acted.

Even after an apology, Patton was still left in the dark by his commanding officers, and he was still relieved of his command for a short amount of time. This action befuddled and infuriated him.

However, this was a shrewd act of using him as a decoy by General Eisenhower, as he misled the German Army into thinking that Patton was in England, getting ready for the D-Day invasion. In all actuality, he was being left to wait where he was and would be used in order to attack the Nazi Army from the south.

At this point, Patton then got his command back, and thank God for that, because his troops marched through the countries of Europe with his tanks, like they were melting butter. This allowed the Allied Army to win the war against the Nazis with the help of their large grit and tenacity.

Tenacity, now that is a good word in order to describe the feelings that a person with PTSD and panic disorder goes through. It is a word of fortitude and strength that many people with these mental problems possess.

A person does not need to have been in the military in order to be affected by these mental issues. A person has only had to go through a very traumatic experience that lingers in one's mind. This includes having an accidental brain injury or having too many concussions in their past.

If a person were in the military, had a brain injury, and had also suffered several concussions, then that person would have received the PTSD Trifecta and probably possess most of these mental issues. Where mental health is concerned, the inner strength of tenacity is the only and best word that is important and most needed in these individuals.

By no means does having PTSD or panic disorder make a person weak. In all actuality, it is quite the opposite, as each person has got to struggle with these thoughts in order to overcome them. Remember, bravery doesn't just happen in nature or with a certain person, particularly. Bravery occurs when a person is fearful and they act, IN SPITE OF, the fear that happens during a certain situation.

A person does this in order to move forward and become more confident and stronger. That is why I believe that it is time to be represented by a hero that has had to deal with these anxiety and mental problems. People with these issues and these problems should no longer be kept in the dark.

Trauma is the other terrible thing that a person with PTSD carries. A person feels very alone with the tentacles of panic that are reaching out from the darkness and trying to hold them down.

Even family, God bless them, pretend that they understand the problems, but they will never truly understand how horrible these mental disorders are. They even seem to make such problems worse, by exacerbating and trying to control the issues and the person themselves. They will never know what it's like to want to be hugged and left alone at the same time.

Here are some things that people without these problems should know about people with PTSD or anxiety issues:

1) People with PTSD are very good workers. A person has got to be a good worker for things to run as smoothly as possible and they have a vast amount of confidence and pride in their workplace. They thrive on good friendships and being liked by others but find it hard to discover them or those qualities.

2) People with PTSD are never late. A person that is suffering from these issues may not make friends easily in the workplace and may be focused on their work, but they won't be late in doing so.

3) People with PTSD will hardly ever lie. Mainly because a lie will always come back and bite a person in the butt. If a person suffering with these mental issues lies, they will worry about any little fib until their stomachs are full of ulcers and they usually feel like they are continually going to get sick. They will only try to work harder in order to cause more pleasure in their own performance.

4) People with PTSD are great lovers. Please read rule number three as an example.

5) Finally, people with PTSD have great senses of humor...they are just fearful of telling certain jokes, and jokes are what we all need right

now. This would probably be the most help to anyone suffering from these anxiety issues. Laughter truly is the best medicine.

Seriously, a person can have the strength of a tiger, but feel like a kitten when it comes to something as simple as even leaving the house. A person with these mental issues is incredibly strong just to roll out of bed and face a non-understanding society each day.

This takes a Herculean effort at times, and I salute such people, as they do not know the strength that they have and the confidence that they exude. There is one more thing that a person must know about people with PTSD. Never misjudge their constant path of redemption and their need to try to do what is right in this world and beyond.

"Nothing worth having,
Didn't come without some kind of fight.
You have to kick at the darkness,
Till it bleeds daylight."
(The Barenaked Ladies)

Chapter One

Just because you quit watching cartoons doesn't make you a grownup.

The attacks were getting worse. Ryan Maxwell was in his easy chair, which felt eerily un-easy at that moment. He slumped backward in the chair, and then he lurched forward, while wishing that his heart would beat at a slower pace. His heart was racing faster than Michael Phelps during a gold medal swimming match in the Olympics. He moved forward onto the edge of his seat while lowering his head, still not getting enough air into his lungs.

He felt as if he was going to fall forward, which would cause a nice looking rugburn to appear on his nose. This caused him to rise to his feet and start to pace the tan carpeted floor. He was afraid of walking as well, because his blood pressure felt so high that his body could blow his head right off his shoulders.

Maybe, just maybe, he was suffering from a heart attack, or even a massive stroke. "Oh, lordy...lordy...lordy!" his mind raced.

However, movement was the only thing that made him feel even slightly better. He had to calm his emotions and exercise. Even if it was just to walk off this unwanted energy and clear his mind from any medical emergencies that may be happening.

Ryan was taller than most men at about 6'2" in height and he was broadly built with light brown hair that was cut short in a business-like fashion. However, he usually covered up his nice head of hair with a baseball cap or a floppy cowboy hat.

He had a bright and inviting smile that he often wore in public, although he didn't feel like smiling most of the time. Several people only saw a tall, broad-shouldered man who had no visual issues. However, underneath this friendly exterior was a person that had a large amount of anxiety and was in a huge amount of emotional pain.

This intensity showed through at times and intimidated some people. However, he was an extremely loving and compassionate man who would give you the shirt off his own back if you truly needed it.

He had inquisitive blue eyes that never tended to rest, as if they were always searching for any hidden dangers or any friendly person in order to share a good word with. On most days, he had a close-shaven jawline and would absent-mindedly clench and grind his teeth if he were in deep thought. Most of the time, though, he was smiling a mischievous grin, as if he was always looking at the world in a funny way or was thinking of an inside joke.

Ryan tried to never be a mean or rude person, unless someone took advantage of him and pissed him off, that is. He tended to be a very protective and pragmatic person when it came to the people that he cared about. When he was happy, he wore his heart on his sleeve and would always try to do anything for others.

However, when he was unhappy and in the grip of anxiety issues, he found solace in self-medication with alcohol. Drinking tended to take away his anxieties and would give him courage and self-confidence in whatever situation life threw at him. That may be a good solution in the short term. However, when alcohol takes control of a person's actions, it truly becomes a liability.

The biggest weakness that had affected him in his 35 years of life had been panic attacks and PTSD. Even though he suffered with panic disorder, Ryan was not one to be messed with. Mainly because, if a fight or flight scenario happened within his surroundings, Ryan would always choose to fight in that situation. He had a strong moral compass and prided himself on always trying to do the right thing.

Suddenly, his pulse seemed to slow at the touch of the warm tongue upon the back of his hand. This was followed by the worried whine that came from his best animal friend, his loving dog Allie.

He reached down and scratched the warm, thick fur that was between her ears, and he asked her, "Do you want to go for a walk with me, girl?"

He was met with only a more severe tongue lashing against the skin of his hand, as well as her bright eyes smiling up at him. She was so excited by this notion that a mild breeze was caused by the exuberant wagging of her tail.

The air outside had a bitterness that cracked across the unshaved whiskers on his chin that morning. As soon as he felt the chilling wind on his face, his pulse started to retreat slowly back to a normal range. As he and Allie began to walk, Ryan breathed in heartily through his nose and breathed out heavily through his mouth. This was a relaxing form of breathing that was supposed to slow the beating of his heart.

"A little bit softer now... A little bit softer now," Ryan thought to himself, which made him grin as this was a little trick for him to slow the super hyped-up messaging in his brain. He could imagine that great scene of singing and dancing from the movie "Animal House."

He still felt as if he could trip on Allie's leash, as he was still uneasy and unbalanced, as if the world was still spinning out of control. He grimaced at the memory of tripping on Allie's leash once before and faceplanting onto the cold, wet ground. Not one of his finer moments, that was for sure, but nothing stops a panic attack faster than the sudden pain caused by a swollen, bloody nose.

On this brisk day, it was just early spring in Montana, and by early spring, I mean the last week in April. The year that this cool spring day occurred was 2005. Ryan had moved away from his small hometown to take over the world. However, the world had beaten him so far. He had recently moved back to the small town that he had grown up in after almost losing everything. This was the kind of place where Ryan could call everyone in town a friend and a neighbor. It was a great place to be living, but how did he possibly get to this point?

Ryan breathed in the cool spring air and said out loud to nobody in particular, "The seasons get later each season, I swear."

In the month of April, Montana could be sunny and 70 degrees one day, and the next day could bring you six inches of snow and freezing weather. At dawn on this very day, the weather had started mostly sunny but had become intensely cloudy, and it was a coldish 50 degrees outside.

Thank God for Allie, though, who pulled briskly on the leash, hoping to explore a new hole that had appeared on the lawn. She was what Ryan's grandfather had jokingly called a 'Heinz 57 dog', as she had a little bit of every dog breed thrown into her, plus a little bit of coyote. She was a mixture of Golden Lab, Golden Retriever, and Springer Spaniel breeds of dog. To Ryan though, she was just a blond-haired, loving, partner in crime, that would always protect and love him.

When Ryan first met Allie, she was a cowering, sad-eyed ball of blond fur. It was an afternoon a lot like this one, except during that time of year, it was the chill of fall that blew across the countryside. Ryan and his friends had met up at the only bar in town, Mike's Bar and Grill, after watching their team lose in the local high school football game.

A smile trickled across Ryan's face with the thoughts of playfully spending time with his friends, drinking some beers, and enjoying a day filled with sports. Ryan truly loved the fun-filled company and sometimes hilariously filthy conversations that only four young men could share.

Mike's Bar was just like any other drinking establishment in small towns across America. Upon entering through the splintered wooden door, there was an older looking wooden bar that stood off to the right side of the room. On the top of the stained, wooden bar itself, there were knife marks where past bar patrons had tried to carve their initials into the wood. Behind the bar, a large mirror was built into the wall and allowed customers to stare at their own reflections.

There were 24 barstools facing the bar itself, but only 16 had four legs that were long enough and went all the way to the floor. Those barstools were called the Bucking Broncos of Mike's Bar because many a sorry ass was thrown out of one of those wobbly seats during the night.

Behind the barstools stood the large, scarred pool table, as well as a jukebox that was blasting out country and rock music. Next to that, there was a scattering of four small tables where pool players sat, as well as the rowdier crowd that tended to mingle around the loud music. Many overserved customers tried to dance along with the songs coming from the crackling sound of the overused speakers.

On that day, those tables were occupied by the 'proper and more upstanding couples' of the community. They had stopped in after the football game in order to have a quick pint of beer or a glass of cheap wine. Plus, they were there to overhear the latest local town gossip and to proudly talk about how their child had played in the football game.

Also on that day, Ryan and three of his best friends were sitting at the last table, which was located by the lone pool table. They were about to start a friendly game of eight-ball that included two of the friends on each team.

First, there was Tommy, who thought of himself as the great jester of the group as he danced around like he had a live trout in his underwear. He liked to throw around jokes as if he were a person throwing a pair of dice in Vegas. Bar jokes, that is. These jokes aren't very funny, but you laugh at them anyway, just to make him happy. He was also his own best audience and laughed loudly and boisterously at much of his own sense of humor.

Then there was Lenny, who was smoothly leaning on the bar while hitting on the waitress and absently throwing Trail Mix into his mouth. He was a well-groomed, skinnier man who liked to think that he was the smooth operator of the group, but in all actuality, he just tried a lot more often. He just didn't count the times that he was shot down by different women and retreated in a ball of flames.

Lastly, standing at the pool table was Monty Alberton. He and Ryan looked very much like each other. They were the same height and had the same color eyes and hair. Many people thought that they were at least cousins, but they were not even related. The biggest difference between the two men was that Monty was two years older than Ryan and had a brown goatee on his chin.

He was also Ryan's best friend, as they had become inseparable ever since they were younger and were able to go on adventures on off-road motorcycles during the summer months and skiing and snowmobiling in the mountains during the cold of winter.

Monty was now bending down and staring at the racked triangle of pool balls in front of him. A mighty cracking sound was emitted from the pool table as the white cue ball was driven hard into the tightly packed group of colored balls. This caused the solid blue 2-ball to fly into the far-left corner pocket. The rest of the balls were scattered around the top of the pool table.

Monty chalked his pool cue, eyeing all his available shots, and he then leaned over the felt covering of the pool table. He did this with a newly lit cigarette hanging from his lower lip like a bat that was grasping at rocks on the roof of a cave. He inhaled on the cigarette, just as he struck the cue ball, and let out the smoke when the four-ball seemed to hang in mid-air, and then it suddenly dropped into the side pocket.

Ryan simply stated, "Nice shot, bud!"

He was sitting at the barroom table and absently fidgeting with the chalk and his own cue stick. His boot-laden foot was absentmindedly tapping along with the beat of the song on the jukebox.

"Yeah, thanks." Monty said, while walking around the end of the pool table.

He blew out more smoke as he continued to say, "I drew first blood, so which partner should I choose? Both these guys are distracted, but I'll take Tommy as a partner. He can make some good shots, if you can hold the pecker down long enough in order to shoot the damn ball."

He took another drag off the cigarette, and then stated, "Fucking, squirely, bastard." He then grinned at Ryan and let some more smoke blow out from between his smiling teeth.

"Hey, Len...You and I are partners, man." Ryan yelled over the jukebox, which was blasting out "Living on a Prayer" by Bon Jovi.

"Quit trying to get a date over there. Come over here and get one of your heads into this game."

"Grab me a beer, too," said Monty, without lifting his head.

His eyes were barely visible above the green felt of the pool table and the smoke that was coming from his mouth. The cigarette was more blackened ash than white paper now, but it was still hanging from his lips.

"Me too, brother," said Ryan, checking the contents of the can of beer and noticing that it was indeed only filled with the last remnants of warm beer and with his own backwash.

This caused Ryan to then yell at Lenny again, "Make mine a bottle this time, though."

He didn't have to add that he wanted to see through the bottle and see how much content was left for him to drink.

The six-ball then hit against the short wall, next to the corner pocket, and drifted slowly out from the short wall, hitting the eight-ball in the middle of the table. This left the cue ball next to the bumper edge of the table.

"What the hell am I supposed to do with that?" Ryan exclaimed.

He was chalking up his cue and walking toward the far end of the pool table, which was next to the front door of the bar. Monty only raised his shoulders and gave Ryan a sly grin.

Ryan looked down at the cue ball lying against the side wall of the pool table and said, "Damn, Monty. You left me nothing to shoot at here. This is just going to be a poke and hope at the nine-ball in the side pocket."

Ryan spun the cue in his right hand, lined up his shot, pulled the cue back, and KA-BANG. Suddenly, the outside door of the bar flew inward, and Ryan was almost knocked down onto the floor as the front door slammed into the back of the cue, causing it to be thrown into the array of pool balls on the table. Along with hitting the cue, the door hit Ryan on the right hip and knee, which caused pain to streak down his right leg.

"Holy Shit!" He blurted out loudly. "What the hell, man."

However, when Ryan turned in pain and anger, there wasn't a man standing there at all; it was Carol Beeman.

A cold gust of wind blew into the bar along with Carol as she stomped across the hard wood floor, scowling around the corner of the door at the angry Ryan.

However, it was Tommy who broke the awkward silence when he looked at her with his mouth agape and said, "I don't remember a freezing wind at the football game, but there is a strong one blowing in now."

Carol stood just 5'3" tall and weighed probably 200 lbs. The nickname that had been given to her when she was younger was "Mailbox," as she was built like one of those blue postal boxes that one sees on the side of the street or in front of a grocery store.

Carol was from the rival town that had just beaten the local high school football team, and most people steered clear of her. She didn't intimidate most people because of any physical attributes, but because she was always in a foul mood. As well as always being rude, crude, and outright mean to other individuals.

Carol glared at Tommy and spat out, "Get out of my way, cheese dick. I need a shot of whiskey."

"Shut up, Mailbox, I hope you...." Tommy stopped in mid-sentence when Carol turned on him and gave him an evil-filled stink-eye that would make the hair on a boar's back rise in fear.

He then continued to say cautiously, "I hope that you have a nice evening here at Mike's Bar."

With these words, Tommy practically ran to the other side of the pool table, hiding behind Monty's protection.

"You hit me with the door, Carol." Ryan said angrily, while testing out the muscles and joints of his right knee and calf. "You damn near knocked me to my knees."

"Well, that's one way to get you there, I guess." She let out a loud cackle and she walked to the far end of the bar, where she ordered a shot of whiskey, and a glass of draft beer. The people sitting at the bar soon moved and gave Carol a wide berth.

Ryan shook like he was extremely cold and then jokingly said to Monty, "I would sue the pants off that woman, but nobody needs to see that."

Monty joked back at Ryan when he said, "What do you expect? She has a face that could stop a thunderstorm."

This statement caused a bout of chuckles between the two friends as they tried to assemble their pool game again.

Carol was the kind of woman that Ryan liked to call 'a bar girl'. She was in her mid-50s, had brown hair that was cut short in the front, and the back of her hair hung down to her shoulders in a Billy Ray Cyrus style mullet. She also had a smooshed-up face, as if a frustrated artist tried to form it out of a block of clay each morning. Of course, she never wore any make-up or even tried to make herself more attractive in any way.

On any given day, she could honestly drink the biggest cowboy under the table. She could then cuss out the local football coach and make him blush… and then she could shovel the shit out of an old barn afterwards. Ryan always stood an arm's length away from her as with his height, and her lack of it, she could change his future family situation with one aggressive punch.

Lenny then came over to the pool table and stated, "I have Michelle bringing your beers over. She loves me! You know, she always begs me not to leave in the mornings."

Monty replied to him, "I don't see how you could leave in the morning, Lenny. Not if you are still tied to her headboard. Be careful, Len; I heard that she can be kind of wild in bed at times." Monty then winked at a grinning Ryan.

The bar went eerily quiet as the jukebox was switching in between songs at that very moment. Lenny ended up shouting, two decibels too loudly, "Nah! Michelle is not wild enough for me; she's too clean for my filth."

'Tequila Sunrise' from the Eagles then started blasting out of the speakers of the jukebox, but not before everyone at the bar had turned around to look at Len. This included a very upset Michelle. The rest of the group of friends broke out into a roar of laughter directed toward Lenny, their newly embarrassed friend.

"It looks like we won't be getting our beers anytime soon," Ryan said while waving to Michelle and trying to stifle a chuckle.

"It's your turn to take a shot, you horny bastard." Monty yelled at Len while trying to hold back a laugh as well.

Lennie walked toward the pool table with the cue in hand, and then he quickly knocked the cue ball completely off the table without it ever hitting another ball.

This caused Ryan to raise one eyebrow at him and ask in an amused but stern voice. "What the hell was that?"

Ryan shook his head, and then he witnessed Tommy racing into the back room and said frustratingly, "Tommy just ran into the bathroom, and I think that this could take a while. I think Carol scared the shit out of him."

Ryan then tossed the pool cue onto the pool table, and he said to Monty, "Let's quit; your partner is all over the place, and my partner couldn't hit a pool ball with a shotgun blast."

Monty said with a frown, "I agree. Let's grab that table behind us and just sit down and relax."

Then he, Ryan, and a blushing Lenny all headed to the table that was the farthest away from the loud music of the jukebox. Monty ended up flipping his chair backwards and sitting on the seat cushion with his arms casually crossed on the back of his chair.

Besides Carol, sitting at the bar were some of the usual local customers including Stubs Smith, who got his nickname from loading a semi full of wheat and cutting off two fingers in the process.

He ended up finishing the job of loading the truck, and then he finally drove himself to the doctor's office, where his hand was bandaged up. Unfortunately, they never did find those two fingers or find out where they were shipped out to.

Sitting next to Stubs was an old cowboy named Frank, who had never met a whiskey he didn't like. Finally, sitting at the end of the bar was a stranger that none of them had ever seen before.

This man was dressed as most people do around the small towns in Montana, anyway. He wore a blue baseball cap on his head, a brown button-down work shirt, blue jeans, and dirty, brown boots on his feet. He also had a very desperate and depressing attitude coming off him, as he wore a scowl on a scraggly-haired, bearded face.

In New York City or Los Angeles, he would stand out like a sore thumb. But not in Montana, as agriculture was the largest commodity in the state. He tended to blend in with the rest of the environment that surrounded him. He ended up chugging the last gulps of his pint of beer, stood up without saying a word, and then left the bar, as if he were deep in thought.

Michelle finally brought the beers to the table, and she gave Len a much-needed dirty look.

"Spank me, honey," Len said cheekily. "I've been bad."

Len was trying way too hard to be charming, which caused Michelle to stick her tongue out at him, and then she flipped him off by rubbing her eye with her middle finger. Ryan laughed at this and was rewarded by a sly smile from Michelle.

"Don't be too hard on her," Ryan said. "She's a nice girl."

Not stating that he had been seeing Michelle for the last couple of months, which proved to Ryan that his friend Lenny was talking out of his own ass about his love life.

"That is for a girl that you find in a bar, anyway," Monty said with a shrewd grin and a joking wink directed toward Ryan.

Monty was the only person who knew about his love affair with Michelle, and Ryan liked to keep it that way. For one thing, she made much more money from tips if men thought that she was single. Secondly, Ryan was never a person to make any announcements about his love life or try to control someone.

"Where else do you find women, then?" asked Lenny.

This statement was met with a rolling of the eyes and some dubious looks at the jukebox as it went quiet in between songs again. Soon, Stevie Ray Vaughn was telling all of them what to do if his "House was a rockin'!"

This choice of song drew smiles from the men at the table. That is one thing that everyone had to be aware of about a bar jukebox: you never knew what kind of song would come out of the speakers next.

That is when the stranger walked back into the bar, and this time, he was not alone. He was tugging at a faded, red-covered leash that held a skinny, scared blond pup on the other end of it. The door didn't slam shut right away, and it almost hung open while he stood there, blocking the fading outdoor light and letting the cold air rush in. The stranger almost dragged the poor blond pup into the bar, and then he only gave one statement.

"None of you know me." He drew the little dog closer to his heel, and then he continued, "I've been working at the Foothill Ranch for the last couple of months of summer, and I got a new job down in the Lewistown area."

He nervously took off his baseball cap, showing a messy brown head of hair, and then he continued to say, "I can't take this pup with me."

He motioned to the small dog, who sat there silently, looking across the room at Ryan with her head lowered and her big eyes shining at him.

The guy finally finished his story by saying, "I'm gonna take her out and shoot her if none of you want her."

Two seconds may have passed by, and immediately Ryan didn't use any other time to even think about this decision, and he yelled out, "I'll take her!"

"What the hell are you doing? We don't know him or his dog. She could be sick." Monty said, almost falling out of his chair.

Ryan ignored him and simply said over the music on the jukebox, "What is her name?"

"Alice," the guy answered back to him, and then he dropped the leash on the floor of the bar. The man spun on his heels, and he left the bar as quickly as he had entered it. Only this time, he had left Ryan with this loving, sweet dog.

Ryan called the dog over, who walked across the length of the bar with her head down and her eyes held low. She walked slowly, with her red leash dragging behind her. Everyone in the bar watched her walk over to her new owner without saying a word. Ryan checked her for any cuts or sores, and then he scratched her fluffy head. She almost smiled up at Ryan, with her tongue lolling out of her mouth thirstily and her large brown eyes glistening up at him.

Ryan looked at her and said sarcastically, "So, Alice is what you answer to. Oh boy, that name really rolls right off the tongue, doesn't it? I have to admit, that truly is an awful name for a dog."

"If I remember right, didn't you date a girl named Alice?" asked Lenny, laughing at the name of the dog.

"Yeah, that girl was kind of loopy, and that name is definitely not good enough for any dog of mine, that is for sure," laughed Ryan.

"How 'bout Allie?" Monty said without laughing.

"Allie it is, then." Ryan said with a grin.

Allie seemed to know that she had gotten a new name, and she stood up in order to lick Ryan's face. After she was done with Ryan, she went over to Monty's face and started licking it, as if thanking him for the better name.

Ryan looked at the two of them and jokingly said, "I would guess that you had better food on your face than I did, Monty."

"I just winked at her. You know how I pick up all the pretty girls," Monty said, in between licks on his face.

Just then, Tommy finally came out of the bathroom, and he started talking a mile a minute, as he always did. He looked down and asked absentmindedly, "Hey, you got a dog... Where did she come from? And, more importantly, is Carol still here?"

This question trailed off slowly as Tommy looked leftward and saw Carol sitting at the bar and staring up at him angrily. Carol slowly stood up and swiftly punched the back of her hand into Tommy's stomach.

She grimaced and said, "You know, just because you bunch of assholes quit watching cartoons, doesn't mean you are all grown up."

"Then it's a good thing that we still watch cartoons, Carol." Ryan said as he stood up and continued, "Because life is way too short for it to be taken so seriously, and we like to have fantastical dreams of the big old world out there."

Ryan then stared down Carol and finished by saying, "Hell, we might even like to have a little fun in the process. Just try to cool your engines and relax a little bit, would ya? C'mon, Allie, let's go and introduce you to some "nicer" farm animals." Allie stood, gave a quick, hard bark at Carol, and then stood there smiling and wagging her tail at Ryan.

"You see that? Even my dog doesn't like you, Carol." Ryan said as he started walking toward the door, only stopping long enough to give Michelle a wink.

Then he said with a grin and a small wave over his shoulder, "Have a good night, boys. Till next time."

Ryan was rarely seen without that lovable dog from that day on, until the day when she was too old to go with him anymore.

"Buddy I coulda gone that extra mile,
For an extra bark or an extra smile
'Cause I never felt so free,
It was just my dog and me."
(John Hiatt and the Goners)

Chapter Two

Do you find love, or does love find you?

Before Allie had become Ryan's best friend and before PTSD had become a grief upon his very soul, the summer of 1985 had been a very special one for Ryan. It was the summer before he was to become a junior in high school; he was a handsome young man over 6 feet tall, and he was also in the best shape of his life.

He was good at all sports, but he enjoyed playing baseball the most, as he played first base with the ease that good coordination can provide a person. Ryan was not the fastest person on the field, and he didn't hit a huge number of home runs, but he did offer a very good defensive glove on the field of play. Plus, a huge number of singles and doubles were being delivered from his aluminum bat.

On the other hand, he was probably very coordinated because he had also been drumming since he was seven years old. By the time he had reached fifteen years of age, he had also been doing many vocal solos in the high school choir. He was not only playing drums in the high school orchestra but was also performing in a rock band and a country-based band.

At that age, Ryan could play a full game of baseball in the early afternoon, go on a romantic date in the evening, and then a person could find him playing drums and singing at a local dance until 2:00 in the morning. Ryan was a very popular and smart young man, and his future looked like it could not get any better. That is when he received the letter that would make the whole summer just that: better. Or so he thought.

The letter was from a company called America's Young Musicians, saying that he had been chosen to travel to Europe in order to play the drums for a nationally organized orchestra. There were supposed to be a little over 100 other teenagers from throughout the entire United States that were chosen to perform and entertain the people of Europe.

Ryan's first thought had been that he didn't want his baseball team to be without him, and he didn't want to let them down. However, after talking to his parents and his coach, he found that they believed that he could not pass up this opportunity.

His whole life would be changed by going on this trip. He felt this with every fiber in his being, and he knew how important this trip would be to his life. However, having a friend on the trip would also make his parents feel better, and it would be great to have a traveling companion.

So that is what Ryan did. One of his very good friends was also involved with the high school orchestra, and Ryan worked hard on getting him included in the orchestral tour as well. After several letters and a huge amount of work from Mr. DePuydt, his orchestra conductor, Ryan and his friend Mike would be traveling through Europe together.

At this time in his life, Ryan thought that he could do no wrong. Now, he was going to have a partner in crime and a traveling companion with whom to share this amazing adventure.

Could things get any better in 1985?

Mike not only played trombone in the high school orchestra with Ryan, but they also played on the same baseball team with each other. Mike and his younger brother Alex had moved to small town Montana from a large city in California. Viewpoints and environments were vastly different between the two places. Luckily, that didn't matter to any of the teenagers that were involved, because shortly after, they had all become steadfast friends.

Mike's mother had moved to Montana with her new husband in order to take control of a local farm, and they were worried because the boys were of Asian descent. They were afraid that the two young boys would not be accepted into this rural community.

However, the opposite thing happened, and the brothers soon became very popular among the people of rural Montana. Rather than any division among the young boys, there was only acceptance and friendship. Why shouldn't this always be the case?

Ryan and Mike decided on riding the Amtrak train to New York City from Montana, as they wanted to see the American cities and countryside of this great country. The journey took three days, and at the end of the train trip across the country, they had made friends with almost every person that rode the train in those three days. They were a very sociable duo that never backed down from approaching anybody.

The next three days were spent in New York City and thank God that Mike had chosen to travel with Ryan. The city of New York is a wonderful place, but it can be incredibly intimidating to a small-town ranch boy from Big Sky Country. They spent most of their time learning and practicing the new music, as well as getting to know their new fellow musicians and friends.

After three days of practice and camaraderie, the boys and over a hundred of their fellow young musicians were off on a seven-hour flight to Europe. This whole experience seemed to happen incredibly quickly and was almost overwhelming at times.

It seemed that in one minute, Ryan and Mike were in the wheat fields of northern Montana. In the next minute, they were flying over the Atlantic Ocean with a group of other teenagers from around the United States. The population of the young people in the orchestra would overshadow the entire small high school that they came from in Montana.

The young group of Americans landed the next morning in Paris, France. Soon they checked into their hotel, which was in one of the older communities of Paris. This hotel had a small metal elevator, which caused a huge amount of wait time as it only held six occupants at a time.

This older metal cage of an elevator seemed to groan and squeal under the weight of each load of teens. The metal grinding of the elevator caused a vast array of concerned faces and wide eyes from the young men and women that were brave enough to ride on it. The stairs were not much better, as they were narrow and clogged with weary American teens that were forgoing the wait for this lone elevator.

They were tired, hungry, and incredibly frustrated at having to wait nearly an hour to get to their rooms. Behind weary eyes and frowns on their faces, the young group of musicians all thought, "Is this what all of Europe is going to be like? Welcome to Paris?"

The elevator finally did its job and led them to a slightly larger hotel room, where our trusty group of travelers fell fast asleep. This was because of over-excitation on the flight over the ocean, combined with cases of overwhelming jetlag.

The group of teenagers didn't awaken until the late afternoon, and the evening was bearing down on them. They gathered a small group of willing teenage Americans and made a walking trek toward the Eiffel Tower. There was not much light left during the day when the group of teenagers arrived at the Eiffel Tower, and the view of the darkening city of Paris that was all around them was breathtaking.

The fading light of the sun turned into shadows, and slowly, street lanterns started to illuminate the busy streets of the City of Love. With a smile on all the young teenagers' faces, they all thought, "Ah, this is more like it. Welcome to Paris!"

The last rays of the sun were glinting off the amazing steeples and the stained-glass windows of the cathedral of Notre Dame. As well as the stone structure of the Arc de Triumph and the extraordinary waters of the Seine River. As far as first experiences are concerned, you could not have had a better experience than this one.

They had been scheduled to have three days of sightseeing in Paris. The first day of tourism included visiting the grand cathedral of Notre Dame, as well as the Arc de Triumph, which they had only seen from a distance. It was amazing for them to learn that directly under the Arc de Triumph is an eternal flame dedicated to the unknown soldier of France.

The second day in Paris was completely attributed to a tour of the incredible Louvre Art Museum. The young students marveled at the works of the world-famous masters who created the paintings and the statues that surrounded them. Their last stop in the museum was a visit to the Mona Lisa, which was painted by the amazing Leonardo Da Vinci.

They were all surprised at how small the painting is in real life, and one visitor even told them that the historic painting wasn't always famous. A critic had at one time panned the painting as just a mediocre work of art. However, it became famous only after it was stolen in 1911 by an Italian man named Vincento Peroggia.

The Mona Lisa wasn't even noticed as missing until the next day, and it was continually missing for two full years after that. It ended up being hidden in Peroggia's Paris apartment, which was located not far from the Louvre itself. A black-market buyer from Florence, Italy, tried to purchase the painting at this time, but Vincento Peroggia had a change of heart. He ended up turning himself in, and he returned the famous painting to the museum.

When this happened, the same art critic pronounced the painting to be a brilliant work of art, and then it became the masterpiece that is known and loved to this day. Thank you, Leonardo, for creating the Mona Lisa and also thank you, Vincento Peroggia, for making us appreciate her.

The last day in Paris revolved around the concert that was performed in front of a large group of Parisians in the newer portion of the city. This was located at an outdoor concert pavilion that was completely different from the historic districts that the teens had encountered since coming to this beautiful city.

This was the first time that the group played in front of an audience, and this was both thrilling and nerve-wracking for all of them. Thankfully, the concert went seamlessly, and the crowds in Paris were thankful for the performance. Things were starting out extremely well.

After the concert in Paris, the tour loaded onto their two rented buses and headed across the border and into Belgium, where they stayed overnight in Brussels. After the first three days in Paris, groups of teenagers who had the same interests began to form. Ryan and a group of six other performers decided to explore the streets of this Belgian city that evening.

The young men and women were joking with each other when they met a group of local young men. Suddenly, the young man walking next to Ryan, who was named Robert from Indiana, quit laughing and shouted out, "Oh my God, I have been cut! Those local bastards just cut me across the arm. I am bleeding badly."

Ryan immediately turned on his heels to confront the local men when he was faced with a switchblade knife being waved in his face. He put his arms out to his sides, stopping the other teens in their tracks, and took a step backwards.

The local young man with the knife spat out words of contempt in his voice. "You fucking Americans! You are so full of yourselves. Go home! Go back to your own country. You don't belong here."

That was the first time that Ryan had been faced with an extremely violent individual who wanted to see harm fall upon him. Ryan didn't turn and run, which seemed to confuse his assailant, and he stared the man in the eyes with a huge amount of intensity.

Slowly, Ryan started to speak, saying, "We don't want any trouble from any of you. We are just here on a concert tour. We thought that this would be a great night to explore your beautiful city. What is so wrong with that?"

Angelo, who was from New York, jumped into the conversation and said vehemently, "If you don't put that knife away, we filthy Americans are going to shove it up your ass!"

Ryan didn't look away from the man's eyes and said curtly, "Shut up, Angelo. He and his friends are going to walk the other way. There is no need to start a fight and keep them from going away…and we are going to take Robert to the chaperones and have his arm looked at. There is no need to start an incident; we just got here. If these men want to push this problem, we are going to fight back and protect ourselves. Do any of you want that?"

The young Belgian closed the switchblade knife in Ryan's face and tried to say toughly, "No, we don't need that. We will go. Just count yourselves as lucky. We are not intimidated by you. Spread the word to any other Americans… stay out of our way."

At these words, the man and his gang of local thugs turned around and walked up the street in the other direction. Ryan grabbed Robert by the neck and said, "Now then, let's have someone look at your arm."

Angelo didn't look happy, but he did look impressed and nodded his head at Ryan. They were all still trying to figure each other out and were from different backgrounds at that point.

The next day, they toured one of the most infamous battle sites of World War II. This battle was named 'The Battle of the Bulge', and it is located next to the small but quaint town of Bastogne, Belgium.

This place in the Ardennes Forest is home to a star-shaped monument that honors the soldiers from every state in America. It is at this location that the allied forces defeated the final large surge of the Nazi Army. The fighting was fierce at this location, as it was being fought in freezing conditions amid troops that had not rested in days of fighting.

Hence, this is the location where General George S. Patton became a general of note. After being used as a decoy, he commanded the Sherman tanks and the troops that had arrived at Bastogne. They became the decisive force behind the victory of the Allied Army against the charging Nazi onslaught.

Ryan and Mike were looking at the memorial when Angelo approached them from behind. He slapped Ryan on the back and then said, "I want to thank you for last night. You kept your cool when I was getting really upset. I would have fought those guys. That probably wouldn't have ended well."

Ryan smiled at him and said, "No problem; we were all scared last night. It didn't need to be escalated into something worse. I just didn't want anyone else to get hurt. Speaking of that, have you heard how Robert is?"

Angelo pointed into the distance and stated, "He is right over there. His arm is in a sling, but he will be alright. It wasn't bad enough to put him in the hospital. He didn't like seeing his own blood and just needed some TLC. I think that he was more scared than hurt."

Ryan smiled again and said, "Good. I am awfully glad. Thank you for not going after those guys. Hopefully, we don't run into another situation like that one. That rattled me as well. I would want you in my corner any day of the week. I hope that you understand, Angelo."

Angelo smiled back at him and said, "I know. I feel the same way."

Over the next week, the orchestra performed three concerts and went on constant tours of battlefields, museums, and cathedrals. Everyone was getting worn out, and they all needed a day to relax and recharge their batteries.

The youth orchestra was finally given a couple of days off at a small, pristine mountain resort town named Lucerne, Switzerland. The lake and the town of Lucerne are surrounded by the towering peaks of the Alps, making it a pristine resort town that is in an extremely secluded area. However, it had now been invaded by a group of musical teens from America.

Our intrepid group of young heroes found a large amount of solace here as they sat and rested atop a rock wall that surrounded a small pond of water. This pond protected an unbelievable monument of a giant dying lion that was carved into the sandstone cliff opposite them.

The dying lion carving loomed over them as it was created by a stone mason in the 1820s. This was created as a monument to the Swiss soldiers who lost their lives while protecting the French royal families during the French Revolution.

This monument was even immortalized by another American in the 1800s. This happened when Mark Twain was quoted as saying, "The dying lion monument is the saddest and most moving piece of rock in the world."

Today it played host to Ryan, Mike, and Angelo, as well as one other orchestra member named Troy Edwards. They were more interested in what the day would offer than in what history had already given them.

"Holy shit, we have been going hard and heavy. We have played so much that my fingers have callouses upon callouses on them," Mike exclaimed.

"Well, you shouldn't play with yourself so much," said Angelo.

Ryan was lying on the wall beside him, and this statement made him look up and smile. The warm sunshine that was beating down on them seemed to start to regenerate the young men.

Angelo had been the first New Yorker, as well as the first Italian person, that either Ryan or Mike had known personally. If he wasn't threatened in any way, he proved himself to be a great guy who had a quick wit as well as a very pleasant demeanor.

Angelo had styled black hair that stood atop a face that had dark eyes, a slender nose, and a chiseled jaw. He stood on a 5'8" muscular frame, and he also sounded like he came right out of the cast of a mob movie. He seemed to exaggerate this accent when he needed to sound tough around unwanted company, or else when he wanted to show it off in front of willing young women.

"Agreed," Troy Edwards said. "You have been fingering the hell out of it lately."

Troy then burst out into a cackling, overproduced laugh, as he was one of those types of people that tries excessively hard, in order to fit in with the crowd.

Troy was shorter than Angelo by a few inches, and he had a skinny frame. He also had an acne-covered complexion and deep-set, dark brown eyes that seemed to scream out in fear and anxiety. He was from Indianapolis, Indiana, and played the bassoon in the wind section of the orchestra.

Troy did not have the body or coordination for any athletics, and he was in love with advanced mathematics and chemistry. In high school, he would have been known as a know-it-all nerd, and he would ruin many a grade curve throughout his educational history.

Ryan was not thought of any better in the group of young teenagers as he was a laid-back farm boy from Montana, and people often thought of him as a rube or a hick. That was according to the thoughts of his fellow traveling companions from across the U.S. anyway.

He was even called a hillbilly at one point, but Ryan tended to let such meaningless statements pour off his back. He knew that you can't really judge a person without getting to know them in their entirety or what caused them to become a certain way.

None of these people would have guessed that he was an all-star athlete, as well as an honor student, and an outstanding musician. People tend to see one thing about a person and define them as that. He had learned that it just didn't matter in the long run. The only thing that mattered was treating people the right way. If they didn't see that in him, that was their problem. He could only affect how he acted, and he had confidence in that fact.

The main difference between Ryan and other people is that he accepted who he really was and where he came from. Other people tended to change how they thought or acted in order to please the other people that surrounded them. Ryan tended to see these people as pretenders as well as followers. Ryan tended to feel sorry for these people because they must not have liked themselves very well if they pretended to be someone that they would never be.

"Fuck you guys!" Mike said. "Hey Maxwell, what are we doing on our day off today?"

Mike was the only one to call Ryan by his last name, but it seemed right hearing the name come out of the mouth of his fellow teammate from Montana.

"I don't know about you guys, but I want to do as little as possible," Ryan said while still lying down with his eyes closed.

He was wearing sunglasses as well as having his baseball cap pulled down over his eyes. He had one arm behind his head that he used as a cushion, and he looked as if he might fall asleep at any moment.

"I heard at the front desk that there is a topless beach at the lake," Troy exclaimed.

That statement made Ryan sit up and take off the shades. "No shit, Troy?" He said, "Don't fuck us over, dude."

"That's what Giovani, or Giovandelo said," Troy suddenly flinched as he was speaking, because Angelo hit him with a hard right punch to the shoulder.

Angelo then said angrily, "It's Giovanisi you blasted nob, why didn't you bring this up sooner?" He said it with grit in his voice.

Troy gave them a sheepish grin, and then he said, "I didn't think that it would make any difference what I said, you guys don't listen to me very often."

The boys were tired of seeing historic landmarks as well as beautiful scenery. On that day, all that they cared about and wanted to see were female beachgoers with their tops off. The run to the hotel, where they changed into their bathing suits, and then the sprint to Lake Lucerne would take an average person 30 minutes.

However, on that day, the boys made the trip in half the time, as they had a huge amount of teenage energy and exuberance built up inside of them.

Upon arrival to the lake, the boys were witness to a large expanse of beach that offered them views that the United States beaches did not offer. Running out into the crystalline waters of Lake Lucerne was a lonesome pier that ran about 40 feet into the waters and had small boats tied to the sides of it.

They all agreed that the first step in their adventure on the shores of Lake Lucerne, would be better off if they all jumped into the waters at the end of the dock. This matter of cooling off would hopefully dampen the boys' raging hormones before they could make total fools of themselves.

This was Ryan's idea, and he led the group of friends out to the end of the pier in order to have them all jump into the cold waters of the lake.

"The best way to get wet and cool off on one of these cold, snow-fed mountain lakes is to just jump into the water directly from the pier," Ryan exclaimed. "Trust me, I'm from Montana, and this is how we go for a swim in the mountain lakes of Montana. We have to get used to the cold of the water."

He grinned widely at the three friends and then continued to say, "Okay, right at the count of three, we all jump in." Ryan looked right and then left and found that they were all ready to go.

"Okay, One...Two...Three." They all jumped into the freezing water, except for Ryan, who started walking away from them and back toward the beach. He was whistling a jaunty tune and waving at them as he walked away.

"No fair, you asshole!" Troy cried out, coughing on a gulp of water, as he tried to catch his breath.

These admonitions and jibes from the three gullible teens only made Ryan smile even wider and giggle harder.

While the rest of his friends were still catching their breaths in the cold waters of the lake, Ryan set up the umbrella and the four beach chairs that they had rented upon their arrival to the lake. He then laid back and relaxed his muscles so much that he fell asleep in the shade of the umbrella.

Ryan had only slept for a short time when he was awakened by a spray of cold water as Angelo shook his head over him and said, "You want us to act like a pack of dogs? I'll give you a dog. What a nasty trick, farm boy."

Angelo then wrung the remainder of the water out of his hair, all over Ryan, who asked in between chuckles of laughter. "How was the swim, boys, and where the hell is Troy? You didn't drown him, did ya?"

Ryan then looked out into the lake and saw that Troy was standing in the water up to his stomach and was just gawking around at the women that passed by him. Mike and Angelo laid down on other beach chairs and started laughing even more at the inside joke.

Ryan then asked them, "What the hell is dipshit doing out there in the lake?"

Angelo and Mike laughed heartily again, and then Angelo answered him by saying, "He can't leave the water. He comes to a topless beach and can't leave the water because he got a boner."

He said this statement loud enough for Troy and anyone around him to hear, and then he continued by yelling loudly, "That guy is gonna die a virgin with a constant hard-on!"

Ryan was still looking out toward Troy and the shoreline that continued past him. He didn't laugh or even react to what Angelo had said, and he responded with only a grunt. He wasn't looking at Troy anymore, who was still standing in the cold water with a perpetual erection poking out.

His attention was now on the most magnificent vision that he had ever laid eyes upon. She seemed to shine and glimmer, just like the waters of the lake behind her. This girl wore a full pink bathing suit that completely covered her slim, taut body. She also had a jaw-dropping smile and long blond hair that cascaded over her slightly freckled shoulders.

She was a very petite young woman, as the well-toned girl was maybe 5'4" tall, and she had an unblemished face with high cheekbones. Ryan also imagined her having large and bright blue eyes. The young blond woman let out a giggling laugh, and when she did so, Ryan heard that lilting tone, and he almost fell out of the beach chair that he was sitting in.

"Who is that?" Ryan pointed at her and felt as if one of his friends had hit him across the forehead with a shovel.

Mike blew her off with a shrug and a wave of his hand, and then he said, "I think that she is in the band with us, but she usually dresses in really frilly clothes. She usually wears her hair up in a bun. I think that she rides on the other tour bus, and she plays the flute or something like that. She looks good in a bathing suit though, but she is nothing compared to these European women."

Mike then gave his friend a very dour and nervous look. That was until Ryan looked back at him and said, "Don't worry buddy, just too much sun, I guess." Ryan then looked back at the blond girl and continued. "She just kind of knocked me for a loop."

Mike just shook his head and mumbled, "Yeah, I know what kind of loop."

"How do you know when it's love?
I can't tell you, but it lasts forever...
How do you feel when it's love?
It's just something that you feel together..."
(Van Halen)

Chapter Three

A first date in Venice is never a good thing if you suffer from seasickness!

The young blond woman happened to be named Karen, before the name had become associated with high-brow ridicule. Ryan just thought that she could light up a room without ever touching a candle or a flashlight.

Usually, Ryan had no issues when it came to talking to members of the opposite sex, but Karen made him stammer and stumble all over himself. In any case, it seemed that Ryan could not find the correct words or confidence, in order to ask her out for the first time. He felt like he was trying to flip hotcakes with his own tongue.

It was lucky that Ryan also had no fear of making a fool out of himself, as he stammered through their initial introduction like a goat trying to climb a chain-link fence. It was even more amazing that Karen said "yes" to his proposition of having their first date happen in three days, when they were going to visit the eternal city of Venice, Italy.

In the meantime, the group of teens were still in the heart of the Alps Mountains, and they were supposed to visit the snowy peaks above them. This day trip was still incredibly beautiful, but coming from the Rocky Mountains, Ryan enjoyed watching other people's reactions to the extremely high mountain peaks. This was just as enjoyable to him as the scenery itself.

Ryan and Mike decided to help a young black man named Kensy Walker, as he was from the Caribbean Island of the US Virgin Islands. He had never seen such high mountains, as well as any snow, ever before.

At the peak of the mountain, the boys from Montana then helped Kensy with another tradition as they joined him as a teammate in a snowball fight against the other occupants of the second bus. It was a joy to watch Kensy laugh and have the time of his life, during which he won his first snowball fight ever. Just the smile on Kensy's face made everyone's heart melt that day.

They then traveled out of the Alps at a place named St. Gotthard Pass, which was located next to Mount Titlis. Now, these names were probably never a second thought to Europeans, but teenage Americans are a totally different story. This ended up being a huge opportunity for several jokes to be told by a group of teenagers who tend to have their brains in only one place.

These jokes were thrown about the bus all the way to Italy. The fear of saying anything rude never seemed to enter the vocabulary that exited their mouths. That fear didn't exist in the 1980s, and people were proud if their joke actually offended someone. After some time to rest and the cheerful atmosphere, the bus ride was truly full of a massive amount of joviality.

The last place that the group stayed before Ryan was to have the big date with Karen was in Verona, Italy. They performed an hour-long concert amid the ancient buildings of the city. This performance happened to be excruciating, as the temperature in Italy that day was 96 degrees. Most of the musicians were sweating like whores in church when they finally finished performing.

However, the next portion of the tour included a mandatory walking tour of the cobblestoned, skinny streets of this ancient metropolis that seemed to be boiling over from the heat. The first stop had been the supposed location of the small balcony that was used by Romeo and Juliet in Shakespeare's famous play.

Along the small alley was a stone bench, as well as a statue of a fair Juliet. Ryan had helped Kensy with the snowy mountains of the Alps, and this time it was Kensy's turn to help Ryan.

The young man from Montana climbed up the stairs and stood on the stone balcony that had been made famous by the Shakespearean damsel. He was suddenly tapped on the shoulder from behind, and upon turning too quickly, he was confronted by the vision of Karen.

She looked beautiful, even with sweat glistening against her alabaster skin and a few strands of blond hair that had been raised up into a bun on top of her head had come loose. These hairs were now hanging down perfectly and surrounding her smiling face.

Ryan started to say his surprised greeting to her when his eyes rolled backwards into his head. He collapsed like a sack of potatoes at the feet of the woman who was now haunting his amorous visions. This happened at the very place where the biggest romance between two teenagers had ever taken place, and Ryan had now made a fool of himself and collapsed on his fair maiden's shoes.

This is where Kensy helped Ryan the most, as the young black man from the Caribbean had jumped to Ryan's aid and had apologized to Karen. He then helped a dehydrated Ryan get down the stairs to the courtyard below.

When Ryan came to his senses, he was joined on the stone bench by Angelo, and Mike, as well as Kensy, who was pouring cold water over Ryan's head in order to cool him down.

Ryan took a large, cool drink out of another bottle of water and said quietly, "What the hell just happened?"

His friends just looked at him with caution and fear on their faces. Angelo then asked, "What hurts more, Ryan, your overheated head, or your damaged pride?"

Ryan let out a deep breath and filled his lungs with a long inhale through his nose, as his head was still swimming in the shallow end of the pool.

Angelo then snapped his fingers in front of Ryan's face and continued by saying, "Are you okay, bud? You just nose-dived on Karen's sneakers up there. Kensy helped you out on the balcony, and he lessened the damage with Karen, but the sun of the 'old country' seemed to knock you out."

Angelo was very proud to be in the 'old country', as he kept calling Italy by this vernacular. To him, it was as if he had returned home in some way.

Ryan looked up at Kensy and said, while coughing, "Thanks for looking out for me up there, Kensy. Did I make a total fool out of myself, or did Karen say anything?"

Kensy laughed and told Ryan, "Yeah, you looked like you had taken a punch from Mike Tyson. Karen was worried about your date tomorrow, but she seemed more concerned about your health than anything else. Hell, I am used to this much heat, and I've seen too many of you crazy white people pass out on the beach from too much alcohol and the heat of the sun. You just need some water and a cold piece of cool cloth on your neck."

After about 10 minutes of Ryan drinking from a water bottle, Kensy helped Ryan stand. Then the crew of teens helped Ryan visit their final and best stop of the day. This is one of the largest and most beautiful cathedrals in the world. The "Santa Maria del Fiore."

The cathedral is in the center of historic Florence, Italy, and Ryan still felt slightly weak from the walk. Because of this, the men sat in a pew and gawked at the enormity of the cathedral and the 44 stained-glass windows that shone down upon them.

Ryan was heard saying, "Wow," and then his head lolled backward, and he looked at the amazing fresco on the dome above them, titled 'The Last Judgment.' This magnificent fresco is probably the second most famous painting on a dome in Italy, besides the famous one that has the same name on the Vatican dome in Rome.

While gazing at this work of art, Ryan seemed to feel himself become stronger and more intuitive. This was as if a powerful force was refueling his body, mind, and soul. Ryan did not understand or think about these feelings until a much more difficult time in his life that would emerge inside of him.

When Ryan knocked on Karen's door the next morning, he hoped that the color had returned to his face, as he still felt off-balance. That was until Karen answered the door, and her blond hair was hanging down and cascading over her slightly freckled, tanned shoulders. The vision of her almost made Ryan collapse onto his knees once again.

She was wearing tight tan shorts and a pink cotton top that seemed to conform tightly to her petite form that morning. Her legs and arms had also been darkened by the large amounts of time that she had spent outdoors that summer.

Suddenly, instead of feeling weaker by the looks of her, Karen instead seemed to light a fire in Ryan's belly as she looked too beautiful to really be a true vision standing before him. She looked as if she may have been a daydream that had appeared in Ryan's mind. It was as if he wasn't strong enough to hold onto her and she may just disappear.

"You look...gorgeous!" He said this while sucking air into his mouth, so that he wouldn't drool like a hungry dog waiting for feeding time.

At this point, Ryan felt speechless, and he only stepped away from the door and welcomed her into the hallway with a bow and a swoosh of his arm. Karen giggled as she stepped into the hallway of the hotel.

Not a word was said, and a nervous silence enveloped them as the young couple simply walked toward the lobby exit and looked at one another curiously.

This was until Ryan finally stated, "Karen, I think that I like you very much."

Karen simply looked back at him and said bluntly, "I hope so."

Ryan had already taken the lure into his mouth, but when she answered, he was totally caught on the hook. He was behaving just like a rainbow trout that had swallowed a fisherman's bait. Ryan led Karen to the group of boats that were used as water taxis in order to enter the city of Venice.

Ryan then stepped into the boat, held out his hand to Karen, and said, "My Lady."

She gave him a serious look and then took his hand in hers and giggled again. Why was he talking and acting this way?

He was still holding her hand when the boat pulled away from the pier, and she asked him, "Are you always this gallant, or are you just acting like a knight in shining armor, in order to impress me?"

This question seemed to almost confuse Ryan, and finally he answered her by saying, "A little bit of both, I guess."

The look of the boats reminded Ryan of the old Woody style of cars that one sees in Beach Boys pictures, except they were in watercraft form. They felt the wind blow through their hair as the boat sped toward an ever-growing group of ancient buildings that seemed to be hovering on the waters themselves.

As the boat slowed in front of their destination at the docks of St. Mark's Square, Karen leaned close to Ryan and asked, "Where are your friends today? You can usually never be found without them by your side."

Right on cue and after that question was asked, Ryan and Karen were then splashed by a cold spray of water that came from the boat directly behind the two young travelers. Ryan then grimaced and tried to protect Karen from the onslaught of water that would spray upon them from the Grand Canal of Venice.

Then Ryan gave her a look that seemed to say, 'My friends are idiots'.

However, in all actuality, he said to her, "Sorry about that; someone let them out of their cages this morning."

Ryan motioned to the guys with his middle finger and then said, in a cheesy fashion, "I may have to protect you from them, so just give me a word if they bother you."

As the two young teenagers began walking across St. Mark's Square, the world around them seemed to weigh a thousand pounds. The beauty, history, and special feelings that only Venice can offer a person were now standing in front of them. Neither of them seemed to know how to feel or even know what to say at that moment.

Luckily, the universe found a way to lighten things up when a pigeon shit directly on Ryan's right temple and the crap began running down his right cheek.

Karen looked at him shockingly and then burst out into a hearty laugh. She tried to stop giggling as she cleaned Ryan's face with a Kleenex that she had found in her purse. Ryan tried to look at the glob of white feces hanging from the side of his face, and he made a comical, wincing face in trying to do so.

This caused Karen to burst out into a new bout of hysterics when she finally said, through giggles, "Thank you for protecting me from these flying sky biscuits! Well, my knight in not-so-shiny-armor anymore, will you protect me from all these pigeons as well?"

"Flying Sky Biscuits?" Ryan teased back at Karen, and then he continued, "I would gladly do so."

She smiled up at him, stood on her tippy toes, and gave him a quick kiss on the lips. Then she returned to her original height and said lovingly, "I'm glad that is out of the way, now we can have some fun."

Ryan didn't answer her; he only gave her a wry grin. Then he picked her up by the waist with one arm and ran through the flock of pigeons that covered the piazza. Ryan yelled like a wild man, and Karen squealed with giggling laughter as he made an exhibition out of the two of them.

He then carried her to an outdoor café, where Ryan put her down beside an open table and asked her, "Ice cream and a soda for my lady?"

He then put his arm out for her to join him. My goodness, he was speaking like that again.

"Why, thank you, kind sir," she answered.

Then they shared a treat of three scoops of ice cream, and they talked for nearly an hour. He told her about his life in Montana, but he wanted to hear everything about her, so he just kept asking her questions in order to listen to her fascinating answers.

Ryan then took Karen by the hand and led her toward a lone gondola, so they could slowly drift through the canals of Venice, only stopping long enough for Ryan to buy a small, single red rose for Karen.

Karen broke off the thorny stem of the rose and stuck the flowering petal of the rose above her right ear. Ryan looked at her and stated, "I didn't think that Venice could get any more beautiful."

As the loving couple pulled away from St. Marks Basilica and traveled up the Rio de Palazzo canal, not a word was said, and only the sound of the gondolier's paddle in the water made a slight splashing sound. The busy locals and tourists that were along the walkways of the seemingly floating city made for a small distraction. However, Ryan was entranced by the beauty that was beside him.

Finally, the gondola operator cleared his throat and motioned to an upcoming bridge that the two young lovers would soon be gliding under. The bridge was made from white stone, and it was almost totally enclosed as it ran between two ancient buildings. There was only one window on the bridge, and it had bars running across it as the gondola slowly drifted under this stone structure.

The gondolier quit paddling, and he said to Ryan with a strong Italian accent, "Kiss her, my friend. Kiss her with passion."

Ryan was holding Karen tightly, and he raised her head with his finger. He then kissed Karen so lovingly and deeply, that her shoulders relaxed so much that she nearly fell onto the floor of the boat.

When their lips first touched, an arc of electricity ran across their mouths, which surprised them both. Then he kissed her again, softly and tenderly, but this time, the electricity didn't spark them. He held her tightly, as if she might loosen from his grip like a cloud of smoke. She looked up at him lovingly, and her face was flushed by the afternoon sun as well as the passionate kiss.

She grabbed the side of the wooden boat with her right hand, lifted her body up from the seat, and kissed him again on the mouth so hard that it took Ryan by complete surprise. However, he didn't sway backward at all; he just pushed onto her welcoming mouth with the same ferocity that she showed him.

The gondolier then said, "This is the "Bridge of Sighs" that you just drifted under, and it is said that if you kiss her deeply while going under it, you will be in love forever. The bond will never be separated between the two of you."

Ryan then held her close again and said to Karen, "You see, we are now bonded forever. At least whenever you eat any Italian food in the future."

She smiled brightly at this, and then her face fell into an expression of confused seriousness.

The romantic connotation of the Bridge of Sighs was made famous by the writer, Lord Byron as the bridge that was built in the 17th century was used by prisoners as they traveled over it. It connected the two buildings, which were the interrogation rooms of the Doge Palace and the prison cells themselves. The prisoners were said to have sighed with despair upon laying their eyes upon the beauty of Venice for the last time.

They then toured the Doge Palace, which was where the Supreme Authority of the city, also known as the Doge of Venice, lived. It also housed the offices of power that oversaw the city of Venice at one time. This building is now a museum and overlooks St. Marks Basilica and the Grand Canal as well. Ryan and Karen were now in the upper rooms of the palace and looking out at the island that housed the Palladian Church of San Giorgio Maggiore.

From the ancient stone window of the Doge Palace, the clock bell was heard to ring out two clangs, saying that it was 2:00 p.m. They saw that other students were now leaving the city via water taxis, and Ryan grabbed Karen's hand and whisked her away to the Grand Canal so that they would not get left behind. They still had a three-hour bus ride to Milan, Italy, where they were scheduled to perform a concert the next day.

Upon arrival in Milan, the hotel hosted the young musicians with a truly magnificent meal. They had fried calamari for an appetizer, followed by an entree of meat-filled Milanese ravioli, and followed by a dessert of cream-filled Panna Cotta.

Alcohol was legal for them to consume in Italy, and they had red wine with their dinner. Ryan was told that it was a very good bottle from a local vineyard. However, the young teenagers had never had red wine before, and they were both a little buzzed when they left dinner for the evening.

After dinner, Ryan led Karen to the La Scala Opera House, where he led her indoors. They sat in a pair of cushioned seats that overlooked the towering, fascinating beauty of the stage and the theater that surrounded them. Ryan was happy that an opera was not being performed that evening. Even though the couple were not bothered by an overcrowded opera house, Ryan and Karen spoke in whispers and hushed tones as the surroundings around them seemed to emphasize this.

Ryan was holding Karen's hand when he leaned closer to her and asked quietly, "On a scale of one to ten, how did our first date go today?"

"I will give you an eight." She ribbed back at him, and then she finished speaking by saying, "You did get shit on, right off the bat. You lost a couple of points because of that."

"Whoa, do you kiss your mother with that mouth?" He pretended to be offended at her curse word.

"No, but I will kiss... you." She said, with a voice just a little above a whisper.

Ryan leaned closer to her and kissed her warmly on the mouth while their tongues danced together at the slow, deep pace of a dream exchange. Ryan finally had to pull himself away from Karen's lips, as he was searching for much-needed air.

After refilling their lungs, Ryan gave Karen one last soft kiss. He then pulled away from her and gave her one last brush of his lips over her slightly opened, accepting mouth. This made them desire more, but they knew that they both had to stop.

After this final show of affection, Ryan tried to stand up but found it very hard to do so. His bulging member was in a full salute, and he embarrassingly glanced down at his crotch.

He blushed and said to Karen, "We had better call it a night. I don't think that I could stand much more loving from you tonight. My brain and my heart are not in control of my body anymore."

Ryan was almost limping Karen back to the hotel, and he walked her to her room where he ended the date by kissing her deeply again. She leaned close to him, feeling his throbbing manhood push against her upper stomach and just below her taut, nubile breasts.

At this close movement between the two young teens, Karen felt the warmth of Ryan's love member giving way. She stood on her tippy-toes again and kissed Ryan gently on the mouth.

She then said, "Remember, we are linked together forever, now."

She gave Ryan another quick peck on the lips and then rushed into her room for the night. This left Ryan to walk uncomfortably back to his room with his small head sliding in his own white, sticky sperm. His large head on his shoulders was reeling in disbelief as well, and he couldn't stop smiling as the memories of the day seemed to wash over him.

"I said life without end wouldn't have any meaning,
The journey to death is the point of our being...
Well, the point of my life is to be with you, babe,
But there ain't enough time in the life that they gave me."
(Lord Huron)

Chapter Four

Give me the smell and feel of a hand-written love letter any day of the week.

There wasn't much sleep for Ryan or Karen on the night of their first date in Venice. Ryan wanted to be with her so badly that he had snuck out once, only to be caught by a dour-faced chaperone close to the elevator of the hotel. Ryan absentmindedly asked him for directions to the snack machine, but only disappointedly went back to his room and screamed desperately into his pillow.

Karen had waited for Ryan to come to her room and see her, but she was also disappointed when she sat by the door for thirty minutes. Sleep did not come to her, so she lay in her bed and sleeplessly watched the quiet image of a talk show on the Italian television.

The next morning, Ryan tried to act cool but found himself rushing to her hotel room. He couldn't sleep the night before, so he had done laundry, as his clothes needed it from the date the night before. He also packed for the coming bus trip that was going to carry them toward Austria and West Germany.

She answered the door after only about ten seconds of knocking, and Ryan immediately grabbed her waist. He lifted her directly up from the floor and gave her a big, sloppy kiss on her lips.

"Hold your horses, you slobbery hound dog," she said, laughing. "I haven't had a chance to brush my teeth yet."

"How are you this morning, beautiful?" Ryan was trying to act charming but was coming across as rather cheesy. However, don't most young lovers make this common mistake?

"Just packing my clothes for the next part of the trip, sweetie." She said, while pushing him away with her left hand and pulling him closer to her with the right one. She looked him over and continued to ask him, "Don't tell me that you are ready to go already?"

"Yes, I tried to come and see you last night, but was rejected by that chaperone with the bad hair piece. So, I did laundry instead. I have you to thank for that." He then kidded at her by asking, "Are you packing underwear this morning?"

"Not for your eyes, Bub!" Karen stated while smiling.

Suddenly, when she finished packing, she jokingly jumped on his back and commanded, "Take me to breakfast, Naif; I'm hungry."

"Anything you order, your majesty," he said, as he pawed his foot into the floor like a horse. They both ate some Italian form of cut up and seasoned potatoes, as well as the best cheese omelet that either of them had ever had.

"Holy shit!!!" Ryan exclaimed, "What do they feed their chickens over here, garlic and gold?"

Karen giggled at the thought of this and then said, "I think that it might be the cheese that they use here. It does taste amazing, though. This is the best omelet that I have ever had."

He then swallowed hard and asked her, "Will the powers that be let me onto your bus so that we can ride together?"

Then he looked at the chaperones, who were eating just a few tables away, and said to her, "It is worth a try, you know, the worst they can say is no."

She looked at him sheepishly and then said, "Let's not ask the chaperones, okay? I don't want to stir the pot. You know, they worked hard on these arrangements, and I don't want to be a pain or anything."

Ryan smiled at her and wondered if he was moving too quickly, then said that he understood. However, he really did not, and he wondered what the big deal would be.

He had fallen hard for Karen, and he could only think about spending more time with her. For the time being, though, he decided that it was better to be within her reach rather than out of it all together.

This seemed like a tightrope act done over a bed of hot coals and razor blades. However, he also had to respect her wishes, and hopefully they would include him. Ryan took Karen's hand in his and lovingly kissed the tops of her knuckles.

Traveling in a different bus was extremely hard on Ryan, as he desperately wanted to explore these new countries with her. He only wanted to be close to the person who had seemed to conquer his mind, his heart, and his very soul.

The young performers of the orchestra had a predetermined bus in which to ride, as well as concert performances that had been scheduled long before they had even left the United States.

At the scheduled stops for each concert, the orchestra would often just unload the instruments and perform the concert. Ryan and Karen would only have enough time to lock eyes with each other from across the concert hall. Then they would have to reload onto the bus and start traveling across the country again.

Evenings were the best time for Ryan to visit Karen, but that was also too short of a timeframe for love to truly blossom, as they were only given two hours of free time. They never encountered any privacy or alone time on their journeys, as they were always in a group. Plus, the chaperones had discovered their young romance, and they were watching them shrewdly.

As more time passed, both Ryan and Karen found it more difficult to even steal away for a quick embrace and a kiss. This also affected the young lovers moods as they became more surly, more irritable, and in a forced foul demeanor.

After leaving Italy, the group traveled to Innsbruck, Austria, and Ryan finally got to take Karen on a daytrip to the Winter Olympic site, which was still standing from the 1976 games. Ryan left Karen alone and climbed to approximately 100 feet above her in order to visit the large Olympic ring symbol that had been placed on the side of the mountain. He gazed and waved down at Karen, as he wasn't afraid of any heights at the time.

However, he did witness what he was most afraid of at the time, as he watched four separate young men approach a beautiful-looking Karen. They all tried their hardest to pry her away from her new, young suitor. Ryan then realized that his biggest fear at the time was rejection or completely losing her to someone else.

With this, he had no control over the situation. Now, this was a truly frightening situation for him. She made him want to be a better person, and he felt like he truly needed her now. That feeling of needing someone and being needed back can be extremely addictive, which is also why some people end up with the wrong partner.

The group then traveled into West Germany from Austria, and they were faced with another scary situation, as at the time there was a West Germany and an East Germany. Even though the buses were entering West Germany, a group of soldiers had to inspect each bus, as well as the occupants.

The teens were commanded not to say a word and to sit very still as a group of soldiers, who carried automatic weapons, swept the bus for any weapons. Dogs even came aboard the vehicles to walk up the aisles in the search for any explosives or drugs. Everybody was so afraid of the situation that all the teenagers were afraid to even move in the slightest way or say a word.

Ryan had heard of the heavy-handed tactics involved between the free countries of Europe and those of the socialist countries. However, this was his first experience with any unwanted relations between the two ideologies. He was more thankful for freedom on that day than ever before. A person has got to truly experience the situations that come from these differences before they can ever understand the feelings that come from being truly free.

The group had to perform a concert in Frankfurt, Germany, that afternoon. After this concert, Ryan and Karen had the opportunity to spend the evening together, during which they ate a meal of the biggest kosher sausages that either of them had ever seen, as well as baked potatoes and sauerkraut. They even brought them a giant, mug of German dark beer, containing at least 32 ounces of the warm, hoppy liquid.

They were supposed to share the beer, but every time Karen took a drink from it, her nose would wrinkle up, and it would make a distasteful grimace go across her face.

Ryan just laughed at her reaction and said, "I guess that I will be gentlemanly and drink all of the beer that they bring us. I have to say I do enjoy the beer better, but the food has gotten worse the further that we have gotten away from Italy."

Karen looked at him with a look of concern on her face and then said, "How gallant of you, Ryan. It has been a long day with extremely intense situations. We had better call it an early night."

Ryan took a drink of beer and then pretended to be drunk and slurred his words while saying, "Why is this? I think that we need to get a little bit of lovin' in tonight, or do you have a secret boyfriend to run off to?"

Ryan knew that he had said the wrong thing, but the green-eyed monster can make people not behave in the correct manner.

Karen looked at him with the glint of tears in her eyes and said, "No...It is just something I have to deal with myself."

Karen started to say more at this point, and she just ended up saying, "I mean, we...just can't."

Tears suddenly started to fill her eyes and spill onto her cheeks. She took in a heaving breath, and she sorrowfully said, "I am so sorry, Ryan. I just wanted to look at your smiling, caring face tonight."

At this point, Karen was crying heavily, and she couldn't speak coherent sentences. All she did was reach out her hand and caress Ryan's cheek. Then she quickly stood and ran from the street café.

Behind her, Ryan was sitting with disbelief and sadness covering his face, as well as a strong feeling of sorrow and confusion in his stomach. Ryan's first and main thoughts were, "She didn't even say good night to me", and "what the hell just happened?"

Ryan knocked and knocked on Karen's door that night, as well as trying to communicate with her through the closed door. Karen didn't seem like the type of person to just sneak out, but Ryan gave up knocking and simply sat on the floor outside her door. That was until he was chased away by the same chaperone, who wore a hideous toupee.

At that point, it being close to midnight, Ryan walked slowly back to his room and was met by worried questions from his friend Mike.

Mike saw the look on Ryan's face and quickly asked him, "What the hell happened tonight, Maxwell? You look like a guy who got his blood sucked out by a vampire. You left here all excited and full of color and energy, and now you are just colorless and bland."

Ryan then looked up at Mike as if he were a beaten puppy who was guilty of soiling the carpet. He raised his shoulders and quietly said, "I don't know what I did, Mike. Somehow, I must have fucked everything up tonight, but I just don't know how. She wouldn't talk to me, and she acted extremely shady, and then...then...she just took off, and I don't know where or why."

Ryan looked at his friend and sorrowfully said, "I swear, Mike, I just feel like I am a lost soul, and I don't know if I should be sad or just pissed off. All I know is that I feel taken advantage of and really scared. Do me a favor tonight, would you, Mike? I don't want to talk about it because I don't know what to say anymore and I just need someone around me. Not to examine my beliefs about Karen, but to just watch this goofy German TV with me and hang out together."

Mike gave him a compassionate smile and said, "Let me go grab some sodas and some junk food. I don't think that we will be sleeping much tonight."

When Ryan finally awoke the next morning, he and Mike were running late and had to skip the tour's breakfast plans. Ryan wasn't hungry at all anyway, as he felt like he could upchuck anything in his stomach. He did try eating a small blintz and drinking a strong cup of coffee from the corner grocery stand.

Soon after finishing the coffee, the acidic liquid bounced around his stomach like it was beginning to boil over. It almost made a triumphant escape from his esophagus when he witnessed Karen hugging a fellow male musician in the distance.

She shyly glanced over at him, and she gave him a weak smile and a small wave. Ryan, in return, gave her a small wave back, but his face did not reflect a smile in any form. The corners of his mouth seemed to hang down to the tops of his shoes.

Karen held up a finger in order to have Ryan wait for her, and then she ran in his direction and sheepishly said, "Good morning. I hope that you are okay today."

Before Ryan even got one word out of his mouth, Karen said quickly, "I need to talk about something. You probably won't believe me, but I only have a short time in order to see you, and I have to try to explain the truth to you."

Ryan looked totally confused and then said very slowly and drawn out, "Okaaay! That doesn't sound like a very nice conversation. Why shouldn't I just tell you to take a long walk off a short pier instead?"

Karen then glanced at an older woman, whom Ryan thought was one of her chaperones from the other bus. The woman wore a yellow, older style dress with wood buttons that ran diagonally down the front of it. She had brown hair that was tightly curled, and a brown wart was on one of her cheeks. She absentmindedly played with it while seeming to prod Karen forward with her body language and her no nonsense actions.

Karen then stood up straighter, looked directly into Ryan's eyes, and said with confidence, "Try to understand Ryan; this is very hard on me as well. I was supposed to leave last night, but I begged for one more day with you, and this is the only chance that we will have some time together. So please, Ryan, don't make me waste any time examining this whole crazy situation, because it would ruin the day ahead for both of us. Let's just enjoy a nice day together, alright?"

She looked at the older woman again, who nodded her head in approval and grimaced in a very regal, stuck-up manner. Karen nodded her head at the very interested woman again and almost pleaded with the young man who had become such a large part of her life.

She almost begged at him by asking, "Ryan, let's just have a nice day together and leave it at that. Don't ask me too many questions about this... please?"

Ryan only looked hurt, confused, and said to Karen, hoping that it would change her mind, "Okay, only because I think that I've fallen for you, and I would have fought off the devil if you had asked me to."

Karen grabbed the back of Ryan's neck and pulled him downward into a series of heartfelt kisses while stating, "Thank you." She said this between each small kiss she placed on his lips and cheeks.

The day started out as a sunny one. However, as the bus traveled in a southern direction to their destination, large black clouds seemed to gather at a certain location that the bus was pulling in front of. This had developed into the gloomiest day that occurred on the entire trip. Not only meteorologically but also mentally.

Ryan found Karen by her bus, and she gave him a big hug with tears welling up in her eyes. "Are you alright?" Ryan asked with concern.

Karen simply nodded 'yes,' and instead of grabbing his hand, she grabbed his entire arm. She walked extremely close to him with his arm held tightly against her chest, as if she may have floated away if she didn't hold on tightly.

Ryan could feel her chest rise and fall rapidly, and he heard her whisper to herself, "Be strong, Karen. You can do this."

They slowly walked around the front of the bus, and Ryan was stunned by what he saw in front of them. As if on cue, the young couple stopped walking, and the brown-haired woman who had egged on Karen earlier in the morning walked by them and said, "Welcome to Dachau Concentration Camp!"

Ryan and Karen stared through the gates of the infamous work camp that was originally built to house political prisoners. However, it had become a concentration camp during the Second World War, holding over 188,000 Jewish people and other political dissidents from throughout Europe. In actuality, the main forced population was from the Jewish community, which lived throughout Europe at the time.

It is said that if people don't learn from history, then we are all destined to repeat it. This can be especially said about the history of Europe. During the medieval period in many of these European countries, the Jewish people were often maligned and killed. They were even made to wear badges claiming their belief in the Jewish religion.

These people living in the dark ages became prisoners or were made to be refugees when they were kicked out of their homes. This has been the case with millions of Jews throughout several millennia of time. Mostly because they loaned money to royal houses that did not want or feel like they needed to pay these monies back to them.

The Jewish people also had a different view of religion that had a conflicting belief against the most popular religion in Europe, the Holy Roman Catholic Church, and the pope himself.

Now, if a person has ever had the distinct pleasure of being around a large group of teenagers, that person would never expect them to be quiet for very long. On this day, in Dachau Concentration Camp, a group of one hundred teenagers were as quiet as a stone for over two hours. The only sound that could be heard coming from the group of young Americans was sobbing.

Included in the tour were some memorial statues of some very emaciated, Jewish prisoners. Also included on the tour were the barbed-wire fences that surrounded the camp, as well as some of the barracks where prisoners were held during WWII.

However, the place that affected the most people with sadness was a type of bunker building that had twin smokestacks sticking out of the roof of it. This is where the youth orchestra entered the building where prisoners were taken to disrobe. They were then filed into showers that were made deadly as poisonous gas was rained down upon the naked prisoners.

After the deadly showers, there was a room that contained two furnaces that were still standing. This is where the bodies of the dead were cremated, turning them into a fine dust that blew out of the stovepipes of the war camp and fell gently upon the prisoners still interred there.

At the end of the tour, Karen was crying profusely. Ryan slowly led her back to the bus that he would be leaving on shortly. Karen wiped her nose with a hankie, and then she hugged Ryan closely, with her arms around his waist and her face held against his chest. She stayed this way and finally quit crying huge teardrops after five minutes.

Ryan did nothing but hold her close, stroke her long blond hair, and whisper words of encouragement. Ryan had totally forgotten about the situation the night before. He had fallen in love with her all over again as he held her quaking head and body against his own solid form.

Karen finally released him, stood on her tiptoes, and gave Ryan one of the most deep and sensual kisses that he had ever felt.

Ryan wiped her red eyes lightly with his thumb and then said to her, "I'll see you later tonight, okay? We still have tonight together, right?"

Karen shook her head in a 'yes' answer, and then she said, "This is the last night that I can be with you on this trip, though. I hope that you understand that. Oh, and don't try to come to my room and see me. I will come to your room tonight. I may be a little bit late, but please just wait for me."

Ryan grinned down at her and said, "I will wait for you for all time...that is... if you ask me to."

Karen reached again for Ryan as he quickly turned and entered the coach bus because she just wasn't strong enough to hold onto him anymore.

Ryan looked back at her through the large window on the bus, and she blew him a kiss and mouthed the words, "I love you."

Ryan never saw her walk around to the back of the bus and enter the passenger seat of a black BMW sedan. This car was driven by the older brown-haired woman that had been there that morning.

In the backseat, there was a demure, saddened, brown-eyed girl that was sitting by herself. She seemed to be a very petite girl who happened to be in her mid-teens as well. However, she was an unknown stranger to anyone who had the perception to notice her. Which no one did.

That evening, Ryan was nervously pacing the floor of the hotel room. He was not a man of patience when it came to waiting for someone else. He prided himself on being on time, and the thought of being late because of what the other person was doing seemed to immensely bother him. This was another thing that Ryan had no control over, and this tended to drive him crazy.

The group of musicians had traveled from Germany to Amsterdam in the Netherlands, that afternoon. They were going to have a formal dinner for the group of musicians that evening, and Ryan hoped that he had brought nice enough clothes. While he was pacing, he picked at the collar of his shirt and the tie that went around it. He always felt almost strangled by the constraints of a tie.

Finally, a knock was heard on the door, and when Ryan answered it, he quickly relaxed. The image that stood before him was the most beautiful sight that he had seen in his entire existence. Karen looked completely grandiose, as her long, blond hair was stacked perfectly over her high cheekbones. To add to her allure, she was standing in the hallway with a shy, but comely smile upon her slightly freckled face.

As he looked at her, all Ryan could say to himself was that he was a 'very lucky guy,' as she stood before him in an almost immortal package. To Ryan, she looked like the Greek goddess, Aphrodite.

She was covered by a glimmering soft white dress that hung over her darkened shoulders by thin spaghetti straps. The fabric of the dress seemed to conform to her shape and hang down to her lower thighs. She also carried a white sheer scarf over her left shoulder and had small, bright diamond earrings dangling from the lobes of her beautifully sculpted ears.

Karen looked at the way Ryan had dressed himself and started to giggle. Ryan tried to look insulted, and then he said too loudly, "Hey, don't laugh; I look sharp. I only look worse than you because you look like an actual angel."

Karen rolled her eyes at Ryan and then turned him to the reflection in the mirror and said to him, "We're not going to the country club dance, you, knucklehead. This is going to be an elegant evening, not a night out with your buds."

She then looked sorrowful and finished by saying lowly, "A once in a lifetime night."

At that moment, Ryan was dressed in a pair of white tennis shoes and a pair of black dress pants that had a blue, wrinkled button-down shirt tucked into them. He had taken off the tie, as the snugness of his collar was driving him crazy.

Ryan looked in the mirror and finally said, "Okay, I have definitely not been blessed with a great sense of fashion, but I do try. I packed these clothes all the way from Montana; the least you could do is be seen with me in public."

She exclaimed back at him, "No way, you look like a really bruised waiter in that. Let me help you."

Ryan grimaced and then agreed to let Karen go through his suitcase. At the end of her fashion experiment on Ryan, he was dressed in the same black dress pants. Only now, he wore polished black dress shoes as well as a dark green button-down dress shirt that his mom had packed for him. She found it in the bottom of the suitcase, and it seemed to have been cleaned and pressed. Then she slowly put a skinny, solid black tie over his head and let it hang loosely around his neck with his collar unbuttoned.

Karen let out a low whistle and said, "Now you look like you can be by my side. I always want to remember you this way. Just give me a smile to make it perfect."

He gave her his best smile, and then bent down and began kissing her moist, waiting lips. Cautiously, he kissed down the length of her neck, and he kissed along her right shoulder until he had run into and lowered the strap of the dress off her trembling shoulder.

At this moment, Karen seemed to snap to attention and take a deep breath as if she had been hypnotized. She then pulled away from Ryan and raised the strap of her dress back onto her shoulder.

Ryan's face looked flushed, and he was totally confused. He didn't know what to think, but he gave her a boyish grin that had a twinge of sadness in it.

They were staying in a remodeled hotel, which is in the older portion of Amsterdam and sits along the oldest canal in the city. This canal is named the Singel Canal, which was an old moat that used to encompass the medieval city of Amsterdam.

The impressive restaurant was located down the stone path that was next to the historic canal of the city. Many people think about Venice when they think about the canals of Europe, but many people don't know that Amsterdam was built on a series of canals as well. These were used as a transportation hub as well as a recreational passage throughout the city.

One of the main delicacies of Amsterdam, besides the edibles, of course, is the seafood and the salt-water fish located there. Ryan and Karen dined on an appetizer of a green salad with a vinaigrette dressing, sauteed shrimp, and a lightly coated herring filet, along with some incredible asparagus spears.

They ate slowly, as if they wanted this night to last forever, and they were eating a desert of lightly sugared, small waffles when Ryan noticed a small amount of sugar on the outer lips of Karen's mouth. He slyly leaned in closer and licked at her lips. He then gave her a warm, sensual kiss, just as the older, brown-haired woman placed her hand on Karen's shoulder.

Karen jumped at the touch of this woman's hand, and then she pushed Ryan's hands and head away from her own and stated, "Quit being so damn charming and funny. Just quit making this harder than it has to be."

She looked back at the older woman and then said to Ryan, "I think that it is time that we talked for the final time."

Ryan let the air out of his lungs at hearing this and swallowed hard as if he had been kicked in the sternum by a feisty horse. He then said gingerly, "Don't tell me you have a boyfriend back home?"

She gasped and said, "NO! NO! NO! Nothing like that; what kind of girl do you think I am?" She squeezed Ryan's hand a little harder, and then she continued saying quietly, "How many Jewish girls do you know?"

Ryan thought about this question and then shrugged his shoulders and said, "I have never thought to ask anyone, but not any, I would guess. There are not too many Jewish cowboys in Montana."

Ryan was still not even comprehending what she was telling him, until she finally had to tell him plainly, "Ryan, I'm Jewish."

Ryan finally understood, and he suddenly exclaimed, "Oh shit! I'm sorry. We were at Dachau today. No wonder you were upset. I understand now. I am such an insensitive boob at times, please forgive me."

She just looked at him with sorrowful eyes and grabbed his hands in order to make him quit talking. This finally made Ryan sit quietly while looking at her quizzically.

She then continued by saying, "Ryan, you have been so wonderful these last two weeks, and I would love nothing more than to stay here with you, but I must leave you tonight. I don't want to...but I have to."

She blurted this message out very quickly, so that it would be like ripping off a band-aid. However, in all actuality, did this approach hurt a person any less?

Ryan simply cried out in exasperation, "I just don't understand. Why? Karen...tell me what is going on."

With this new confrontation that he didn't understand, Ryan began to sweat profusely. His stomach seemed to rise into his throat, and his pulse quickened to that of a rabbit that was being chased by a fox. He started to breathe heavily, as if he couldn't get enough air into his lungs, and the room began spinning out of control.

Ryan had always loved the feelings given to him by the fair ride called the 'Zipper'. In this case, he didn't care for this queasy feeling when he was just trying to enjoy a nice evening at a restaurant.

Suddenly, most of the blood seemed to leave his head, and he turned an ashen white color. He had to grasp onto the table in fear that he might fall out of his chair. He looked at Karen with bulging eyes, and he simply blurted out to her, "I have to go outside...Now!"

Karen followed him out of the restaurant and tried to console Ryan, as he was really scaring her. He began pacing beside the watery canal at a very rapid pace. Whenever she came close to him, he looked at her as if he might jump into the waterway and swim up the current, until he reached the ocean.

Suddenly, Ryan stood up straight and walked to a stone bench that was along the canal. He sat down and finally lifted his head, looked at Karen, and asked her simply, "Why?"

She started speaking very quickly, and then she stopped herself and started to speak more slowly. As if, by doing so, she would make fewer mistakes and the truth behind her reasoning would make more sense.

Karen swallowed hard and then told her story to Ryan. "You see...right after I got chosen to go on this tour...I started to have some visitors. I don't even understand this, so I hope that you will believe me. Well...I started dreaming about this older brown-haired woman who seemed to be protecting this young, skinny, brunette girl. Then, one day before I left for New York, the same young girl came to visit me at my home."

This didn't help Ryan's feelings any, but he patiently listened to her in silence as he sat next to her on this cold, stone bench in Amsterdam.

She looked at Ryan, trying to see if any understanding was coming from him, and then she continued, "The last thing that I ever wanted to do was to hurt you. This girl who visited me spoke very knowingly as she talked at me with the most passion that I have ever heard before. She told me about where I came from and about what I was meant to do. You see, she claims to be a relative of my family."

Karen stopped talking and swallowed hard again. A grimace came across her face, and she cautiously said, "The young girl claimed to be an older relative of mine that was killed during World War II. She and this brown-haired woman that accompanies her need my help."

Karen started to cry again, and then she said through her tears, "I can't believe I am trying to explain all of this. I never thought that I would meet you, and this is the first time that I have said this out loud. It feels as insane as it sounds to me, too. I also feel...almost urged forward in order to help them. I truly do believe that she is a part of my family's journey, and I promised her that I would help. You probably think I am off my rocker, but she knows things about me that are very personal. I honestly do believe in her."

Ryan looked at her with incredulity and then finally said, "What about me, Karen? Am I a part of your fantasy world as well? Do you even hear yourself? You are going away, and I have no idea where or why. I just know that a ghostly relative told you that you had to. What the hell, Karen?"

While Ryan spoke to her, the fear and anxiety that he felt made him even angrier at Karen. He screamed out into the night sky, which caused passing tourists to pause and gawk in their direction.

Karen sat quietly and then said angrily back at him, "This is why I just wanted to leave and not have this talk with you. I asked for more time, just to be with you for a few more hours. They are here now, waiting for me. I wish that I could make you understand how important this is for me, you big jerk! Can't you see them?"

Ryan followed her finger and saw the older brown-haired woman holding the hand of a smaller, skinny, brown-eyed girl that looked about the same age as Ryan and Karen. The older brown-haired woman looked sternly at them, but a wide grin was stretched across the face of the young girl.

Ryan put his head back in his hands and stated roughly to Karen, "Well, if you are going to go, just get up and leave with them. They seem anxious to get out of here."

Karen was crying when she stood up and began walking toward the woman and the young girl. She was half of the way to them when Ryan blurted out behind her; "Remember this, you made me a broken person tonight."

Karen did not even turn around, as she may have run back to Ryan if she had done so. She only said quietly, "Goodbye, my love!"

Ryan didn't know this at the time, but this was the first of many panic attacks that would affect Ryan's entire life after this. This is also when the visions started as well...because Ryan should not have been able to see the women who were waiting for Karen.

"Juliet, the dice were loaded from the start,
And I bet, then you exploded into my heart,
And I forget, I forget the movie song,
When you gonna realize, it was just that the time was wrong."
(Dire Straits)

Chapter Five

If it wasn't for love or heartbreak, we would only have one-tenth of the songs we listen to.

The vision was of a knight who was riding a horse down a muddy road as the last light of the day was slowly disappearing behind him. This knight looked downward, and his shoulders slumped like he had just lost his only friend.

Suddenly, the knight raised his head, and his brow furrowed; his mouth hung down in the most sorrowful frown; and his green eyes spilled silent tears onto his slender, ashen cheeks.

Upon those cheeks was the stubble of an unshaven beard, and his long bangs of chestnut-colored hair hung down beneath a darkly stained metal helmet.

While sleeping, Ryan's forehead crinkled like he was trying to see the man closer, even though the knight was just a vision in his mind. He should be able to get a closer look at the man, shouldn't he? Ryan thought that it was important to know as much as he could about the knight.

Ryan then noticed that the knight had a sharp and skinny nose that was crooked, as if it had been broken several times and seemed to have been put straight by only his own hands. The knight also had broad shoulders under his gray armor. His upper body fell downward to a smallish waist, and his armor-clad legs hung listlessly on either side of the steed.

At this time, the knight seemed to look directly at Ryan, and he only said one word... "Princess!" Ryan awoke with that one word echoing in his mind. "Princess," he said to himself.

When Ryan fully awoke, he shook the dream out of his conscience, not noticing that he had overslept that morning. Then he thought of Karen, and the most important thing was to find her by rushing down to the entrance of the hotel. He had so many more things to say, and he just wanted to see her one more time. As a matter of fact, he felt like he needed to see her.

Ryan was jumping up, hoping to find her over the crowd of teenagers, when suddenly he felt a tap on the shoulder. He felt a surge of excitement go through him as he turned around. His excitement quickly turned to sorrow as one of the chaperones was facing him, and he said to Ryan, "She's gone, but she left you this."

He handed Ryan a letter and then turned on his heels and walked through the crowd of young musicians. Ryan opened the letter, which was soiled in wet drops that Ryan believed were teardrops, and it said:

> *My Dearest Ryan*
>
> *I can never feel more sorrowful for putting you through this. I don't know how else to explain this to you. I can't even tell my parents about this. I have told only you. I don't blame you for not believing me.*
>
> *Just know that I care for you deeply and that I may be in love with you. As crazy as this all sounds, I just feel like I need to try and help them. I write this with every bit of love in my heart, and I hope that you will find me again.*
>
> *Goodbye, my love!*
> *Karen*

Ryan's eyes dropped downward, along with his youthful spirit. He didn't even feel like he deserved the light and the warmth that the sun gave him that beautiful summer morning in Amsterdam. The tour was scheduled to stay in the Netherlands for only two more nights.

They were then scheduled to travel across the English Channel to London. This was going to be the last stop on their tour of Europe. They would be in London for three more days of sight-seeing and concerts, but Ryan felt as if his journey had ended then and there.

This was a first for Ryan, and he didn't know how to grieve the loss of someone that he had loved and trusted so much. This seemed to make Ryan much harder, more cynical, and much more guarded toward the world that surrounded him. All he knew was that he was disappointed and mad at the world. He made a vow right then and there that he never wanted to feel this way again.

Ryan loaded his luggage onto the bus, and they traveled to the amphitheater where they would perform their next concert. At this location, the performance fell way short of the excellence that was expected from the orchestra. They were now missing a talented flautist, as well as Ryan screwing up several important parts of the music.

His heart and mind were not into the music, which caused confusion among the other members of the orchestra. This caused the band to sound like they had not ever practiced playing together before that day. When one of the musician's performances falls short of expectations, the rest of the musicians follow suit.

After the concert, Ryan was confronted by the conductor of the orchestra, who sneered at Ryan and said, "What the hell was that piece of shit performance out there. Have you been sampling some of the local drug dens?"

Ryan only looked at him angrily and snarled back, "Get out of my face, you pompous, high-brow windbag! I lost the love of my life today, and the last thing that I need is to be yelled at by a dickless douchebag like yourself!"

Mike and Angelo heard Ryan's angry rant at the conductor of their tour and came to Ryan's rescue by grabbing each of his elbows and pulling him backwards.

Mike then apologized to the leader of their orchestra, "I'm sorry, sir. He has had a bad morning, and he is acting like he has gone out of control. His love life has really affected his mood and his ability to play. We will keep him away from you and will make sure he is ready for the last concert in London."

The conductor screamed back at them, "He better not screw around anymore… and he better be ready for our last four days of the tour. This is on all your heads now, not just his. I don't like to be made a fool of, and I don't care about his feelings or any of your social lives. I will call off the last concert and send the whole troop home if this keeps happening."

Ryan started to yell his reply to him, but Mike put his free hand over Ryan's mouth and silenced his disdain toward the conductor of the tour.

Mike then said to the man, "Don't worry, sir. He just needs to walk off this horrible frustration and anger that is bothering him this afternoon. He won't bother you again, sir. We promise."

Mike and Angelo then marched Ryan away from the conductor and away from the other curious rubberneckers in the group.

When the young men were safely away from the others, Mike asked Ryan angrily, "What the hell is wrong with you, Maxwell? You were acting almost out of your mind back there."

"Never been better." Ryan insisted sarcastically, while raising a stoic face and clenching his jaw.

"Bullshit!" Mike exclaimed quickly. "What the fuck is wrong with you?"

Ryan took several deep breaths, and when he became more relaxed, he stated, "She's gone. Karen is gone from the tour and out of my life."

Angelo then spoke and said, "I heard that she left because of some family problems. That is what the chaperone with the bad toupee told us at breakfast, anyway."

Ryan then looked over at him and said to his two best friends on the tour, "Left for family reasons, my hairy ass! She probably had to go into some booby-hatch. She told me last night that she had to leave in order to help some ghosts or spirits that had been haunting her, or some bullshit like that."

Ryan spit out his contempt and finished saying, "That's right. I got dumped because of visitations from dead people. I don't know whether to laugh or cry. This isn't in the 'getting your heart broken handbook,' and I don't know how to react at all. I feel like I am horribly angry, confused, and in deep despair at the same time. I can't even think straight right now."

Angelo was the first to speak when he said, "I am sorry, Ryan. I can't give you any guidance on your love life or your crazy girlfriend, but don't fuck up the rest of this tour for the rest of us. We understand that you are hurting and angry right now. Please don't rock the boat with the conductors or the chaperones. You will go down with this ship alone if you continue to go off the handle like you did this afternoon. We are your friends, but this crazy shit is not going to ruin the rest of my trip. I will tell you that with certainty."

Ryan looked angrily at Angelo and said, "This coming from the guy who almost got into a fight and fucked the whole thing up when we first got here."

Mike then chided Ryan, "Knock it off, Maxwell."

Angelo then looked seriously at Ryan and asked, "Who are these ghosts that she is supposed to be helping?"

Ryan then looked at him and stated, "I don't know. It is some older lady with brownish hair that is piled up into a bun on her head. There is also a young, skinny girl with shoulder-length brunette hair and big brown eyes. That is all I know, and this whole situation is completely against everything rational."

Mike then said something that made Ryan's skin crawl as he stated, "Listen, Maxwell, I want to believe you, but what you are saying is outright bullshit. I have been around Karen a lot since you have been seeing her, and I never saw her with anyone that looked like that. I have just seen her with you, and that is all. So, I don't know what the hell is happening."

Mike lowered the tone of his voice and then said, "Now, I have never thought that you were off your rocker, but this whole thing is absolutely nuts. Somebody has got to be lying here. I don't know why she is doing this, but it looks to me like she just felt out of control and ran away from you. Were you two getting too serious, or did you come on too strong where she just had to leave for some reason?"

Ryan thought about this and then stated, "Well, we were getting extremely close, and I was kind of pushing at her. However, it was because of the reasoning that she was giving me and the final story about the ghostly relatives. Hell, I saw her leave with this older woman and this young girl. If this isn't a true story, then she went out of her way to make me believe that it was the reality of the situation."

Mike then stated it plainly to Ryan by saying, "Listen, bro, doesn't it make more sense that she was just trying to get out of this whole relationship by telling you all about these weird ghost stories? I wouldn't want to be with anybody that is crazy, would you? I think that this was just her way of getting away from you. I hate to say this, but doesn't this seem more plausible? I am sorry, man, but I think that you got kicked to the curb and she found some others to help her."

Ryan was silent for several minutes, and then he apologized to his two friends by saying, "By God, I think that you are right. She has been acting weird for the last week. I am sorry, you guys. Boy, do I feel like a fool, and I just feel horrible that I pushed her so hard that she felt like she had to make up this goofy story in order to get away from me."

Mike then asked Ryan, "How do you feel now?"

Ryan answered him by saying, "I feel relieved that nobody is losing their mind, but I am very pissed off right now. How could she do this kind of thing to me? I mean, just be honest and upfront with me; don't tip-toe around the subject and blame a promise made to a bunch of ghosts. Now that I say it out loud, the wackier it all sounds. Damn, how could I have fallen for this? Dead people... shit!"

After dinner, the young boys had two more hours left in the day, and they decided to walk and see the women of the Red-Light District of Amsterdam. Upon arrival to the infamous prostitution zone of the city, the first thing that the three young men noticed were all the windows that the women posed in.

Angelo's eyes glistened, and he said gleefully, "My God, it's like window shopping here."

Mike looked at Angelo and reminded him, "Remember, we only have about 45 minutes until we have to high-tail it back to the hotel."

Angelo pointed out to Mike with a smile, "Dude, if I get into one of these rooms, it won't take me 45 minutes to do my business."

Mike and Angelo laughed heartily at this statement, but Ryan's eyes only flitted over these several glass windows. He could see that they housed more women of every age, color, and nationality than he had ever seen before. He had never felt a stronger urge in his life.

Besides the local prostitutes, the Red-Light District of Amsterdam was home to peep shows, sex shops, and even museums dedicated to human sexuality. Mike read from a tour guide about the prostitution zone, and he pointed out that all the women would pull the curtains of the rooms closed and a red light would turn on over the door if they were 'entertaining company.'

Ryan was still angry with Karen, and he was also extremely lonely. This combination of feelings often leads people to do things that they wouldn't usually do. If Ryan had been drinking that night, he would have had the perfect storm of dubious decision-making brewing inside of him.

Ryan then pointed at the window of a beautiful, nubile woman who was probably in her early 20s. She had long, dark brown hair, and she had a smallish face with a cute button nose that seemed to turn up at the end of it.

She gave Ryan a perfect smile and motioned at him with her slender hands to come closer to her. Her body was very athletic-looking, and she had a smaller build. Along with this, she also had a slender pair of long legs that were covered by red-laced stockings. She ran her fingers from her small breasts to her tightly toned stomach and thighs.

Because of the happenings of the day and because of how Ryan felt, he took a step toward the young woman's window.

He was grabbed by the arm by a worried Mike, who asked, "You're kidding, aren't you, Maxwell?"

Ryan only looked wounded and then said blatantly, "Why not? This will make for a great story someday. Imagine telling someone about how you lost your virginity. Plus, I'm not dating anyone right now, am I?"

Ryan then took a deep breath and said to his two good friends, "She is the one. This is it, boys. Wish me luck!"

In the next minute, Ryan was up at the glass of the window of the small apartment. He pointed at the girl and rubbed his fingers together in a universal payment signal.

The young woman then walked out of sight, and a newly painted wooden door was opened for Ryan to enter. He looked back at Mike and Angelo with a surprised gesture upon his face. Ryan then gave them a mischievous grin, and he winked at Mike and Angelo.

The boyish Ryan Maxwell disappeared into that room, leaving his friends standing on the street with their mouths agape.

Mike looked at the door and simply said, "I have known Ryan for six years, and I have never known him to do something like this."

Angelo shook his head and just looked back at Mike and said, "What is there to say? Women can sometimes drive men to act totally batshit loopy."

Ryan forked over the money that he had saved for food on his train trip back to Montana when he returned to the United States. Right now, he only had one thing on his mind, and it wasn't about the food on the train from New York to the Rocky Mountains.

His first act was to ask her name and if she spoke English. She said that her name was 'Paulette' in a broken, heavily accented English that sounded almost like a Russian accent to Ryan. He then wondered where she was from, but thought differently about asking her.

He then thought that he would make a bet that her mother hadn't named her 'Paulette', either. He liked the name very much anyway, and he told her so after introducing himself under his own fictitious name.

'Paulette' smiled at him in a very flirtatious way that made Ryan sit down weakly at the foot of a small bed. He then tried to cover up the very elongated and rigid boner that was growing in his pants. To conceal his excitement, he gingerly tried to cross his legs, but to no avail.

'Paulette' walked sexily in front of Ryan and waggled her finger while saying, "No."

She dropped to her knees and carefully uncrossed Ryan's legs while staring up at his own nervous eyes. She looked at his face and said to the young man, "You...first time...I be nice...take care of you."

Paulette then removed Ryan's shorts and underwear and began kissing the tip of his throbbing shaft. It seemed to be beating along with the rhythm of the blood coming from his very heart.

At this time, Paulette stuck something in her mouth and then dove her head forward, over his almost-pleading member. While sucking on Ryan's pulsating appendage, she unrolled a condom on top of his wanting cock with her tongue and made it safe for them to continue further.

Paulette never said another word to Ryan at this time, and he never said another sentence to her either. The silence between the two young lovers seemed perfect in that situation. He wasn't here for a conversation anyway.

The only glorious words and exclamations that came from Ryan were words that he had only used in church before this day. Paulette sucked on his fully erect penis until she sensed that Ryan's body was fully relaxed and hard as a board at the same time.

During this period, she slowly and tenderly laid Ryan's shoulders on her bed. Paulette then stood up and opened her red lingerie in order to show Ryan, her small yet perfectly rounded breasts.

Ryan was still lying on the bed, and Paulette then joined him by swinging one leg over his body. She straddled Ryan's prone form with her knees on either side of his waist. She lifted Ryan's hands up onto her firm breasts, and she began to writhe back and forth at his touch. She then pulled aside the bottom of the red-laced lingerie that she wore and slowly slid herself onto Ryan's almost pleading, erect cock.

'Paulette' began lifting herself up and then down over Ryan's stiff member. Ryan suddenly surprised her by taking his hands off her breasts and placing them on the firm curves of her upper thigh and the tight figure of her splendid buttocks. He acted like someone who had done this before because he began guiding her movements along his rigid member.

These movements only happened for close to two minutes, but in these two minutes, time seemed to almost slow down. The passion in the room seemed to explode around the two complete strangers until they finally collapsed into one heap together on the bed.

After Ryan erupted with pleasure in between Paulette's thighs, she leaned down to him until her lips kissed his ear softly.

She then said, in broken English, "You make American girl very happy someday."

'Paulette' was trying to adjust her red lace stockings when Ryan opened the door to leave. He looked back at her and said faintly, "My first," as if he were trying to take a mental photo of her.

Mike and Angelo watched Ryan leave the apartment, and they stared at their fellow fifteen-year-old friend as if he had just come back from the moon. Suddenly, they began to ask him several probing questions about his experience.

Ryan only stared back at them and said, "I can't tell you boys about this; you're just going to have to experience it for yourselves. I will tell you one thing, though. This is the best that I have ever felt in my life."

Ryan then led his friends out of the Red-Light District and back to their hotel. He was walking at least two inches taller that evening.

For the first time in about a week of relationship problems, Ryan finally slept throughout the night. He finally had a good night's rest without dreaming of any knights or even of any young blond woman named Karen.

He was proud of himself the next morning. He would never have had the nerve to visit 'Paulette', if he had not been hurt and felt betrayed by past relationship woes.

He had also awoken with an ever-growing hunger for the next great challenges and adventures that life would throw at him. The young troupe of musicians had one more day of sightseeing in Amsterdam. Then they were scheduled to travel across the English Channel on a ship that ran from there to London, England.

Mike and Angelo joined Ryan for breakfast the next morning, and Mike said, "That was a wild thing that you did last night, Ryan. I have known you for six years now, and I have never seen you act that way before."

Angelo then asked him, "Do you feel any better today?"

Ryan leaned back in his chair and lied to Mike by saying that he "never felt better" and that he "felt invigorated and was ready to experience life in a new way".

In all actuality, the sleep had helped him immensely, but his heart was still heavily damaged. At that moment, he was deeply cynical about the entire world around him.

Mike then said doubtfully, "You just seem different, Ryan. You seem a lot darker in how you look at things and how you treat people. You aren't your usual positive self. You are kind of... scary in how much you have changed."

Ryan gave Mike an angry look and stated, "Yeah, I am not your happy-go-lucky pal anymore. What do you expect? I got dumped for a fucking ghost! Compassion and truth are two of the farthest things from my mind right now. I am just basically trying to survive this whole situation, and I don't really want to be your responsible buddy right now. I also do not want or need your pity."

Mike didn't say a word to Ryan. He simply lifted the plate that contained his breakfast and left the table, while Angelo sat there as if in shock. They both finished their breakfast quickly and in silence. When Angelo had finally left the table, Ryan put on sunglasses in order to hide the hurt in his eyes. He then leaned back in his chair and sipped his morning coffee.

The friendship between Ryan and Mike was never the same after that moment. They both had too much stubborn pride in order to speak about this again, and neither of them had the sense to try to admit that he was wrong.

Angelo was still speaking to Ryan after the whole breakfast fiasco with Mike. He and the always attention-seeking Troy joined them as they walked the short distance to the Anne Frank annex, where the teenaged Jewish girl was hidden during World War II.

In 1942, when the Nazi army occupied the Netherlands, Jewish citizens lived in constant fear of arrest, imprisonment in a concentration camp, and being put to death. There were reprisals against them just because of who they were and what they believed. During this time, Anne Frank's father worked in an office that was in a warehouse that had a small, roomed annex built on the upper floor.

The four members of the Frank family, as well as the three members of the Van Pels family, and a single man named Fritz Pfeffer, lived in hiding in this small, roomed dwelling. In this annex, Otto Frank had put in a small amount of living provisions, including a small stove, single beds, a small living area, and a bathroom. These families stayed hidden for over 700 days, or almost 3 years.

In August of 1944, the annex was raided by the Nazis, and the Jewish families were discovered. To this day, no one knows who turned them in or why the raid was administered by the Nazis.

However, the young, fifteen-year-old Anne Frank and her family were sent to Auschwitz Concentration Camp, where they were held as prisoners.

Soon after, Anne and her sister, Margot, were then moved to Bergen-Belsen Concentration Camp, where Anne died due to a bout of exhaustion.

During her time in hiding in Amsterdam, though, Anne could not ever leave the confines of the warehouse or venture outdoors. Anne wrote in her diary to pass the time, and she did this as a way of escaping her confined and overcrowded conditions.

The diary was rescued by a group of sympathizers who also worked in the warehouse. They tried to help the families by hiding the diary in order to show the world the Nazi Party's crimes against humanity.

Upon walking toward the building, Troy asked one of the most stupid questions that Angelo and Ryan had ever heard.

He unknowingly asked, "So, we are going to this museum where the "Diary of Anne Frank" was written, right? What famous author lived there and did the writing?"

This question made Angelo stop in his tracks, and he looked at Troy with incredulity and stated plainly, "You really do have shit in between your ears, don't you?"

Troy shrugged and said, "What? I have never heard of this book before."

Ryan had always loved history, but at that point, he really grieved for the education that was being taught to young Americans. The trio then entered the museum, and Ryan was almost bowled over by what stood before him.

Ryan's mouth dropped open, and he stopped coldly in his tracks. He said, almost silently, "That is her! Oh my god, that is the young girl that Karen left with."

Ryan was standing in front of a large photo of Anne Frank, who was smiling widely at the camera. Her large, brown eyes seemed to bore a hole into Ryan's very soul. At the sight of this young girl, Ryan dropped the bottle of water that he had been holding in his hand, and he began to shiver uncontrollably.

Angelo looked back at Ryan and asked cautiously, "What do you mean, Ryan? This girl died in one of those concentration camps that was like the one that we were at on Wednesday. She's been dead for over 40 years. She must remind you of someone on the tour because she is not the girl that you saw with Karen."

Ryan's face had lost all its color, and he stated again flatly, "That is the girl. That is the girl that I saw Karen leave with, along with that older brown-haired woman. If she isn't the girl, then I saw someone who looks exactly like her. The only difference between this girl and the one that I saw was that she had very sad and anguished eyes when I saw her. This girl has eyes filled with excitement, but I swear, this is her. I am going back outside; you two go ahead and count me out. I suddenly don't feel very good."

"And watching lovers' part, I feel you smiling
What glass splinters lie so deep in your mind
To tear out from your eyes:
With a thought to stiffen brooding lies
And I'll only watch you leave me further behind."
(Duran Duran)

Chapter Six

"I heard the executioner was very good, and I have a little neck."
(Anne Boleyn: the day before being beheaded.)

The next day, Ryan was sitting next to the glass window that overlooked the waters of the English Channel. The wind was blowing a light rain against the window, and outside a darkening sky was beginning to grow on the horizon.

He had convinced himself that Karen had told him an incredible falsehood in order to protect both of their feelings. However, that was until he stared at the face of Anne Frank in any old photo.

That evening, a lot of the reverie among the teens was at the dance club that was aboard the ship. Ryan had been asked to join in on the festivities several times but had turned down each offer. Each time the door opened to the party, Ryan could hear electrified drums of a European pop group. Ryan would have enjoyed the attention that he would draw at the dance club, but tonight he wanted to think about all that had happened. Even if it drove him insane in the process.

Ryan closed his eyes at the sound of the billowing wind on the glass of the ship, when suddenly he was standing on an older bridge that overlooked a muddy river flowing beneath it. The bridge was made of stone and was constructed with several arches that descended into the waters below it.

On top of the bridge, there was a span of roadway that ran over the river. Along either side of the bridge, there were houses that were skinny row houses that were maybe 12 feet wide and two or three stories tall. Ryan frowned as he had never seen houses built on a bridge before, and then he noticed two bulbous forms seeming to float over one end of the bridge.

A thick fog was rising from the water below him, and Ryan could hardly see the ghostly appendages ahead of him. However, they almost beckoned him to walk in their direction. As Ryan carefully stepped forward, he noticed that no one was bustling around the street on the bridge. The only sound that Ryan could hear was the torrent of water that was flowing beneath him.

As Ryan approached the two bulbous items at the end of the bridge, he saw that the objects were implanted on slender pikes of wood that were covered with a dark, reddish liquid. At seeing this thick liquid, Ryan's stomach seemed to lurch upward, and he slid his hand down the closest sharp stake of wood. He wasn't surprised at the feeling of warm, sticky blood on the palm of his hand.

He pulled his hand away quickly when a sliver of wood embedded itself under the skin of his calloused palm. He was tempted to suck on his wound and pull the sliver out with his teeth. Then he noticed the amount of blood that was covering his palm and beginning to run down his wrist.

At this point, Ryan knew that the pieces of wood were ancient wooden pikes, and the bulbous forms were human heads that had been driven down on them. The blood from the heads was now intermingling with his own. The only question that Ryan had to know now was whose heads had been placed on either side of this old stone bridge.

Ryan walked very slowly past the entrance to the bridge and looked upwards at the gruesome images of the swollen, bloodied heads that dangled above him. The first thing that Ryan noticed were the faces of the men, which were drawn back in a horrible sneer of a bloody death mask.

Their eyes were closed, and their hair hung limply down and almost reached the pike that it was placed on. Ryan took a closer look and recognized one of the heads as that of the knight that he had dreamt about the week before.

This other head carried some of the same similar features as the other knight's head, except it was much more wrinkled and had fewer teeth in the mouth. He had an open mouth and seemed to be screaming out from inside a heavy gray beard.

Suddenly, the younger knight's eyes flew wide open, and he muttered with a guttural voice four new confusing words, "Princess o' the Tower."

A bloody scream escaped Ryan's lips, as if he had been suddenly struck in the face by an invisible fist. Then he felt his shoulder being shaken back and forth, and he heard one more time those blood-filled sputtering words, "Princess o' the Tower."

Suddenly, Ryan was once again sitting in the seat overlooking the English Channel. He was being shaken awake by a young girl who had red hair pulled back in a ponytail. It stood atop a freckled face that looked worried and scared at that moment.

The girl's name was Laura, and she was from Cleveland, Ohio. Most importantly, she had been Karen's roommate throughout the tour of Europe. Laura quit shaking Ryan's shoulder when he looked at her, but she kept a firm hand hold on his arms, as if he might lash out at her.

Laura then looked even more concerned at Ryan and said, "Are you okay, Ryan? You were shivering and starting to yell quite loudly."

Ryan looked at her concerned face and fumbled out a quick apology, making the features on her face relax a little bit. She then gave Ryan a slight grin and said to him, "Well, you should know that it almost killed her. I mean, when Karen knew that she had to leave you and the tour."

Ryan looked at her suspiciously and said more sharply than he intended, "Well, it has been no picnic for me either."

He then shook his head and apologized, "I'm sorry. You had nothing to do with it. Did she explain why she left to you?"

Laura looked embarrassed and said back at him, "Well, her story didn't seem quite true to me. She told me that she needed to leave for family reasons, but I don't think that she was being completely honest with me."

Ryan gave her a completely shocked look, and then she continued, "One night, I caught Karen talking to someone in our room. At first, I thought that she was talking to herself, but this was like she was carrying on a full conversation with someone. I couldn't see anyone there, but Karen told me afterwards that she was talking to someone called 'the girl'. She said that she was just practicing a conversation that she had to have. It was all very strange."

She gave Ryan a curious look with one raised eyebrow, and she got up to leave, which made Ryan ask her one more question: "Did Karen ever say anything about a 'princess' or anything like that?"

Laura looked at him quizzically, shook her head, and then said, "Nope, good luck though. You look like hell boiled over, Ryan. Do yourself a favor and get some rest."

However, sleep would have to wait, as Ryan's hand began to throb with pain. When he looked at his palm, he was horrified to find a sliver of wood embedded in it.

When the ship pulled into London the next morning, Ryan went out onto the upper deck and watched the ship dock onto a large stone pier that was on the outskirts of the city. He immediately put a baseball cap over his messed-up hair, pulled up the dark black dress pants that he was wearing, and put on his sunglasses.

He looked out at the skyline of the city and said to no one in particular, "London Town, what do you have to offer me?"

Ryan had only drifted in and out of sleep while sitting upright in the seat of a human transport ship. He looked as if he had been a drunk that had been rolled by a gang of thugs over his spare change.

His eyes seemed to be drawn inward, as if he had not found sleep in several days. Also, his clothes were crumpled and wrinkled from the very top of his white button-down shirt to the bottom of his dark black dress pants. Luckily, he had his trusty blue baseball cap pulled down over his wild head of hair, and he had his sunglasses on in order to hide his weary eyes.

At the bottom of the gangplank, there were two buses parked that would whisk the young musicians to their final hotel in Europe. This is where they would be staying for the final three days of the tour, and he sincerely hoped that this hotel was nicer than the rest of them. He also prayed that the surroundings would give him ample opportunities for his mind to be distracted.

Ryan looked at their new bus driver and asked him curiously, "So, where are you going to take us today?"

The driver winked at the young American, and then he said, with his best Cockney accent, "Ta de ead ut off inn."

Ryan stopped in his tracks, and he was rammed from behind by a chaperone of the tour, who wearily said to Ryan, "Watch yourself, Mr. Maxwell. It was a long trip last night for all of us, and I think that we all want to get to the hotel and get some rest."

Ryan looked back at the chaperone and asked him, "What did the driver just say?"

The chaperone looked at Ryan like he was wasting everyone's time, and he said very harshly, "It is his accent, Mr. Maxwell, he said 'the head cut off inn'. He meant that we are staying at 'The Tower Plaza Inn'. It is right next to the Tower of London. Now then, would you please get on the bus so that we can get there and get some sleep."

Upon arrival, Ryan was very impressed by the Tower Plaza, as he believed that this was probably the finest hotel that they had stayed in during the entire trip. As he entered the beautiful lobby, he was surrounded by windows, as this location looked out upon the famous Tower Bridge and was located directly across the street from the infamous Tower of London.

Ryan looked upward at this point in this luxurious lobby, and he was positive at that very moment that his room would overlook the Medieval Prison on the Thames River.

A restaurant was also in the same building, and it provided seating outside of the hotel on a large patio. This provided them with another fantastic view of Tower Bridge and the ancient river that flowed beneath it. Ryan could not wait to have dinner in an al fresco atmosphere surrounded by such interesting historical sights.

First off, he traveled up the elevator to the fifth floor, and upon entering his room, he was not surprised by the scenic view of the city and the Tower of London below him. Ryan looked down at the tower for several minutes...not moving...until he heard a jingling sound coming from the door. He turned around, expecting to see Mike. However, the acne-faced Troy entered his room.

Ryan looked confused at the sight of Troy and asked him, "What the hell is this, Troy? What are you doing here?"

Troy kicked at the carpet uncomfortably and then said shyly, "Well, I was rooming with Angelo, but Mike and I traded rooms. They wanted to hang out together, I guess. So... Mike and I did a trade."

Ryan looked at Troy in a hurt and shocked manner for several seconds and simply said to him, "Okay...right...well, welcome to the room, Troy. I didn't get much sleep last night, so I am going to lay down before I fall over. Don't worry about waking me up. I think that I could sleep through a bomb blast right now. I will be listening to my Walkman through the headphones anyway, so I will talk to you later."

Ryan didn't have any more words to say to Troy, and soon his ears were filled by the sound of Bono singing, "Sunday, Bloody Sunday". He fell directly into a dreamless world and was sound asleep very quickly.

Ryan awoke at 5:50 in the afternoon, as he had slept through almost the entire first day in London. He was alone when he awoke, and he knew that he needed a shower and a new set of clothes. He felt like a complete slob, as he had slept in the wrinkled clothes from the night before.

The night was warm outside, so he decided to wear a pair of black shorts, a red polo shirt, and a comfortable pair of high-top tennis shoes. The first stop that Ryan made was at a table in the outdoor restaurant, where he felt like he needed to eat a huge amount of food. He was surprised to discover that they had a steak, a baked potato, and some cooked carrots. To sit outside on this warm night and enjoy a steak sounded like heaven to Ryan.

Ryan had ordered his dinner, as well as a pint of dark ale, when he was joined by a sorrowful Angelo, who said, "I am sorry to throw Troy at you like this. Mike was insistent that he didn't want to stay with you. He says that he just wants to enjoy the rest of his trip and not be drawn into this weird soap opera that you are involved in."

To make Angelo's point about being involved in something that he did not understand, Ryan began to hear a loud group of people cheering and yelling at something entertaining. The sound of the crowd seemed to be coming from up the river, where the Tower of London is located.

Ryan was still talking to Angelo while this noise kept getting more boisterous. Ryan began to compensate by speaking louder and louder. This caused many people near them to stop eating, and they gave Ryan an extremely cautious look, but Ryan paid no attention to them.

Finally, the waiter brought the steak, which was quite disappointing to Ryan. This was not exactly beef country.

Then he asked the waiter, "Is there a concert or a soccer game going on around here?"

The waiter bowed and then asked politely, "I beg your pardon, sir?"

Ryan took in a mouthful of potatoes, and then he said after swallowing, "You know, all the people yelling and cheering at something up the river from us. What is going on?"

The waiter gave Angelo a strange, almost sad look, and then he left the table without saying another word.

Angelo, however, gave Ryan a worried look and said, "There is no yelling out here; there are no sounds of anybody even talking loudly, except for you. Mike thinks that Karen may have pushed you over the edge. Are you okay, Ryan? You have a lot of people worried about the way you have been behaving."

Ryan leaned forward, put his head in his hands, and then answered him by saying, "I just don't know, Angelo. Something is happening to me, and I don't know what it is. I may have fallen out of the crazy tree and hit every branch on the way down, but I just don't know anymore."

Ryan let out a deep sigh and then continued by saying, "Don't worry. I am going to finish this trip, and then I am going to the doctor when I get home. Tell Mike that I am sorry. I will try to figure this out on my own and won't ruin the trip for any of you. I think that I will have another ale and see if that quiets the voices that I am hearing."

Angelo gingerly stepped away from the table as if he might set off a mad ranting episode of alarm from his depressed friend. Angelo truly wanted to help, but he just didn't know exactly what to do or say.

He finally said to Ryan when he was about ready to leave, "You have been through a lot. You will be home soon. Your parents are going to be so glad to see you. Just be strong and take care of yourself, Ryan."

Ryan let out another deep breath and then said aloud to himself, "So my choices are that I am either going stark raving mad or I might have a tumor. What other choice is there? It will probably not be a believable one, that is."

The ale had worked a little bit, as Ryan still heard people cajoling and yelling, but the loud noises had been tamed down quite a bit. The ale had helped him with the voices, but it had also hindered him as his stomach became very nauseated and he could not quit belching. Before Ryan could make an even bigger jackass out of himself by getting sick in the restaurant, he decided to walk out onto Tower Bridge and get some fresh air.

He had only walked 40 yards across the bridge when Ryan had to stop and rest himself against the railing. He suddenly felt horribly dizzy and nauseated. Luckily, the wind did not blow this evening as Ryan had to lean over the side of the bridge and let loose a powerful stream of steak, potatoes, and dark English ales.

He leaned against the railing with his head lowered, and he wondered to himself if this was it. Was his life going to end in London? Would his body have to be shipped back to his mother?

Ryan's head was still lowered, and his breathing had just gotten back to normal, when he heard the yells and screams coming from his right again. He turned his body and looked at the Tower of London itself, only to find what he saw to be unbelievable. All the concrete and sidewalks had disappeared, and only grass and a dirt-covered trail ran between the river and the walls of the tower itself.

These walls and the area in front of them were now illuminated by torches that were hung on the sides of the walls. The sounds of a crowd ranting and screaming came from inside the large gates that had been opened, where Ryan could see a gathering of torch-wielding peasants.

Suddenly, a woman who was in her mid-60s and had grayish brown hair piled on top of her head in a bun came running out of the gate and up the dirt trail. She was wearing a white dressing gown, and she was holding her left shoulder and screaming at the top of her lungs.

Ryan squinted his eyes, and he could see now that blood was running from a wound on her shoulder. The white dressing gown that she was wearing had begun to turn a ghastly color of red. Behind her was a young, fat man who was wearing a dark black mask on his face, and he seemed to be chasing her while carrying a large, bladed axe.

As he ran out of the gate after the hurt woman, a mass of people carrying torches started running after him, as if they were cheering him on in his pursuit of the woman. The woman was grasping at her bloody shoulder and trying to look behind her as she ran. When she did this, her feet got tangled together, and she fell harshly onto the dirt road.

The fat man with the axe caught up to her at that point. He violently grabbed her, hoisted her over his shoulder, and carried her back to the open main gate. The crowd of onlookers made a pathway for the fat man carrying the much smaller woman, still chanting and yelling at either the fat man wearing the mask or the woman herself.

Ryan began to shiver, even though the summer night was warm. He closed his eyes at the horrors that were unfolding in front of him. While his eyes were closed, the loud rants of the people seemed to drift off into the night sky, and Ryan could not hear them anymore. When he opened his eyes, all that he saw standing before him was the closed edifice of the Tower of London and the city skyscrapers behind it.

Ryan stood in disbelief, and then he said out loud to no one in particular, "What the fuck just happened?"

He then tried to take a step toward the tower when his legs gave out from under him, and he fell directly forward onto his protecting arms. This fall gave him a pair of bleeding elbows in the process.

Ryan's heart almost leapt from his chest when a young man with a backpack strung across his back tapped him on the shoulder and said, "Ghet es dir gut?"

Ryan looked at the young man and shook his head and said, "No, sorry...I don't speak German."

The young man wasn't traveling alone and looked back at a young woman, who was also hoisting up a large backpack. He said something to her in German, and she replied in the same language, along with a shrug of her shoulders.

The young man looked back at Ryan and then said, in very broken English, "You...Good?"

Ryan let out a coughing laugh and then stood up and said sarcastically, "Am I good? Physically, I am okay."

Ryan showed his bloody elbows to the young German couple, and then he finished his statement, "Mentally, not so much."

Ryan then pointed at the Tower of London and placed his forearm horizontally. He tried to represent running to the Germans by using his forefinger and his middle finger in a parody of running across his forearm. He then gestured to the German couple, pointed to his eye, and then to the Tower of London itself. Hopefully, he was trying to make them understand what he had seen.

The German couple only shook their heads, and the man looked back at the woman. He said one word several times, "Verruckt."

The man then patted Ryan on the back, shook his head, and he and the woman walked down the bridge and into the night. They were both shaking their heads in a concerned manner.

Ryan walked back to the hotel room, and when he arrived, he asked Troy, "Do you still have the translation book that we used in Germany?"

Troy looked through his suitcase and then tossed Ryan the translation book. Ryan gave his thanks and then started reading. When he was finished looking through it, he looked at Troy and stated, "Did you know that crazy in German is pronounced, Verruckt?"

Troy looked at him seriously, and he then asked him, "Are you doing okay tonight, Ryan?"

Ryan didn't even change clothes again and simply crawled into his bed. He turned over on his side and answered Troy, "Oh, I think that I am just, Verruckt!"

When Ryan awoke the next morning, he laid in bed until Troy decided to get a chaperone to visit him and see how he was feeling. Ryan pretended that he may have food poisoning and that it made him extremely weak to walk too much. It wasn't exactly a lie, and it probably wouldn't be a good idea for him to join the rest of the tour that day.

The chaperone tried to talk Ryan into going, as they were supposed to visit Big Ben, Westminster Abbey, and Buckingham Palace that day. However, proof that Ryan should stay back at the hotel and rest was up his sleeves.

They were the scrapes and bruises on his elbows, and he told the chaperone that he had fallen because he had been extremely weak. He blamed it on the English cooking that he had eaten the night before and said that he didn't want to ruin the day for the others on the tour. This was very believable to the chaperone, and they soon left without him.

The time was now 8:00 a.m. Ryan checked with the chaperone and learned that the tour was not scheduled to return until 5:00 p.m. That gave him an exact timeline by which he knew they were planning to be gone. Ryan waited an additional hour, just to make sure that everyone had left. Then he went out of the hotel by the side entrance and walked to 'The Tower,' as he liked to call it now.

He had to try and figure this whole situation out, and the only thing on his brain were the new mysteries involving the contents of this intimidating medieval structure. Ryan slipped across the busy street and stood outside the large, open wooden doors that seemed to loom above him.

Ryan was standing there, having trouble moving his feet forward, when he heard a cheerful voice asking him a question in a perfect Old English accent. The voice cheerfully asked, "Can I help ye, young master?"

When Ryan looked up, he had been confronted by a round, very large man who had a gray beard, and he was wearing a bright red uniform. This form of dress was highly inquisitive to Ryan, as the man was wearing a long, red tunic that ran down to his knees. The Tudor crown of England was embroidered on the chest in golden colors, and the initials of E and R were placed on either side of the red uniform.

Also on the front of the uniform were the symbols of a thorn, a rose, and a shamrock. On the top portion of the red uniform, the man had on a frilled white collar that went around his neck. He also wore a taller, black hat that had a colorful hatband on top of his head. Under the waist, the man wore highly polished, black shoes that covered long, red socks pulled up high on the leg.

Ryan was taken by surprise by the red-clad man, who stood nearly 6' tall and he probably weighed 320 pounds. He most definitely wasn't the fastest guard in the tower, but he was probably the strongest. He was not a man to be trifled with, by any means.

Ryan jumped back at the sight of the man and spoke out in surprise while he was in mid-sentence by saying, "I sure hope you can help me. I need to know the… HOLY SHIT! YOU'RE A BIG GUARD!"

Ryan blushed after he said it and apologized to the gentleman. The man chuckled out loud, grabbed his profuse belly, and said jokingly, "Ay, never have I turned down a good meal or a pint of grog. My name is Mel, and I will help you all that I can."

Ryan looked at the way he was dressed and asked Mel, "I have seen other men dressed like you, but why are you all dressed like that?"

Mel looked seriously at Ryan and said, "Well, I am a Yeoman Warder, or a guard of the tower. We are also called Beefeaters. I think that they call us by that name because we used to guard the royal families. We got large amounts of beef that was left over from their meals, but that is just an old story. This is our dress uniform."

A beefeater is an ex-military person who wears traditional military dress. They guard the exhibits, the royal jewels, and the historic buildings that enshrine them. Mel was squinting his wrinkled eyelids into the bright sun, and he rubbed his scruffy, white beard.

He looked seriously at Ryan and asked, "You alright, Mate? You look out of sorts."

Ryan answered him morosely, "I am just having a nervous breakdown, I think."

Mel looked concerned and then said, "Well, let me give you the tour and teach you about the tower. Maybe I can lift your spirits and give you an ear to listen to."

Ryan followed Mel through the gate, and he gaped in awe at the intensity of the buildings and the walls that surrounded him.

Mel looked at Ryan's face, and then he said slowly, "Now, there are many things that I have to teach you, but I am going to start you out with the basics of the tower itself. Then I will show you some of the more ominous, secretive aspects of this old castle. Do you understand what I am telling you? I'm only telling you this because you look kind of overwhelmed and scared of this place."

Ryan protested back to Mel that he was fine and that he wanted to learn everything about the place. Ryan even used the words that he felt like he really 'needed to learn' the brutal history of this famous locale.

Mel gave Ryan a cautious look and then simply grabbed him by the shirt collar and pulled him along while saying, "All right then, mate. I will give you the complete story as well as the most gruesome tour that we give. If you have any questions, I am at your bidding."

Mel started to say something else, but Ryan dug his heels into the ground. When they stopped, he firmly asked Mel, "Did you guys have a play out here or something that was very loud last night?"

Mel gave him a curious look and stated, "Laddie, we are a military, historic landmark, and museum. We don't act out plays or anything like that. We shoot off cannons and have parties to commemorate special events, but we don't host any wild parties."

Mel then chortled out loud and continued saying, "Look at how I am dressed, young man. It took me half an hour to squeeze into this damned uniform; I'm not doing any costume changes or trying to run in these blasted clothes. Why do you ask?"

Ryan said that it was nothing to talk about, even though it was the most important thing on his mind.

Mel looked at Ryan's face seriously, and then he started to give the tour to Ryan again by saying, "This, young man, is the main gate into The Tower. These walls have been the homes of Kings and Queens; coronations of the Royals; a home to the Crown Jewels; a royal mint; and, of course, a prison and place where many tortures and beheadings took place."

Mel took a deep breath and then continued saying, "These buildings, laddie... actually, this entire place is like a complete tour of English history in one stop. You might say that this place is an actual "Time Machine" into the glamour and the savagery of the men and women throughout our history."

Mel finished saying his opening monologue to his youthful listener, looked at Ryan, and said, "This place is also home to many ghosts as well, lad...many, many ghosts."

Ryan smiled weakly back at Mel and asked him directly, "How do you not become overwhelmed by all of the history that comes from this place?"

Mel seriously said back at him, "I like to look at myself as being a part of the history of this entire medieval structure. When you see yourself as a part of the action, you tend to act and think in a certain way. I see myself as a part of the story."

Ryan truly enjoyed this answer, and with this knowledge, his whole body seemed to relax. Plus, he also enjoyed hearing it said in an original English accent, as this tone of voice seemed to relax his mind. It was extremely comforting to Ryan.

Mel then started speaking as a tour guide again, and he said, "All right, lad...I think that I am going to show you some of the grounds and landscapes outside of the buildings of this remarkable place first. Then we will go back in time from there; does that sound good to you, young master?"

Ryan finally smiled widely, and he said, "That sounds perfect to me. Lead away."

Mel began the tour by pointing out the oldest and tallest castle keep in the center of the walled fortress. This nearly 100-foot-tall structure was once the tallest and most formidable structure in all of London. This white-washed, stone monolithic castle is named 'The White Tower'.

Mel then told Ryan the story of William I, 'The Conqueror', and how he had invaded England from northern France in 1066. He and his army had defeated the English troops at the Battle of Hastings. He had not just conquered England; he had also changed the entire course of human history as well.

Upon reigning over a new populace, William wanted to show the people of England that he was their new ruler. He wanted to instill fear into their very hearts, as well as into the hearts of any armies that planned on attacking English lands again.

Mel continued by taking Ryan for a walk around the massive White Tower. He then pointed out that the castle keep was four stories tall, and they were all built to have three rooms on each floor.

All the upper floors were designed the same way, as there is a large room in the west area of each floor. This room provided entrance to the two square defensive towers at those corners. There is a smaller room in the northeast corner of each floor that is connected to the circular tower that holds the main staircase.

The ground floor, otherwise called the basement, was used for storage and was also used as an armory and prison chamber. Weaponry and armor from kings of the past have been put on display here in the main large room. Directly below the grand Cathedral of St. John's was a room called the crypt, where prisoners were detained. Also, the smaller rooms were used for the torture of the many prisoners that were interred there.

The first floor was raised and became the main entrance to the building. A wooden staircase rose on the outside of the castle to the main entrance doors of the mighty fortress. The entrance to the grand Cathedral of St. John's is also located on the first floor. This chapel's ceiling rises all the way to the top of the third floor. It was mainly used as the floor where the constable of the tower and his officers were located.

The second level of the keep is made up of the main, larger room, which was used as a banquet hall. The smaller room in the northeast was used as a court, where many prisoners found out their fate. Lastly, the middle section of St. John's Cathedral takes up the rest of the space on this floor.

The third and final upper floor had a small office in the northeast section that was used by the king. The larger room was used as a council chamber, where the king's advisors would make decisions regarding the country. Finally, on this floor, there was an overlook of the chapel and the people that were attending the Holy Roman Catholic masses.

Above these four floors, the roof was remodeled and fortified to add heavier weaponry to it. First, cannons were placed along the roof in the 16th century, and eventually, larger gunpower was placed there to shoot at the Nazi bombers during World War II.

Mel raised his arms outward, as if he might give Ryan a large bear hug. Then he said proudly, "This, laddie, has been arguably the most formidable and strongest fortress in all of Europe for nearly 900 years."

Ryan seemed to have the breath almost driven from his body by the mere brilliance of the place. Then he noticed statues that depicted lions, tigers, and even a statue of an elephant.

Mel smiled at this astute observation, and then he stated, "This was, in all actuality, London's first zoo as well. They began bringing animals here in the 1200s and they were housed here until the 1800s. There were many lions and tigers and bears..."

Ryan cut Mel off by saying loudly, "Oh, my!"

Mel only gave Ryan an annoyed look and continued by saying, "They even had that bloody elephant here at one time. People traveled from all over England to see these creatures, and the royals thought that the animals made the place look even more perilous."

Ryan then looked around the grounds and asked, "What about the large crows that are seen all over the place? They walk around like they own the palace. Why don't you ever shoo them away?"

Mel smiled at Ryan and said knowingly, "You mean the large black ravens? They are not supposed to ever leave the grounds. It is said that if the ravens ever leave the tower, then the kingdom and the royalty will fall out of favor, and the country will be lost. That is why the ravens don't fly anymore...they clipped the wings so that they can never fly away or leave the tower."

The last place on the landscaped grounds of the Tower of London that Mel took Ryan was a location west of the White Tower. It was named 'Tower Green'. In 1985, the site was marked by large tiles of granite that had a small brass plaque placed on a pole. It stuck out of the ground and said:

The Following Nobles Are Known To Have Been Executed At Tower Green:
William Hastings, 1st Baron Hastings,
by order of Richard, Duke of Gloucester, in 1483

Queen Anne Boleyn, 2nd Wife of King Henry VIII, 19 May 1536

Margaret, Countess of Salisbury,
the last of the Plantagenet dynasty on 27 May 1541

Queen Catherine Howard, 5th Wife of Henry VIII,
by a bill of attainder on 13 February 1542

Jane Boleyn, Viscountess Rochford
by order of King Henry VIII on 13 February 1542

Lady Jane Grey, "The Nine Days Queen," Wife of Lord Guildford Dudley
by order of a special commission of high treason, 12 February 1554

Robert Devereux, 2nd Earl of Essex, for Treason on 25 February 1601

Ryan looked confused and said, "I thought that a lot more people were beheaded in the Tower. I mean, this place is kind of well-known for people getting their heads lopped off."

Mel gave a little chuckle to Ryan's observation and told him, "You see, laddie, if a person was beheaded here, it means they were of a higher rank than everyone else. They were given the opportunity of being killed inside the tower walls, so that the general rabble of peasants couldn't watch them being executed."

Mel wrinkled his brow and then continued by saying, "These people thought that they deserved more privacy than the other people in England. Three of these folks were Queens of England. All but Lady Jane Grey were accused of adultery or treason against King Henry VIII. All of them were beheaded with an axe except for Queen Anne Boleyn, who was beheaded by a professional executioner from France. He used a sword to 'lop off her head', as you put it."

Mel then finished this story by saying, "They were all buried in the chapel that stands just north of here, St. Peter ad Vincula. The rest of the executions took place outside of the gates at 'Tower Hill'. This place is located outside the walls and behind the famous chapel. These were the people that the public was invited to watch die."

Ryan looked confused at the place where the gallows were and the place where Tower Hill was located. He couldn't quite imagine the fascination with watching someone die.

Mel then gave Ryan an ominous look and said, "In those days, it was quite an event to come to an execution. If the people were rich, they cut off their heads. If the people were poor, they hung the poor bastards. Welcome to life in medieval England. If the plague didn't kill you, then you could be persecuted at any time. They did this just for speaking their minds."

Mel gave Ryan a joking wink and then said, "Well, the tour is done for today. If you come back tomorrow, I will take you inside these historic towers. I will also show you the Crown Jewels. Do you want to come?"

Ryan's mouth rose into a large grin, and he said back to Mel, "Tomorrow would be great. I want to learn all that I can about this place. I will have some tricky questions to ask you as well. Thanks, Mel, I will see you tomorrow morning."

Ryan arrived back at the hotel at 4:35 p.m. This was a brief 25 minutes before the rest of the tour was supposed to return. He entered the hotel by the side entrance again, as he saw the bus pull into the parking area as he was waiting to cross the busy street to get back to the hotel.

He scrambled up the stairs as he avoided the lobby and the elevators, or any place where he could be seen. On the stairs connecting him to the second floor, he heard the loud chittering of other young people who had entered the stairwell just below him. He knew that he would have to sprint up the stairs and into the room of his hotel on the fifth floor.

Ryan burst out of the stairwell just as the dinging sound from the elevator echoed down the hallway. Ryan was standing at his door, trying to awkwardly slide his key into the keyhole as quickly and quietly as possible. Suddenly, he heard the familiar voices of Troy and the older male chaperone.

Finally, the key found a home in the door, and a frantic Ryan burst into the room. He then stopped and reached behind himself in order to close the door as quietly as possible. Ryan was still panicking in the middle of the room when Troy's key clanged against the metal knob on the exterior door.

Ryan's first thought was of the clothing that he was wearing, and he unbuttoned the white dress shirt that he was wearing, as quickly as he could. A thread of the fabric got caught on the last button of his shirt, and he cussed out, "Oh, shit!"

The door was starting to open when Ryan tore the button off with a heavy yank of his arm, and he flung the shirt into the corner of the room. He then jumped into the single bed at the far end of the room, pulled the blankets up to his neck, and pretended to be asleep.

Maybe 10 seconds passed when Ryan heard the voice of the chaperone saying, "Well, Mr. Maxwell, how are we feeling this afternoon?"

Ryan pretended to yawn, and put his bare arms above the blankets, and replied. "Still kind of weak. I feel hot and flushed right now."

Ryan didn't lie to them because sweat was raised on his brow and on his neck from the climb up the stairs.

The chaperone smiled weakly, as if he looked skeptically at Ryan's condition. He then asked about dinner, but Ryan said that he would stay in the room and eat a little something. He promised to do this, just so that he would be strong enough to visit some of the local sights the next day.

Ryan then finished by saying, "I will go on walking tours, I mean. I don't think that I will stray too far from the hotel."

Ryan did go to sleep that night, but it was a restless sleep as he kept thinking about the many executions that had happened across the street. Most importantly, he tried to figure out a way of asking Mel about the visions that he had been having. All without making himself sound completely insane in the process, that is.

"On my deathbed, I will pray to the gods and the angels
Like a pagan, to anyone who will take me to heaven
To a place, I recall, I was there so long ago
The sky was bruised: The wine was bled
And there you led me on."
(Audioslave)

Chapter Seven

"The world is but a large prison, out of which some are daily selected for execution." (Sir Walter Raleigh)

Ryan walked through the gates of the Tower of London when they opened at 9:00 a.m. That morning, both excitement and apprehension controlled his inner thoughts and actions. The recent visions and dreams had really shaken him. He was surprised that he had not had any dreams the night before.

Also, these recent, strange occurrences had really caused a bad reaction with the other teenagers on the tour. Ryan had become almost an outcast among his fellow peers. It was tremendously nice to have a smiling face await him, even if that joyful face belonged to an older, very large Englishman.

Mel looked at Ryan and said, "Good morning to you, laddie. I've been waiting for you."

Ryan responded to the morning's greeting, and then he asked Mel, "Can I see inside the towers today?"

Mel chuckled and then answered him by saying, "We will look inside all these towers today. The White Tower is just the oldest and largest, but there are many places to explore in this place. As I told you, this structure started with William I in 1066, but towers, moats, and walls have been added by several kings and queens since then. We have lots to see."

Ryan then looked confused and asked Mel a question that had been bothering him: "Mel, why do you give me a guided tour by yourself and not as part of a group, like the other guides?"

Mel smiled back at Ryan and said, "Because you are not like most tourists, and these have been my days off work. I get extremely lonely here. Most people want to just see the easy lessons of history that happened here...but you seem to want to absorb all the past that this place has to offer. I can tell the difference. Now then, let me show you the meat and potatoes of what this place has to offer you."

Ryan and Mel then began walking up the wooden staircase that led to the entrance of the White Tower. The first thing that truly stood out to Ryan was the thickness of the walls of this ominous castle. Mel had told him that they were up to 15 feet thick of hardened stone in some places. This fact had amazed Ryan, but now he could see that it was true.

Mel could see the astonishment on Ryan's face; he leaned closer and said, "Remember, this was built as an impenetrable castle. Plus, you need walls this thick in order to hold up the chapel and some of the rooms above you on the third floor."

This first floor was also used to welcome people to the castle and astonish arriving guests from the upper class of society. If a person is astute, they can tell this by the large, ornate fireplaces along the walls and the private privies that were located here.

Ryan then curled his nose and asked Mel, "By privies, I would guess that you mean medieval indoor toilets, am I right?"

The response that Mel gave was only a smile and a nod of the head. Ryan then jokingly asked him, "So did historians have to sift through the royal shit as well?"

Mel smiled wider and said, "Not the historians themselves, but their underlings did. Remember, shite flows downhill, laddie! In this corner of the massive building, there is the small circular staircase that will lead us to the chambers above us."

Ryan gave Mel a confused look and asked, "Aren't we going to start with the basement?"

Mel frowned and said bluntly, "You are more than welcome to go down there by yourself, but I do not like it in the crypt. I will not go down there."

Going through the main doors of the ancient church, the two men entered the back end of a large, stone Romanesque Chapel. Ryan looked astonished, and Mel proudly said, "Welcome to St. John's Chapel. This is actually 'the mostly unused and overlooked chapel' of the Tower. The main chapel was the one that I pointed out to you yesterday, the St. Peter ad Vincula chapel, where Queen Anne Boleyn and other nobles are buried. I will show it to you later in the day."

Ryan almost didn't hear Mel as he looked down the inner aisle of the historic chapel. Wooden pews stood on either side of the inner aisle, and a smaller altar was raised above the pews on the far end of the building. Vaulted stone archways ran along each side of the chapel, not only on the bottom of the chapel but also on the upper sections as well.

The whole chapel was lighted by the larger windows that stood above the parishioners. Ryan walked slowly toward the altar, and he rubber-necked at the massive archways that surrounded him. Mel only stood in the doorway and grinned proudly to himself, as if he were the cat that had just caught and eaten his first bird.

Mel then led the young American to the second level of the tower. There, he showed Ryan the large banquet hall that was used by royalty. He also showed him the court, where many people were sentenced to death outside of these walls.

All these items were very interesting to Ryan, but he found himself most interested when they went to the third level of the castle. On this floor, there was a block of wood that had a depression in the wooden top that was running down the middle. In this depression, many cut marks were made into the wood.

Leaning next to the wooden block was a thin, sharp axe that was on display in front of a huge display of a large group of people cheering at the beheading of a knight.

Ryan looked over at his large personal tour guide and stated gravely, "I have seen an axe like this before."

Mel gave Ryan a confused look and asked him, "Are you positive of this, laddie? There are many kinds of axes. Some are used for chopping wood, some are used in building, and this one here is an executioner's heading axe. It was made for chopping people's heads off."

Ryan then glared at Mel and said, "I am sure that it is used for cutting people's heads off. It looks very sharp."

Mel made a hushing sound with his finger across his lips. He sensed that Ryan needed to talk and led him to a bench that was next to a window that looked across Tower Green, where seven people had lost their heads.

After sitting down, Ryan breathed in and out heavily, and then he told Mel about the vision that he had seen the other night. He also told him that he had "witnessed," a fat man carrying that form of axe, and how he had been chasing a woman who was bleeding from the shoulder and neck.

After the story, Mel scratched the graying beard on his face, and he asked Ryan, "Could you pick out the woman that you saw from a picture?"

Ryan thought about the situation for a second, and then he said truthfully, "Yes, I could. Plus, I have also been having dreams about a very sorrowful knight. I saw this knight's head and another older man's head that had been driven onto wooden spikes. Their heads hung over the entrance to a stone bridge. This has been a nightmare for me recently, Mel. Please tell me that I am not losing my mind."

Mel only looked over at Ryan, shook his head, and said, "I don't think that you are going insane. Many people see the dead in this place, and there have been many reports of ghosts throughout the years. Don't worry, lad."

Ryan seemed to relax at the thought that he wasn't alone in seeing these visions, but he also didn't tell Mel about his experiences with Karen and her guiding spirits.

Mel then surprised Ryan when he pulled a curved, brown, wooden pipe out of one of the pockets in his shirt and loaded it with a stringy wad of tobacco. He then lit the pipe and blew out a thick plume of smoke.

Mel then leaned back against the backrest of the bench and looked over at Ryan and said thoughtfully, "Don't look at me so harshly about me smoking, laddie. I like to have some relaxing time to think. Don't forget, we are all addicted to something."

After Mel enjoyed his smoke, he led Ryan to the Gentlemen Geoler apartments, as Mel called them. They are also known as the 'Lieutenant's Lodgings'. The Gentlemen Geoler was also known as the Yeoman of the Tower in medieval times.

Lady Jane Grey, the Queen of England for a mere nine days, was held here before her execution on the orders of King Henry VIII's firstborn daughter, Mary, in 1554.

In these apartments, Lady Jane Grey was held before her execution because she was an unwilling pawn in the pursuits of power chased after by her father and her beloved husband's family.

She was a seventeen-year-old girl who married the man of her dreams. Her only crime was listening to and believing in her unscrupulous family.

From these prison apartments, she witnessed her young husband being led to Tower Hill for his own execution. Then she watched as her beheaded husband's body was brought back into the tower grounds while only being covered by a bloody sheet. She was beheaded later in the day. Mel lowered his head in reverence at the plight of the young queen.

Next to Lady Jane's prison apartments was the 3-story stone Beauchamp Tower. This is where her husband, Guildford Dudley, was held prisoner. He was imprisoned here along with his three brothers, who were also jailed because of their father's rebellious ambitions.

The young couple was offered one more night together before they were executed. However, Lady Jane refused, saying, "Their meeting would only increase their misery and pain, and that they would be better off meeting shortly elsewhere."

At the time, in 1985, the Crown Jewels were held in St. Martin's Tower. That was the next location on the tour inside the Towers. Inside, Ryan marveled at the immensity of the collection of valuable diamonds, rubies, emeralds, pearls, and sapphires.

Included in the crown jewels were some of the crystal blue sapphire gemstones that were named 'Yogo' sapphires. These gems only come from his home state of Montana and are named for the mine that they come from. Ryan had known that an English company had owned the mine at one time.

However, he had no idea of the extent or size of the gemstones that they had discovered there.

Also, in this collection of royal gems there were the ones in a large crown called St. Edward's Crown. There was also a smaller crown called the Imperial State Crown, which held 2868 diamonds, 17 sapphires, 11 emeralds, and 269 pearls.

These were all fascinating to look at, but the grand masterpiece of all the gems stood atop a gorgeous scepter that was given to a king or queen during their coronation. On top of this silver scepter was an amazing diamond, which was 530 carats large. Ryan made a fist and compared its size to this gem. He was not disappointed by the size comparison between the two of them.

Ryan looked seriously at Mel and asked, "Has anyone ever tried to steal the Crown Jewels?"

Mel said, "Aye, it has happened. There was one man who attempted to steal the jewels in 1671. His name was Colonel Thomas Blood. He dressed up as a "parson" and became friends with the keeper of the keys to the jewels. He came to visit him many times and even brought a woman pretending to be his wife and a young man pretending to be his nephew."

Mel smiled to himself and then continued. "One night, they knocked out the keeper of the keys, and he and two conspirators shoved the jewels into a bag. They had to smash down the large crown to make it small enough to hide in a coat, and the young man tried to saw the scepter in half because of its length. One of the conspirators even tried to shove that orb into his pants. It was like a bloody circus."

Ryan was mesmerized by this story and asked, "Were they caught and beheaded?"

Mel laughed harshly and said, "The Irishman got away with it. Nobody knows how or why it happened, but the king pardoned him. King Charles I, unbelievably, was impressed by the bravado of the man and even gave him property in Ireland. Of course, after that, the jewels were always guarded by armed soldiers."

Ryan and Mel visited many towers that day, but Mel had saved the most interesting for last. That was when he showed Ryan 'The Bloody Tower'. This was originally named the 'Garden Tower', but Queen Elizabeth I renamed this infamous tower because of all the bloody history that occurred there.

First, Mel led Ryan to the large, two-roomed prison of Sir Walter Raleigh that was on the upper floor of the Bloody Tower. This was where the man lived for 13 years of his life. Sir Walter Raleigh was an important part of three histories: the English, the American, and the South American colonies.

Sir Raleigh was a very eloquent and extravagant man who lived his life in a very large manner, as he tried to act as a very important person, among the nobility of England. He made very famous friends, including Queen Elizabeth I, and very serious enemies, like King James I. The latter king had him imprisoned for the second time and eventually beheaded.

He tried to establish a colony in the new world named Roanoke, whose people disappeared in an unknown manner. He also traveled to the South American colonies that were held by Spain. It was there that he claimed to have found a city made of gold, named El Dorado.

From the new land that would become the American colonies, he brought back one of the first ships filled with tobacco to England. Tobacco would first be used for medicinal purposes in the 16th century. In medical history, that ranks right up there with leaches or bleedings of the bodily fluids.

Sir Walter had been imprisoned the first time for treason when he married Elizabeth Throckmorton. She was the 'Lady in Waiting' or courtier of Queen Elizabeth I. He married her without asking permission from the queen.

Sir Walter was a favorite of Queen Elizabeth I, and it was truly demeaning to have one of her favorite men reject her and marry her 'Lady in Waiting'. This did not look good in the eyes of her subjects or the kingdom of England.

However, some people think that others liking him had more to do with his elaborate, boisterous personality and charm. His mannerisms made women, such as the queen, like him an exorbitant amount.

On the other hand, men tended to dislike him because of this same confidence that he exuded. He had a hugely powerful personality, and it cost him 13 years of imprisonment and eventually his life in 1618 at Westminster Abbey. That is when King James I had him beheaded.

The last item that was shown to Ryan in Sir Walter's cell was a portrait of the man himself. Ryan could see the deep set of intense eyes, the brown hair that was cut short, the handsome face, and the well-groomed beard that ran down his cheeks. This beard was styled into a pointed end running downward as if his beard had been styled like an upside-down triangle on the bottom of his chin.

Ryan asked Mel, "Why the hell do all of these portraits from the 1500s have men with these silly-looking beards?"

Mel chuckled gruffly, and he said, "It was the style of the time, much like having a haircut of short hair in the front and long hair in the back that is popular today. What do you Americans call it, a mullet?" It was the mullet of the 16th century. Only it was on the face."

Mel and Ryan walked down the ancient spiral staircase, where Mel directed the young man to sit on a stone bench that was opposite the stairs and against the far wall. Mel told Ryan that he had to go outside and enjoy a small dab of tobacco smoke in order to feed his hungry appetite.

Usually, the Bloody Tower is one of the most visited and crowded sites in the Tower fortress, where a person would never have an easy time resting, but not that day. Incredibly, Ryan heaved out a breath of air as he sat down, and he put his head in his hands and closed his overwhelmingly weary eyes.

Suddenly, Ryan heard a sound that echoed around the rocky chamber as if he were listening to a slow trotting horse. It went clop...clop...clop. Ryan opened his eyes when the sound changed to a rolling, dribbling sound that seemed to grow closer as it made a clop...thrrrrrp...clop...thrrrrrp...clop, echoing stream of sound.

Ryan didn't move his head and look up; he only opened his eyes and could see an old, leather tennis ball that had been neatly stitched along the seam. The ball slowly rolled to Ryan and stopped when it ran into his unmoving left foot.

Ryan slowly picked up the small ball and rolled it in one of his calloused, long-fingered hands. Ryan then stood up and slowly started to ascend the stone stairs again. Ryan was straining his ears and walking tentatively, as if a step might collapse under his feet as he climbed the medieval staircase.

Ryan suddenly stopped walking up the steps. Standing on the landing in front of him were the images of two young boys. The boys were holding hands and looking down at him sorrowfully.

The two young boys were wearing long, pure white bed dresses, and they had long blond hair that hung down over their white, sunken faces. With unblinking eyes, the boys let go of each other's hands and reached out toward Ryan.

Ryan tried to scream, but the sound seemed to be caught in his throat. Then the older of the two boys said the words, "Help us, Sir Knight!"

The younger boy started to join in by repeating the chant, and they started speaking faster and louder, those same four words. "Help us, Sir Knight...Help us, Sir Knight!"

Suddenly Ryan's shoulders began to shake, and his eyes grew even wider as the figure of Mel's face came into view. The large man was desperately saying, "laddie...laddie!"

Ryan then felt a stinging pain claw at his cheek when Mel concernedly slapped his face.

Ryan blinked his eyes, as if he had been awakened from a strange dream, and he said to Mel, "That is it for today; I don't want to be in this place anymore, but I do have some additional questions for you. Can you go get a cold drink with me outside of the tower?"

Mel grinned with a worried look on his face, and he said slowly and carefully, as if he were thinking this over, "I would be happy to hear your tale and have a refreshing drink. I will take you to a cafe near here."

Ryan and Mel sat at an outdoor table of a small cafe that looked out over Tower Bridge. Ryan was white as a freshly washed sheet and looked like he could be sick to his stomach at any moment.

He looked at Mel and told him the story of the lonesome-looking knight. He also told him of the knight's message to "Save the Princess" that he had passed on to Ryan. He then told him again of the bleeding woman, the executioner, and the cheering crowd that was chasing her from the gates of the tower.

Finally, he told him of the two young boys who had just reached out to him with those ghostly visions in the Bloody Tower. With a great deal of worry, he passed on the message that they had given him.

Ryan shuddered when he repeated the words, "Help us, Sir Knight."

Mel listened intently to him and somberly asked, "Have you heard any tales about the young royal boys in the Bloody Tower?"

Ryan shook his head in a "no" answer, and then Mel told him the sorrowful tale of the pre-teenage boys that had disappeared in the Tower in 1483.

Mel began the story by stating, "You see, laddie. British history can be very heroic and gallant, but it can also be very sorrowful and full of cruelty. The boys in the tower would be a case of the latter example."

Mel stopped to see if Ryan was paying attention and then said, "These boys were two young brothers whose father happened to be King Edward IV. He died unexpectedly when they were very young boys. They were taken to London for the older of the two brothers to be coronated as the new King. These boys were named Edward V and Richard, Duke of York, and they were just 12 and 9 years old at the time."

Ryan had goosebumps crawling up his arms, and he simply asked, "Brothers?"

Mel nodded a "yes" answer as he paused the story to build suspense in his intriguing tale. He then continued by saying, "The dead king's brother, Richard, Duke of Gloucester, was named the boys protectorate. He ordered the boys to travel to the Tower for Edward's coronation. Well, that is what the young boys were told, anyway."

Mel took a cool drink and then continued with his story by saying, "The members of the Parliament then declared the young boys illegitimate to be crowned as royalty. This was at the suggestion of the dead King's brother, Richard III. He declared himself to be the King of England. The boys were never seen in the Tower of London after Richard III became king. They simply disappeared, and no one knows the truth about what happened to them."

Ryan was leaning closer to the large Beefeater, and then Mel finished by saying, "On the way to London, the boy's protectors on the journey, Anthony Woodville and Sir Richard Grey, were arrested and beheaded. This left the boys unprotected from their uncle's soldiers."

Ryan burst out eagerly by asking, "Well, what happened to the boys? Somebody has got to know the truth."

Mel smiled patiently and said, "Nobody really knows. Workers ended up finding the skeletons of two young boys when they were working on the small, stone staircase in the White Tower. The skeletons were unceremoniously shoved into a trunk and hidden under one of the steps. Did Richard have the young masters murdered? That is one of the great mysteries about this place, and it is for you to decide."

Ryan leaned back in his chair and let out a big breath while he silently thought about this true tale. Mel then broke the silence by asking Ryan, "Was the knight that you saw in your visions the same man that you saw a portrait of today? Was it Sir Walter Raleigh?"

Ryan shook his head and said flatly, "No, the knight I saw had longer, more wild light brown hair and a scruffy bearded face, not a styled, fully pointed beard."

Mel then asked if Ryan would be coming to see him the next day. Ryan said that he could not, as he had to fly back to the States in the morning. Mel then said his farewells to Ryan and walked back into the Tower of London complex, shaking his head.

"The world was on fire, and no one could save me but you
Strange what desire will make foolish people do
I never dreamed that I'd love somebody like you
And I never dreamed that I'd lose somebody like you..."
(Chris Isaak)

Chapter Eight

"People are often like art: Originals are way more valuable than imitations!" (Doris Anderson-Western landscape artist)

Ryan packed his suitcase and his backpack wearily the next morning. Their airplane left at 11:00 a.m., but the group of teens had to be ready to board the buses by 9:00 a.m. After packing, Ryan traveled down the elevator at 8 a.m. in order to have a good breakfast and drink some coffee.

When the door opened in the lobby, Ryan was surprised at the sight of Mel standing there. He smiled and said startlingly, "Mel, this is unexpected. I hope that you have good news. You are wearing your Beefeater uniform already; aren't you supposed to be working?"

Mel wiped the sweat from his brow and said, "I figured out some interesting things last night. I hope that you have some time to discuss them with me."

Ryan almost beamed out a large smile and said, "Yes, let's get a sausage and egg breakfast and some go-juice or maybe some tea for you. I have a little less than an hour, but I am anxious to get any answers that I can. I'm just glad to have you join me. I've been damned lonely among this judgmental bunch of wankers."

Ryan and Mel sat at an empty table in the hotel restaurant, and then Ryan asked Mel, "So what is the exciting news? Did you find any answers about the visions that I have been having?"

Mel looked at the young man in anticipation and replied, "I didn't find anything on the knight that you have been seeing. However, I think that I have found out why he wanted you to see and hear him. You said that he wanted you to "Save the Princess". I do not think that is what he meant."

Ryan squirmed in his seat, and he asked, "What do you think this means, then?"

Mel looked very proud of himself, and he stated, "I don't think that he was saying 'Princess'. I think that he was really meaning 'The Princes'. I think that he meant the two boys that you were in contact with yesterday."

Ryan looked distant and said both words out loud as if he were trying out how they sounded: "Princess...Princes'. I will be damned! I think that you are right. Did you find anything on the hurt woman and the crowd that I saw?"

Mel looked even prouder of himself, and he asked Ryan if the young man knew anything about British history. Besides the American Revolution, that is. "No," Ryan said with a shake of his head.

Mel then pulled a piece of parchment paper out of his uniform and asked Ryan if he recognized anyone in the drawing. The drawing was of a skinny, shallow-faced woman who was looking back at an executioner who was dressed in a leather robe and mask. She seemed to be running away from the executioner, and they were surrounded by a large crowd of cheering people. She looked very frightened, and she was holding her neck as if she were protecting it.

Mel looked at Ryan seriously and asked, "Ryan, have you ever heard of a woman named Margaret Pole?"

Ryan shook his head and said, "No, I haven't, but this woman does look like the one that was being chased by the executioner. The man I saw chasing her seemed fat and oaf-like, though."

Mel smiled and asked Ryan, "Do you want to hear one more story before you fly back to the States?"

The breakfast came to the table when Ryan gave Mel a wry grin and said, "Yes, a good story is just what I need to pass the time on the airplane. I need something to think about."

Mel then cleared his throat and started his tale: "You see, Margaret Pole was a woman who lived in the 1500s. She was an older, very petite, and proper woman…who also happened to be a devout Catholic. At the time, people didn't understand what she had done to upset the King so much, but she did try to throw her weight around about the Pope and the Catholic church. The King had broken away from the Catholic Church and this made him feel extremely vulnerable."

Mel gave Ryan a knowing smile and then continued his story: "She was also the 8th Countess of Salisbury, the last member of the Plantagenet family with any political power. The king feared a revolt may happen, so he had her quietly beheaded in the tower."

Mel took a bite of a sausage, or banger, and then continued to say, "For some reason, they had a very shaky, overweight, and hungover executioner that day. Anyway, during the first whack of the executioner's axe, Margaret flinched, and the executioner missed badly. He cut into Margaret's shoulder instead of her neck. Rumor has it that she escaped from the executioner's block and ran for her life that day. I guess that she didn't want to be beheaded."

Ryan smiled and then exasperatedly asked, "Who would?"

Mel chuckled and said, "Just checking to see if you were paying attention."

Mel then continued the story by saying, "Well, the story goes that the executioner caught the Lady Pole and returned her to the execution block. She kept trying to get off the executioner's block, and he missed again…several times. It took a total of 11 swings of the axe for her head to leave her body. She was alive for much of it."

Mel finished the story when he proudly said, "She was beheaded inside the Tower, without very much pretense, and with only a small group of people in attendance. It is unknown if they were cheering, but it was a smaller group of onlookers. Tower Hill had all the rowdy crowds, and there were large groups of people at those executions. However, not all beheadings were horribly botched, nor did the victims run. That may have caused the excitement. Does any of this sound familiar to you?"

Ryan sat quietly and coldly said, "I don't know if this is what I saw, but it sounds almost exactly like it. I would haunt this place if this horrible thing happened to me, too."

The grin fell from Mel's face, and he asked Ryan worriedly. "You don't sleep at night, do you, laddie? You have been thinking a lot about all this shite, haven't you?"

Ryan looked at Mel tiredly, placed his hand on top of Mel's, and said, "Thank you for looking all of this up, my new friend. Also, thank you for caring about what happens to me, but I will sleep over the Atlantic Ocean, I promise."

Ryan got up and started for the glass door at the entrance of the hotel. He seemed to remember something, turned around, and asked one more question of Mel. "How were the two young princes killed, anyway?"

Mel looked down solemnly, and he said, "I remember hearing somewhere that the boys were smothered while they slept in their beds. A man confessed to the crime, but he was tortured first, so no one really knows this as being a fact. Study up on the two young boys when you get home; maybe you can solve the crime. First, however, you will probably have to make up your own mind on what actually happened to them."

Mel then stood, watched Ryan walk out the door, and said quietly to himself, "Goodbye, laddie. Have safe journeys."

The melee of young musicians trying to board the plane for the flight home was chaotic at best. This seven-hour flight was going to be the last time that many of these new friends would see one another. There were more tears than laughter for most people on this exhausting flight home.

Ryan sat in the back row of the plane, where he was alone in his row of seats. He watched the other members of the teen orchestra hug one another, wipe away tears, and promise to see one another again.

Ryan frowned at the rest of the teenagers with an expression of feeling left out. This is when and where Ryan started to become an even more cynical and sarcastic person. Deep-down, Ryan still cared about other human beings a huge amount, but he found it a lot harder to show it to them. He didn't know it at the time, but he also became largely untrusting of others that surrounded him on that day.

Ryan did fall asleep while sitting along the window of the last row on the airplane. This was much harder because a person experiences the extremely loud sounds of the jet engines of the airplane. Not to mention the smell of the lavatory that was behind these seats.

At least a Walkman helped with the noise as he listened to a new band from England named "The Cure." The music didn't help Ryan with the dark mood that he was in, but at least the music covered up the droning sounds of the jet engines. Within ten minutes, Ryan's eyes started to quiver back and forth in a R.E.M. sleep pattern, or were the quivering eyes caused by the nightmares that had invaded his mind.

First, Ryan heard the clanging sound of the armor that the knight was wearing. Then he felt the weight of the metal coverings that hung across the man. Ryan was in the knight's body, and he was walking rather noisily across the mud-filled grounds that were surrounded by the towers of a great fortress.

He could also see through the eyes of the knight and experience his visions. He was marching toward a raised wooden scaffold that stood ahead of him. The only sound was the clanging of the weighted suit of armor that the knight was wearing, as there were no crowds surrounding the gallows. The only person that could be seen was the executioner checking the sharpness of his axe blade.

Ryan was still seeing through the knight's scared, green eyes when he looked down at the ground, and Ryan only saw his own figure staring back at him. This was in the reflection of a mud puddle, where he saw his own image staring back at him. Ryan was now dreading what would happen next and felt completely out of control in this incredibly bizarre dream. This was a dream, wasn't it?

Suddenly, Ryan's sight shifted away from what the knight was looking at, and he could see out of his own body once again. Ryan saw some movement out of the corner of his eye, and he raised his view up to a window in the looming, White Tower.

Behind the glass, an extremely pale, white-skinned man with shoulder-length brown hair stood there looking down at him. When the man behind the glass knew that he was being watched, a sneering reptilian smile crept onto his face.

Ryan's view drifted back to the executioner once again, where the knight was giving him coins, as if he were tipping or bribing the man with the axe to not miss his neck.

Ryan started to panic, as he could see through the eyes of the knight once again. This time, he was now looking down at the executioner's block, where the knight would soon be placing his head. Ryan seemed to not have any control as the knight fell onto his knees and placed his head on the cold hunk of wood. Is this what it really felt like to be beheaded?

Without the help of any movement, Ryan then tried to scream, but only a loud gasp escaped his throat. Suddenly, Ryan only heard the violent sound of a wet, thwacking noise, and his vision went totally black. He awakened with a hard jolt that came across his entire body and made him almost jump out of his seat.

A female voice was heard saying to Ryan, "Are you alright, sir?" Then, the younger blond woman shook Ryan's shoulder, and she repeated her concern when she asked, "Can I do anything for you, sir?"

Ryan rubbed his weary eyes and then said back to her, "Please don't call me sir. I was just in London, but I didn't get knighted by the queen. I just need a massive amount of caffeine right now… so please just bring me some coffee and a couple of sodas. I really need to just stay awake and make it home to the Rocky Mountains at this point."

Ryan had just thanked his kind flight attendant when Angelo came to the back of the plane.

He sat down next to Ryan and said, "You have a lot of people worried about you, bud. You started out on this tour as if you were a king and nothing could faze you, but then you got involved with the 'Blonde Yoko Ono', and everything changed."

Angelo looked up at the other teenagers and then continued to say, "Karen decided to leave the tour, and the word now is that she left because of you. I don't know. You seemed like you had everything going on when I first met you. Ever since she got her grip on you, though, you changed a lot. I liked you quite well when we first met; you were a very stand-up guy. I will think about you very fondly in the future."

Ryan grinned emotionally and said back, "Even if I end up being fucking batshit insane?"

Angelo smiled back kindly and said forcefully, "You see, this is what I mean, Ryan. Since all of this has happened, you have become more standoffish and, in a way, a lot more like an asshole. All that the rest of us have wanted is to have a nice trip, and this is how you acted throughout half of it. We put up with it for a long time, but you are just not very fun to be around anymore. Get some help when you get home. Find the fun inside yourself again."

Angelo then stood up and walked back up the aisle of the plane. While he was in the back of the plane speaking to Ryan, the passengers on the entire plane had grown quiet. Now, the teenagers became boisterous again as he passed their seats.

Ryan took a deep breath and let out a large sigh. Then he said to himself, "Well, it is hard to find your fun side, when your emotions feel like they have been run over by a bus."

Upon landing in New York City, the rest of the young men and women were all in tears as they bid their final farewells to one another. Ryan only grabbed his suitcase off the baggage carousel while searching for his traveling partner, Mike, whom he was extremely nervous about talking to.

He approached Mike anyway and said, "Well, I am sorry if I ruined your tour, but we have a little further to go, and we should stick together."

When Mike didn't answer him, he asked, "Do you want to wait at Grand Central Station for the outgoing train with me? We could share a taxi, and then we will have a three-day ride back to Montana, you know?"

Mike looked at Ryan seriously, and then he said, "You put a woman before our friendship. It fucked you completely up. I will ride with you to the train station, just because it is cheaper, and I have just enough money to get home. Beyond that, you are on your own. I don't think that I want to hang around with you anymore."

Ryan only felt a grimace go across his face, and he simply said quietly, "Okay. If that is what you want… you got it."

They boarded the train that was heading west for Chicago. Ryan turned left and sat in the back of the train car. He sat down in the passenger seat and looked up the aisle, as if he might see his friend following behind him. Unfortunately, Mike had turned right and was traveling in the car that was ahead of him. Neither of them was going to speak to each other on their three-day journey to the large state of Montana. That was now obvious.

Soon after leaving the city, Ryan checked his backpack, where he kept his money. He found the pocket with only a rolled-up lint ball inside of it. His money was now gone and had been spent. He then stood and checked his pockets and his wallet, but he only found a small dime in his hip pocket.

Ryan then sighed again and said to himself, "This is going to be a damned long three-day trip back to Montana."

Luckily for Ryan, the visions of ghosts had vanished, along with the hopes of having several hamburgers along the way home. Damn, he was really craving a good, old American bacon cheeseburger and fries.

Ryan felt incredibly stupid, as he had spent extra money in the Red-Light District in Amsterdam. Now he was paying for it by having only water to drink and no food for the next three days. Was losing his virginity to a sultry woman named "Paulette" in Amsterdam worth three days of no food? Lying back and smiling knowingly, Ryan thought that the experience had been.

Ryan was offered a lunch or dinner by kind strangers who listened to his story. However, he always refused the offers, as he had enjoyed the cause of his not having money to spend. He was willing to accept the consequences that his pleasure-seeking actions had caused. Ryan was raised to 'pull himself up by his own bootstraps', and no amount of hunger would stop him from believing in this principle.

The train pulled into the station in northcentral Montana, and Ryan could hardly wait to see his parents. He missed the hard-working lifestyle, the more laid-back view of the world, and especially his mother's home cooking.

Hell, he missed any Montana cooking at this point. He would not even tell his parents any stories about his time in Europe. Not until they stopped by a fast-food restaurant for some much-needed burgers and fries.

Ryan's parents were anxious to hear of his trip, and it was hard to understand him in-between the rushed gulps coming from his zealous lips. After he had nearly eaten the left-hand side of the menu, Ryan loaded into a blue pickup truck. He still had to travel an extra 100 miles by road between the train station and the farm that he was raised on.

When Ryan's mother brought up the topic of his friendship with Mike, she knew that she had struck a very hard nerve with her son.

He simply said to her, "The trip was amazing, and I had an unforgettable experience, but I don't think that Mike and I will be friends anymore. This tour changed both of us...we just don't think the same way about life anymore. Our friendship is a sad deal, and I really don't want to talk about it. It is nobody's fault. We just don't get along anymore. Please, just leave it at that, mom."

Ryan's mother looked confused and kind of hurt, but she didn't talk about Mike again after that day. Except for one question when she asked, "Does this deal with Mike have anything to do with a girl that was on your trip?"

Ryan only smiled at her and said, "Yes, mom, you would say that this whole situation with Mike is over a girl. That is for sure."

Ryan never told her of his problems with the visions of long-dead people. This seemed like a very taboo conversation to have, and he didn't want to open this can of worms.

Ryan had one month left in the harvesting season at the farm. His next year of high school was about to begin in one month, so the rush to get the grain stored in the bin was a big deal. Thankfully for Ryan, harvesting season was a very hard-working experience.

He either drove the combine that cut the crops or drove the truck filled with wheat or barley grains. He would then unload these grains for storage in the grain bins at the farmstead. All this work didn't allow Ryan any time to focus on his problems.

This always ends the last few months of summer. The fall started with going to two grueling football practices per day. These were held once in the dawning mornings and then later in the evenings as well.

Once again, Ryan was too busy to worry about any of the problems with his friends. If he did dream about Karen or the sorrowful knight, he was too exhausted to remember even having these dreams.

Ryan could hardly wait until school would start so he could finally focus his mind on his scholarly duties again. This was followed by the once-per-day football practices after school, where he starred as a wide receiver on the local high school football team.

During this time, Ryan's hectic schedule would finally be cut in half. His mind could once again explore the mysteries of the universe that surrounded him. Sometimes, a person just has to be careful about what they wish for.

The last year of Ryan's high school career was an absolute blur of high school activities as well as a busy social schedule. Did he live these years, or does a person just go along for the bumpy ride?

Even though Ryan was very involved with many school activities, he still found time to entertain crowds with his drumming and singing talents. He performed in several country and rock and roll bands throughout a vast area of Montana's bars and crowd gathering festivals.

Many of these events included massive amounts of alcohol, and Ryan soon found a new way of dampening the voices and the visions that plagued his mind. Besides the physical activities that Ryan was already involved in, he began to go to parties involving kegs of frothy beer, shots of rum, or even strong whiskey drinks.

This became a much easier way for Ryan to relax, as the alcohol would cause him to dream less and allow him to make many new friends.

During this final year of high school, Ryan started to think of the seasons not as a change in weather but as a way of following his activities. Spring was a time for golf, swimming competitions, and planting crops on the farm. It involved many hours on the links of a golf course as well as being behind the wheel of a large red tractor.

Summer was baseball season, where Ryan excelled at playing in the infield and getting on base ahead of his larger homerun-hitting teammates. Fall was harvest and football season. Also thrown into this spate of activities were hunting and fishing excursions with his friends.

Finally, the winter months were completely about the basketball team and ski season. In between all these activities, Ryan found that a full-time partying season took place in every small town in Montana. A person just had to look for it.

There were mountain keggers...house parties...park parties...graduation parties...traveling parties...and the good old-fashioned sit around and complain that there is nothing to do but drink parties. Life was so busy, but alcohol took the edge off all that.

Ryan played drums in bands every weekend and throughout the entire year of 1986. By the time Ryan started college in the fall of 1987, he had become a seasoned veteran at drinking and a professional party boy.

It was very fortunate for Ryan that he had been raised in a very rounded manner in all things. This included changing his own oil in any mechanical object or making a mouth-watering dinner. He only hoped that he had listened more when people were trying to teach him about the maintenance of his own body and soul. He felt himself walking a fine line.

Besides common sense, Ryan was also well-rounded and hard-taught in almost every category in school. He was hoping for an athletic scholarship but was surprisingly offered a collegiate scholarship instead.

Ryan was also never afraid to work for what he wanted, as he had two jobs in college. This included being the college representative of a tobacco product and the leader of all the intramural athletic sports held on campus.

Both jobs worked perfectly for Ryan, as he was actually paid for playing sports during the day and going to parties in the evenings. The first two years at the university were perfect for Ryan, as he received respectable grades, developed several good friendships, and had a very successful social life. He had almost forgotten about any bad dreams or visions and the loneliness that he had felt on his trip to Europe.

Ryan's schedule was the only problem, as he went to class in the mornings, after 9 a.m., of course. He played sports all afternoons and then practiced what he thought was 'controllable partying' during the evenings.

The visions of the past and the ghosts that had bothered him still tried to appear to him. Whenever they did, Ryan would tamp them down by having another round of drinks or by playing an extra round of golf.

Ryan's teachers and family thought that he did well but had not ever lived up to his God-given potential. However, sometimes fate will force 'potential' onto a person, no matter if they want it or not. Especially if a person's pride and humility will be tested along the way, no matter the consequences.

Dudley's Bar was a perfect college bar in Ryan's eyes. It was his favorite place to relax, play, and just hang out with friends. Dudley's was a series of three taverns, all of which were located on one large property. Each style of tavern that Ryan and his friends hung out in was completely different. Hanging out in one portion depended on their mood for that evening.

The front bar was a rowdy, hard-drinking man's bar. Included in this large wooden bar area were three electronic dart machines, four pool tables, and an arcade that held such machines as Pac-Man, Donkey Kong, and Galaxia. Peanut shells covered the floors around the wooden tables, which were strewn around the floor with half-empty pitchers of warm beer left on them.

If a person was not in the mood for such a rambunctious atmosphere, they simply walked through a small walkway that led them to a more casual, laid-back bar. This place served drams of Scottish whiskey and fine glasses of wine. A small jazz quartet even played casual music in this tavern. The lighting was dimmed much lower, the chairs were made of leather, and candles lit the dark, relaxing atmosphere.

Two French-style doors exited this section of the tavern onto the outdoor patio of Dudley's. In this portion of the bar, there were picnic tables and more of a beach theme, with tables that surrounded a large sand volleyball court. Dudley's had everything that a college student needed in a tavern.

It was the perfect place if Ryan wanted to have a night of sporty fun, a night of wild carousing, or even an intellectually relaxing night of conversations with a pretty woman. Dudley's was like a convenience store in this respect. It was a one-stop shop for everything that involved parties. This location was also where the next horrible chapter of Ryan's life was about to begin.

The celebration on this one unfortunate night at Dudley's had been that the last day of the college semester had ended for the year. This meant a month-long break during the Christmas holidays.

The date was December 15th, 1990. Ryan and his nicknamed friends and roommates, Hog and Weasel, were excited to enjoy the holidays to their full extent. Even though a storm had moved in, and the streets were frozen and snowy.

They were going to be met at the tavern by two of their other good friends, Greg and Randy. Greg was a fellow intramural sports coordinator who worked with Ryan. He was probably the most rambunctious and adventurous of the three close friends. If he were your good friend, he would always be there to protect you from anybody who wanted to do you harm. He was an excellent man to have in your corner.

Randy was a college gymnast that stood proudly at 5' tall. He made up for any lack of height by having one of the biggest hearts that a person could ever have. He was not only a voracious gymnastic champion but was also the most amiable and fun-loving person in the group of friends. He had the ability to get the attention of some of the most attractive women with his impromptu backflips on the dance floor.

Ryan has always considered this group of friends to be a force of nature to deal with. He considered their bond to be what true friendships were supposed to be like, as they fed off one another's abilities and attitudes. Only his best friend from when he was a youth would ever hold a candle to these great friendships.

When all of them were together, Ryan felt as if they were all indestructible. However, tonight would mean that this group of friends would find out how vulnerable each of them really was. They could not be protected from all the horrors and fates that surrounded even one member of their group.

The group of friends entered Dudley's with their heads held high in confidence and their mouths incredibly dry with anticipation for the evening. They sat down at two tables that had been moved together on the louder and more boisterous side of the bar. They were soon joined by two more college friends named Dusty and Steve.

Now, this was not the evening that any of them imagined, as they wanted to have some female company to entertain and celebrate with. Quickly a game of quarters began at the table of young men, but Ryan and some of his friends had other thoughts on their minds.

First Ryan, and then Greg and Randy slipped away from the table of juvenile miscreants and joined a table of three women in the more relaxing section of the tavern. These women were enjoying the sounds of a smooth jazz trio and drinking a glass of Pinot Grigio.

The women were all known from the classes that the young people shared. Their names were Haley, who was over 6' tall and pretty. She also played on the women's college volleyball team. Greg had fallen hard for her and was extremely happy to see her out that evening.

Then there was Amy, who was shorter and was also very pretty. She had a large, 1980s-style hairdo, which made her look taller. Her thick head of hair stood out high and in several different directions. She and Randy both had the same sense of humor, and they immediately gravitated toward each other.

The final woman was named Lisa, and she was more of a natural beauty. She was less flamboyant, more intelligent, and just a down-to-earth type of woman. She had a shorter brown hairstyle, freckles that covered her small nose, and a great sense of humor with a contagious sounding laugh.

Ryan sat next to her and started the conversation by asking her if the average college male had a better fashion sense than the common Neanderthal. He knew that she was training at a high-end furniture store so that she could become a designer.

The evening started out slowly for the young couple. However, their time together seemed to really gather steam as Ryan enjoyed truly speaking with the highly intelligent woman. He gained speed when he quit trying to force his own agenda onto the poor girl and started to act like his more enlightened self.

After two hours of simply talking about history, authors, music, and even the uplifting spirit of being younger. Ryan was so encouraged that he ordered a taxi for Lisa and him to continue the conversation back at Ryan's house.

Ryan lived with his friends Hog and Weasel, whom he knew were still out playing quarters at Dudley's. That meant that he and Lisa would have the entire house to themselves. They said goodnight to their fellow friends and then sat close to one another in the back seat of the taxi, exchanging thoughtful glances, which were only interrupted by brief bouts of kissing.

Ryan had his arm around Lisa's shoulder when the taxi roared away after dropping them off at Ryan's house. The young couple started to walk toward the front door of Ryan's house when they turned at the sound of a man's voice coming from behind them on the street. The man yelled out in Spanish, "Espera gilipollas!"

Ryan took one more step back toward the street, when six young men and one woman walked out of the shadows of the trees that stood around them.

The young woman and one of the men grabbed Lisa by each arm and pulled her ten feet away from him.

Ryan found himself surrounded by five young men who marched up to the much taller Ryan while swinging away with two baseball bats. The leader of the gang of thugs stood as tall as he could in front of Ryan and said flatly, "You cut us off, asshole!"

Ryan stared him back in the eyes and replied angrily, "We were in a taxi, you piece of shit! We couldn't have cut you off. But if the driver cut you off, we apologize, and we don't want any problems happening here."

This time was different than in Europe. Ryan could just feel it. The leader with the Latin accent said to Ryan, "Callate, you pencil-dicked college boy."

Ryan's mind was working overtime at this point, not wanting Lisa to be harmed in any way. He tried to remain calm and talk his way out of this situation once again. However, Ryan didn't think that he could talk either of them out of any violence at this point. Mainly because a blazing fire can be lit when the smallest of sparks is tossed on a pile of dried kindling.

Ryan locked eyes with Lisa, and then he mouthed the words to her, "I am sorry."

The lone Latin woman let go of Lisa's arm and open-handedly slapped the side of Lisa's face, which drove her to the snow-filled ground. Ryan took one step in Lisa's direction and was surprised by the thud of one of the aluminum baseball bats that came across the side of his head. It hit him all the way from his temple to the hard lower part of his right jaw. At that point, all hell broke loose, and time held no meaning to Ryan.

When Ryan had been hit across the face by one baseball bat, the end of the other one was jabbed into the softness of his belly. A large "OOOPHING" sound exited Ryan's throat, and he found himself falling to his knees while trying to cover his outer head with his arms.

If Ryan had been knocked unconscious, it would have been a truly nice blessing. However, Ryan stayed on his knees, wide awake, and yelling out spiteful epitaphs.

He was shouting out such colorful phrases as, "You mother fuckers, that is enough already! You spineless dick holes! Quit kicking me, you rotten little pieces of dog shit!"

The louder that Ryan yelled and the worse language that he used, the more severe the beatings were coming at him.

While Ryan was throwing out curses, his head was continuously being kicked violently backwards, as if it were a football used in the practice of a field goal kicker. How many times had he been violently kicked in the face? Ten times?... twenty times?... more? He had lost count.

The blood-curdling curses being thrown from Ryan's mouth had grown into a slurring, blood-filled sound of agony, and Ryan finally noticed that the beatings on his head had stopped. He then heard the accented English words of men, mixed with a few Spanish words, who were beginning to argue with each other above his lowered head.

Ryan felt a cold cylindrical piece of metal push into the rear of his skull, and he clamped his mouth shut hard at the feeling that he now endured.

A voice suddenly said closer over him, "You don't have anything to say now, do you, Punto?"

The cold feel of metal left the back of his head, and one more violent foot in his face made his head harshly snap back. It was as if his head were on a swivel, and he fell backward into the blood-filled snow. A red-faced Lisa crawled over to Ryan's side and helped him sit forward. Ryan tried to keep kneeling by her side but found himself slumping further into her lap.

Lisa gently caressed his face with her hand and then said, with worry in her voice, "Oh my God, Ryan. Can you stand? I don't think that I could lift you."

At this point, an older golden car named a Malibu raced down the street beside them. They knew that the thugs were fleeing the scene, and the car sprayed them with the gravel that was covering the icy road. After the gold Malibu had raced past them and was only a few hundred feet away, Lisa could see lights coming from up the road and was coming towards them. A new car full of teenagers pulled up quickly beside Ryan and Lisa.

Thankfully, some of Ryan's friends and roommates were coming home from their own nights' adventures. It was their arrival that had scared away the violent gang of fiends and brought them to the aid of the increasingly ailing Ryan.

At first, Ryan refused to go to the emergency room, and the group of friends helped him into his home. They were mainly doing this for him to grab a few items to be taken to the hospital. Ryan was barely awake when his friends walked him into the emergency room at 1:00 a.m.

Ryan vaguely remembered going into the emergency room in a wheelchair. The doctors and nurses then took off his mainstay baseball cap, his gray winter coat, and his green-colored sweater. They left on his bloody jeans and his high-top tennis shoes. Ryan was trying to speak, but only a mush-filled group of sounds escaped his throat.

Suddenly, a sharp pinching pain came from a shot in his arm, and he muttered, "Ow!" He finally collapsed onto the emergency room table.

When Ryan awoke, he was still lying on the hard emergency room bed. His roommates, Hog and Weasel, were sitting in chairs next to the door, and a quietly sobbing Lisa was sitting next to him while holding his hand.

Ryan placed his hand on hers and whispered groggily and rather mushily, "Are u o'ay, isa?"

With these words, Lisa's head was thrown upwards, and Ryan could see the tears running down her cheeks. Hog and Weasel got up and stood on either side of Lisa, looking down at him while smiling with uneasy looks on their faces.

Ryan looked at the three of them and then tried to say, in an unintentional Porky Pig imitation, "Isa, why id ya bring ese charac...charact...I mean...unch o ya-hoos wit ya?"

Lisa let out a small laugh and looked at both of his friends in astonishment. She smiled down at Ryan and then stated, "I…I…I thought that they may have killed you, Ryan. You were beaten so badly."

Ryan tried to give her a half-hearted smile, and then he tried to sit up. This caused his two friends to grab him by his shoulders and push him back onto the bed.

Hog then said, "They fucked you up really bad, buddy!"

Weasel added to it by saying, "We have got it under control for now, so just lay back. A cop is here and wants to talk to you; is that okay?"

Ryan nodded 'yes' and then asked Lisa to stay in the room, as she would remember what had happened to them much better than he ever could. Officer Pachek entered the room and grinned sorrowfully down at Ryan with an open notebook in his hand.

He introduced himself and then asked, "Do either of you know what happened tonight?"

Lisa told the story of the taxi ride home and how they had been followed and beaten when they had exited the taxi. She had only received one blow, which hit her on the side of her face. She didn't have to point out that most of their violent outbursts had been directed toward Ryan.

Officer Pachek then turned his attention to Ryan and asked again if he could ask him a few questions. Ryan gave him the approval to do so, but all that he could remember from that night, besides the huge amount of injury and pain, was the fact and embarrassment that his assailants seemed to pounce upon him like a pack of rabid wolves. No matter how much he tried, he had no control over their senseless beating of him, which brought him near death.

He remembered screaming at them, but he couldn't remember any of the words that were used. In all reality, he was extremely embarrassed to repeat what he had shouted at them. He remembered their accented language, but he could not remember any of their specific faces. Worse of all, he remembered the horrid crime of being unrepentantly beaten, without any means of giving any retribution back to them.

Officer Pachek then told him that he was the sixth person to be beaten that night, but none of them were beaten as badly as him. Probably because of how he had yelled at them and his ability to try and fight back at them. He then told Ryan that he had been the victim of being caught in the middle of a gang war. The gangs had an initiation to get into the group, and this initiation was to find an unknowing person and beat them within an inch of their lives.

The officer just looked sadly at the floor and said solemnly, "Ryan, you were just at the wrong place, at the worst possible moment."

The doctor then entered the room and gave Ryan one more look-over and said, "Well, Mr. Maxwell, we are going to let you go home tonight."

Ryan and Officer Pachek both said back to the doctor at the same time, "Are you kidding me?"

The doctor shrugged his shoulders and then said, "Yes, you have been severely injured, Mr. Maxwell, but I don't think a night in the hospital would help you any. Plus, you seem to have lots of friends and nurses to take care of you at home anyway. We can't have all of them stay in our hospital halls overnight."

Ryan looked confused and asked him what the hell he was talking about. The doctor slowly pulled the shades away from the windows, showing Ryan an emergency room filled with at least sixteen people. They were all waiting to see if he was okay.

The doctor then shrugged and said, "You have quite a concussion and a broken nose, but other than that, your tests all came back good. Plus, I might add, you also have probably the hardest head that I have ever seen...and that is not a compliment, Mr. Maxwell. You got very lucky this time."

Ryan then tried to snap his fingers but couldn't have them make any noise. He then said to Officer Pachek, "The car… the car that they were driving was a beat-up gold Malibu. Please find those bastards and put them away."

Do you ever wake up halfway and lie in bed with half your brain still in the dream world. All while the other half of your mind slowly awakens to the actual reality surrounding you. Your eyes never open at this point, and it is the most serene feeling in the whole world. That is how Ryan awoke on December 16th, 1990.

His bed at the time was a queen-sized waterbed, and he lay silently while thinking out loud, "Thank God, last night was a dream."

Ryan began to feel someone sloshing back and forth in his bed, as if he were not alone. He tried to open his eyes amid a blinding flash of pain that filled his head.

After the pain subsided a little, a female voice was heard saying, "Try to relax and look up at me."

Ryan concentrated on opening his eyes, and his left eye would only open half the way because of the massive amounts of swelling. His right eye was completely swollen shut, and he could only see blackness when he tried to use it.

Ryan then tried to speak worriedly and found out that his mouth would only open a quarter of an inch. A grunting "Uungghh" sound could only be emitted from his vocal cords. Even his teeth hurt at this point, and he was just lucky that he still had his original teeth still in his head. Lisa sat above him and slowly lifted him out of the warmth of the bed.

She then carefully led him into the bathroom, where he tried to look at his reflection in the mirror. In a panic, his hands flew up to his face, and he felt at his large, extremely swollen facial features that protruded from his head. He was unrecognizable to even himself. He felt the warm tears try to spill out of the slits that had once been his wide blue eyes the night before.

After pulling himself together, Lisa led Ryan out into the living room, which was scattered with two couches, a chair, and two bean bag chairs that did not match each other at all. On all this mismatched furniture were the forms of 12 other people who had slept there the previous night. They had even laid on the carpeted floor during the night, just in support of him.

The crowd of friends started to wearily surge into an awakened state. Ryan heard several people showing him their proud support and others gasping out their horrors at the sight of him.

Ryan whispered quietly into Lisa's ear, and then she spoke for Ryan and told the living room full of young college students, "Ryan wants me to tell you all thanks for wanting to be here for him. However, this is all a bit overwhelming. I am going to take him back to bed now, and when he gets up later, he will like it if you all had gone home. Unless you live here, of course. Me and his other roommates will take care of him today, but come and see him later in the week, okay?"

A voice rang out from a chair, and a young man said, "We are all going to be leaving for the holidays today or tomorrow. We just want to know that Ryan is all right before we leave. We are here to help him in any way possible."

Ryan then whispered once more into Lisa's ear, and she said, "Ryan says that he really appreciates all your concern and friendship. Merry Christmas to you all."

Ryan whispered one more thing and then shuffled back to his bedroom, leaving Lisa to say, "Please don't come back until after the new year and give him some time to heal. God bless you all, and please just go to your families and let him rest."

Ryan laid back in his sloshy waterbed and almost fell directly into a deep sleep. Ryan barely noticed the bed move when Lisa crawled over him and then laid down beside him. She put her head on one of his shoulders and wrapped her arm around his stomach. When she did this, she felt Ryan's muscles tighten harshly with pain, and she began to sing a Poison ballad about a 'rose having a thorn.'

She continued singing until she heard Ryan's breathing slow and his tightened muscles begin to relax. The last thing that she heard from Ryan before she fell asleep herself were the words that tumbled from Ryan's lips, "Stop...I can't help!"

Behind Ryan's furrowed brow and in the mists of his mind, Ryan was walking toward the lone knight standing in front of a river that was flowing rapidly. The knight was looking at the tree line across the river, and he did not turn around when Ryan approached from behind him. Ryan moved next to the knight and noticed how much shorter the muscularly toned knight was. Of course, he was also standing next to the over six-foot frame of Ryan.

The knight looked up at Ryan and said, "I am sorry about last evening. I wish that I could protect you more in your physical world. I can't interfere with that plane of existence, though. Not like my enemies often seem to do."

Ryan gaped in disbelief and asked in exasperation, "Woah, there. You can't interfere in my world? And they have already caused things to happen that have involved me? Did your enemies have anything to do with what has happened to me...say, like last night?"

The knight looked solemnly at the ground and then said plainly, "Yes... they will try to stop you anyway that they can. They use fear and people that they can control to do their bidding."

Ryan then thought about his time in Europe and asked the knight, "What about when I was younger and on the trip around Europe. Did they interfere with my life, then?"

The knight thought about this warily, and then he said firmly, "Yes, they did. Every time that I tried to help, it was as if you had blocked me out somehow."

It was Ryan's time to look full of remorse, and he thought about those years. He then asked the knight, "How do I know that I should trust you? How do I know that you are the one trying to help me?"

The knight simply said, "You are a very good man who has a very good soul. Just listen to that soul, and you will find the right path on which to go.

My name is James, and I swear to give you all the help that I can. I will also bring along some extra trusted help when we need it. Please, just be patient with us. Please, Ryan...we all need you and I think that you may need us too. All of us think this to be true."

Ryan looked at the Knight and could only say confusedly, "Wait...who are all of us?"

The knight smiled and said one word, "patience." Then his body seemed to turn into steam, and he dissipated before Ryan's eyes.

"Silence now the sound, my breath the only motion around
Demons cluttering around, my face showing no emotion
Shackled by my sentence, expecting no return
Here there is no penance, my skin begins to burn..."
(Creed)

Chapter Nine

Some of the best ideas on the planet began as thoughts written down on a bar napkin.

The following week, after Ryan had been beaten so badly, was just as debilitating as the assault itself, as it was the beginning of his battle with panic attacks and PTSD issues. Ryan could feel this pressure in his entire body. The die had been cast, and Ryan had rolled a pair of snake eyes when he was trying to climb toward the stars.

Since Ryan had been severely beaten on the 15th of December, many of his friends had scheduled trips home in order to celebrate the holidays with their families. This meant that many of Ryan's friends had disappeared from his bedside. Because of his isolation, he became extremely lonely, depressed, terrified, and horribly paranoid.

Everyone had left to go see their own families and had left Ryan completely alone. Sometimes, you get what you ask for. His mother and father were not scheduled to arrive until another five days afterwards. Ryan's parents had made plans to pick Ryan up and take him with them to his brother's house in Colorado. However, they had not scheduled this trip until the 22nd of December.

Ryan was flabbergasted and extremely scared at the thought of spending this week alone. He had no one to count on for nearly a full seven days. Ryan's mother wanted to go to her son immediately, but for some incomprehensible reason, his father would not change the plans that he had already made. This would be a source of contention between Ryan and his family for many years to come. It would affect the relationship that Ryan would have with his parents from that day forward.

However, the conditions of people who suffer from panic attacks and PTSD were unknown in 1990. Ryan's family would never understand the intensity and life-changing consequences that these mental disorders can cause. The worst part of the whole situation is that his family never seemed like they would make any attempt at understanding his mental health problems at all.

This is one of the most difficult problems that many people afflicted with mental health disorders have. That is when their own family and friends would rather pretend that these problems don't even exist. They think that if they just ignore the situation, maybe these problems will just go away in time. At this point, friendships and family dynamics begin to implode from within, and the only person that is really left out to dry is the person dealing with these horrid mental diseases.

Without being able to explain what is happening to them, it is impossible for others to comprehend how badly these feelings are affecting them. It is maddening to the individual who is suffering, and this is when relationships erode.

This was also the time when Ryan started to have the unnerving dreams and visions again. Reality had once again turned into a shitty horror show. Only now, Ryan had to deal with his ever-growing visions and surreal nightmares while also trying to recover from physical injuries.

Ryan had tried to go for walks in order to get some exercise and try to control his fear. Each day, he walked the six blocks to the nearest video store in order to rent movies for the day. Whenever a car would approach him on these walks, he would find himself having to hide behind a tree or bush that was close to him. He was just waiting for them to pass and for him not to be seen. Paranoia was now controlling his mind.

Each day was beginning to be the same. Ryan's heart would start to beat at an uncontrollable rate, and his pulse would quicken. He would then break out into a cold sweat, and his stomach would lurch and make him want to vomit.

Ryan would return home from his walks each day breathing heavily and shaking uncontrollably. He would then lock the door behind him and lie on the couch in front of the television.

He had some visitors, but Ryan never answered the door because he did not want anyone to see him like this. He couldn't explain how he felt at all. If Ryan did not have to go to work at the gymnasium in the evenings and pretend that he felt okay, he would almost always be alone. Everyone else was away during the Christmas break. When he was alone, alcohol seemed to always be his constant companion.

Besides his daily dose of movies and alcohol, Ryan was positive that Looney Tunes and Underdog cartoons had saved his life during these horrible times. They came on the television each afternoon, and Ryan never wanted to miss any of these programs. Laughter was truly the best medicine for Ryan these days.

Ryan was told by doctors not to drink during this period of his life. He saw this as a huge disadvantage because alcohol seemed to tame the savage beast that was rising inside of him. Plus, this type of forced sobriety caused the nightmares and visions to return. This time, Ryan truly felt like he was going completely insane and didn't know if he would live through them.

Upon falling asleep on the couch while listening to a classic Pink Floyd CD, Ryan found that he was lying in a beautiful grassy meadow.

Sitting next to him and playing in the grass was a very young girl with long blond hair running down her back. She also had a pink ribbon holding her hair back from falling into her face. She had wide blue eyes and an almost cherub-like round face. The young girl glanced over at Ryan and smiled a wide grin where he saw that she was missing several baby teeth. On her shirt, the name "Ellie" was written in sparkling pink glitter.

"Grasshopper," she said proudly, and held the bug up for him to see.

The grasshopper jumped away when Ryan shifted his head to look at it closer. The small girl laughed at the funny feeling that the grasshopper's legs had made on her fingers.

Ryan wrinkled his nose at the girl and playfully said, "He got away from you."

Ryan then noticed that the girl was wearing a skirt that was glistening white, except that it was covered in colorful decals of butterflies. She also wore a large hat that matched the color of the dress, and the girl had pink sneakers on with white stockings that were pulled up to her kneecaps.

She got up and followed the grasshopper through the grass, giggling as she went. Ryan lifted himself onto one elbow and leaned his closed fist onto his cheek in order to just watch the girl.

For the first time in a long while, Ryan felt peaceful. When Ryan looked back at her, the girl had a plastic bubble wand in one hand and the container that held the soapy liquid in the other. She seemed so happy as she blew out bubbles in the warm, sun-filled meadow.

She would blow these bubbles out of the wand and then chase after them as they slowly floated to the ground. Ryan laid back in the grass and just enjoyed listening to the little girl's laughter emanate through the crisp spring air.

Slowly, the sky started to get extremely cloudy, and the young girl would blow out a large bubble and then break it in midair. She would do this while yelling loudly. "Higher...Die!"

With each bubble that she blew, she became more insistent and yelled louder, "Higher...Die!" Ryan tried to get the girl to come over to his side again, but she just kept yelling, "Higher...Die!" "Higher...Die!" "Higher...Die!" As she hit each bubble.

Ryan lay back down and covered his eyes again, until there was only silence and the sound of a small stream flowing through the meadow.

Then, Ryan lifted his hands out toward a blue, cloudless sky above him and found that the clouds had dissipated. He was still lying in the grass, and the only difference in the meadow, that Ryan could tell anyway, was the sound of a small creek running over ancient stones. Also, the younger girl was no longer destroying any bubbles and had disappeared from his view.

A female voice broke the silence in the air when she said, "I really like babbling streams."

This voice scared the living hell out of Ryan; his eyes sprung even wider open, and he also sat up in shock and surprise. Ryan slowly turned his head in the direction of the voice, and he immediately smiled and said excitedly, "Karen."

At that point, Ryan had never been so happy to see anyone in his entire life. He leaned closer and started kissing her warm lips, all while crying profusely at the same time.

Ryan pulled himself away from her lips and said impatiently, "Karen, please don't ever go away from me again."

She simply quieted him by making the calming sound of, "SSShhhh!" She took hold of his upper body in a deep hug while cradling his upper torso with his head against her chest and neck. Karen wore the exact same thing that the child was wearing, except she did not have the name Ellie that was imprinted on the front of the young girl's shirt.

Ryan pulled back, looked into her eyes quizzically, and asked, "Karen...why am I experiencing all of this?"

She just simply put her finger on his lips, and then she said to him, "Ryan, I don't have much time, but you are going to have to be courageous and strong, my love. You must be strong for me. You must also be extremely grateful and gentle toward her. You know who I mean. We will always be here for you, but you must be patient. I can't answer everything now."

Ryan then said quietly, "I promise you."

Karen then pointed to the little girl waving at them from across the meadow. Karen threw the girl invisible kisses, and the little girl caught them and held them to her heart. Ryan tried to say, "Don't go," to Karen, but when he looked back at her, he found that she had already disappeared.

He then looked back toward the small girl, and she was gone as well. Ryan heard a faraway cry of "goodbye" and found himself waking on the ugly brown couch that was in his college living room.

Ryan didn't remember much from his ghostly vision of Karen except the smell of her hair. "Lilacs," Ryan had ended up screaming out loud to the empty room. "Her hair smelled of lilacs." He lay back down on the couch, hoping that he would be transported back to the meadow with the smell of lilacs in his nose and the visions of beauty that surrounded him. Damn, he loved that smell.

He did fall back asleep, and he did once again open his eyes to another world. Surprisingly to him, the environment around him had completely changed. He was no longer lying in a grass-filled, pleasant meadow. This time he was standing on top of a snowy mountain pass, and aspen and pine trees were surrounding him in each direction down the mountain.

Ryan could only hear the brisk wind as it swirled and moaned all around him. Besides the wind, Ryan could hear nothing else that surrounded him. Suddenly, he realized there was another noise in the distance that seemed to be coming his way and getting louder.

Ryan stood there and then looked in the direction of the lilting noise as the sounds of approaching tinkling bells became louder. Slowly, coming up the mountain pass and toward Ryan, was a white carriage that was being pulled by two large white stallions.

Driving the carriage, was a very pretty, petite woman. She looked like she was a little bit bigger than a teenaged child, except her mannerisms gave her away as being a much older woman.

She wore a white, skin-tight dress with black gloves and shoes. She also had a thick, flowing mane of black hair that sprawled out behind her and down her back. She stopped the carriage in front of Ryan, and the abrupt stop threw her body forward in the seat.

That made Ryan notice the pearls that were hanging from the necklace that the woman wore, and that there was a large golden B in the middle of this necklace. After stopping the carriage, Ryan also noticed that this was the jingling sound that he had heard as it danced across her chest.

Ryan thought that she was pretty, but she did not seem beautiful to him. She was very plain-looking, but also very seductive and intentionally sexy in the way that she acted. The woman then looked at Ryan with her large, dark eyes, and he found himself almost falling into those hypnotizing, dark brown pools. They stood above a smaller, pert smile that seemed to rise instinctively into a seductive grin.

She said slowly toward him, as if drawing out the sentence, "Do you see anything that you like, sir?"

She caught Ryan looking into her eyes, and then at her heaving breast. Ryan blushed and said to her, "I like your necklace."

"Oh, I thought you might be looking at something else, maybe something behind my necklace," she said flirtatiously.

Ryan only smiled at the woman and thought about the smell of lilacs.

"I heard that you might be able to help me," she said to Ryan, as she leaned back into the seat of the carriage.

Ryan then replied to her quickly, "It depends on what you want help with."

Her eyes grew bigger still, and they hypnotically pulled Ryan closer into them. Then she said, "I want jewels...I want furs...I want to be rich...but mostly, I want something that you carry with you."

Ryan tried to make a joke and said back to her, "Bad credit? I have lots of that. You are more than welcome to it."

The woman either didn't understand or she was just dismissing what Ryan was talking about, as she waved her hand at his last statement.

She then sat up and got within inches of Ryan's face and said, "I want your seed."

Then she slowly licked the bridge of his nose from the tip of it up to between his eyes.

Ryan stammered back in surprise and asked while wiping her saliva off his nose. "You want my what?"

Then she raised her voice and belted out loudly, "I want sons...and I will get sons. You will give them to me."

They both let those last words echo across the pass, and neither of them said anything for quite some time, letting the words reverberate around them.

Ryan finally broke the silence and asked her bluntly, "What if I don't want to sleep with you?"

She made a face as if Ryan had slapped her with an invisible glove, and then she smiled seductively.

While caressing her smooth, white breasts, she said, "Men have found it hard to say no to me. Don't make that mistake."

"Listen," Ryan said, while sneering at the woman. "I like your eyes, and you have nice tits. However, I have stepped over better-looking women than you just to go and pleasure myself in the corner. No Thanks."

She sat up and covered her breasts as if she had been hugely insulted. Then she said, "I gave you a chance to lie with me. You would get great pleasure from doing this...but now I will have to take your seed by force. I will get what I want."

Then she gave the horses' backs a brief crack of the reins and went on her way down the mountain.

"Good luck on trying to force yourself onto me," Ryan yelled after her as she disappeared down the far end of the mountain pass.

As the woman disappeared from his view, Ryan was awoken by the pounding on his front door. His living room was completely dark, but he could see light entering the room from the windows in the back of the kitchen. Ryan stumbled to the door and was greeted by the worried but excited faces of his two good friends, Greg and Randy.

Greg said to Ryan while entering the room, "The swelling around your eyes has gone down, and it looks like you could eat solid foods again. Now, the white areas of your eyes are a blood red color. You look like you've been possessed or something. Other than that, you look a whole lot better than you did before. Are you really alright, buddy?"

Ryan thought about his answer and said, "I am getting better slowly on the outside, but internally I am still a hot mess."

Randy then spoke up when he said, "Ryan, I have been in gymnastics for as long as I can remember, so just be careful with any head injuries. They can really screw you up, and if a person isn't careful, they can take over your entire life."

Ryan looked at his friends and said back to them, "I really appreciate it. Thanks for just looking out for me. Please sit down. Is it time to have a drink, yet?"

Greg laughed at his damaged friend and noted, "Well, it is only about 2:00 in the afternoon, but I don't see any 'no drinking' or 'no smoking' signs around here."

At this statement, his friend pulled three nice Cuban cigars out of his inside jacket pocket.

Ryan looked at him incredulously and said, "Where in the hell did you get these?"

Greg only smiled, offered the cigars to his friends, and said, "It was a Christmas miracle. However, it is a sin if we smoke these cigars while drinking cheap college beer. We will have to go to Dudley's and drink a snifter of brandy to go along with these beauties."

Ryan's smile disappeared, and he said fearfully, "I haven't been back there since the beating happened. I'm not sure that I want to go back there."

"Bullshit!" was the only reply from both his friends, and then his gymnast friend said, "Get back on the horse, my friend. Get back on the horse!"

Ryan finally agreed to his friends demands and then asked to get cleaned up before they left for the tavern. He nervously stood in the shower, and he almost forcibly had to make himself leave the warm waters and get dressed. Not to mention the negative thoughts that he continued to have while riding in the car to get to their destination.

When they arrived, Ryan stood outside the doors to the tavern, and he began shaking in fear and stopped moving forward. Greg took his left elbow, and Randy took his right elbow, leading their friend into the dark, casual section in the back bar of Dudley's tavern.

One of his friends picked out a table that stood in the darkened corner of the tavern and was only lit by dimmed lights and a candle upon the table. They sat down in the leather chairs provided, ordered their drinks, and then prepared to relax and casually smoke their illegal cigars.

Greg looked over at him and said, "It is good to have you by our side again, compadre."

"Hear, hear," said his gymnast friend. "We have both been so worried about you. My family did nothing but fight. I should have stayed here with you. You are more like my brother than those two knuckleheads that try to pick on me."

Ryan only grinned at his two friends and then took a long drink of brandy. In all actuality, he drank almost half of his large snifter of expensive liquor in one large gulp. Greg puffed out a huge plume of smoke, and he reached over and rubbed Ryan's head, mussing up his freshly brushed hair.

He then said, "I was truly worried about you over the Christmas break, buddy. If you need anything...well…you know. We have got to look out for each other."

Greg then continued by saying cautiously, "Speaking about any help, we wanted to bring you here and discuss something with you. How do you feel about getting revenge on those bastards?"

Randy then spoke up and asked, "Do you remember Dusty Tintinger, the manager of these fine drinking establishments?"

The gymnast looked over at Greg and then finished by saying, "Well, we have been talking with Dusty, and he thinks that we can find these assholes that beat you up. He has ears on the ground and surveillance cameras inside the bar that could pick out these jerkoffs. You said that it was a gold Malibu, and with the help of Dusty, we think that we can find these guys."

"No!... I appreciate it, guys...but...but," Ryan shook his head and tried to figure out the best way to say the next statement that he had to make to his friends.

"It's ok, buddy! We will blast them for you, just give us the go-ahead," his coworker and close friend said, with fiery eyes.

Greg was a very funny individual with a very good heart and a witty personality. However, he was also fiery and lived his life with an extremely protective and vengeful attitude if he or his friends were wronged in any way.

Randy leaned closer to him, placed his hand on Ryan's arm, and said, "We are only looking out for you buddy. We want to get back at this group of assholes! They could have easily killed you. We aren't the only friends of yours that want them to pay for what they did, and they all want to go after these guys."

Ryan let out a deep sigh, and then he said sorrowfully, "I appreciate your intensity and your willingness to go after these guys...but it was just my turn to step in the horseshit."

The immediate response from both of his friends was answered in one word, when they almost yelled out, "What?"

Ryan then made his point very clear when he answered them by saying, "I don't want this to get out of hand. Listen, if we all get too ballsy and go after these guys just on an emotional response, this whole thing is just going to end up being a battle between a bunch of gang bangers and a bunch of college kids. I am so proud to call you both my friends, but I don't want anyone else to get hurt, or even worse."

Ryan did explain himself about the pile of horseshit and pointed out, "When you are standing in a field of horseshit, you have got to look for the pretty pony. That is an old farm saying, kind of like a cloud having a silver lining. This time, I just happened to be the one who stepped in a big pile of horseshit."

Greg started to loudly object when Randy calmly said, "Well, you know how we feel, Ryan, and you may be right. We may be in over our heads, but we just want to get revenge for what they did to you and to make sure that this doesn't happen to any of the rest of us."

Greg then said more calmly, "Now then, since we got this horrible subject out of the way, let's try to have a good time. We don't have any classes to go to for a week, and besides a little bit of work, we have nothing to tie us down. Speaking of tying someone down, when do you expect to see Lisa again?"

Finally, Ryan beamed with excitement, and he answered back that it would be right after New Year's Day. He was incredibly anxious to see her. He felt safer and more protected when she was with him.

On New Year's Eve, soon after this conversation between friends took place, an off-duty police officer was jumped by a group of men. He was sitting on a bench and waiting for his wife while she shopped at the local Kmart store. He called for backup over a walkie-talkie when they started to surround him like a pack of hungry wolves. He fought back at the gang of thugs with a terrible force of reckoning, and all the young men were soon arrested.

Ryan read this article about this gang-related violence on the third page of the local newspaper. The article was all about how the police officers had protected themselves against the gang of thugs and had apprehended seven suspects in the process. Ryan smiled widely when he read that the police had also impounded a gold-colored Malibu sedan in the process.

"There's something inside of me that pulls beneath the surface
Consuming, confusing
This lack of self-control I fear is never ending
Controlling, I can't seem…"
(Linkin Park)

Chapter Ten

Don't sweat the petty stuff, and don't pet the sweaty stuff!

They have said that the world would change for a person with a big, booming sound. For Ryan, however, his world changed at the sound of the sticky, slushing sound of a Slurpee machine at a 7-Eleven.

Ryan was waiting behind a rude, insolent boy of about 10 years old, while waiting for a plastic glass full of an icy, cool, berry-flavored drink. Without any notice, the most extreme of his daily severe panic attacks started to develop inside of him.

It was 7:06 pm on January 7th, 1991, when the first pangs of something in his chest and stomach told Ryan that something was 'not right.' His heart was pounding hard and at a quicker rate than that of an older man who was trying to make love to a much younger woman.

He also felt as if his stomach had taken up residence in the back of his teeth, and his mind swirled in a dazed, off-steady sort of way. Ryan had walked to a 7-Eleven that evening in order to rent new movies and get the wonderful, sweet goodness that only a Cherry Slurpee could provide.

However, right now, Ryan felt like he had to get out of there...Oh, God, he had to get out of there. He had to do it now...bad things were going to happen! Everything felt so wrong at that moment. His whole existence seemed to be slipping away from him, and that is exactly what Ryan did. He got the hell out of there.

Ryan had left the movies and the Slurpee sitting on the counter. There is no way that he could go back into the store now. Not tonight by any means, and perhaps not ever again. He started walking back towards his home while asking himself, "What the fuck just happened?"

Ryan had gone to a different store, and now he had 11 blocks in which to walk back to his house. The cold air of the outside world made his breathing slow, and he felt as if his heart may stay inside his chest.

As soon as he was away from any busy streets and in a residential neighborhood, he dropped to his knees in a snowbank. His stomach lurched and gurgled out what little food or drink he had in his body. After throwing up, Ryan then laid on his back in the freezing snow and looked up at the constellation of Orion. He made one simple wish and forced himself to his feet in order to carry on.

Only 10 blocks were left now, and Ryan could see little stars that were in his vision, but they were not in the night sky. They seemed to dance across his field of view and make him unsteady and weak. At this point, he had to stop and put his head down. He bent at the waist until they had vanished from view.

Ryan then began walking again, with only 9 blocks remaining now. He could envision himself lying on his couch, and this vision soothed him a small amount. That was, until a thought passed across his mind, and he became paranoid and thought that he could have been followed by someone.

At this thought, Ryan's heart began to race faster again, and his breathing started to become shallow. At this point, he started counting his steps and focusing on the white breaths of air that were expelling from his lungs.

Only 8 blocks now. In his mind, the young men who had beaten him so badly, or others like them, were now following him; he was positive of it. At this thought, Ryan's mind began to race with horrible thoughts that convoluted his thinking.

Ryan then thought that if they couldn't see him, then they couldn't hurt him, could they? Ryan tried to travel faster, but there was one thing that was slowing him down immensely. Whenever a car came toward him or from behind him, he had to hide behind a tree or a shrub again, as if he were a convict fleeing a mob that was coming after him.

Six blocks were left now, and Ryan was counting the steps that he was taking at a faster pace. This seemed to be a compulsion, and he had started to count his steps out loud, "56...57...58."

Ryan stopped in his tracks and screamed to himself, "Stop it!"

Maybe he was going batshit crazy this time. It sure felt like he was. 4 blocks left... "92…93…94…95."

Suddenly, there was a car coming from behind him, and it was slowing as it approached him. They had found him; they had to come to get revenge on him. For heaven's sake, they knew where he lived.

Ryan then said to himself, "Get behind a tree... get behind a tree...they can't hurt me if I am behind this tree. Oh, God...the car is slowing down...the car is slowing. Holy crap, the passenger window is rolling down... Does he have a gun? Will I hear the fiery blast of the gun. This tree will have to protect me. Please God, let this tree protect me."

"Hey Ryan…Ryan Maxwell, is that you? You want a ride?" A familiar voice of the male who was driving came from inside the black truck.

Then the voice continued to say, "What are you doing buddy? You must be freezing out there. Come here and get in."

Ryan peered out from behind the tree and saw that an ex-bandmate named Anthony was driving the black pickup truck that had a white scrape on the front quarter panel.

Ryan tried to say casually, "Thanks...yeah. Thank you, Anthony. I will take you up on getting that ride."

Then he thought that he had better explain his hiding behind the tree, and he finished by saying, "You almost caught me draining the main vein over here."

Ryan did not know how cold he was getting until he climbed into Anthony's truck and felt the warmth of the heater blowing on his face and especially on his feet. The ride back to Ryan's house only took the young men two minutes, but not a word was spoken during that time as Anthony seemed kind of freaked out by Ryan's actions.

Anthony and Ryan were not close friends, as Ryan tended to not like Anthony's personality too much. Tonight, however, Ryan was sure glad that he had been spotted by someone that he knew.

Ryan figured that he had better call Lisa when he got back to his house. When he did, he asked her to pick up a pizza, any movie that she would want to watch, and maybe grab a 12-pack of beer or wine coolers as well. He told her that he would pay her when she got there and that he really hoped to see her shortly.

After getting off the phone with Lisa, Ryan went to the refrigerator, grabbed a couple of cheap beers, and returned to the living room. He threw one of the frothy, cheap college beers to Anthony, who was sitting on the couch and thumbing through a girlie magazine that was laying open on the coffee table.

Tony caught the can of beer out of the air and then said to Ryan, "This girl is lookin' very nice. Why can't we find any women like this around here?"

"I'm glad that you approve of her. You wouldn't know what to do with any woman that looks like her." Ryan said, remembering suddenly why he didn't like Anthony very much.

Ryan then furrowed his brow and said, "Hell, you hit on all the women that came to our rock shows anyway. They looked nothing like her. I didn't think that you were picky."

However, Anthony had gotten Ryan safely back to his house. Ryan was also glad to have him stay and keep him company for a while, so I guess he couldn't be too bad to have around. He had better mind his manners and not be rude.

Anthony was the same age as Ryan, but he was stuck in the fashion of the 1950s for some reason. He was a good guitarist and played newer music, but he had jet black hair that he combed back with the help of styling mousse. He also wore a white T-shirt, blue jeans, black leather boots, and a black leather jacket worn over the top of his out-of-date clothing.

"So, has everything been going well for you, Anthony?" Ryan asked out of making conversation, as his tongue felt like it weighed eight pounds, and his thirst was insatiable.

Ryan then cracked open the pull tab on the beer and breathed in that wonderful aroma. Most people didn't like the smell of beer, but Ryan found it quite inviting. He drank the first can of beer in less than two minutes and had to make another trip to the kitchen in order to get another round of beverages. This time he brought back a 6-pack of beer, so that he wouldn't have to keep getting up and down at a frequent pace. The more that Ryan drank, the more he started to feel better and more like his former self.

Lisa was worried when she spoke to Ryan before, as he did not sound like himself. As a matter of fact, he only sounded like a shell of the man that she had gotten to know and really started to care about. Even though he seemed very lonely and scared at the time.

So, she was completely shocked when she showed up at Ryan's house to find an inebriated new boyfriend who was partying with a man that neither of them liked very much.

Lisa stormed into the house and immediately took the pizza into the kitchen. Then she leaned in anger against the kitchen counter.

Ryan entered behind her and stupidly asked, "Are you mad that I started to drink some beers?"

Lisa's face turned red, and she railed in anger at Ryan, saying, "Of course I am mad. We were going to have a nice evening together, and I get here, and you are drinking with 'Slicked Back Anthony'? I was really worried about you, and I just don't understand any of this. You know that Anthony took advantage of one of my friends."

Ryan put out his hands in defense and tried to explain by saying, "When I called you, I had every intention of having a nice evening with you. I got incredibly sick when I tried to go to the store earlier, and I really felt like I could have a heart attack or something. Then Anthony came by and offered me a ride, and that is how he got here."

Ryan then tried to sound calm and in less of an arguing mood. He then was totally honest and stated, "Now then, I don't understand what the hell is going on either. I only know that I begin to feel better when I drink some alcohol. It tends to slow down the fears and pressures that I am feeling. I do want you to be with me as you slow down the blood pressure running through my body as well. This all started that night when we got jumped by that gang."

Ryan then almost pleaded with her, saying, "Please, I will kick Anthony out...and tonight will be all about us. If you want me to, I won't even drink anymore. Just please stay with me. You are the healthy alternative to alcohol for me."

Lisa tentatively gave Ryan a half-grin, and then she conceded by saying, "Well, I did pick out a romantic comedy that you would never watch with me otherwise, and there are veggies on the pizza, so I guess that we are even. The only thing that you can drink tonight is some wine coolers that I picked up, okay?"

Ryan pulled himself closer to her and kissed her neck while saying, "Let's go get rid of Anthony and go from there, veggies and all. I promise that I will be good from now on tonight."

Ryan simply walked out into the living room and said to Anthony, "Dude, you've got to go. I really appreciate the ride and the company, but Lisa and I would like to spend some time together. We haven't seen each other since before Christmas. So, I don't mean to be rude, but you really must get out of here."

Anthony was rising off the couch when Ryan asked this, and he only said, "Both of you have a good night. You just take care of yourself, Ryan. You didn't look very good when I first picked you up. You kind of scared me."

Anthony then stopped at the door, looked back at Ryan, and said, "I hope that it gets easier to deal with for you."

At these words, Anthony left the house, and Ryan never saw him again. However, he often thought about this horribly eerie scenario and the words that Anthony had said to him. Ryan dismissed Anthony's words right away, but in hindsight, his words were extremely prophetic. He was just glad that Lisa was there now.

The two young lovers curled up on the couch together, watching Tom Hanks and Meg Ryan gripe about their relationships. They enjoyed the warmth, safety, and compassion that each person gave to each other.

Ryan was laying down with his head in Lisa's lap when he looked up at her and said very seriously, "If I fall asleep, please don't leave me tonight. I really need to have you here."

Lisa stroked his hair and said thoughtfully, "I am not going anywhere."

When Ryan's eyes opened slowly the next morning, the panic that had encompassed him the night before was back with a vengeance. He didn't realize where he was at first, and maybe this was caused by a small hangover that he was having. Alcohol could really make him feel better, but it could also cause him to feel extremely worse the next day.

His heartbeat and blood pressure began to surge again. He then felt Lisa shuffle her body underneath his head, and his anxiety immediately calmed down.

He said his thoughts out loud, when he fondly stated, "Thank God for someone to hold onto. The world might swallow me whole, otherwise."

"Good morning" Ryan said to Lisa as he sat up onto the couch cushion and let out a large yawn.

"Good morning" she said, and then she rolled her stiff neck and her hair smacked Ryan in the face. She giggled and continued saying, "What are you making me for breakfast?"

Ryan gave her a small kiss and then said, "I'll go get something to eat. Just lay here for a while and relax." He then sleepily closed his eyes and tried to nuzzle up to her again.

She said emphatically, "No way. Get up. I have to take a pee, and I want bacon, so get going, mister."

He got up and put on his winter boots, coat, wool scarf, and matching stocking cap. He then opened the door to leave when Lisa yelled at him from the bathroom, "Don't forget to get me some coffee."

Ryan didn't answer her and stepped out into the cold air of the morning. What Ryan didn't know this morning was that he was about to ask for an ambulance for the first time in his life.

Ryan owned a blue Chevy Baretta at the time, and he trudged through the snow toward his car, unlocked it, got in, and sat down. The massive panic attack hit Ryan like he had been struck in the face by a snow shovel. It was so bad that he was frozen with fear, and he couldn't even turn the key in order to start the engine. There was nothing wrong with the car, as it was in perfect working order, but there was everything wrong with him instead.

His stomach wretched again, and a large belch was forced from deep down in his diaphragm. He tried to look toward his home, but he was partly blinded because of the tears and the sweat that were running from his eyes and onto his face. He suddenly felt as if he would pass out or have something happen to him that was even worse.

"What is wrong with me?" Ryan screamed in frustration at the inner ceiling of his car.

It took every bit of strength that he had in his arms and legs just to get the manual car started. The engine roared to life, and he felt the cold shudder of it underneath his own butt as the snow and cold made the engine emit a low grinding sound.

His heart was thumping faster again as he turned his defrosting heater on high. Hopefully, in a short amount of time, he would calm himself down enough for him to see his way to his favorite fast-food restaurant to grab a hearty breakfast. After about 5 minutes, Ryan checked his mirrors and slowly pulled the car out onto the street.

Ryan did not drive any faster than 15 mph that morning. He tried heartily, but he could not physically push the gas pedal any farther down in order to make the car go any faster. His mind wouldn't allow him to do this.

Ryan made a right turn at the next street and corrected the car as the rearend slid out from under him and into the wrong lane of the icy road. Ryan then slowed the car even more than he had been going and crawled the car up the middle of the street. Ryan took another right turn at the next street and then checked all the lights on his dashboard, as well as the speedometer.

Ryan then thought frantically, 'Did I accidentally almost hit another car? Oh God, I hope that no kids are out playing in the street this morning. What if I hit a child?'

At the next street, Ryan took another right turn, and he made sure that his blinker worked properly. Then he slowed the car even more and checked all his mirrors again. Oh God, his eyes were off the road for a second; Did he hit something? The paranoia was becoming almost uncontrollable now.

The next street came up in front of Ryan, and he took another right, where he pulled up in front of his house again. Suddenly, he realized that he was crying at an agonizing rate. There was no way that he could try to drive anymore.

When Ryan opened the car door, the cold air hit his face, and he couldn't see anything. His vision had become totally blurred and his tears froze immediately. He couldn't stay in the car even though the air outside was freezing. Ryan practically fell out of the car and onto the street. He crawled his way up to the steps that led into his house, and he slammed himself into the door as he tried to turn the doorknob and let himself inside.

"Lisa?" Ryan yelled, "Lisa, I need your help."

Lisa ran out of the bathroom with a wet head of hair, and she was buttoning her blouse clumsily. She opened the door wider, and then she stopped at the sight of him. All the blood left her face, and she fell on her knees and tried to pull Ryan into the warm house. After closing the door, she started to hug his shoulders and wipe the frozen tears away from his eyes.

Then she said to him, "What do you need...Ryan...Ryan...What can I do?"

Ryan couldn't see the vision of her, but he grasped for her knees and her hands. Then he pleaded with her by saying, "Lisa, call an ambulance.... I need help of some sort. I feel like everything is breaking all at once on me. Help me, please help me, Lisa."

Lisa got a concerned look on her face and said, "Hang on!" She then got up and raced for the home phone in the kitchen.

For the first time, Lisa rode with Ryan in the clunky ambulance and held his hand. The paramedics had given Ryan a shot of something wonderful at his house, which had finally calmed him down. He wasn't feeling any pain when they arrived at the hospital.

At one point, Ryan had even called her by the name of 'Karen' a few times, and this really made Lisa angry. She had never heard Ryan even mention a woman named Karen before.

He had also asked Lisa if, "She was a messenger for the knight?"

Whatever that may mean, Lisa had no idea. The doctors and nurses then asked Lisa what had happened to him and her relationship with Ryan. At first, she couldn't remember that anything was wrong with him, and then she remembered how he had gotten badly beaten a few weeks before. She told them the abridged version of that horrible story, and that was when all of this started. As for what her relationship was with Ryan, she honestly could not answer them.

However, this seemed to be a fresh pain that Ryan was going through. No one seemed to know what was causing these new, fresh pains. Not Lisa, not the nurses, not the doctors, not even Ryan himself. It seemed as if the athletic, strong, confident man that Lisa had begun to know and care for had been sucked out, and what was left was a quivering version of himself.

It tore her apart, seeing him like this, but how long could she handle taking care of him. It seemed like he was a cracked egg. He had been dropped and broken, and she had no tools to put him back together again. She was now dating Humpty Dumpty.

The doctors left Lisa sitting in the waiting room for too long....way too long. Lisa was crying uncontrollably now, and all that she wanted was the man that she had begun to have feelings for. She wanted to have him hold her in his strong arms and smile rather goofily. She wanted him to just ask her about her day or tell her a stupid joke.

Lisa jumped at the sound of the opening emergency room doors as Ryan came out of the swinging doors. She was completely surprised when she found him laughing hysterically while sitting in a wheelchair. She imagined him to be lying on a hospital gurney and raving wildly.

Ryan also wasn't the heroic man that she had been daydreaming about when he first appeared. Instead, he seemed to be drunk or sleepy, and he would laugh at the smallest of jokes that he made at his own expense.

He looked at Lisa and said, while yawning, "They gave me a prescription for some pills that we have to pick up on the way home."

Lisa's heart was broken and sank a little that day. Then she asked the nurse if there were any notes or directions from the doctor.

The nurse only said unapologetically, "Nope, he is in your hands now. We can't find anything wrong with him… physically. We don't know what to do to help him, but we can't keep him here. Good luck."

The nurse then left Lisa standing in the emergency room lobby with nothing to hold onto but a wobbling shell of a man.

God bless Lisa. She did the very best that she possibly could, especially with what she had been given to work with. She did not know what was wrong with her man, but she did like the idea that Ryan was her man.

The world was looking up for the young couple as the new pills, Xanax, that the doctor had put Ryan on were working. Ryan seemed to have his fearful attacks figured out for the time being, and Lisa had moved in with him. During this time, they were trying to make it a home.

One thing that Ryan had accomplished, even with the disorder that had hobbled him so badly, was that he had received his degree as a historian. He hadn't literally been going to his classes, and only showed up to take the exams in his final two years. However, he did receive his diploma.

Ryan was not stupid in any way; he was simply damaged. Ryan was drinking much less, as he had switched from hard alcohol to beer or wine. He often cooked, and they would have friends over for games or movies at night. Sometimes, they would go out to a nightclub and dance until 3:00 in the morning, but not as often as Ryan had done in his earlier life. Life was how it was supposed to be. Life was fun again.

Lisa never seemed to mind that Ryan was taking one Xanax pill each morning to have him survive the day unscathed. Then he would drink a few beers in the evening, just to help him sleep throughout the night. However, she watched closely to make sure that he never mixed the two. The doctors made sure that she was aware of doing this.

A person may disapprove of these habits, and some people did. However, he was sure that if he ever mixed these two addictive items, his life would be severely cut short. Often, he felt that if he didn't use these two items, he would have to be put in a psychiatric hospital for the rest of his life.

This was a terrible paradox for Ryan to feel that he had to do these things in order to have control over his own mind and body.

For the next six years, Ryan worked for a local telecommunications business called Deluxe Cable. He was an excellent salesman and an installer of television and phone services. Lisa was also working as an interior designer for a large real estate company. Everything was coming up roses for the young and upcoming couple.

After this opening period, the next three years were rather rocky for the young couple. Ryan thought that he was still doing very well at the company that he was working for, and he was still making a good living doing this.

However, the company felt the other way about Ryan because they saw him as a liability for their future endeavors. Because of these fearful feelings, Ryan was called into the boss's office one day, and he was let go. This was done by the same boss who had hired him nine years earlier. How could this happen? What had he done wrong?

However, after not having constant work, Lisa seemed to mind when Ryan would take a Xanax in the morning, a Xanax at noon, and then drink with his buddies at a bar until at least midnight each night. Ryan's severance payments would soon run out, as would his unemployment. Soon, Lisa would be the only person bringing a salary into the home.

Plus, the economy wasn't the best either, so people stopped buying houses. When that happened, business for her was not going very well either. Between Ryan's welfare and Lisa's small income, there were not too many smiles between the young couple. Everything seemed to be coming up weeds for the couple, who were now in their early 30's.

Finally, the last year had been outright lousy. Lisa had been fired from her good job, and she was now cleaning a school to have any income coming in. Ryan was detailing cars at the local Chevy showroom and was working next to a kid who was still in high school. This young man aspired to someday make over $12.00 per hour.

Also, Ryan had gone to a bar with a friend and been arrested for a DUI when he tried to drive home without his headlights on. He tried to call Lisa from the jail, but it only went to voicemail, so he had to spend the night in a cell.

Ryan came home in the morning after spending the night in jail, just to find an empty living room and a note taped to the outside door. Ryan grabbed the note that was on the door without even reading it...turned around...and drove to his favorite bar. Ryan knew that his time with Lisa had officially ended.

"'Cause I'm broken when I'm open
And I don't feel like I am strong enough
'Cause I'm broken when I'm lonesome
And I don't feel right when you're gone… away"
(Seether with Amy Lee)

Chapter Eleven

"I never met a drink that I didn't like"—Norm Peterson (Cheers)

Ryan woke the next morning, and he was lying on the carpeted floor of his empty house. Somehow, he had made it home, even though he was pretty sure that he hadn't driven his car at all.

He checked the pockets of his blue jeans that he was still wearing and discovered a receipt from a taxi ride home and said lowly, "Thank God for that."

Ryan looked around at the floor and noticed that he had made a pillow out of the sweatshirt that he had been wearing the night before. His blanket was the coat that he had worn the night before as well. He smelled like cheap beer and even cheaper cigarettes.

Ryan then grabbed all his clothes out of his closet, loaded up his car, and then filled up the gas tank of his old sports car. Lisa could have everything else. Was this life his fault? In his own mind, he didn't think so.

Ryan drove an older Triumph TR7 at the time, and luckily for him, it was a small sports car that did not take much fuel to fill up. Unluckily for him, though, Ryan found that with having a much smaller car, it did not hold very many garbage bags full of clothes or even fewer suitcases.

A Triumph TR7 was a small British car that was a two-seated sports car. It looked like it could go very fast, but in all actuality, it was standing still compared to any American-made Camaro or a Mustang that passed easily by him.

Ryan's car was bright green, and it also had fold-away headlights, which would fold down into the hood of the vehicle. This happened when he shut off the headlights, but this was only occurring on the driver's side of the car. The passenger side had a headlight that remained fully upright, as if the car were winking at someone.

Ryan had to get out of the car whenever he stopped and physically push the passenger side headlight down into the hole that was provided. This car was an older, cheaper alternative for Ryan, who still wanted to look like he could afford a sports car. He was getting what he paid for at these moments.

Ryan thought about his present situation, shook the sleepiness out of his head, and drove his car directly over to Dudley's. He wanted to say goodbye to the groups of friends that would hopefully be coming there. Ryan stopped at his favorite watering hole and had downed two beers when the doors swung open, and Greg and Randy emerged.

Besides the bartender, Ryan and his two old friends were the only people in the bar. Ryan ordered the alcohol, but Greg and Randy refused to drink with him. They had heard about how he had reacted the night before, and they were both desperately pushing Ryan to get some help. These were the only friends out of Ryan's mass group of them that had shown up to see him depart, and these friends seemed to be preaching into deaf ears.

Ryan said lowly to himself, "I can't believe that only two people showed up to see me off, and my best friends are trying to change me."

However, Greg and Randy knew that a person must want to quit on their own and couldn't be forced into it. They were Ryan's good friends, yes, but they could not make him do anything that he didn't want to do. Unfortunately, many people do not come to this understanding.

After a half hour of almost preaching to Ryan, his two best friends from college offered him their best goodbyes and well wishes. With a lowered head and a depressed mood, Ryan drove off into the distance.

Ryan had to make a stop 60 miles later to drain his bladder and fill it up with some additional shots of vodka. He thought that no one could smell this alcohol on his breath. Two hundred miles later of driving while not drinking anything but water, Ryan parked in front of the first bar that he had ever known in his small hometown, 'Mike's Bar'.

Ryan was now living in the early 2000s, and he said to himself, "You can go home again. This place hasn't changed a bit since the 1980s, and I don't think I will, either."

Ryan walked jauntily into the bar and was greeted loudly by some of his high school friends who still lived and worked in the small agricultural community. He was now in his 30s and on his way to another drunken evening at his hometown bar. Eventually, this would lead to a night spent sleeping on his oldest friend's couch. Was this life his fault? It may well be his fault.

Ryan got a job and began working at the local grain elevator with his good friend, Monty. They purchased and sold the grain at this location from the local farmers. This included unloading massive farming semi-trucks and storing the grain there in the elevator bins. They then loaded the grain onto locomotive cars and shipped the grain out from there to consumers.

It was very hard and dirty work, but it was also honorable and good physical labor. Agriculture is the lifeblood of America, and he was proud to provide those products to this great country and to the entire world.

Because of Ryan's lifestyle, he had become estranged from his family, and they had moved away from his hometown. This is when Ryan was rescued and lived in a small room in the home of one of his best and oldest friends from childhood, Monty. The house was older and small, but Ryan was happy to have a roof over his head. Ryan's life story had now circled back through three decades to his old friends and to the home where he had been raised since childhood.

Monty was glad to have Ryan stay with him, as he had gone through a bad divorce, and misery truly does love company at a certain point. They needed each other's company at that time. Both of their failed relationships were nothing to be proud of, but neither man relished the past. They only liked to look forward to the next fun opportunity that would be offered to them.

Ryan and Monty were living life as hard as when they were teenagers in high school. The two of them worked hard and seemed to play even harder. Time went by very quickly, as the two men had reunified their high school friendship as well as their love of all things, which included having the best time that they could find in this life.

During the next fall season, Ryan had met Michelle at 'Mike's Bar,' and they had started dating. In the middle of fall, Ryan had also fallen in love with that same little yellow dog, which he had named Allie. Ryan couldn't think of it, but why did that name sound so familiar to him?

If it hadn't been for suffering from panic disorder and the binges of drinking, things would have been looking up for Ryan. Was this life his fault? Yes, it was probably his fault.

One night in the January of 2005, Ryan hadn't felt like drinking any alcohol. He lay in a bed that had been given to him by his best friend from high school. Of course, sleep would not come to him that evening, even though he was comfortable lying in the bed that had been provided to him.

He heard the cold, hard wind whipping the branches of the trees against the sides of his windows. Michelle was laying on her belly next to Ryan, with her arm hanging over his nervous, growling stomach.

Allie was sleeping on the floor at the foot of the bed, which was the usual spot for her dog bed. She was snoring loudly and dreaming about either swimming or chasing a chipmunk down a hole, as her legs were flailing around wildly.

On the walls, there was a white wallpaper with ugly yellow flowers covering it, and Ryan often had the urge to tear it down and paint the entire room. Hanging on one wall was an old, framed poster of the 3 Stooges playing golf. On the other wall, there was a panoramic print of a train, that was pulling a heavy load of wood and belching out thick black smoke.

Ryan ran his fingers through Michelle's long, blond hair. She nestled closer to him and mumbled an incoherent group of sentences.

Ryan gave her a quizzical look and hushed her, as he did not want her to awaken for some reason. Ryan had never paid any attention to the locations of his paintings on the walls before, and then he looked more closely and said in a whisper, "Holy Shit!"

The paintings had switched positions and stood on the opposite walls. Nobody had entered the room. How the hell had this happened?

Suddenly, when Ryan lifted his head in order to examine the two wall hangings again, he noticed a movement in the corner of the room near the doorway. As if it were out of the blue, he then heard a low growling noise, and he saw Allie raise her head and her ears perk up.

He cleared his throat and whispered quietly, "Come out from there."

The knight stepped out of the shadows in the corner of the room and motioned for Ryan to follow him out the bedroom door. Ryan slid out from under Michelle's hanging arm, pulled on his ugly plaid pajama bottoms, and he and Allie followed the knight out of the door.

When they got out of the room and shut the door, Ryan said amazingly, "Holy blast from the past. Where the hell have you been, James? I haven't seen you in a long time."

"I have been busy and have not been able to make contact with you." James pointed to the bedroom and said, "I see that you have been quite busy, also."

He sounded as if he did not approve, and then he finished by asking, "Is that not the same woman as the last one that you were with?"

Ryan thought about the last time that he had seen the knight and answered, "No, that last woman couldn't be around me anymore. I wasn't the best companion to be around. I have been down an extremely long trail, buddy. But I am glad to see you. It has been several years, James. What does a knight do for nearly 10 years?"

James the Knight looked at Ryan and spoke solemnly. "Recruiting... my...friend." James said this slowly, drawing the words out, as if he were being careful with how he answered.

And then James continued when he saw Ryan's reactive face of shock: "It will be happening soon, Ryan. I say this just so that you may prepare yourself. I have been building an army to fight by our side."

Ryan stopped him from speaking with a "Whoa!" He then continued with a raised hand, and he asked a serious question, "An army, for what purpose?"

James' mouth turned up into a slight grin, and he said, "I told you that we need them to fight with us, Ryan. Isn't that what armies still do?" Just then, James the Knight started to fade in and out of vision.

James then looked back over his shoulder as if he were listening to an invisible person that was behind him. He then turned back to Ryan and said with a solemn tone in his voice, "I wanted to say this to you though...no matter how you feel...you are never alone."

James looked over his shoulder at someone again, and then said as if he were passing along a message, "We are all here for you. Never give up on us."

Ryan started to ask another question, but James had vanished from his view.

"Thanks a lot," Ryan said, while putting his head into his hands. "Any other helpful hints from the ghost world tonight?"

A familiar female voice answered that question for him and said, "I don't have any other words of advice, except for you to be strong and to be ready very soon."

Ryan's hands dropped quickly away from his eyes, and he shook his head as if he were seeing things. He then said to her, "Karen, is it really you? This can't be happening."

Ryan then tried to reach out to her while continuing to say, "The last time that you visited me in any of my dreams was way back in 1991 with that young girl. That was 5 years after the trip where you disappeared from my life. Now it has been 20 years since the last time that I physically saw you in Amsterdam. Why and how are you visiting me again?"

Karen looked at him gravely and said, "Well, you couldn't see me during those times in your life...but I could see you, and I tried to help you along the way."

Ryan's eyes flew wide open, and he started to say, "Karen, I nev..."

She stopped him with one raised hand, and she only said, "I am very disappointed in some of the choices that you have made. However, I am also very happy with the man that you have become. Do you understand?"

Ryan lowered his head and quietly said, "No, I don't."

Karen looked at him with patience on her face and then said, "A lot of bad things have happened to you, and you haven't been the perfect man. However, you have remained a very good, trustworthy, and protective man throughout all these hard years. You are a man who believes in doing the right thing. Even if doing the right thing causes you to have your own heartaches and disbeliefs in the process."

Ryan had never felt so badly and had also felt very proud of himself at the same time. If Ryan remembered correctly, Karen had a huge gift at this attribute. She could make you feel like you were one of the dredges of society in one minute, and the hero of humanity in another.

It was as if Karen enjoyed lifting a person's confidence, just to be able to tear it to the ground and rebuild it from the floor up again. Ryan resented the thought of her actions, but at the same time, he loved her and wanted to make her happy and proud whenever possible.

However, on this night, pain and anger began to boil up in Ryan once again, and he said to Karen angrily, "You were my first love, Karen, and I would have done anything for you at the time. I felt so lonely and betrayed by you. I could never get a straight answer from you."

Karen started to speak, and Ryan made her stop talking with a raised hand. He then continued saying, in an irritated manner, "I kept getting promises from you, and then I ended up being the horrible, insane person that nobody trusted. I was accused of chasing you away by being a stalker. I was shunned by the rest of the teens in the orchestra, and I lost very good friendships, all because of listening to you and believing in you."

Ryan dropped his head at this last sentence, and he began to pace across the room as if someone might hold him down if he did not.

Karen let out a deep sigh and finally asked lowly, "So, what do you want Ryan? Do you have no desire to help us anymore? Do you not want to be visited by me or anyone else in the future?"

Ryan looked over at her incredulously and then said to her with a huge amount of impatience in his voice, "I think that it is a little late for that. It is not a matter of me wanting to help. I just want to know how this whole problem involves me?"

Ryan began pacing and speaking louder by saying, "It seems like I have given away so much of my own life. All for something that I have no idea if I believe in at all. Damn it, I have given away my own self-confidence for this whole situation, and nobody will tell me what I will get out of it. Is this just trusting in blind faith? Because I do not like it."

Karen then said quietly, "You have every right to be angry, Ryan. We could have handled this whole situation so much better, but unfortunately, we did not. Believe it or not, there are a huge amount of people involved in this whole fiasco, and you are a huge, important cog involved in this entire situation."

Karen then began to cry and said sorrowfully but forcefully, "You are not the only person to give everything up in order to battle for this cause. I was extremely scared when they explained it all to me at the very beginning. I nearly bolted away from my responsibilities...especially when I got involved with you."

Karen snuffed in loudly and continued to say, "I am sorry! I truly am incredibly sorry that I got thrown into this mess and included you. However, it is because of your many attributes…your loyalty...your resolve...your compassion...and most importantly, your burning desire to do what is right that makes you so important. These are all the knightly qualities that make you integral to this world-changing event."

Ryan looked sarcastically important and said, "My knightly qualities? My world-changing attributes? Karen, I think that you may have the wrong person in mind. I have been labeled as a 'drunk' and as an 'eccentric asshole', not to mention a stalker and a complete loon. I have heard all the jibes made at me, and 'knightly' was not one of them."

Ryan sat down at this statement and looked dejectedly into his open palms. He then said lowly, "I don't know how you can think that I am so damn dependable."

Karen then walked behind Ryan and wrapped her arms around him. She comfortingly said, "Pay no mind to what other dullards say. We all know the truth about you, and you will once again have to act like the honorable person that we all know that you are. Promise me this, Ryan; promise me that you will keep your vigilance and that you will be here when we call upon you."

Ryan raised his head and looked at her beautiful face. He then stared into her blue eyes and said, "I promise you, Karen, I could never say no to you."

With these words, Karen's body evaporated into a white mist that dissipated into the atmosphere.

Ryan raised his head to the heavens and exclaimed, "Karen, do you truly believe in me, or are you just betting that a longshot like me will actually come through?"

Michelle's voice broke the silence when she said behind Ryan, "I don't know about this Karen woman, but I don't think that I can depend on you anymore. You are a wonderful man, but you are a complete longshot. I have a ten-year-old son to think about. He does nothing but look at you like you were a rock star, but I can't afford for him to get disappointed again. Neither can I, for that matter. I really like you, Ryan, but you are not a sure bet. I need that right now in my life. If we were both younger, most probably, but not now."

Ryan smiled knowingly and slowly walked over to Michelle. When he reached her, he held her hand in his, leaned down, and kissed her forehead.

He then said in a whisper, "You deserve everything that the best love can offer you and your son. I hope that you and your son find that someday. I really do. God bless you, Michelle."

Ryan slid by her and held her hand until he was almost in the bedroom again. He then looked back into her eyes and dropped her extended hand. At that point, he blew her a kiss and sauntered quietly back into his bedroom. When Ryan awoke the next morning, Michelle was gone, and only the flowery smell of her hair on his pillow was left.

In the next three months, the weather was cruelly windy and cold. It was also as if it wouldn't end anytime soon, as Montana winters are known to hang on for dear life.

However, today was April 20th, and it was sunny and neither hot nor cold. It was also a day that Ryan and Monty had been looking forward to ever since the first snowfall of the year back in October. Today was the opening day of the golf course at the local country club.

This included an entire day of drinking beer and chasing a little white ball around in the spring sunshine. Golf had become both men's therapy. Even the most stubborn, stupid asshole on the planet would have no impact on Ryan and Monty that day. It was as if they just pretended that all their problems were in the golf balls, and they were driven away from them with each hit of the ball.

Ryan and Monty drove the 20 miles to the golf course in about 16 minutes. They listened to an old AC/DC cassette tape to get themselves hyped up, where they sang along with Bon Scott, the first singer of the Australian rock band.

They had met Len and Tommy at the golf course so that they could have a foursome of golfers. Then they drove to the first tee, where the first golf drives of the day would show each of them their promising or disheartening skills for the upcoming year.

Len was the first to hit the ball, and he drove it about 200 yards, straight down the middle of the fairway. Then Tommy drove the ball, and it made an indirect, sharp turn to the right in a nasty slice. This errant golf ball nearly hit another group of golfers on the other fairway.

Monty then hit the ball next and hooked it to his left, almost to the out-of-bounds line. However, he did hit the ball hard, and it went approximately 280 yards, just not in the correct direction.

Ryan was the last one to hit the ball, and he seemed to follow Monty, except he didn't hit the ball as hard or as far. It looked like both Ryan and Monty were going to be landlocked within a group of trees inside the rough that was next to the left side of the fairway.

Ryan wrinkled his nose and said to Monty, who was sitting behind the driver's seat of the golf cart, "Well, it seems like our golf balls went in the same general direction. It looks like I am riding in the right golf cart after all."

Monty chuckled softly and said back to Ryan, "Damn straight, Skippy! Off to the trees we go. Please don't let us find our balls out of bounds. That is not the way to start off the golf year."

When they found Ryan's ball, they found that his next shot would be out of a group of trees. Monty asked him sarcastically, "Are you using that special tree iron for your next shot, buddy?"

Ryan's ball was on a tuft of grass that was surrounded by these trees in every direction. He had zero shot of getting out of there, but that never stopped Ryan from trying anyway. Ryan playfully flipped Monty off because of his comment, hit the ball as hard as he could, and then watched as the ball ricocheted between several tree branches. His ball shot off to the left, rolled out of sight, and ended up out of bounds.

They both started to laugh at this horrible situation, and then Ryan stated, "Well, I lost my first golf ball on the very first hole. This isn't how I wanted to start."

Monty started to drive the golf cart forward to his ball and then jibed at Ryan, "You couldn't hit a bull in the ass with a snow shovel."

Monty then jabbed at him by asking, "Do you want to place a bet on our score at the end of the day?"

Ryan then took a drink of beer and joked back at him, "I will make a friendly wager on your next shot. Now it is your turn to make a fool of yourself. You are as much of a hack as me. Don't be bragging too early."

Monty also hit a tree with his second shot, and the ball also went out of bounds. Still, this was a very fun day, and one that had to be repeated as much as possible by the two friends. It was just a shame that they were not better at the game. They both started off the year, with bad results.

Ryan and Monty were still laughing at how badly they had played the game when they arrived home. The men were extremely buzzed when they finished playing, but they at least had the good sense to pay the sixteen-year-old son of a friend to drive them safely home from the golf course.

On their arrival home, Ryan dropped his clubs onto the floor and let Allie slobber and kiss his cheek. Monty carried his clubs back to his bedroom, and Ryan stated loudly to him; "I will be back, I am going to get the mail and let Allie go out for a pee."

Ryan went outside, and sure enough, both Allie and he peed in the backyard, at the same time. Ryan laughed at this predicament until he got to the mailbox, and inside was an invitation.

ATTENTION: AMERICAN YOUTH ORCHESTRA
CAN YOU BELIEVE THAT IT HAS BEEN 20 YEARS?
JOIN US AND CELEBRATE: IN LONDON
JULY 13-20, 2005
COME SEE OLD FRIENDS AND MEET SOME NEW ONE'S!

Ryan became much less jovial and extremely quiet after reading this invitation. He did not feel that getting invited to this event was a coincidence.

Allie looked up at him quizzically, with one ear raised and her pink tongue hanging out of the side of her mouth.

Ryan asked his dog, "Should I go, girl?" In which his reply was the vigorous wagging of her tail.

Ryan led Allie inside and showed the invitation to Monty, who only asked the same question, "You going to go?"

Ryan thought about this question and walked across the living room and sat down on the couch. He then said, "For some reason, I think that I am supposed to go."

Monty only said, "I think that you have to go as well. You are still haunted by that trip to Europe and by that girl who broke your heart."

Ryan quietly said back, "Yeah…I will definitely consider it."

The sun-filled day and the beer had taken their toll on Ryan and he quickly got very sleepy and excused himself into the bedroom. He also had a lot on his mind.

Ryan and Monty only got the opportunity to golf together one more time. This was when June started out with beautiful blue skies and plenty of sunshine. This time, though, Monty had brought a date along for Ryan.

Ryan looked at him skeptically and said, "A date to the golf course? That will make a good impression on her. We don't really act like gentlemen when we are out here."

Monty came back at him and said, "Hey, I had a date, and I at least brought a woman for you as well, so no bitchin'. Just don't have temper tantrums or cuss too much. This could be nice for both of us."

Ryan laughed at Monty and said, "You make her sound like a breakfast burrito that you just happened to pick up for me on the way to the golf course."

Monty looked at Ryan and said, "You like breakfast burritos. Just shut up and your welcome for the nice surprise."

The women finished loading their clubs onto their own golf cart, and then they finished by loading a case of beer into a cooler as well.

Ryan then said to Monty, "Okay, I like them already. Plus, they are a lot cuter than Tom and Lennie."

Monty drove up to the first tee, while his date swung and missed hitting the ball entirely. She yelled out in exasperation, "Shit!"

Monty looked over at Ryan and asked, "Do I know how to pick 'em or what?"

Ryan only gave him a shy smile and answered back, "Well, she does have the golf expressions and vocabulary down to a tee. Pardon the pun."

Whenever the women shouted out a curse word throughout the day, Ryan found himself biting his tongue, and he seemed to become sadder and less talkative himself.

With these feelings, he thought to himself, "I really need to quit getting so angry and cussing as well. I don't find it very attractive. For some reason, this is just not sitting right with me."

After the day of golfing, Ryan sat alone, pondering the invitation that he had received in the mail. He was sitting on the back deck of the clubhouse, which overlooked the muddy Missouri River. He could also see the 18th green, where other golfers were finishing up their day of play.

He toasted the golfers that were just finishing their rounds of golf and took a long pull from his aluminum beer bottle. The women who had joined them for the day had gotten too much sun and alcohol and had to retire for the evening. The sun was just going down over the western mountains, and Ryan was joined by Monty on this brilliant warm evening.

Ryan didn't even look over at Monty and he said solemnly, "I have an extremely bad feeling about this trip to London that I am going to go on. You know I didn't leave there as the most liked or well-respected member of the touring orchestra."

"Yeah, I know I have a mixed feeling about it too, man. You were in a bad place when you got back from that trip last time," Monty added.

The two sat in silence for a while longer, and they looked out at the divine image of the distant mountains that were dazzling in the last light of the day.

"Do you want to come with me, dude?" Ryan suddenly asked Monty from out of the blue. "You know, keep me from getting into any trouble."

Monty didn't even blink an eye and answered quickly, "I have a lot of vacation days that I need to use up, and this part of the year is damned slow in our business. You got it, Bro."

Ryan blushed and nudged his good friend Monty and said, "Good, I am glad that you feel that way. I owe you some back rent for letting myself and Allie stay with you...so...I already bought you a ticket."

Monty looked kind of shocked and asked, "To London?"

Ryan shook his head in a "yes" motion while allowing his friend to think this over. Then Monty said, "Sure, I think that we would have a blast over there, and we can watch each other's backs, as well."

"You know, there are a lot of women that were involved in this tour." Ryan joked with his good friend.

Monty got up for another beer and said, "Hey, all you have got to do is get me to London. I will work my own "mountain man magic" when I get there."

Ryan let out a chuckle and then parroted it back at Monty. "Mountain Man Magic?"

That made the men laugh at the thought of this statement, but there was still a dark pallor over their choice to go on this trip. Even with them both going to London and watching out for one another.

That night, James the Knight visited Ryan in his dreams again. Ryan was sweating profusely and breathing heavily, while all around him were the sounds of the wailing of nearly dead soldiers. James confronted Ryan from the rear with his helmet off and his armor smeared with dark red stains of blood.

James then walked to Ryan's side as though he wanted to speak to him, which caused Ryan to finally look over at him. Only a trickle of blood came out of the corners of James' mouth, and he made a kind of "Urrggh" sound as an arrow had struck James the Knight in his left cheek.

The arrow had run clear through his mouth and had exited in the back of his right cheek. James then sheathed his sword and grabbed at the tip of the arrow while pleading at Ryan with his eyes. He pushed at one end of the arrow and pointed at Ryan. When he did this, another "Urrghing" sound came from his injured mouth.

Ryan got the gist of what James was asking of him, and he stepped to the feathered end of the arrow and began to push. James made his legs steady and pulled at the sharpened head of the arrow. Finally, James pulled the arrow out of his bloodied mouth, and the Knight dropped it onto the cobblestone road at his feet.

His face had two holes on either side of it that oozed blood down his chin. James spat out a glob of blood and then carefully said, "You could have been a knight who knows how to heal others, Sir Ryan. We would have needed someone like you. You have the metal for it."

Ryan then clapped James on the back and said, "Please don't call me by that 'Sir' title. I don't feel very chivalrous at this moment."

James then bent over and grabbed an English longsword that was lying among the dying soldiers. He handed the molded piece of mayhem to Ryan, letting him feel the weight of the sword in his hand. Ryan held the hilt of the sword tightly and tried to swing it wildly. He was amazed at the great amount of strength that he had to use to do this.

James looked at him confusedly, and then he said, "Look here, Ryan. Hold the hilt of the sword firmly, but also with grace and fragility. Right now, it looks as if you are trying to choke it to death. Then, let the blade guide and control some of your actions. Try not to be so stiff and wild with it. Use your instincts."

Ryan then turned toward James the Knight and amazingly said, "I took a lesson in a game called golf one time, and he gave me the same techniques and lessons. He told me to grip the club like I was holding a baby bird. Firm enough so that it wouldn't fall from my grip but also not with enough pressure for me to crush it. Also, he told me to swing the club slower and with more precision and control."

James raised his eyebrows and then spit out some more blood and stated, "He sounds like a wise man."

Ryan then swung the sword with a graceful motion, and he seemed to slice the air with a deadly arc of natural motions.

Ryan then stopped his swordplay, and he looked at James seriously and asked, "James, why are you showing me all of this?"

James spit out more blood and then said, "It is in your blood, and you will need it. Feel and hear how the sword makes a swishing noise as you whisk it up and down and from left to right. Try to have the weapon become a part of you."

Ryan gave the swordsmanship a try and then stopped after he almost hit himself in the face. He then said back, "This whole kind of coordinated effort reminds me of drumming. It may look great to the unknowing bystander, but it takes a whole lot of practice for it to be just right."

James looked at Ryan solemnly and said, "Well, keep practicing."

The knight said one more thing before Ryan woke from this odd dream. "Remember, all this is in your blood. Use it."

With this statement, James the Knight started to rise, pulling away from the earth like he was black smoke that was floating away. The smoke slowly rose into the atmosphere until he was completely gone. All that was left was Ryan standing there, looking at smoldering fires, smoke, and dead bodies.

"James....James?" Ryan said to an empty field as he took in a deep breath. However, the air was smoky and acrid and made him cough with a rasp in his throat. Slowly, with each raspy breath, Ryan awoke to find he was lying in his own bed with Allie lying beside him.

He thought he heard a distant voice saying, "It is in your blood...Use it!"

"What a shame, what a shame
To Judge a life that you can't change...
The choir sings, the church bells ring
So, won't you give this man his wings?"
(Shinedown)

Chapter Twelve

Is it called stealing if you plagiarize from the Bible?

July 12th, 2005: 2:58 P.M.- Ryan and Monty were waiting at the bar/restaurant inside the terminal of the local airport in Montana. It was going to be a long day of traveling, interspersed with the running between terminals. They had to do this on their two layovers in which they would have to change planes.

They had to leave earlier in the morning as Ryan had to drop off his loving, faithful dog at the kennels. Allie had wagged her tail, given him a small whine, and given him a slobbery lick to the face. He was about to leave her, and she acted as if she may never see him again.

Of course, he and Monty also had to stop by a local sports bar to have a bowl of soup, a ham sandwich, and a couple of pitchers of beer. Now, Ryan had become very fearful of flying after so much damage had been done to his head. The pituitary gland that was in his brain had been irreparably damaged throughout the years and by the many injuries.

The pressure in his head seemed to be filled with pain, which often caused him to be off-kilter and unsteady. After a pitcher full of beer, he was just starting to feel comfortable taking to the skies again.

They began boarding their plane when Monty asked Ryan with concern in his voice. "Are you ready?"

Ryan was putting in earbuds that were connected to some of his favorite music. He answered back with even more concern in his own voice. "Nope, but I am here anyway."

Barely a word was spoken between the two friends until they reached the eastern coastline of the United States. Monty had delighted in some much-needed sleep because of the libations of the night before. Ryan sat with his music blaring in his ears and his eyes closed in deep concentration and breathing techniques.

His seatbelt, which he checked often, had been pulled extra-tight, and his sweaty palms were rarely leaving the armrests. Thankfully, Ryan did make it to his first destination on this trip with no incidents. He sighed heavily and let out a shaky breath when the plane finally landed in Philadelphia.

Ryan awoke Monty with the nudge from his elbow, and he pointed at the city that they were landing in. He then said, "We're there, Monty. Weren't you here for four years in the Navy?"

Monty stretched, yawned, and then simply said, "Yeah, there is not much to tell you though. I was assigned to a ship that was stationed here and it ended up in dry dock for all four years that I was in the Navy. There is still a lot to do on a ship that is being repaired, though.

Monty saw the look on Ryan's face and said more intently, "A person does as much work for this country at home as they do in other countries or in international waters. I just went to more Phillies and Eagles games than most sailors get the chance to."

Ryan laughed at the thought of being in the navy and never going out to sea. Then he asked his good friend, "I know that you worked hard in the military, and I'm proud to have a friend who is a veteran. But can you also remember any good places to eat and partake in the local community? We have two and a half hours to kill."

Monty's eyebrows rose as if this was the first time that he had thought about this scenario. He winked at Ryan and confidently said, "I got this."

At 9:15 pm, Ryan followed Monty out of the airport, and they took a short van ride to a local restaurant/bar called 'The Flying Pig'. This tavern and restaurant looked exactly like the kind of place that they needed for the evening.

Ryan looked the menu up and down and was about to order a cheeseburger with fries and a nationally known draft beer.

Monty cocked his neck in Ryan's direction, and he said, "Don't order the same old shit that you would eat in Montana; you are in Philly now. Enjoy one of these amazing cheesesteak sandwiches that they make here and try one of the local microbrews."

Ryan had an original cheesesteak sandwich, and he could immediately tell that he had eaten a great sandwich. It tasted amazing, just like the strong local ale that he had tried. At the end of the meal, Ryan ordered three fingers of an Irish whiskey that he was supposed to sip slowly and another glass of craft beer.

Monty looked at Ryan and then said warily, "Remember, you are in Philly for God's sake. You are in a bar, and you are in a city that is kind of tough. I think that there could be a rowdy bunch of partiers in here, so be careful."

Ryan then looked at him and said curtly, "I just hope that their booze works as quickly over here as it does in Montana."

Monty laughed and ordered another glass of the local microbrew. He then sat down quietly and said, "Are you telling me everything, Ryan? You have been acting like a suspicious weirdo so far on this trip."

"Yeah." Ryan began to say more, but then he changed his mind and said, "I mean, no... I just have had a real bad feeling about this trip in my gut. I have been worried about you as well, and I can't tell you why. I guess that I have been overthinking everything, and it is putting me in a bad mood. I have been known to overthink things, as you know."

Monty blew air out of his tight lips, which made a farting sound. This made the people sitting at the table next to them look over and give them a strange look.

He then said surely, "Well, buddy, you ain't leaving me safely behind. Someone has got to watch out for you and your weird feelings. Probably the best lesson that I learned in the military is that you never leave anyone behind, especially a friend that is in harm's way. This includes a friend who has been left hanging too many times and has not had anyone believing them or trying to help them. Even from themselves."

Then Monty smiled and said jokingly, "Plus, you need me. You wouldn't admit it or especially say it, but you do need me to help you fight these battles."

Ryan then raised his whiskey glass, made a toast, and said "Well, here's to a couple of needy farm boys from Montana, I guess."

Ryan then knocked back the entire glass of whiskey and made a screwed-up face. The harsh liquor seemed to burn his entire insides, from the back of his throat, down his esophagus, and into his stomach, where it seemed to land with a sharp thud.

It was now midnight: After three whiskeys and four beers, Ryan was finally ready to fly to London. He had a large tolerance for alcohol, and it didn't seem to affect him strongly. Except in the way of calming his entire nervous system down and giving him a lot more confidence. It wasn't true inner strength, but that is what he felt like he needed to do to accomplish this.

However, this behavior is most definitely not well liked or supported in any way by other people. Ryan found himself socially excluded from activities because of this way of thinking. Ryan's face and actions looked as if he was sober, but he probably smelled as if he had bathed in a vat of cheap beer or whiskey.

Ryan and Monty entered the plane together and found the assigned seats that they would call home for the next seven hours. Monty immediately began flirting with the very attractive, smiley, brunette flight attendant. When Peggy, the flight attendant, had moved up the aisle, Monty poked Ryan in the elbow and gave him a thumbs-up sign.

Monty seemed like he was just getting riled up by the alcohol, and Ryan smiled widely at his good friend. However, Ryan's plan regarding the alcohol in his own body was starting to take effect, as he felt like it was time to fall asleep.

Ryan was falling asleep with his head lying on his hand. His head seemed to be drooping lower with every passing second. Monty didn't know that Ryan was so sound asleep until Ryan's baseball cap fell off his head and landed in his lap. Then Ryan let out a loud grunting snort, causing other passengers to look disgustedly back in the two men's direction.

At 1:53 am, Ryan suddenly sat up fully awake in the middle seat of his aisle on the plane. Everyone else aboard seemed to be fast asleep and lying with their heads cocked and lilting to the left and right sides of their shoulders.

This was even the case with Monty, as Ryan nudged his friend only to be met by silence in return. Monty had a pair of dark sunglasses on that were covering sightless eyes. His mouth hung open, and Ryan could see that it contained a lump of chewed spearmint gum lying on his tongue.

Ryan opened and closed his own eyes in a rapid blinking motion. After he shook his head, he looked forward at the other passengers on the plane. He then noticed the curtain that designated the seating between the economy-class customers and the uppity first-class seating was moving slightly. A wisp of smoke seemed to be coming from underneath it and spilling into his compartment.

Ryan leaned in and looked closer when the barrier sheet started to ruffle more abrasively, and it started to slide open. Smoke then billowed out of the first-class seating area and crawled up the central aisle toward Ryan. Through the smoke stepped the raven-haired and wide-eyed young woman who had wanted Ryan's seed in one of his previous dreams.

One beautiful eye, which had an almost black pupil, bore right through him and almost hypnotized him again. She had tried to cover the other eye with her dark hair. It also had a dark piercing pupil in the center of it; however, half of the cornea of the eye was pure white, and the other half was a bright red color.

Ryan could then see all of her, and the woman wore a bright red dress with a long flowing mane that seemed to just keep coming out of the curtained first-class area of the plane. Her lips were also painted bright red and stood out against her extremely pale skin.

She winked with her good eye, blew Ryan a kiss from her pursed mouth, and said seductively to him, "Hello, my sweet."

Ryan said nothing and could not take his own eyes off her half-red beating orb of an eye. It was as if he were disgusted by it and awkwardly drawn to it at the same time. It was as if it were one of those paintings in which you were supposed to see a picture of a sailboat hidden in a painting of an open meadow. That is, if you looked long enough at it and relaxed your eyes.

She was almost perfect in how she looked, except for that ugly, glowing eye. She strode slowly up the aisle toward Ryan.

She held out her hand as if he should kiss it and asked, "Have you missed me? Have you missed your queen?"

"No, I have not even thought about you at all, let alone missed you." Ryan said this coldly, and then he glared closer at her imperfectly red eye and finished saying, "You know, you may want to have a doctor look at your eye; it is really nasty looking."

Ryan started to raise his open hand and lift his index finger closer to her eye. She quickly covered it up with her own hand and spoke at him harshly. "Do not be rude, sir. Also, do not stare at your queen. I did not give you permission to do so."

Ryan gave her a sly grin and then said, "I don't understand. I get the feeling that you really enjoy having people look at you. You love to show off your beauty whenever or wherever you can. Why not now? Do I sense a chink in the armor of your imperfection?"

She smiled cruelly and then put her black hair over her eye once again. She then arrogantly said, "People enjoy staring at me, to this very day. You, sir... well... you either like boys or are just an absolute dullard who is just rude. Maybe you don't have the tackle anymore, like you are one of those eunuch servants?"

Ryan's mouth started to form a stinging comeback, when suddenly a high-pitched, shrill screaming noise came down the aisle of the plane from behind him. His hair began blowing forward, which made the baseball cap that he was holding fly forward from his hands to the front of the cabin.

Ryan braced himself, trying to grab at his hat as it flew away, but this screaming wind made him grab the backs of the seats on either side of him instead. He lost his balance and almost fell forward from the hard wind that was blowing from behind him.

He then witnessed a pure, bright light flow through his own body and ram into the beautiful but dangerous woman. It seemed to fling her body backward through the dividing curtains.

The white light and wind disappeared, along with the dark-haired woman, into the first-class seating area. Ryan was almost certain that he had heard a woman's shrill scream come with the wind when this happened. It was an icy sound, like the scream that a mountain lion makes when it is upset or protective.

This loud roar of a mountain lion sounds amazingly like a woman's scream. Ryan had heard this several times, coming from the large cats that surrounded the camping spots in the mountains of Montana. This wild scream had also frozen him from moving for a short period of time while he had been hunting deer or elk.

Ryan became aware that he was fully awake when he felt a sharp pain jab into his left ribs, as Monty had poked him in the gut. Ryan was now out of his seat and was walking on top of Monty's feet.

Monty looked at him and said with annoyance, "What are you doing, bud? Are you sleepwalking on an airplane?"

Ryan looked down at Monty and turned beet red from blushing at how this had to look. Ryan mouthed "Sorry" to Monty and then noticed something laying on the floor next to the dividing curtain between the seating areas.

This made him raise his hands and say loudly, "Sorry folks, but I lost my hat, and I think that it is laying on the floor up there. I was just motioning for the flight attendant with it, and I lost grip of it. Could somebody please pass it back to me?"

The pretty flight attendant picked up the hat and brought it back to their seats. When she got there, she asked with annoyance in her voice, "Now then, what were you gentlemen trying to get my attention about? We do have a buzzer to use for the passengers to call me back. You don't have to throw anything at me."

Ryan blushed and asked her if she could make him a 'Bloody Mary' drink. She disappeared and then brought him a cup full of tomato juice in a clear plastic cup and a small bottle of vodka.

At 2:27 am, Ryan finally sat down after getting his hat returned, and he whispered to Monty, "Oh my God, that was so messed up."

Monty looked at him strangely and said back, "No shit, Ryan. You got up and began stepping all over my feet. You had this far-off look in your eyes, and you started talking gibberish. What the hell were you doing?"

Ryan looked at the people that were all around them and then said lowly to Monty, "Dude, I really don't know what just happened. That really scared me, though."

Then Ryan began rocking in his seat and saying to himself, "Just don't panic...Please, don't panic."

Monty looked over at him with concern on his face and spoke cautiously, "Calm down, bud. You are not alone. I am right here. Now you are scaring me. I thought that you were asleep, and then you started walking all over my feet. What can I do for you?"

Ryan then thought about his dream, or whatever a person wanted to call it, and asked Monty, "Did you see any beautiful women with me just now?"

"Are you high?!?!" Monty exclaimed loudly, and then he said it lower and with a lot more concern in his voice. "You need several more reasons for you to relax and for you to go back to sleep. I would recommend it as soon as possible."

Monty motioned for the beautiful flight attendant again and asked her, "If you can, please let us have about six of those little bottles of booze, please. My friend really needs something to help knock him out, and I left my sledgehammer in my other bag."

Monty gave her his best smile as he added, while motioning to Ryan, "He is really a nervous flyer."

The flight attendant looked at the other passengers and knew that most people aboard the flight had been sleeping. Against her better judgment, she gave Ryan and Monty seven small bottles of rum and vodka. She then made them promise to not bother the other passengers any further by motioning with her finger to her lips at the two of them.

Ryan instantly drank the first little plastic bottle of rum in one quick drink. Then he had another small bottle opened soon afterward, and it only took him about two minutes to drink it down. He had to suppress this damned anxiety that seemed to be crawling into his mind and trying to drive him insane.

Halfway through the third bottle, Ryan had started to fall asleep in his chair again. Monty took the small bottle out of his friend's relaxed hand, and then he joked to himself, "I should have been a dentist."

He then looked at Ryan and put the rest of the small bottles into the pocket of his carry-on bag.

At 7:03 am, the next sound that Ryan heard was the pilot over the intercom saying, "Please sit down…fasten your seat belts…and thank you for flying with us. Welcome to London, England."

Ryan sat quietly and held his breath in order to try and clear his head and make his eardrums 'pop' and work properly again. He felt as if his head was swimming and pounding out a Neil Peart drum solo. The thought of a great drum solo made Ryan smile through his discomfort.

His stomach then started to do somersaults inside his body, and his breathing became shallow. This all happened until the plane safely touched down on the ground.

He could feel Monty looking over at him every now and again. Monty probably had to make sure that Ryan wouldn't stand up screaming and push his way to the door.

Monty finally said to him, "We made it, partner. We made it to London safe and sound. We only had a few bumps on the ride, but we are no worse for wear."

He then lied to Ryan when he told him that they didn't have to worry anymore.

"I woke up today in London
As the plane was touching down
And all I could think about was Monday
And maybe I'll be back around…"
(3 Doors Down with Bob Seger)

Chapter Thirteen

> ***If you wake up and you're not dead, then shut up and live your life, dammit!*** (Herb Klinefelter: 96-year-old WWII Veteran and my friend)

They strolled down the walkway of the plane and had entered the main terminal at Heathrow International Airport when the sounds of people talking filled the air. Monty was almost yelling while trying to carry on a conversation with Ryan about where to go.

Suddenly, Ryan realized that he could no longer hear Monty's voice or feel him by his side. Ryan had only walked an additional ten steps before he stopped and looked around for his friend.

Monty was staring with his mouth agape at the newspaper stand that stood across the sea of people that was in front of them. Then he looked over at Ryan as if he had seen a ghost. He pointed, gave Ryan an aghast look, and then shook his head as if he had just seen something that he did not understand at all and was completely unexplainable.

Ryan walked back and looked in the direction that Monty had been pointing and said with caution in his voice, "What's wrong, Monty?"

Monty didn't speak; he simply grabbed Ryan's shoulders and moved him until he was looking at the people standing at the newspaper stand across from them.

Ryan stared at them and then jokingly said, "Insanity must be infectious; now you are catching it."

Then he stopped himself cold. He could then see what Monty was looking at. How could this be possible? He rubbed his eyes, as if that might have made her go away, but that was to no avail.

Her plump body seemed to be squeezed into a tan pantsuit that was two times too small for her. She also wore a plain white cotton t-shirt underneath, and a red rose was above her ear in her kinky brown hair.

She stood by a group of young people who were all talking and laughing with one another. Then she looked in Ryan and Monty's direction with a mean grin of disdain upon her face. "Do you see her, Ryan? .... Can you incredibly see...Carol Beaman?" asked Monty.

"I do," said Ryan in return.

He then continued by saying, "Congratulations; you're now just as insane as I am. Now then, let's go see what she wants from us."

Monty grabbed Ryan's arm and said, "No, the only crazy thing that I can even think of is going near her. Man, there is some funky shit going on here and I don't want to just walk up to it and say, 'Hi, how you doing'?"

Monty turned white as a sheet and continued to say, "Let's just go to the hotel, I have seen enough for today, and I believe you. I will never second guess you again."

The short hair on the backs of Ryan and Monty's necks now rose, as if they had been electrocuted in some manner. The two men started walking slowly towards the doors while glancing at Carol as they walked along.

"How did you...get...here...?" Ryan said it out loud as if he were trying to figure the whole situation out. He was coming up with nothing but a blank slate.

The men could tell that they were extremely tired, and they both agreed that they wouldn't discuss this hot mess of a situation. Not until they had relaxed, settled down, and maybe gotten a few more hours of sleep.

Monty put his head down and kept walking until he and Ryan were standing on the curb, and Ryan was stretching tall and hailing a taxi. They quickly loaded their luggage into the trunk and jumped into the back seat when Carol walked out of the front doors of the airport. She gave the departing cab that awful smiling sneer that always seemed to be on her face. She continued to give the taxi a glowering stare and pointed one bony finger in their direction.

This caused Monty to close his eyes and ask, "Did you see that awful look on her face? That awful fucking grin? Ryan, what the hell is going on here?"

Ryan nodded sleepily and then answered, "I am still trying to figure this whole shitty situation out. This has been happening to me for 20 years, and I never know who will show up next. I never had anyone else experience it before though. I have always been alone in this fight. I am so sorry that I got you involved in this nightmare, Monty."

The taxi pulled up to the Tower Inn, and Ryan and Monty unloaded their belongings on a baggage dolly. The first person that both men looked for was an evil grinning, Carol, who was luckily nowhere to be seen.

Then Ryan pointed out the graceful splendor of Tower Bridge, and he 'introduced' Monty to the medieval Tower of London. He did this as if it were his personal arch-nemesis and an object to be revered and feared at the same time.

Monty only squinted at the ominous tower and said tiredly, "I will have to be astonished later. Right now, I just need a great big bed, and since there doesn't seem to be any ghosts bothering us right now, I am going to get some sleep. Then I will need a drink, and I would like you to tell me what the fuck is going on. Tell me everything, won't you, buddy?"

Ryan only made a "yes" nod of his head and followed him into the hotel, not knowing what he would tell him. Hell, he really didn't know what would happen next.

Monty only stared seriously into Ryan's eyes and said, "Listen, if this is the kind of shit that you have been dealing with, I am the one who is sorry. These feelings are absolutely nuts, and no one should ever have to handle them alone."

Ryan thanked him and then said, "You have helped a huge amount already today, Monty. You have always been my buddy, and you never ran away from me when I was going batshit insane at times. You have never made me feel lonely."

A young man from India then spoke to them from the opposite side of the hotel check-in counter. In a perfect English accent, he asked if he could help them in any way. He had thick, slicked-back black hair, a slim build, and a nice cordial smile. He was wearing a neatly pressed black vest with the name Binu emblazoned on a name tag.

Ryan gave him his credit card and said, "Binu, could you actually get us a room with two beds on either the first or second floor?"

Ryan could feel the weird look that was coming from his best friend, and Ryan turned and said to Monty, "What? Remember, I don't like heights, and I have already been on an airplane all night that had no atheists riding aboard it. Now, I want to feel as comfortable as I can be, especially now that I am here. You don't want me to face all my fears in one day, do you?"

Monty said lowly back, "As long as we can get a bottle of Scottish whiskey delivered to the room. Ryan, you have your demons, and I also have my own, so don't judge me."

Ryan smiled at his friend wearily and said, "I am right there with you, buddy. Just save room for the get-together that is supposed to be happening tonight."

Ryan and Monty both laid down on their respective beds. Exhaustion washed over them like a hot, wet blanket had been thrown over each of them. Sleep came upon each of them quickly and deeply.

Monty was incredibly jet-lagged and lay there as if he were a large sack of potatoes. However, Ryan seemed to become restless in his sleep. His muscles seemed to jump as if they had gotten a spark of electricity charged through them.

Suddenly, an arc of pure blue electricity started to cover Ryan's body like a pulsating cocoon. It then fell downward toward the end of the bed and enveloped Ryan's complete body. He suddenly disappeared and left only a wisp of smoke where he had once been lying.

Ryan found himself kneeling on top of the roof of the Tower Inn, where he and Monty were now staying. He could see the Thames River curling through the city, as well as Tower Bridge standing elegantly over it. He cautiously stayed away from the edge of the building, but he could see the tops of the old stones of the Tower of London that were standing below him.

His first impulse was to curl himself into a ball as his fear of heights tried to strengthen its grasp over him. The only thing that seemed to help was the sudden smoke and fog that were surrounding him on all sides.

Soon, the fog started to thin, and a large glass building seemed to be looming over the entire city of London. The White Tower was the tallest building in London for centuries, but now 'The Shard' has taken that honor. The building does look down upon the city like a giant piece of glass that has been driven into the ground.

The noise of scuffing gravel made Ryan turn around quickly, and he saw James the Knight standing twenty feet from him. He was leaning on his sword, like he was either hurt or very exhausted.

James gave Ryan an intent look, and then he said, "It will be happening very soon."

Then he continued with passion in his voice by continuing to say, "I am glad that you are here. I know that you have your fears and worries, but can you handle the training and the fighting that we will have to go through?"

Ryan looked at the knight intently and said honestly, "I will push myself, if that is what you mean. Bravery isn't just about action. It is a matter of being frightened and doing the things that scare you anyway. It is about doing the right thing, and I am a huge believer in that. I am just going to put my trust in you and in my own confidence and skill."

Ryan stood up and found a sword now hanging from his hip. He grabbed the hilt of it and pulled its heavy steel blade out of its sheath. He tried to get used to the weight of the sword, and he struggled to hold it out in front of him.

Ryan looked at James and said, "This blade is way too heavy for me. I can swing it, but I would rather have a smaller, shortened blade that I could move with more precision and speed. I may not be able to break a man's leg bone with one swing of the sword, but I could give an enemy several hundred smaller wounds that would sting at him profusely."

James then began to laugh out loud and said, "You are a talented knight, Ryan. It is in your blood. You are only lacking knowledge on how to use a sword. However, you have passed the first lesson in learning which is the right weapon that you should use."

The knight then walked to a part of the building that was secured from view, and he drew another sword from the ground that was covering the roof. He then tossed it at Ryan's feet.

He grinned at Ryan and said playfully, "See how you like this sword. It is lighter, but it can still pack a hell of a wallop on your opponent. You want to make your enemies bleed like a stuck pig that has been chosen for slaughter. Make it so they are fearful to fight you back."

This time, it was Ryan's turn to laugh at the knight, and he rolled the lighter sword in between his hands. It seemed to almost dance across his palms. Ryan could make very quick arching motions across the air.

After a short amount of practice, Ryan smiled confidently and then said, "Are you ready to fight, old man?"

James the Knight drew his larger sword and motioned for Ryan to come closer. Then James began to feel out Ryan's strengths as well as his weaknesses behind the sword.

Ryan spun the sword in his hand and stepped cautiously towards the knight. Ryan looked as if he may be fast with this sword, and the knight was greatly impressed by him. Especially how he lowered his balance of power and agility onto his legs. The style in which he fought was rudimentary, but Ryan truly was a natural.

In his first attempt at swordplay, Ryan swung the sword wildly at James the Knight. The knight, who had so much more experience, easily pushed aside each thrust and blow that Ryan attempted. Ryan was not horrible at sword play, but he lacked control and needed much more practice in the art. He tended to project each blow and was easily blocked when he did this.

Ryan and James stepped back from each other while catching their breaths. Then James asked, "Where did you learn such a strange and different fighting technique?"

Ryan said, while slightly panting, "Well, I am pretty good at the sword fighting game that is on the video game console that I play."

The knight gave him a confused look, and he shrugged and adjusted his sword for another battle.

Ryan tried to push the point of his sword onto the knight's lower left armor that was covering his stomach. Easily, the knight knocked this blow off to the left side of his body. Ryan then tried to counter off to the right side of the knight's body, but he was easily rebuked again.

Ryan then said, while grunting loudly, "In the video game that we play...it is not a real fight...it is mainly used as a fun way to exercise."

He then lunged for the legs, and the knight kicked his sword away with his armored boot, and the sword skidded across the roof top.

"Let me make you aware of one thing; this is not a make-believe scenario, Ryan." The knight said this seriously, and then he continued, "This is the real thing, and you could be killed if you do not perform to the best of your ability."

Ryan then picked up his sword and came in high and from the left. The knight went upward with his sword, as well, in order to block this blow. Suddenly, Ryan changed his swing in mid-slice, swung lower, and hit the knight in the middle of his right thigh. Loudly, the clanging of his metal armor made the knight stop and bow to the young man.

Ryan stopped fighting as well and smiled at James. This blow had surprisingly struck the knight with a large amount of force. Ryan stopped because he was afraid that he had hurt the knight in the process of fighting. James had quit because he was clearly amazed and impressed at what Ryan had just done.

James the Knight shook his head unbelievably, grinned at Ryan, and said, "Do that each time, and don't tell your enemy with your vision where you will be striking him next. That was good swordsmanship, my, my..."

James stopped speaking abruptly and then looked around as if they were being watched. He then finished by saying, "...my good friend."

Ryan bowed his head to the knight who said back to Ryan, "I wish that I could work with you more in order to make you even better, but this will have to do for now. I will see you shortly and be very wary. You are being watched, and they will do anything to control you."

Ryan then began to ask more questions when he could feel electricity flow throughout his body once again, and he began to disappear. This made him close his eyes tightly, and when he opened them, he was lying on the bed in the Tower Inn. His ears suddenly popped as if he had relieved pressure in them.

He looked over at Monty with a strange look on his face, and he asked, "What the fuck just happened to me?"

Monty gave him an even more fearful look in return. He rubbed his eyes and then told Ryan, "When I woke up, you were nowhere to be seen. I thought that you may have woken up and left me sleeping away. However, your shoes were still here, and nothing else was missing. I was then about to go down to the bar and see if you were sitting down there. Suddenly, I saw a blue light and a charge of electricity go across your bed. When it had disappeared, you were lying there again."

Monty was now flinging his arms in all directions, and he continued saying unbelievably, "You just fucking disappeared and then reappeared back into the room. Shit! Tell me, Ryan! Tell me what we are facing here. Start from the beginning and tell me what you know. Because right now, I feel like I am going out of my fucking mind."

Ryan then sat on the edge of the bed and told Monty everything that he knew. He also told him the things that he couldn't explain. Monty only listened in silence and then looked at Ryan in astonishment.

Ryan sat on the bed, lifted one of his feet, and began pulling gravel out of the fleshy sole of one of them. Ryan was still absent-mindedly picking the gravel out of his feet when he looked at Monty, who had turned as white as a freshly washed sheet.

Ryan then stated, with great importance, that the two of them were going to have to be extremely careful and vigilant. He expressed that they would have to watch each other's backs from now on.

Monty then rubbed his hands together and sarcastically asked, "So then, Sir Ryan, what is on the agenda for tonight? Having cocktails with the undead? Maybe playing poker with a pack of werewolves?"

Ryan smiled a little and said casually. "I had my eye on a couple of she-devils that are waiting for us downstairs. We just don't want to be around them at midnight. Do you have more jokes to throw in my direction? I am not in a joking mood at this moment."

Monty laughed, and slapped Ryan on the back. He then, not so jokingly, asked him, "Well, how about some liquid courage then?" He then grinned and said, "God really hates a quitter, you know."

Ryan laughed back and then said, "Well, liquid courage will have to do for now. Tonight, we are going to have a reunion and a dinner party in the hotel. It is going to be one of those name-tag shindigs, but there should be several single women for you to chase after, Casanova."

Ryan looked as if he were in a different world again and continued saying, "I have one woman that I am going to seek out. I haven't seen my great love in twenty years. I can't wait to see Karen again. Not only because of my feelings, but because of this whole weird situation that I have been dealing with for all these years. All this crap began with her, and hopefully, it will end with her. Plus, I think that I am still in love with her, and I think that I always will be."

Monty took a swallow of his Scottish whiskey directly from the bottle and jokingly said to Ryan, "Well, from what you have told me, her farts must smell like a field of blooming roses, and she probably shits out rainbows. Otherwise, I am going to be highly disappointed."

It was Ryan's turn to have a drink out of the bottle, and he said back to his good friend, "Fair enough, but it's not like her ass has a pot of gold in it. Please try to behave yourself when you meet her, okay?"

Ryan looked at Monty seriously and continued to say, "This really means a lot to me, and I have been carrying around this torch for this woman for way too long. Tonight's party is supposed to be casual but dressy. Put on your 'Sunday Best' and remember, this isn't the wild west of Montana anymore. We are going to be surrounded by some people that think that they come from high-brow stock."

Monty had been pulling on his dress pants and had put on his nicest button-down shirt when Ryan said this to him. He unzipped his pants and pulled one shirttail out of the open hole.

He then said back to Ryan, as if he were an uneducated huckster: "Well, dang, I sure hope these highfalutin folks over here will 'cept me fer who I is!"

Ryan laughed at this and called Monty a "smart-ass". Then he started to get dressed himself, still chuckling at his dorky friend's antics.

Monty was wearing his black dress pants with a dark blue shirt and a pure black tie. Ryan wore a nice pair of blue button-fly jeans with a lighter green shirt. He kept his collar open, as he did not like to wear a tie. Ryan finished out his look by also wearing a gray sport coat over the top of his open, button-down shirt.

Ryan decided to show some country style by also wearing gray riding-crop cowboy boots. He usually wore a baseball cap, but on that evening, he wore a gray cowboy hat upon his head. The hat was well worn and broken in. He wore it more while fishing the river than while riding a horse. It was a great hat for keeping the sun off his face.

Upon entering the convention center in the hotel, Ryan had to stop by a check-in table in order to receive his name tag for the event. The woman behind the desk was not recognizable to Ryan, but her name tag said that she was 'Gwen'... and she certainly remembered Ryan.

He and Monty overheard her rudely saying to a friend seated next to her, "He is the one who nearly ruined the trip for the rest of us."

Ryan stepped away from the table while rolling his eyes and said to Monty, "I think that this is going to be a very long night. Let's hit the open bar, but remember, we must be on our guard tonight, so don't overdo it on the drinking. We must watch each other's backs, so let's have fun but also maintain ourselves."

A grin came across Monty's face, and he asked, "Is this like 'calf patrol'?"

Ryan laughed and said back to him, "A little bit, but it is not the calf's life that we are trying to save. This time, we are trying to protect our own skin."

Monty liked to refer to the ranching process of calving as "calf patrol." This was exactly what a cattle rancher would do during the cold temperatures of the early spring months of the year. A ranch worker would always have to stay with the cattle and help the cows give birth to the calves. These men and women would also have to protect the new livestock from predators. They especially had to clean the newborn calves so that they would not freeze to death under the frigid cold winds of the upper Rocky Mountains.

The ranchers would often stay in a sometimes dangerous, barely heated wagon and would stay alert in case they needed to be of any assistance to the needy cattle. Drinking was sometimes involved in these wagons to keep the ranch workers warm and to help them stay alert.

However, these ranch workers also did not want to overindulge in case they were needed during the day or night. It was like walking a tightrope at times, and there was a huge gray area in which a carefully maintained rancher could work effectively and stay warmer. Otherwise, he or she could cross over that edge into drunken sleepiness.

This could not happen, or lives among the herd of cattle would be lost. Many ranchers personally believe that this is how Irish coffee began. This was a manner of containing themselves with whiskey, as well as getting a swift kick in the ass of strong caffeine.

As Ryan and Monty leaned against the side of the open bar at the reunion, many people joined them. They then read Ryan's name tag, made a disparaging remark about him, and ostracized the young men.

Monty finally said, "Man, these people really piss me off. They all pretend to be this better group of people, when they are the phoniest pieces of shit on the planet. They wouldn't pee on a less successful person than them, even if that person were on fire. Why do you want to be a part of this group?"

Ryan thought about this question and could only say, "I just wanted more, Monty. I have felt like I was destined for more, anyway. I almost feel like I am between different societies of people. It just seems like the harder that I try, the more God throws obstacles and assholes in my way."

Ryan's head fell forward onto his chest. Monty then punched him hard in the shoulder and said, "Don't you give up on me now. You have been through a world of shit and never stopped believing that this is going to get a whole lot better for you. Just be strong and keep fighting.

Ryan raised his head and spoke strongly. "You are right, Monty. I feel like I have been through a large portion of hell, and part of me is still standing there. Maybe I have been wounded and scarred throughout life, but I am not going to let this group of assholes try to take advantage of me or my feelings anymore. Thank you, Monty. Thanks for the strong kick in the ass. I need it at times."

Ryan then firmly shook Monty's hand and said with more confidence, "I am going to leave you here at the bar and I am going to go out there and try to find a couple of old friends."

"Mostly, I need to find the woman that I once fell in love with. I need to see if it is still there."

Monty slapped the top of the bar and shouted over the crowd noise. "Atta' Boy! I will be here holding down this position until you return. Good luck."

Halfway across the room, Ryan finally ran into a friendly face when Angelo slithered through the crowd. He gave Ryan a large handshake, which turned into an awkward hug.

Angelo then smiled broadly up into Ryan's face and introduced his wife of fourteen years, Bridgette Marie. Ryan congratulated them, and they engaged in friendly small talk until Angelo finally asked about the 'health issues' that had made Ryan almost leave the tour early.

Ryan answered him by saying honestly and with a matter-of-fact tone in his voice, "I am still being affected by those health problems. That is why I have never been married, unfortunately. I haven't met a woman yet who could handle all my kooky disorders."

Ryan then curiously asked, "Speaking of that, have you by chance seen Karen around this place?"

Angelo said "no" and then told Ryan to speak to Gwen at the front desk again, as she was the main ramrod of this whole big reunion.

Angelo then asked about Mike, and Ryan said sorrowfully, "We weren't friends anymore at the end of the trip. The last time that I saw him was at our high school graduation, maybe eighteen years ago."

Angelo and Ryan exchanged another strong handshake, and Angelo wished him all the good luck in the world. Then he and his bride stumbled forward into the crowd. Ryan, however, made a beeline toward the front door and the 'all-knowing' Gwen.

Upon approaching the front door, Ryan put his best 'fake' smile on his face and asked. "Excuse me, Gwen. I understand that you are the person who is in charge here, and I was wondering if you remembered a girl named Karen Klippenstein from Michigan?"

Gwen gave him a fake grin in return and said, "Of course, I remember Karen. She is such a sweetheart."

Ryan could hardly contain himself and asked her, "Did Karen come to London? Is she here?"

Gwen then glowered back at him and said curtly, "Well, I don't think that she would want to see you...so please leave here... I am not afraid to have you kicked out of this celebration."

Ryan lowered his hands onto the table and then lowered his eyes until they were staring directly into Gwen's. He cautioned her by saying, "I don't want to cause any commotion, so please don't forcefully push me in that direction. I really don't like anybody forcing me into any such situation. I just want to know if she came here or not. After that, none of this business concerns you."

Ryan then moved even closer to her and almost whispered, "Unless you want me to make a total shambles of your get-together and point my finger directly in your direction as the problem. Remember, I don't care if I look or act like I am not a wonderful person when I am around these people. I will bet that you do. Now then, should I raise a huge ruckus or go away happy and quietly?"

Gwen looked back at Ryan as if her eyes were daggers about to stab him directly in the face and throat. He called her bluff and refused to flinch or even move backward.

Finally, she cleared her throat, looked through her files, and said to Ryan, "All that I know is that she was sent an invitation and an R.S.V.P. was returned. We did receive a return letter that said that one person would be attending, but that is all that I know. She could be here, or she may just show up tomorrow night for the medieval banquet. Now then, I believe that drunken cohort at the bar is here with you."

She shuffled in her seat and asked nervously, "Do I need to watch him as well?"

Ryan then stood away from her and said coldly, "Oh, God, yes! That guy over there is even worse than me. He is my best friend, and he is very dangerous and absolutely looking for any excuse to show his disdain for a lot of these assholes around here. However, he also does listen to me, and if I get wrongfully blamed or mishandled in any way, he will have no choice but to protect my back and cause an even bigger ruckus."

Ryan let a curt smile go across his face, and then he said nicely to Gwen, "However, I can also tell my friend to relax. If that is the case, we will just have a good time and cause as little damage as possible. I will leave this ball in your court."

With these words, Ryan turned and walked slowly back toward the bar.

Monty grinned at his return and asked, "Well, did you find your true love… or did you at least find out where she is?"

Ryan ordered a strong Scottish whiskey and then sat back and said, "I never saw her, but I did disturb 'Gwen the Organizer' into telling me that an invitation was sent to her. They also did receive a reply that one person would be here, but she wasn't sure what day she would show up."

Ryan then poked his friend in the ribs and said amusingly, "By the way, Monty, you are now my enforcer. You will have to raise a royal ruckus if we ever feel the need that we are not welcomed here."

Monty grinned broadly and said, "Cool! Can I cause a huge ruckus otherwise, or do I have to wait for your orders?"

Ryan nudged his friend's elbow while laughing and said back to his new guardian, "Please don't cause a fuss unless you see me in any trouble. I can intimidate the hell out of people when I want to, as you well know...so, please just watch my back. Just in case my ass can't cash a check that my mouth has written."

Monty simply said back to him, "You got it, Ryno!"

Using an old nickname that Ryan had not heard in a long time but still liked. Mainly because it reminded him of the nickname of his favorite baseball player.

Ryan downed his drink and then ordered a couple more to be delivered to a table on the patio that was outside of the hotel. Ryan and Monty were about to load their plates with food from the banquet table.

In all actuality, each man would end up loading up two plates for their meal, as neither had eaten anything since the following night. That was also airline food, which didn't really count, did it?

Ryan and Monty gorged themselves on various meats, cheeses, salads, and finally, a fine cheesecake for dessert. After the meal, the two men ordered another drink and looked out at the splendor of the Thames River and the famous bridge that ran across it.

The plates were cleared from the table when Ryan stood up and leaned on the railing of the patio. He was mesmerized at the sight of Tower Bridge and a corner of the Tower of London that stood across the street from them.

He didn't turn around but said to Monty, "This truly is a magical place, isn't it?"

Ryan was met by a snort coming from Monty, as he had fallen asleep under the warm full moon of historic London.

To his surprise, he was instead answered by a lilting, tender voice that said, "Yes, this is a truly mystical, wonderful place."

Ryan jumped with surprise, as he wasn't expecting the voice that answered him to be tender and with a tone that sounded vaguely familiar.

Ryan turned quickly and was nearly knocked to his knees by the vision of beauty that stood before him. She stood about 5'8" tall and had long blond hair that nearly hung to the base of her spine. She had deep blue eyes, a small, slightly curled-up nose, and a bright, wholesome smile. Her face had high cheekbones, and she had slight dimples that seemed to softly highlight her tanned, alabaster cheeks.

She smiled precociously at Ryan and then introduced herself by saying, "I am so sorry to scare you. Hi, my name is Ellie!"

"Oh, now feel it comin' back again
Like a rollin' thunder chasing the wind
Forces pullin' from the center of the earth again
I can feel it…"
(Live)

Chapter Fourteen

Electricity is really, just organized lightning. (George Carlin)

Ryan stammered through his own introduction to the young, beautiful woman. Then he introduced his sleeping friend who was snoring lightly in the chair between them. Ryan had to swallow hard, and he noticed that he was suddenly sweating.

He cleared his throat and said, "Ellie, that is such a nice name. My dog back home is named 'Allie'."

After he said this, Ryan clapped his hand against his forehead. He rambled on in an embarrassed fashion, saying, "Oh, gosh! I am so sorry. I was just reminded of her when I turned and saw you. Not because you remind me of a dog, but because of the color of your hair."

Ryan took another drink and tried to talk himself out of sounding like a total idiot by continuing to say, "She is the love of my life, right now. She is very blonde and has extremely blue eyes, much like you. Please slap me across the face or pour a drink on me at any time. Just give me my final coup de grace so that I quit talking. I just ask if you will put me out of my misery quickly."

Ellie unbelievably giggled in response and then said in return, "I have never actually been compared to a dog before. I am kind of honored to be a remembrance of a pet that you hold so dear. I will take this as a compliment, does that make you feel any better?"

Ryan smiled and said, "Tons." Ryan then shook her hand and continued to curiously ask, "Well, you look fairly young to be a part of this group, and by your accent, you sound as if you may be from the Midwest in the United States somewhere?"

"Nice ear." Ellie said in return. Then she continued while smiling proudly. "I just graduated from Indiana this past fall. Well, this is my second university graduation anyway; this last diploma was for my master's degree. That is why I am here in London. I am going to do my doctorate thesis on the Tower of London. It is a group of fascinating buildings, don't you think?"

Ryan was almost floored at hearing this news, and he answered her back unbelievably, "You have no idea. I was a part of this musical reunion, but I am here to study the Tower of London more deeply as well. You could say that I am rather haunted by the place. My sleepy friend and I were going to go on an extensive tour of it tomorrow, but I am sure that he wouldn't mind if I went through it with you instead."

He anxiously asked her, "Would you like to go through it with me tomorrow? I give a good tour."

Ellie's blue eyes grew wider, and she motioned at Monty and asked, "What will your friend do then?"

Ryan winked at her and said enthusiastically, "This is a big city, and there are a lot of things for him to see. He will be just fine. Plus, I tend to trust my gut feelings, and my gut is telling me to ask you if you would like to join me tomorrow?"

Ellie blushed and then said, "I would love to. I will meet you in the lobby at 8:00 in the morning. You can take me to breakfast first. It was so nice to meet you, Ryan, and I look forward to seeing you in the morning. However, I am going to have to leave you for tonight and go to my room. Also, get your friend to his bed; he looks like he needs it."

The next morning, Ryan was waiting at a table when Ellie arrived at the hotel restaurant, and he waved her over. He stood up when she pulled out her chair for herself, and she gave Ryan a curious look when he didn't sit until she did.

She took a deep breath, and Ryan broke the silence and said to her, "I took the liberty of ordering these warm, fluffy scones that come with this amazing honey butter, for starters."

Ellie tried one and let out a 'yummm' sound and rolled her eyes back into her head at the deliciousness of these small rolls.

Ellie then covered her mouth and asked, "Are we going to be joined by your friend Monty?"

Ryan smiled and then said, "He was just rolling out of bed and into the shower when I left the room. He promised to stop by and meet you again this morning, when he will be fully awake. We have both been known to have too much fun at times. I would not want to call any other person my best friend or have anyone watch my back more."

Ellie smiled shyly and spoke softly, "That is very honorable and very rare."

Ryan then said to Ellie, "You never told me what you are getting your doctorate degree in. Please...fascinate me. It must be something that you love very much."

Ellie blushed slightly, and then she proudly said, "I am becoming a doctor in forensic anthropology. The mannerism of death and the reason for it have always intrigued me. I don't know why, but I am consumed by the whole ritual of death and how it has evolved over the years. Plus, I have an almost ghoulish interest in how death happens, especially on battlefields or by political reasons and treachery."

Ellie then looked embarrassed and asked, "The bones of the people that came before us have so many tales to tell, don't you agree?"

Ryan looked at her in fascination and then said, "Yes, I do know exactly how you feel. I just tend to look at death in a slightly different way."

Ellie took control of the conversation again and said sadly, "You see, my mother was hit by a car and died when I was seven years old. I had torn myself away from her hand and had run ahead of her. She was yelling at me to stop when a teenage girl was trying out her new phone and blew through the intersection and hit her."

Ryan stopped eating and said, "I am so sorry."

Ellie's voice grew quieter and staggered a little when she finished the tale by saying, "Well, I turned around and witnessed the car bearing down on her and finally..."

Ellie quit speaking about her mother at this point, and then said, "I never knew my father; my mother had me as a teenager. I was kept kind of sheltered and hidden, but he took off shortly after I was born. I think that he was one of her teachers, though. This has never been confirmed, and my mother's parents won't talk about him."

Ellie took another bite of one of the scones and then continued by saying, "I think that it was kind of a fiasco at the time. I just know that he was quite a bit older than her, and he was never involved in my life. My mother's parents, my actual grandparents, did step up and raise me after her death, and I consider them to be my slightly older parents. As far as I know, they never acknowledged that I even had a father. He was never spoken about."

Ryan looked at her sorrowfully and then said to her, "That is one of the saddest stories that I have ever heard...no child should ever witness what you have seen. Thank God that your mother's parents had the good graces to raise you well. You seem like a very strong, confident, and wholly well-adjusted human being."

Ellie let out a burst of sharp laughter and said quietly, "That is really a façade. In all actuality, I am really a very insecure dumpster fire on the inside. I just hide it well."

Ryan laughed boldly and loudly at this, which surprised Ellie as she had never received this response before.

He said back to her, "You are even stronger than you know. You just don't know it yet. You are an interesting and lovely person. I would guess that you are incredibly popular."

"Well then," Ellie said back, emboldened and somewhat angrily. "Explain this to me, then. It is because of this that I have become fascinated with death for all these years. This has *really* hampered my personal life. I went through a very dark, gothic phase when I was a teenager and was called 'Death Knell El', by most of the people in the school. That is probably why I am single and why I probably always will be. People don't like to be surrounded by other people who are dark, cynical, and obsessed with ancient death and forgotten bones."

Ryan smiled calmly and warmly back at her. He then said plainly, "I am one of those people...I find you very fascinating and quite refreshing. Believe me, I have been through my share of ostracizations and false accusations made against me by other people. Even people that I have called my dear friends or held incredibly close to my heart. Nobody likes to have that heart broken."

He continued to say, "However, my point is that we have both been affected by a whole lot of shit throughout the years. We have survived up until this point, right? If a person has been blessed by good fortune all their lives, then they must suddenly deal with even half of what you have been through. Well, they tend to fold up like a rickety lawn chair. This is only because they are not strong and can't handle those feelings. Believe me, I see a lot of stubborn tenacity in you. That is an extremely big compliment."

Just then, Monty walked up to their table and grabbed a scone from the middle of it. He looked at them both and then said, with a lilt in his voice, "Good Morning."

He then did a double take at Ellie and asked as smoothly as he could, "And who might you be?"

Ryan stood up suddenly and said, almost protectively, "This is Ellie. She has been kind enough to agree to tour the Tower of London with me today. I know that you like battleships, and I did some research. There is one docked right across the bridge called the H.M.S. Belfast. Would you mind if I spent the day with Ellie and met up with you later?"

Monty winked at Ryan and then smiled at Ellie and said, "I would be offended and think that you are an absolute dumb shit if you didn't. Don't you two give me a second thought; I can entertain myself for the day. We have that medieval banquet tonight, and I will meet up with you right before we head over to that...and don't forget to bring your charming companion with you."

Ryan then gave Ellie a broad smile and said, "I could never forget her. Will you please be both of our dates this evening? Everyone would be jealous just to see you walk into the room with us tonight."

Ellie blushed even more, put her head down, and said, "Let's see how today unfolds, shall we? I don't want to put the cart before the horse, as my grandpa used to say."

Monty took one more scone off the table and then left on his merry way. Ryan paid the bill and stood up with Ellie. He then escorted her out of the hotel and across the busy street that ran in between them and the foreboding tower.

Ryan walked alongside Ellie among the throng of tourists. When he came to the main gate, he stopped in his tracks and swallowed hard. It was as if he were thinking about the repercussions of entering these regal grounds again.

He almost felt like this was a one-way trip as his panic started to boil up from the depths of his very soul. Ellie walked a few more steps; she then stopped and turned around while looking at Ryan. She said nothing to him. She only offered her right hand out for him to hold onto.

He looked into her eyes and reached out for her hand. When he grasped it, his fear and panic immediately dissipated, as if it hadn't existed at all. While still holding her hand, he simply said, "Thank you, Ellie."

With this helpful gesture, he stepped past the gates with a growing amount of confidence welling up inside of him.

She only smiled at him when he stepped beside her, and she grasped his hand even harder. She looked around voraciously at the history that seemed to envelope her in this place. It was a different feeling when you experienced this for the first time. Ryan knew exactly how she felt.

She smiled even wider and said to Ryan, "So, today I am totally in your hands. You have been here before, and I haven't. Teach me what you know will interest me the most."

Ryan thought about these words and then started to lead her around the grounds, telling her of the royal zoo that had been there since the 13th century. He then told her of the ravens that still lived on the property and the tale that if they ever left the grounds, then the royal house was destined to fall.

Ryan could tell that these facts pleased her, but that she really wanted to explore the proverbial 'blood and guts' of the location. He then decided to take her to the location where so many people lost their heads within the tower grounds.

Ryan led Ellie to the memorial erected at Tower Green, where many famous individuals were beheaded. He suddenly turned into 'historian mode' and told her that when he had visited there 20 years earlier, the place was only a display of tiles and bricks on the ground. There was also a smaller bronze sign coming out of these tiles saying who had been executed there.

Now, though, there was an actual memorial that was made of a circular piece of black marble, and over this was a circular piece of glass. On the very top, there was a sculpture made of glass to look like a pillow.

Ryan then pointed out that some people think that the actual site of the beheading scaffold was on the dirt-covered parade ground that was there today. They think that a yeoman at the tower informed Queen Victoria in the 19th century that this was the spot. So, this is where they erected the monument.

He then told her that six people had been beheaded there with a sharpened axe. However, one woman was beheaded with the use of a sword wielded by an expert swordsman from France.

With that thought, he began to trail off from his train of thought. Ryan said slowly and softly, "This was Queen Anne Boleyn...I think that I have something that will really interest you...Follow me."

Ryan put his arm around Ellie's waist and then led her to the Chapel Royal of St. Peter ad Vincula.

Upon entering the main holy chapel of the Tower of London, Ryan felt as if he had walked through an invisible, protective bubble. He looked at Ellie and asked her absently, "Did you just feel that?"

Her response was given in the form of a 'no' motion that she made with her head. All though, in her excitement, she looked on at Ryan with giddy anticipation and astonishment. Ryan then told her that a chapel had been at this holy place for an extremely long time, but this was not the original building.

He then said excitedly, "This church burned, was rebuilt, burned again, and was rebuilt again. However, the way that we see this church today was built around 1520, when King Henry VIII ruled over England."

Ryan absentmindedly took his hand off her waist and grabbed her hand again. He led her to a green and red marble floor that was laid in the sanctuary along with several coats of arms upon different marble tiles.

He turned to Ellie and said, "Well, here you go. This should really get your interests flowing."

Ryan was a little disappointed when he only received a look of confusion from Ellie, who said, "I don't understand, what is this?"

Ryan let out a sigh of patience and then told Ellie the story of this chapel by saying, "Well, this is a very important place. As you can tell, in this chapel were buried many famous British figures from history. This includes Thomas Cromwell, Earl of Essex, and even two martyred bishops of the Catholic Church, those being John Fisher and Sir Thomas More."

Ellie still didn't seem to be impressed, so Ryan continued to say, 'Three Queens of England are buried here as well. Two of which were married to King Henry VIII and the nine-day queen, Lady Jane Grey. All of whom were beheaded at that spot out there on the lawn. Around you, there are many more tributes and monuments to other important people who lived during these times or later. I thought that this might begin to wet your interest in the important significance of this place. This is their main burial site."

Ellie could tell that Ryan was on a roll, and she enjoyed listening to him speak. With this same enthusiasm, he continued by telling her, "I told you that this building wasn't built until around 1520, right? Well, in the 1860s, under Queen Victoria's rule, she had the chapel renovated. In this very spot, they found several skeletons that were buried under the tiled floor of the church."

Ryan looked at her to see if he still held her interest and continued, "Now, most of the skeletons had no heads, and they had been buried rather abruptly and sloppily, it would seem. Well, one of the skeletons that they found was just a few feet below the floor. The skeleton had its skull placed under one of its arms, almost lovingly. Many skeletal remains were found in front of this grand altar, but after much examination, they thought this one to be Queen Anne Boleyn's skeletal body."

Ryan looked at the alter as if he were deep in thought and then finished his history lesson by saying, "None of the bodies were ceremoniously buried, but Anne Boleyn's headless body was taken from the scaffold by her ladies in waiting. It was reported to be placed inside a box used for storage and then carried to the chapel. As I recall, her remains were thoroughly examined by a surgeon in the 1800s, who found them to be of 'excessively delicate proportions'. I wonder..."

Ryan then stopped speaking as if he were concentrating on something else that Ellie could not make out from his facial expressions.

"Well?" asked Ellie. She then asked impatiently, shaking Ryan from his daydream. "Was the skeleton really Queen Anne Boleyn's?"

Ryan tapped his chin and then confirmed himself by saying, "Yes, they think so. They found the person to be very short and very delicate. She stood maybe 5' tall or maybe just a little taller. She was also twenty-five to thirty years old. This size and age are consistent with Anne Boleyn's description at the time. She was also said to have a long, slender neck and large eyes. The skeleton also had a very well-rounded and an almost perfect skull, while having a slender, short spine. Luckily, her description was well documented."

Ryan then looked again, as if he were trying to imagine the person when she was alive. Ellie seemed to awaken him from a daydream when she asked him, "So what happened to all of these skeletons?"

Ryan shook his head and answered her by saying, "They were all identified and then reburied in the crypt under the tiled floors of this current chapel. I don't remember exactly how many bodies there were in total, but I do remember that the Queens of England- Lady Jane Gray, Catherine Howard, and Anne Boleyn were all entombed here."

Ellie then acted incredibly enthused and said, "Now those are the kinds of tales that get my blood pumping. Ryan, how the hell do you know all these details?

Ryan pretended to be modest and then said, "Well, you aren't the only one who ever wrote a paper about the Tower of London. I have a degree in history, and I have been drawn to this place throughout the years for one reason or another. I am quite haunted by these ancient rock walls and the spirits that inhabit this place."

Ellie smiled broadly and then asked Ryan. "Do you have any more amazing stories about this place?"

Ryan then smiled back at her and said, "I sure do. I hope that you can handle the truth about this place. To paraphrase the best rock band out of Australia, "If you want blood..."

Ellie joined him in finishing the song's lyrics by singing with Ryan. "You got it!"

Ryan gave Ellie a surprised grin and then asked, "You know AC/DC? How else are you going to surprise me today?"

Ellie winked her big blue eye at him and said flirtily, "You will be amazed. I know things that are beyond my years."

As afternoon came upon them, Ryan then took Ellie on a tour of the grand White Tower in the middle of the formidable complex. He promised her another amazing story at the end of his walking tour that he had first taken twenty years earlier. This was, of course, with the help of his own guided tour provided by the older Beefeater named Mel.

With his inexplicable experiences inside his head, he didn't tell Ellie that this place had also changed his life forever. His only wish was that visiting this place would not do the same to her. They spent hours stepping back in time as they walked from one amazing building to another. Ryan had reached the last building on his own impromptu tour, and this is the one that scared him the most… 'The Bloody Tower'.

Ryan stopped outside the gate that a person had to go under in order to enter the Bloody Tower. He kept thinking about the two small boys that he had seen the last time that he had visited there. The blood must have escaped his face, as Ellie had mentioned how white he had become. She tried to cajole him forward, but he only stood fearfully at the unknown that was awaiting him inside the building.

Finally, even though he was almost crippled with fear. Ryan shook his head and said to Ellie, "I promised you one more really great story, and the next stop is where I think that I should probably tell it to you."

Ryan then thought to himself, "Am I really afraid of the restless spirits in this place, or am I actually afraid of how Ellie might look at me if I told her the truth?" Ryan didn't know for sure, but he took a deep breath and trudged forward anyway.

Ryan gave Ellie a weakened smile and then told her that this was going to be a damn scary, but truthful, tale that he was about to tell her. He started by warning her about his own experiences that had happened there in the past.

He didn't say the words about having her believe in him, but his eyes must have been pleading with Ellie. She suddenly said, "I will believe anything that you tell me happened here, I promise you. I can handle all of this, and I am with you. Amaze me!"

Ryan immediately felt the courage and the confidence that Ellie gave him. He felt rejuvenated, and he grabbed her hand gently in his own once again.

He then led her into the Bloody Tower while saying, "I think that I should show you the upper level first. Have you heard of Sir Walter Raleigh?"

Ellie rolled her eyes and said, "Of course I have. We learned about him when I was in middle school. He tried to create one of the first settlements in America. Roanoke, right?"

Ryan nodded his head, and then Ellie continued. "He also supposedly found a 'city made of gold' called El Dorado in Central America. Because of this, I know that he fought extensively with the Spanish. Oh, and he was also one of the first big-time smokers of tobacco, am I right?"

Ryan laughed and then told her, "You are right. However, that is a simplified version of his story. You have the gist of who he was, though. There are also some things that you probably don't know about him. Such as the fact that he was once a prisoner held here in the Bloody Tower. He was held here for thirteen very long years."

The tower is quite large, and the lower floor was Sir Raleigh's study, where he wrote and did scientific research. His living quarters were on the upper floor of the tower. Outside of this tower, they even allowed him to have a garden where he experimented with different plants.

At this point, Ryan didn't tell Ellie about the two young boys who had resided there nearly 150 years before Sir Walter Raleigh. The vision of them still haunted him, and he was afraid to tell her about this experience.

Ellie stood in absolute amazement and then said, "He was imprisoned in this tower? This place is nicer than my apartment when I first started at the university."

Ryan laughed again and then told her, "He even had servants to help him with everyday chores. He was given fine food and slept comfortably in a feather bed. Of course, he could never leave the tower grounds, but prison here for the rich and famous was quite different from any place that we ever think about today.

Ellie then said, "Yeah, but people would also have their heads cut off."

Ryan laughed again and then said, "This is true!"

Ryan then told Ellie about the first short time that he was imprisoned here. "He was actually first imprisoned here because of love."

Ellie gave him a sideways look like she didn't believe him and blurted out, "Shut up! How can anyone be imprisoned because of love?"

She then playfully punched Ryan in the shoulder, much harder than what she intended.

Ryan grabbed at his arm and then continued by saying, "That is also true. He was one of the 'favorites' of Queen Elizabeth I, King Henry VIII's daughter. They got along smashingly well. Anyway, behind the queen's back, he fell in love with her main courtier, Lady Elizabeth Throckmorton, and they were secretly married. Queen Elizabeth threw them in here because she didn't give her permission for them to be married. That is why he was imprisoned the first time. He was imprisoned because of love."

Ryan could tell that Ellie was politely waiting for him to continue with the story. Then he told her, "The Queen's heart softened, and she finally released them, where they retired to the country. However, Sir Walter was not the kind of person to just sit around the house. That is when he first sailed to South America. That is also when he became an enemy of the Spanish government and the future King of England, James I."

Ryan checked to see if Ellie was still interested and then continued by saying, "In 1603, when Queen Elizabeth died, her successor, James I, became King of England. He hated Sir Walter so badly that he had imprisoned him in this tower for those thirteen years."

Ryan cleared his throat and then continued to say, "Sir Walter Raleigh was one of those people that people either loved or hated, much like today. He was handsome, adventurous, strong-willed, and witty. Women seemed to love him. Men, however, really disliked him because of these same qualities."

Ellie looked at Ryan with wondering eyes and asked quietly, "What happened to him? I have known of his exploits but have never known what happened to Sir Walter Raleigh."

Ryan finished the story by telling Ellie, "Well, he was finally released from prison. He sailed one more time to South America and King James had him arrested again for treason. The king did this in order to appease the Spanish government. He was beheaded at Westminster Abbey, right around Halloween in 1618. His portrait is hanging right over here."

Ellie looked at it and stated, "Besides having that funky beard, he was handsome."

Ryan blushed slightly and then bravely said, "Now then, that actually isn't the scary story that I wanted to seriously tell you about."

Ryan swallowed hard, and then Ellie squeezed his hand even tighter. He led her back downstairs to the same bench that stood against the wall that he had sat on 20 years earlier.

She was completely quiet when Ryan told her about the two boys that had disappeared and were believed to have been murdered inside that very tower. Ryan then lowered his head and told Ellie about his experiences with the ball that came bouncing down the stairs. He then told her of the two young boys that were dressed in medieval night shirts and were standing at the top of the stairs.

One of Ellie's hands gripped Ryan's forearm tighter, leaving white marks when she loosened her grip. The other hand was planted seriously under her chin as she sat on the edge of her seat, listening to Ryan.

She was quiet for several minutes, making Ryan nervous about his strange occurrence, when she finally asked lowly, "You actually saw the two young princes?"

Ryan then nodded his head slowly and said, "I have questioned my own sanity several times, but I think so. You realize, I have never told anyone about that day for 20 years."

Ellie said, with an emboldened tone in her voice, "I believe you, no matter how crazy it sounds."

She then asked Ryan two questions that caused the hairs to rise on the back of his neck. She asked excitedly, "Have you had dreams about this place or anyone significant that seem extremely vivid and important?"

Ryan looked up at her with wide eyes and a very surprised look on his face. Ryan felt like he had been suddenly slugged in the gut, and he realized what Ellie was telling him.

He asked her quizzically, "Who have you had dreams about?"

Ellie got a serious look on her face and replied, "I have had dreams about my mother, but that is no surprise. However, she was with me in this courtyard outside, surrounded by the ravens. I also dreamt about a sad knight who was in full battle armor."

Ryan looked astonished and then he asked quickly, "Did he speak to you?"

Ellie then looked into Ryan's eyes and said warily, "He tried to, but every time that he opened his mouth, only blood ran down his chin. It looked like his throat had been cut and his tongue had turned blue."

Ryan stood and held out his hand to Ellie, who took it when Ryan said; "Come with me, you have to see one more place in the central castle keep."

Ryan almost ran toward the White Tower in the center of the ancient complex, with Ellie holding his hand and trailing behind him. He stood outside the medieval castle keep and looked at the stairway and the upper entrance into the building itself.

He was almost panting when he asked Ellie, "Did you ever have any dreams of this tower?"

Ellie concentrated her thoughts and then said, "I seem to remember a stone, circular staircase in my dreams when my mother died, but that was when I was seven years old. It is hard to remember any of the dreams, or I may have only remembered parts of them. I tended to try to cancel that part of my life out. I didn't have any friends, and I had just been through a horrible loss. I was going through an extremely hard time…Why? What happened here?"

A wind was starting to blow, and Ryan spoke above the gusts while saying, "The two princes disappeared in 1483, when their father, the king of England, suddenly died. They were transported here by their uncle, Richard III. He brought them here supposedly for the coronation of the elder boy to become king. Now then, think about the stairs that you dreamed about."

Ryan led Ellie up the outside staircase to the entrance doors of the oldest of the medieval towers. Inside the White Tower, Ryan led Ellie to a small, stone, circular staircase and asked, "Does this look familiar to you?"

Ellie's face showed an immediate sign of recognition, and she looked at Ryan with an alarmed look on her brow.

This caused Ryan to say to her, "This is the staircase where they found the skeletons of two young boys buried beneath it. This was nearly two hundred years after the boy's disappearance. Workers were renovating these stairs, and they found a wooden trunk with two small human skeletons inside it. This trunk had been hidden ten feet below the older, ancient staircase that had once been here."

Ellie looked excited and then asked, "Now, this is the meat and bones type of anthropology of what I am passionate about. Can we see these bones?"

Ryan shook his head with a "no" expression, and he said remorsefully, "They were stored for a long time, and then they were moved by the royal family to be reburied and interred at Westminster Abbey. This happened just a few years ago. However, the last time that the skeletons were ever examined was back in the 1930s, and there has never even been a DNA test done on the bones, as far as I know."

Ellie looked frustrated at this fact and said angrily, "It seems we have hit a roadblock. Shit, I feel like we are just on the cusp of understanding a lot of mysteries, and then we run into brick walls. I hate that."

Ryan then looked at his watch and said, "Well, I know of one thing that we are on the cusp of...We must meet up with Monty and go to the 'Medieval Experience' restaurant tonight. Did I pass any test that you may have had today? Will you join me tonight?"

Ellie gave Ryan an almost shy smile and said back to him, "I would love to be with you tonight. Just give me an hour to freshen up first."

Ryan then mouthed the words "thank you" to Ellie and gave her the largest smile that he had given anybody in over ten years.

"Your faith, like the pain
Draws me in again
She washes all my wounds for me
The darkness in my veins
I never could explain
And I wonder if you ever see
Will you still believe?"
(Fuel)

Chapter Fifteen

"Does a child that has been blind since birth dream of a multi-colored universe?" (Gary Anderson-Mountain Man Philosopher)

Ryan and Monty were sitting at the tavern in the hotel while they waited for Ellie. They did not have to wait long when Ellie literally ran into the bar, sat down next to Ryan, and ordered herself an energy drink and a shot of vodka.

She slammed down the shot of vodka and then started drinking the energy drink. Ryan smiled and said to her, "Whoa there, if you aren't careful, you will get even more hyped up and explode. I certainly don't want that to happen."

Ryan leaned toward Monty and asked him sarcastically, "Does a person explode or implode from those combinations of drinks?"

Monty looked at Ellie and then said, "If you are young like her, you just wake up with a mule in your head trying to kick its way out. If you are our age, the mule kicks our skull outward, and we would explode and implode at the same time. It is very messy. She will be okay though. With any luck, maybe she will forget your age."

Ellie was breathing heavily, and in between pants she excitedly said to Ryan, "After I took a shower, I thought that I should call my grandparents for more information about any dreams that I may have had when I was a young girl."

She held up one finger and drank a tall glass of water in three large sips. She then finished her story by saying, "It was mid-morning there, but they told me that I mostly had dreams and even some nightmares about my mother, which is understandable. Now then, when I first went to live with my grandparents, I had it rough, like I told you. I didn't have any friends, so instead, I made up my own friends, and I started talking to two invisible young companions."

Ellie paused to build suspense and then continued to tell them, "This went on for two years, until I was 9 years old. After they told me about this, I started to remember all of it. I was very good friends with two young boys who were my imaginary friends. I completely remember them now, we played such amazing games, especially in the backyard."

Ellie could see the interest and excitement rise in Ryan as well, and he asked her, "Do you remember what their names were?"

Ellie's face turned serious again, and she looked as if she was thinking desperately. A smile suddenly crept upon her face, and she said two names: "I called them Eddie and Rich. One was about my own age, and the other was a little older than us.

Ryan ordered a double shot of Irish whiskey and turned rather pale when he drank this heavy, sour liquid in one big gulp. He turned to Ellie and whispered, "The two princes names were Edward V, and his younger brother was Richard, Duke of York."

Ellie's jaw fell open, and she turned pale as well at this news. She stared into Ryan's eyes and then said one word, knowing that this was not possible at this point, "Coincidence?"

Ryan shook his head emphatically in a "no" manner, and he said back to her, "Coincidence is just de ja vu in disguise. I think both coincidence and de ja vu exist for the same reason. They both teach us something of great importance."

"Holy Shit!" Ellie exclaimed loudly, which made several other customers turn in their direction.

Ryan then looked at her seriously and said, "I think that you and I were destined to meet, and I think that we should be attached at the hip throughout this whole shit show. I think that we need one another right now. What do you think?"

She looked at him with fear in her eyes and then said, "Wherever I go, I would like you to be by my side. Ryan, I also feel like I want and need you by my side. Lead the way, and I will follow. Just don't leave me behind...alone."

Ryan smiled confidently at her and said one word: "Never!"

Ryan, Ellie, and Monty began the short walk along the busy streets of London to the dinner party that was held for them that evening. The restaurant was named 'The Medieval Experience', and it was themed after the court of King Henry VIII.

Ryan and Ellie could tell that Monty had started drinking alcohol ahead of them at the tavern, as he was incredibly more boisterous and talkative than usual. Liquor had a way of making him think that he was hugely funnier than he really was. It also gave him the no-nonsense self-confidence to not be very politically correct, as it does for a lot of people.

Of course, this always made his friend roll his eyes and chuckle uncontrollably. Ryan believed that the biggest problem in the world today was that too many people took themselves entirely too seriously and didn't know how to laugh enough, especially at themselves.

In Ryan's experience, a lot of people like to look for something to be constantly wrong with everything that is surrounding them, and they look for something to be upset about. However, neither Ryan nor Monty felt this way, as they had been on the losing end of too many of these quarrelsome individuals. They preferred not to give these people any of their precious time or argue with them.

Ryan then looked like he was thinking about something from his past and said out loud softly, "When you are standing in a field full of horseshit, you have to look for the pretty ponies."

Ellie looked sideways at him and just asked, "What does that mean?"

Ryan chuckled and then said to her, "It is just a saying that I like and remember from a difficult time in my past. Kind of a Montana version of 'Every cloud has a silver lining'."

Ellie looked seriously at him, and she asked him, "Have you found a pretty pony yet?"

Ryan only smiled over at her and simply said, "You!"

Ellie could not seem to wipe the grin from her face until later in the evening.

Ryan was dressed rather casually that evening, as he wore black shorts and a red polo golf shirt that hung untucked on his torso. He also wore white high-top tennis shoes and the same floppy, cowboy-style hat upon his head.

Monty was wearing almost the same outfit as he had worn the night before, except he had no dress coat on and his button up shirt was laid open at the top, showing off the small amount of hair on his chest.

Both men cleaned up rather well, but Ellie put them both to shame as she wore a low-cut pink blouse, a tan skirt, and shiny black spaghetti strap sandals upon her feet. She had her long blond hair pulled back in a ponytail, which showed off every striking feature of her beautiful, oval face and strong chin.

She was very tanned and had a slight dusting of freckles on her nose, which seemed to make her even cuter. Ryan was a big fan of cuteness. He would take a woman who was naturally cute over a dolled-up princess any day of the week.

Before entering the restaurant, Ryan took off his floppy hat and brushed his unruly hair with his hand. He then said, "I wish that my hair had been cut; I have a bit of a mullet going on here. You know the hair style: business up front and party in the back."

Ryan's hair was a dirty blond color and stood up in a cow lick on the back end of his head with it this long. On that evening, each man was cleanly shaven, except Monty, who had a goatee growing on his face that had begun to turn gray in parts.

Ellie put out her arms in a stop motion in front of each of them and said, "Quit fidgeting, I think that you both look very handsome."

She entered the restaurant in between them and linked their arms in hers at the elbows, and she stated, "Well, let me make my appearance as the luckiest woman at this gathering."

Ryan then looked over at Monty and said, in a bad British accent, "I could go for a leg of turkey and a large ale right about now, how about you, Sir Montross?"

Monty looked back at Ryan and said, in another hokey British accent as well, "Yes, that sounds outstanding, my good man. Do you thinketh that they have a gin and toniceth?"

"Cheerio, and let's go." said Ellie as she led the two cowboys into a medieval themed restaurant. The men grinned at her for being such a good sport and playing along with them.

"Shall we?" Ryan asked, and he got a "we shall" in return from both Monty and Ellie. They let a loud laugh escape their lips after this happened.

Ryan didn't think of her immediately, but then he scoured each wooden table that was standing before him for his lost love, Karen. He felt almost like he was betraying her by being there with Ellie, but his mind seemed to ease when he could not find her anywhere. Did she not come? An RSVP card was sent back, saying that she would be here. So, where was she then?

Monty had gotten a large mug of beer from a passing waitress who was carrying one on her tray and passing near him. He then unlinked arms with Ellie and began following the pretty brown-haired waitress across the faux medieval hall of a restaurant.

Ryan yelled "Good Luck" to his disappearing best friend, and he then looked at Ellie and asked her to lead the way into the crowd of ravenous people. She led him to a sturdy wooden table at the front of the group of people. This caused many heads to turn when they saw that she was holding hands with Ryan, a much older man than she.

Ryan could feel the eyes upon him, and he suddenly asked Ellie, with apprehension in his voice, "How old are you, Ellie?"

Ellie acted shocked and then answered him by saying boldly, "Old enough to make my own choices and spend my time with who I want."

Ryan smiled slightly at her answer and then said, "You know that I have had a lot more experiences in this crazy world?"

She paused, as if she were thinking about her answer, and then she leaned forward and said back to Ryan, "I have found that this is the best way to learn in this life. Otherwise, it is like throwing a child that doesn't know how to swim into the deep end of the pool and praying for the best."

Ryan laughed at the vision that came before him, and he joked back at her, "I have been called the shallow end of the pool, or even the wading pool at times. But you are the first person to think of me as very deep."

Ellie leaned closer to Ryan and whispered, "Fuck 'em all!"

With these words, Ellie gave Ryan a long, sultry kiss directly on the mouth. She then sat back and said strongly, "Don't you agree?"

Ryan only gave her a strong, confident smile in return. One that made his chest swell and his heart, beat faster.

A lot of the tables were in long rows, where some of the other members of the tour sat together. Ryan and Ellie sat away from these groups of people at the long tables so that they could speak privately to each other. They were soon joined by Monty before the dinner was served and the entertainment began. It somehow turned out that his new love interest, the waitress, would be serving them that evening.

She was dressed in a period costume with a billowy skirt and a white top that was pulled down off her shoulder blades. Monty claimed to have nothing to do with her being their waitress, but Ryan knew differently about how his friend's brain worked.

Suddenly, an actor portraying King Henry VIII and an actress portraying one of his six queens, who still had her head anyway, sat at the main table and clapped their hands. All around them, wherever there was room available, entertainers dressed as serving wenches, clergy, beefeaters, and even jesters began to mill through the crowd.

Minstrels began playing music, couples dressed in period costumes danced merrily, and even men dressed in suits of armor began having sword fights all around them.

"Holy hell in a handbasket!" yelled out a startled Monty.

He then looked at all the people prancing and fighting around him, and he started to giggle almost wildly. The serving woman who was helping them was one of the people dancing, and out of the blue, Monty decided that he needed a new drink. He suddenly yelled out, "Wench!"

His boisterous voice could be heard throughout the restaurant, and then a funny sounding giggle fell from his mouth. Ellie looked at Ryan and then asked in astonishment, "Is he allowed to do that?"

Just then, Monty's favorite serving girl quit dancing, stepped forward, and refilled Monty's large mug. She must have overheard Ellie, because she then said to the table, "In all actuality, they want patrons to yell out 'Service' or even 'Wench'! It is supposed to add to the overall original experience of the Medieval Ages."

Monty then nudged Ryan's elbow and said, "We really need to have one of these in Montana." Then he said to their server with a slight wink, "Thanks, Honey."

"Where did you learn that trick?" asked Ryan, trying to be louder than a nearby lute player.

"You know," Monty yelled back loudly, even though the lute player had stopped playing, "I learned this up at the bar, and you know what? They encourage you to be loud and boisterous like that here. By God, I think that I may have been born in the wrong century, as my uncouthness knows no bounds."

Ryan looked at Ellie while pretending to be exasperated and said sarcastically, "Have I introduced you to my rowdy and sometimes embarrassing friend Monty, I believe that he is in-between hangovers right now."

Ellie giggled, and then Ryan continued by saying, "Hell, I can't say much. I have partied like a rock star as well...and I will probably do it again in the future, but right now I don't like to be out of control. Do you want to hear anymore awful things about me?"

Ellie shrugged her shoulders and then said compassionately, "We all have a past, and we are all addicted to something. Most of these things are only superficial anyway, but you...you have shown me what kind of person you are on the inside. That is indeed a rare, good thing… believe me."

Ellie looked seriously at Ryan and continued to say, "You have shown me what makes you excited, which is many of the same things as me. You have shown me how kind you can be, as well as incredibly vulnerable. You have put a huge amount of trust in me, which I am not used to at all. You are an excellent person who believes in doing what is right. Am I wrong in any of these things?"

Ryan blushed wildly at her answer, and he said back to her with ever growing reverence, "I try to be that kind of person. How did you become so wise and perceptive?"

Ellie looked down at her tingling hands and then honestly said, "I started at an early age, right about 7 years old. I grew up very quickly. I had my mother's things that she left me and her ideas. I wanted to be just like her. I slept with her white lace nightgown at night, and I tried to dress like her in high school. I even listened to the music that she loved, even though I have strayed away from her 1980s pop-loving tunes for edgier and angrier music. I wanted to be just like her."

A single tear ran down Ellie's cheek, and Ryan wiped it away with his finger, causing her to grab his hand tightly, and she said lowly, "I guess that I still do."

Ryan leaned closer to her and kissed her gently on the cheek where her tear had just been. Suddenly, she looked up at him seriously and said, "What I like most about you, though, is that you really listen to me and care about what I have to say and the feelings that I have. I like that a lot. Most guys my age don't make the effort to listen."

Monty suddenly yelled out loudly, "Wench!"

When his favorite waitress refilled his glass, as well as those of Ryan and Ellie, he looked at the waitress and then at Ryan and stated, "I think that I may be in love with this girl."

"Thank you, Miss... you are really a good sport to put up with some of us tonight." Ryan said to her, and then she replied to him, "Your friend said there would be a nice tip at the end of the night if I was nice to him. Plus, I really have a thing for the whole 'wild west, cowboy vibe."

Ryan looked closer at her and then asked, "Are you okay? Your eye looks rather red."

She rubbed it instinctively and said, "Oh, my dearie, I was on the wrong end of a flying elbow up at the bar. As you can see, some people can get rather rowdy here."

Suddenly, Beefeater guards marched through the tables filled with people and stood guard behind the fattened actor pretending to be Henry VIII. Ryan was looking at Ellie when they marched through the aisles, but he thought that he recognized someone that he hadn't seen in a long time, so he yelled out the name, "Mel? Mel, is that you?" Could that possibly be true?

However, if an older gentleman that Ryan had known twenty years ago had been there, he would probably be gone now. Mel was quickly forgotten when a whole, crispy, baked chicken, along with fresh vegetables and various cheeses, were put on the middle of the table and each of them was given a replica pewter plate and silverware.

Monty yelled out at this, "Hark, our dinner has arrived. My stomach feels like it has taken up residence in the actual Dark Ages."

Ellie yelled out a, "Boo Yaa!" Which left Monty to tear off one of the chicken's legs for himself and one for Ellie. He then started to gorge himself on the seasoned meat.

Ryan looked at him and then said to Ellie, "I am glad to see that you are not a vegetarian? You may be offended by us two ranch loving carnivores."

Ellie licked her lips and said back, "Oh, hell no, now, cut me off some of that juicy, breast meat, please."

They devoured their meals while using their fingers and not as many utensils. They were supposed to be in the medieval ages, for crying out loud. Juices and grease ran down each of their jowls, which caused Ryan to grab his large napkin and blot them from his face. Then he leaned over and did the same to Ellie's chin while she held onto another chicken leg with her hands.

She looked over at Ryan and said to him with a half filled mouth, "Now you can see me at my worst. Well, what do you think?"

Ryan leaned back in his chair and gently stated, "Crude, but you are still enchanting."

At the end of the meal, Ellie let out a slight burp and then turned red and apologized, leaving Ryan to say, "No need to apologize to either of us; we are cattle-herding mountain men, remember?"

Monty piped up and said, still with a mouth full of chicken, "I would actually have been offended if you hadn't let out a nice burp."

Ryan could really tell that the ale was starting to affect Ellie when she then leaned back and, surprisingly, pushed out a loud belch and then laughed heartily. Monty and Ryan, both gave her a large ovation, and Monty even stood up and gave her a high five and saluted her.

Ellie looked pleased with herself as her cheeks had turned rosy, and then she said to Ryan, "Boy, that felt good. I would have uncomfortably sat here in silence before tonight. Do you know what I really like about Monty and, of course you? You don't like to hold anything back… you live free and have fun. Hardly anybody does that now-a-days."

Ellie then took a drink of her ale and said to Ryan, "I especially like how you speak to me. You get excited when you talk about something that is passionate to you. You make me excited to listen. And you speak to me plainly and truthfully. Tell me a true story, Ryan...Please?"

Ryan looked at Ellie and then asked her unbelievably, "You want to hear a story, now?" Ellie took another drink of her ale and only answered him by saying, "Yup."

Ryan thought for a short amount of time and then told Ellie a little story about how he saw and interpreted life. "Ellie, let me tell you a little secret... besides what is in your head and your heart, nothing really matters much in the grand scheme of things. Take your nice belch at the table tonight, was it embarrassing for you?"

Her response was short and curt when she answered him by saying, "A little. I had a hard time building up the courage to do it."

Ryan then continued by saying, "Now then, the burp that you just belted out may make for a funny story between the three of us someday. We would probably think about it years from now and smile. However, none of the rest of these people will even remember that it happened. I believe it is what is in your soul that really matters in the long run. Always remember, it is not just how you act, but what you strive to be throughout your time in this crazy world. Of course, it really matters the most in whatever mysterious realm that comes next. Hold on to that."

Ryan raised a hand to stop Ellie from saying anything, and then he continued, "When I was a little kid, I had an old uncle that lived close to us out on a farm in Montana, and I called him, 'Old Uncle Eric'. He was 75 years old then, and he attributed his good health to 'throwing a bull, over the barn every morning.' Now, I always believed him when I was a child, and when I got older, I realized that he was throwing around a lot of bull. Just not over the barn."

Ryan stopped talking in order to have a nice, cool drink. Then he realized that not only was Ellie listening intently to him, but the whole table next to them was also listening.

Ryan nodded at this table, made a quizzical look at Ellie, and then continued with his story, "However, I tended to grow older and have other interests, as did he. One day, though, my family visited his homestead out in the middle of nowhere. There is nothing but the sounds of blowing stocks of wheat and barley and the coyotes howling in the distance out there. 'Old Uncle Eric' was 96 years old now, and lying in his bed, slowly dying. He told me about his time in WWII, which he had never told anyone before. He said that he was shot once, and he thought that he was going to die as a young man. He was amazed that he had lived through this point in his life, but he could never explain to anyone why he had lived."

Ryan threw Ellie a wink and then finished up his story by saying, "Old Uncle Eric was lying in bed at the age of 96 and telling me that throughout the years, he really never could understand the mysteries and the meaning of life, but there was one thing that he said he did discover. He had ended up marrying a woman that he loved very much and having several wonderful children that he was so proud of...AND he was also very proud of the sparkle in my eyes whenever he told me about throwing the bull over the barn each morning."

Ryan stopped for effect and then continued by saying, "Old Uncle Eric, then gave me a toothless grin and said, "Ryan, if you wake up and haven't died, then consider yourself lucky, live life to the fullest, and laugh with all your heart. And damnit! Try to make another person's eyes sparkle, each day. Those were the last words that Uncle Eric ever said to me."

Ellie was crying softly when Ryan finished his story, as were three other women and one guy at the table next to them.

Like on cue, Monty yelled out, "Wench!" Then he giggled, and Ryan and Ellie laughed heartily with him.

Slowly, all the other people started looking around at each other and started laughing as well. Ryan got a little red-faced, and then he ordered two more ales.

He then smiled and said to Ellie, "You see, your actions can be contagious, and I see a little sparkle in each of these people's eyes. Maybe they will think about this night fondly."

Ellie said to Ryan in between bouts of laughter and smiling fits, "I hope so; I am sure that I will."

Ryan leaned closer to her and then said, "I know that this sounds like a line, but you really have nice eyes...they remind me of someone's eyes that I knew a long time ago. You have a way of seeing through all my bullshit, and I can make your eyes sparkle incredibly. You have that in common with her."

Ellie had red spots enter her high cheek bones from laughing so hard. She then said, "Thanks, and I don't want to see through your bullshit. I enjoy every part of you, especially your bullshit. I easily see through that rough exterior."

The actor playing King Henry VIII decided to give a speech during this time, and he bellowed out appreciation for the fine meal. He also bellowed out about the fine entertainment which all got rousing applause and made people bang their tables with their beer mugs.

Right after the speech by the King and when all the other patrons had settled themselves, a voice broke through the silence and Monty yelled out, "Wench," which caused a huge amount of more cheers.

Ryan stood up and said loudly to Monty, "No more ale for you, not unless you are willing to sing us a song tonight, knave."

Monty started to sing out a dirty limerick song when Ryan leaned over to Ellie and said to her, "We had better pour him out of here."

Ryan then lifted Monty out of the chair and put Monty's arm around his neck. He then started walking him toward the door, which caused Monty to say rather loudly and embarrassingly, "Come on, Ryan, you know that I am not the worst looking thing that you have ever taken home."

Ellie spoke for Ryan when she said, "Who said that he was going home with your hairy ass."

This caused many men to cuss under their breath and made many women give each other disturbing looks. Ellie again smiled widely at Ryan and then moved herself to the other side of Monty, where she placed his other arm over her own neck.

Ryan became serious after they had walked out the door, and he asked Ellie dourly. "Did you feel like you were being watched when we left there?"

Ellie laughed sarcastically and said back, "With how we left the party? Who wasn't looking at us?'

Ryan hoisted his buddy up a little bit taller and said flatly, "I guess it is just my uppity gut feelings acting up on me again."

"She woke in the morning...
She knew that her life had passed her by
And she called out a warning
'Don't ever let life pass you by..."
(Incubus)

Chapter Sixteen

True friends are much like automobiles: A person only has a few great ones in a lifetime!

Ryan and Ellie held hands behind Monty's back while they supported him. They kept giving each other flirty little smiles as well as making goofy faces, trying to make the other person laugh. They had to stop once, as Monty gave them the warning sign that he may have to get sick.

As Ellie helped Monty walk behind the pillar of a building that was there, Ryan looked back toward the restaurant from which they had come. When he did this, he noticed a large man that was peering at them from out of the shadows of an older statue.

Ryan could tell that the man wore a pair of puffed out striped pants, a dirty white button-down shirt, and a tweed flat top hat on his head. He only saw the man for a quick second, but Ryan was sure that the large man had ducked behind this ominous statue. He was also positive that this man had been following them from the restaurant.

"Is everything okay, Ryan?" Ellie asked, which caused Ryan to look at her. He then looked behind them again, but the man was gone.

He turned back toward Ellie when he heard her say, "Um, Ryan, I probably need your help with Monty. He was leaning on this pillar and has just gotten horribly sick. I think that there is blood in his vomit."

Ryan surprisingly exclaimed, "What? How much blood?"

Ellie looked at him as if she had done something wrong, and then she said, with a look of disgust on her face. "We can check out his puke when we get back to the hotel, though. It splattered on my feet and my nice pair of new shoes."

Ryan gave her a revolting look in return and said, "Oh my god, I am so sorry. That should have been me over there with him, but my paranoia is peaking tonight, and I thought that we were being followed."

Ellie looked almost frantically at him and said, "Somebody following us? Does this happen often?"

Ryan looked embarrassed and answered her back, "Well, I have been followed before. Because of that one time, my strange gut feelings get ahold of me now. Don't worry, it is probably nothing but too much ale and chicken."

The threesome of U.S. travelers arrived at the hotel, and Ryan took Monty to the second floor and threw him on his bed. This prompted Monty to yell out "Wench," and then giggle again.

Ryan smiled down at his good friend and watched him curl up on top of the bed's covers. He then snuggled into the pillow while mumbling something incoherent. Ellie had gone to the outdoor cafe to get a glass of wine and examine and clean her shoes. All while waiting for her new wonderful companion to return.

Ryan looked down at his best friend and said absently, "Wish me luck, Monty. Dream of beautiful, half naked women, my friend."

Ryan was about to close the door of the room when he heard Monty say sleepily, "Thanks for bringing me to London, buddy."

Ryan smiled in return and said lowly, "Thank you for coming with me and having my back."

Ellie had gotten a glass of wine at the outdoor cafe of the hotel, and she was sipping on it when Ryan walked up behind her. He placed his arms around her waist from the back and asked, "How are your shoes?"

She put out a bare foot and said, "I decided to take them off and clean myself up first. I didn't want to walk around in a pile of vile smelling goo for the rest of the night."

Ryan spun her around with the lights awakening on the Tower Bridge behind her. He pulled her close and kissed her perfumed neck, and then took her head in his hands and kissed her softly and passionately.

He leaned back and stated, while trying to look knowingly, "That tastes like a Chardonnay that you have been sipping on."

Ellie looked back at him deeply and stated, "Nope, I don't like such dry wine, you had better try again."

He kissed her passionately again and then leaned back and guessed, "Is that a Pinot Grigio?"

Ellie smiled seductively and said back at him. "Try once more, that is still too dry of wine."

Ryan leaned closer again and kissed her even more deeply. He did this with more emphasis, while exploring her mouth with his tongue, which was sailing lightly across her own tongue and cheeks.

He then pulled away and said jokingly, "I got it, you are drinking 'Boones Farm, Country Quencher. You can't drink any wine-flavored drink that is sweeter than that."

Ellie playfully slapped his chest and said, "I don't even know what kind of wine that is, but it sounds like something a wino might like. This is just a French Port that was made to sip on during a warm, full-mooned evening."

Ryan chuckled and then said, "Well, you caught me, I don't really know very much about wine, but that is a very specific drink. I mean, tonight is a warm, full-mooned night in London."

He kissed her softly again and finished saying, "You seem to be in the perfect demographic for that specific kind of drink."

Ellie giggled, threw her head back, and howled at the full moon. She then looked at Ryan and said, "I have been missing America since I got here. Did that wolf howl make you homesick for Montana?"

Ryan looked at her seriously and then said, "I actually feel like I just found my home."

Ryan turned Ellie toward Tower Bridge and whispered in her ear, "Isn't it the most beautiful bridge that you have ever seen?"

Ellie wasn't as impressed as Ryan, but she was still enchanted by the beauty of the old bridge. The two of them stared at it in silence while Ryan thought about his walk down here between dropping Monty off in their hotel room and joining Ellie out on the patio.

While his mind was on getting to Ellie, Ryan had started to completely forget what had happened on the way to be by her side. While absent-mindedly walking through the lobby of the hotel, the pretty young waitress from earlier had literally run into him.

Ryan had noticed the long black hair, and he had almost knocked her over as he was trying to find Ellie. He had noticed Ellie standing by the railing, having her glass of port, and looking amazing. For some reason, he suddenly couldn't stop thinking about slamming into the pretty young woman now. Maybe he had been paying too much attention on getting to Ellie, at the moment.

Ryan thought to himself, "Quit acting so weird. You are here with a beautiful woman. Just drop it, shut your mind off! You have seen Monty come home with women several times. This time is no different."

However, Ryan couldn't drop it, and for the first time, Ryan thought about how attractive she really was. Even though she wore a large amount of makeup, had very white skin, and was wearing very bright red lipstick. She also had put a red rose in the hair behind her ear. Her only flaw was the red color that covered half of the white cornea of her left eye where she had received an elbow earlier in the night.

Ryan had given her directions to their room and then said as he was walking away from her, "I think that you overserved my buddy tonight, so take it easy on him."

She looked at Ryan, smiled, and said, "He will be like putty in my hands. I promise."

Ryan had to get his mind off her, and asked Ellie a rather impromptu question, "Can you take a walk with me while you are barefoot, or do I have to wait for you to go change your shoes?"

Ellie glanced at him suspiciously and then answered him by saying, "I could walk and carry these shoes with us, I cleaned them up, but they probably still stink and are rather gross. However, I am not going to leave them lying here, by any means."

Ryan looked at his watch and said casually, "It is into the nighttime now, and I am still full of energy. Will you walk out onto Tower Bridge with me?"

Without looking around, they began to slowly stroll, hand in hand, out onto the outside walking path of this illustrious bridge. They never noticed the two men that began to follow them or the leering eyes that were upon them.

A loud knocking sound awoke Monty as he was laying comfortably on his bed. He didn't realize how drunk he had gotten until he tried to raise himself from the bed and walk to the door. When he got to the door, he checked his breath using the palm of his hand, cringed at the smell, and then opened the door widely.

As Monty opened the door, a smile began to spread across his face as his attractive 'beer wench' had found him. Monty invited her into the room and slapped his forehead. He suddenly realized that he didn't even know the girl's name. She giggled lightly at him and then told him that her name was Anne. Monty motioned for her to sit on the bed, and then offered her a glass of wine that was included with the room upon his and Ryan's arrival.

Ryan was severely apprehensive, but since Ellie had been so understanding, he told her all about his severe panic disorder. This included the horrid attacks that had seemed to affect him almost every day since he was beaten so badly. They stopped half the way across the Thames River and leaned upon the railing while Ryan told her of how he felt like he had been cursed by these awful feelings.

He didn't tell her of the ghostly encounters that he had experienced or the ostracization that they had caused him. Especially about the one on an ancient bridge that was outside the Tower of London. He thought that this may be too much information to instill on her. Plus, that had been twenty years ago, correct? To Ellie's credit, she held his hand even tighter at his description of these awful disorders, looked up at him intently, and with complete sympathy.

Ellie's face then became even more somber, and she asked, "Ryan, do you still have these dreadful feelings or these strong premonitions?"

Ryan swallowed hard and said back to her, "Yes...I actually am having one right now."

Ryan fidgeted with his hat by taking the floppy-brimmed chapeau off his head. He then awkwardly said, "I don't know why. I tend not to do many things when I get this strong gut feeling inside of me. It may be that I just like you too much. I also don't want you to think less of me...but...but...I feel like I should be incredibly on guard right now. I also feel like I should prepare both of us against...something."

Ellie looked rather scared and then said confidently, "I have every bit of faith in you."

Ryan smiled warily back at Ellie and said truthfully, "I don't have a wife or even a girlfriend anymore. I did have an important woman in my life, a very great woman, and I fucked the whole thing up. I was selfish, wounded, and I pushed her away in favor of making myself feel better. I did this with alcohol and fun times out with my buddies. I don't want to be 'that guy' anymore."

Ellie then grasped Ryan around the waist, held him tightly, and asked him, "Do you ever feel like you would do that to me?"

Ryan hugged her in return and stated, "That is absolutely the most fearful question I have of myself. All that I know is that I would never want to hurt you in any way, Ellie."

Ellie pushed her cheek onto Ryan's chest and said quietly, "That is good enough for me, just promise me to try your best. If you don't do that, then I can't guarantee what will happen between us."

Ryan then held her away from him while looking into her eyes, and he said happily, "Holding onto promises is exactly what I am best at. Bonds of sorrowful truths and unexpected secrets are very dear to me. They just have to be truthful and honest, that is. Don't ever use me as a weapon to spread nasty rumors. Also, if I am ever a total shit to you, I promise that you can never talk to me again. Which is a fate worse than death, in my humble opinion."

Ellie looked sad and then asked, "What if I am a total shit to you? What will you do then?"

Ryan pulled her closer again and then said, "Well, I guess that I would promise that I would try to forgive you. Trust is very important to me. If I grant you my irrevocably trusting heart, I just ask that you please be kind with it. It can be fragile at times."

Ellie looked up at him and said, "I bet your heart can be pretty unforgiving and stubborn when it wants to be."

Ryan simply said strongly, "I don't give it away very easily and I can guard it very well when I have to."

Ellie threw her head back and said, "Awwww, the truth." Ellie then smiled slyly and asked, "Since you are in such a truth telling mood. How old are you exactly?"

Ryan laughed at this and said proudly, "I'm 35, and I am guessing that you are much younger than that."

Ellie smiled up at him and teased, "Oh, you are much too old for me. I have got to leave you and go back to my room now. Good night."

Ryan pretended to be very hurt, and he said, "All right, you are now being a total shit. I suppose that I will have to forgive you."

Ellie twirled once and then remembered that she wasn't wearing any shoes. She stopped and tiptoed the rest of the way around and said, "I am 22, you nasty cradle robber. You are the lucky number of 13 years older than me. Does that bother you?"

Ryan blinked his eyes and then said, "The age difference would bother me normally. However, for some reason it doesn't with you. Maybe destiny doesn't believe in age differences?"

Ellie stood on her toes again and simply said, "I guess that the fates are too busy with other things, rather than be bothered by a mere baker's dozen full of years."

She then flung her arms over Ryan's shoulders, kissed him hungrily, and said, "I think that you are the perfect age for me. I can't stand the guys who are my age. It must have happened when I had to grow up too quickly, but they act like they are just horribly self-absorbed. They act like they should live their entitled lives inside an inclusive bubble. In my opinion, you can't live life that way or trust a person who thinks that way either. And another thing, they would rather hold everything or everybody else accountable instead of taking blame for their own stupid actions or decisions."

Ryan's eyes grew wide, and he said shockingly, "So, tell me how you 'really' feel.

Ellie blushed instinctively and then said, "Sorry, I tend to go off on rants every now and again. Especially when I tend to get pissed off. I guess it is better if you see one of my rants now, rather than later. I have a bad temper when it comes to stupidity, either mine or especially other people's actions."

Ryan smirked at Ellie and then said strongly, "Well, I still have a bad feeling, keep hold of your anger for the time being. We may need it."

Monty had led his guest, Anne, onto the balcony overlooking the Tower of London, and he opened the red wine that had been offered to him by the hotel. He poured each of them half a glass of red wine. They clinked glasses in an unspoken sign of cheers, and then drank heartily.

After Anne had taken a drink, her eyes opened wider, and she said, "This is good, much better than the swill I used to drink."

Monty's brow furrowed at her response, then he noticed her half of a red eye and offered to get her some ice from the machine. This offer from Monty was on the table, and he was preparing to go out the door. That was until Anne dipped her middle finger in the glass of wine, and then seductively licked the red juices from her longest appendage.

At that point, Monty grabbed her by the arm, spun her closer to him, and kissed her with every bit of wanting in his soul. One of her legs lifted off the ground, as she acted like she had not been kissed with such vigor in a very long time.

Anne closed her eyes when she kissed Monty with great passion. When she opened them, the eye that had been half red, had grown redder still, as only a quarter of it was now white. The rest was that bloody red color now.

Monty grabbed Anne around the bottom of the ass and lifted her easily off the floor. This caused her to be surprised by him and to let out a moan of pleasure. Soon, while still kissing Anne's mouth and neck, Monty clumsily carried her from the balcony, onto his own rumpled bed.

Monty then fell onto the bed backwards so Anne could straddle his body on top of him. He pushed himself upward on the bed with his elbows, so that he could lay his head upon the pillows.

Then, he lay there and waited for Anne to crawl on top and take control again. Anne slowly took off his shoes and socks and then lowered Monty's pants and black boxer briefs down to his ankles.

She then crawled onto the bed and over his erect cock. She sat directly on his hardened crotch, and then leaned forward and whispered directly in his ear, "I have a little surprise for you. Close your eyes."

Monty did what he was told to do and slammed his eyes shut, hoping that she would be completely naked when he opened them.

Monty then heard a female voice, but it didn't sound exactly like Anne's anymore. It said, "Open your eyes, lover!"

With this order, Monty's eyes flew open, and instead of Anne sitting on his hardened member, he was greeted by the homely vision of Carol sitting on top of him.

Monty started to cuss, but only got out the phrase, "What the Fu..." before all hell broke loose.

The hideous version of Carol leaned upward while arching her back backward. She was still wearing that horrible tan pantsuit that he had seen her in at the airport. Her one eye was glowing wildly with a reddish orange color.

She reached her hands above her head and pulled a dagger out from under the back of her loosened pantsuit. Monty saw her hand on the heel of the dagger and saw the glint of steel as it came down toward the right side of his head.

Monty instinctively moved his head leftward and felt searing pain hit him directly on the right ear. His right ear wasn't just pierced by the blade, but it was completely cut off. It was held on to his head by a single flap of skin. However, the damage had already been done, and Monty felt the warm blood start to flow out of the open hole on the side of his head.

Carol then tried gashing down at Monty again, aiming for his left eye socket. Monty quickly moved his head to the right, causing her to hit him on the left side of his forehead. The dagger glanced off his skull and buried itself in the pillow, causing foam to begin to rise out of the tear.

Monty yelled out loudly, "Stop… You, miserable gashing whore!"

Carol/Anne knew that Monty was being entirely too loud during the late hour. She couldn't tolerate his screams causing any undue attention. This caused her to grasp the handle of the dagger in between both of her hands, and thrust downward, with every bit of strength that she could muster.

Monty quit letting out any screams, and his body went completely stiff. Then he fell back into the mattress of the bed while his body became completely limp. Carol/Anne looked at the hilt of the dagger in her chubby little hands and saw that it had been driven into the hollow of Monty's throat. The entire blade of the dagger had gone completely through his throat and into the mattress underneath him.

The white foam inside the pillow was rising and sticking to the warm blood that was pouring not only from the hole where his ear had been, but also from the gash on his forehead and the death gash in his throat.

She lifted her one leg over his body and crawled gingerly off the bed. She stood there, looking over the body of Monty, as the image of Carol. She then shook her head vigorously, and by doing this, she turned back into the image of 'Anne, the Beer Wench.'

She gave one more glance at Monty's body and flicked the heel of the dagger with her finger. This made it vibrate back and forth in Monty's throat. An evil grin then appeared on her face, and she opened the door and looked both ways down the hallway. After seeing no one, she exited the room without even a casual look behind her.

Ryan was kissing Ellie passionately, when a glint of reflective white light flew across her field of vision. She pushed Ryan away from her, which confused Ryan and made him look at her in dismay. When she had pushed Ryan away from her, she had also pushed herself in a backward motion. By doing this, Ellie had saved her own and Ryan's lives that night.

Right in between them, the axe head of a gleaming weapon called a halberd came down hard upon the railing. Ryan was still in a state of confusion and didn't know what was happening when the sharpened blade came down in front of his nose. However, just by using his reflexes alone, he was able to grab the wooden handle of the medieval weapon that was lying upon the railing of the bridge.

A halberd was a weapon that soldiers used during the medieval ages. It was a long wooden pole that had a metal spear point on the end of it. There was also a sharpened axe head that extended outward, directly below the spear point. A person could use it to repel their enemies either by using a sharpened metal spear or by swinging of the axe head.

A hand suddenly grabbed at the collar of Ellie's shirt, and she was yanked backward. She fell directly onto her backside, making a muted thudding sound. This also caused her to make an "Ooophing" sound as the air was expelled from her lungs.

She sprawled out onto the bridge, caught her breath quickly, and then she began to shuffle herself backwards while using her hands and her naked feet. A hardened metal ball that had several sharpened spikes coming out of it, crashed down at the floorboards directly between her legs.

This weapon was called a mace, and it had a wooden handle that was attached to several links of chain. At the end of the chain, was the deadly ball that almost struck Ellie in the head.

The halberd's wooden pole that Ryan was holding onto pulled him backward and to the right. When Ryan was pulled in that direction, the metal axe head came back with his motion and cut him shallowly across the right side of his stomach. Luckily, the cut was rather superficial, but it was deep enough to cause blood to start running into the waistband of his tan shorts.

Even though Ryan was cut, he barely seemed to notice any pain. The backward motion and jerking sensation of holding the pole also threw his right elbow backwards. With a large amount of momentum, he swung forward with his fist, as mightily as he could deliver a blow. Ryan felt the hard strike of his fist against the nose of his unwitting assailant.

He then looked in the direction of Ellie and saw her flailing backwards as a medieval mace was almost driven into her skull, but instead impacted the floor of the bridge instead. At the sight of this, Ryan then jumped forward and saw the dirty looking man trying to pull the mace free from being embedded in the wood walkway of the bridge.

He punched the man directly in the throat, making his hands rise upward. Ryan only curled his fist half-way while holding his knuckles extended. When he hit him, it was as if the man was not able to draw in any air, swallow, or even yell out in distress.

The man slowly swayed on his feet, and then he fell onto his knees, while still holding onto his throat. His body then fell forward onto the protruding spikes of the mace. His face disappeared and blew outward onto Ellie's lap and lower stomach. Ellie screamed and could feel the warm liquid dribbling down her legs. At this point, she began trying to wipe her stomach and thighs.

When her breathing slowed and she became composed again, she noticed that two of the spikes had gone into the man's eyes. One spike had protruded into the man's nose and pushed the cartilage back into his face. She tried to scream again, but only a weeping sound seemed to escape her lips.

Ryan still held the halberd's wooden handle with his left hand. He felt the slivers of wood enter his palm as he pushed his hand up the protruding handle. He then used his other hand and put it directly beneath the axe head. He then lunged with the metal part of the spear directly toward the larger attacker that was coming after him.

This made the axe blade swing at a downward angle from the upper right-hand side of Ryan's face and slice left. The whole move would have looked graceful to any bystander who happened to witness it, and luckily for Ryan, it was also very lethal.

The axe head had entered the left side of the larger man's throat, and it sliced deeply downwards toward the right nipple on the man's chest. The man fell to the walking path of the old bridge while making a rather sickening sloshing sound. With pain in his eyes, the injured man looked up at Ryan.

Laying mortally wounded in front of Ryan was his old friend from 20 years ago, Mel, the colorful Beefeater.

Mel opened his mouth as if he wanted to say something to Ryan, but only blood poured out from between his teeth. Ryan then carefully looked at the carnage of Mel's body lying on the ground before him, and he couldn't believe that he had sliced open and killed his old friend.

Ryan then fell downward onto his knees, bowed his head, and took off his floppy cowboy hat. He then brushed back his sweat-filled hair and let out a huge sigh of exasperation and confusion.

He suddenly turned toward Ellie's dirty assailant, who had impaled himself on his own sharpened mace. He looked over at Ellie's face, seeing the blood on the mace and the splashes of blood on the front of her blouse. At that point, Ryan had to see if she was injured and scrambled to her on his knees.

Ryan searched her for any wounds and then asked if she had been hit or if she was okay. When she gave him the news that she was alright, he then felt the pains extruding from the cuts on his stomach and rolled onto his back.

Ellie reached out for him, kissed him sharply, and cried sobbing tears over his own face. Then she said with a small amount of relaxation in her voice, "Thank god, for your apprehensive and untrusting gut."

Ryan looked up at her and stated sourly, "Then why hasn't my stomach stopped telling me that something is horribly wrong and that we are still in danger?"

Ryan's eyes suddenly flew wide open, and he exclaimed, "Monty!"

Ellie helped Ryan get to his feet, and then he looked down at the two men that had attacked them. He told her that he did not know the one man who had come after her, but the other man was an old friend of his-from twenty years ago, to be exact. Also, Mel looked exactly as he had done twenty years earlier, and he hadn't aged at all.

Ryan said out of exasperation that Mel had to be in his mid-70s by now, but he looks like he did back in 1985. Ryan then whispered to himself, "Impossible!"

On the way to the hotel, Ryan then told Ellie the story about Mel and about his other visions around the Tower of London. He also told her how Mel had been his only friend during that time period in 1985.

"How could this be possible," Ryan cried out. Then he pointed to the hotel, where they were limping toward as quickly as they possibly could, and he said lowly, "Hang in there, buddy."

While they were on their way to the hotel, Ryan also told Ellie about running into the 'Beer Wench' in the hotel lobby. If he was wrong, they ran into the possibility that Monty may be very 'busy' when they got there. This caused them to laugh nervously when Ryan opened the hotel room door.

However, the laughter ended very abruptly as soon as the door to the room swung open. Ryan rushed to the bed and the lifeless form of his best friend upon it. This sight made him fall onto his knees beside the bed. Ryan yelled out angrily, "Oh, No... No!... No!"

This was all that Ryan would say, as his head was lowered on the bedspread next to his best friend. Ellie came forward and placed her hand on Ryan's quaking shoulder and whispered, "I am so sorry."

When she did this, Ryan started saying loudly, "No, I'm Sorry...I'm Sorry...I'm Sorry...I am the one who is Sorry. I got you all involved in this. This is all my fault."

Then Ryan stopped talking suddenly, put his head down again, and started weeping quietly. Ellie went over to the telephone and called the main desk, in order to have them send police officers and an ambulance.

When Ellie finished her call, she walked over to Ryan and knelt beside him. She then calmingly put her arm around Ryan's shoulder and stayed with him until the police knocked on his door. This caused Ryan to jump as if he were startled, and then he never even looked up or moved an inch.

"Your mind tricked you to feel the pain
Of someone close to you leaving the game, of life…
So here it is, another chance
Wide awake you face the day
Your dream is over…
Or has it just begun?"
(Queensryche)

Chapter Seventeen

"Many people die at twenty-five years old and aren't buried until they are seventy-five." (Benjamin Franklin)

The first police officer that had entered the room, closed Monty's eyelids and pried Ryan's hand from his friend's own appendage. Ellie then led Ryan out of the open balcony door, where they sat quietly in the night air. The ambulance crew tried to put a blanket over Ryan's shoulders, as well as another one around Ellie's. However, Ryan had drawn her so close to him, and was holding her so tightly that the paramedic had to finally drape a single blanket over both of their shoulders.

A 'Bobby', as police officers are called in London, came out onto the balcony and started to ask for their statements. Ryan and Ellie told him of the tale of the waitress from the Medieval Experience and about how she had gone up to the room earlier. Ryan and Ellie also had to tell him about their own connection to Monty and about their reasons for being in Britain.

The 'bobby' then asked in a thick British accent to Ryan and Ellie, "Is this all that you have to tell me, then?"

Ryan looked dourly at Ellie and then said, with a large bit of depredation in his voice, "You will also find two bodies on the walking path of Tower Bridge."

The officer then clicked his pen open again and started new notes. He asked them extremely seriously, "Now then, how did these bodies end up there?"

The two Americans told him what they honestly knew about the attack on the bridge. However, they also left out a huge amount of the incredibly unbelievable details of the story, just to make themselves sound sane.

The officer then spoke into a microphone attached to his shirt collar. The police officers that were now standing over two dark shapes on the bridge were now pointing in their direction.

The officer soon came over to Ryan and Ellie and asked, "Was Monty the only one that was meant to be attacked tonight, or were they after the two of you as well?"

Ryan hadn't thought of that scenario before and started to speak more rapidly. He then stopped talking abruptly, and his eyes rolled back into their sockets. Suddenly, he blacked out and slid off the chair and onto the balcony floor, causing Ellie to scream out his name loudly.

In another time and place, Ryan sat up and looked around at where he was at. All that he could tell was that he was alone and surrounded by a thick fog. Ryan could barely see his hand in front of his face as the very air seemed to push down upon him.

He turned his head and cocked it as he heard different sounds coming in his direction. He seemed to hear a metallic tinging sound, followed by hollow, clopping sounds. 'Ting, clop, clop, clop...Ting, clop, clop, clop.' The sound was getting louder now: 'Ting, clop, clop, clop...Ting, clop, clop, clop.' Finally, the sound was almost right on top of Ryan. He could not see what it was, but he could feel something's presence. Louder now: 'Ting, clop, clop, clop...Ting, clop, clop, clop'.

Ryan started to panic, as the thought of him being sightless was almost overwhelming, and he hated this feeling. This was bothering him even more than the fear he felt when he was at a high altitude.

Slowly, out of the fog, came the welcoming vision of James the Knight. He looked very forlorn as he walked toward Ryan. James's hair was wet, and it clung to his face in lumps as it hung down on his head because of the damp weather.

James was making the strange noises because he was leading a beautiful bay pony. The horse's hooves made a hollow sound on the old cobblestone streets, and the clanging noise was one that his armor and spurs made while he was taking a step on these hardened roads.

Ryan smiled with relief when he saw James come out of the fog, and then, as if remembering Monty again, he fell back to his knees and began to openly cry. James kneeled next to Ryan, put his hand on his shoulder, and let the tears flow out of him.

Ryan finally stopped weeping when the horse began nibbling at his ear, which made Ryan sniffle hard and push his nose away from him. The horse leaned his long nose against Ryan's head, and he petted him softly as he lowly nickered at the smell of him. He seemed to know that Ryan needed to pet his nose right at that moment... He was a very intuitive horse.

Ryan looked up at James and simply asked, "Why?"

James thought about what he was going to say, as he ran a hand through his brown, scruffy beard. Finally, he knowingly said, "Tomorrow night. The main battle will begin tomorrow night at midnight. We will be arriving for you and your lady friend, at 11:00 p.m. Be ready for a battle".

James the knight then looked down at Ryan with a furrowed brow, and continued saying, "As for your question, the simple answer is that our enemies are afraid. They are trying to take you and your lady out of the battle before it even begins. They missed their opportunity to do this to you… and thank God for that. Unfortunately, they did get at your friend, and he will be sorely missed."

James looked intense again and then said, "However, you will need to be especially hardened, so be ready for a tremendous battle. Look for a boat beneath Tower Bridge tomorrow night; we will be picking you and your lady up by way of the river."

James and his horse started to disappear, and Ryan rubbed his eyes with his wrists in frustration. Ryan was unfortunately reaching his boiling point and was feeling that he might be going insane again.

He yelled out with exasperation in his voice, "Just tell me what the fuck is going on, James!... Please...I am tired of all this secret bullshit. Please just tell me what you want from me."

Ryan looked up at the vanishing form of James, who looked back at him pensively, and he tiredly said, with extreme importance in his voice, "11:00 p.m. tomorrow. The battle starts at midnight. You will be given more understanding, and all your questions will be answered then. Don't forget or be late."

The knight then disappeared, and Ryan woke up on the balcony floor. A paramedic was just then trying to clear his airway. Ryan tried to let out his disagreement at the man trying to claw at his open mouth, but the sound only came out as an "Unghh" noise. He pushed the young man away with all the strength that he could muster.

He then heard the muffled sounds of Ellie crying and the paramedic saying, "I think that he just had a seizure, and we will be bringing him in for further tests."

Ryan suddenly sat up, took a deep breath, and said, "The hell you will. I am not going to any damn hospital. I just found my best friend stabbed to death in this room. It was all just too much for me, and I blacked out for a little while."

Ellie's face was full of fear, and she started to protest. However, Ryan looked over at her seriously and said, "I will be fine, I just need to get the hell out of this room, do some grieving, and get comforted by my girlfriend."

Ryan looked again at Ellie with a look of importance on his face, and he said, "Just the two of us! We need to be alone right now and get some sleep. Please just leave us to grieve by ourselves. We promise that we won't leave town."

The police officers and the paramedics tried to overpower Ryan's decision and force him to come with them. He and Ellie had to escort and almost push them out of the door. They were not very nice in dealing with the men, but Ryan had lost all patience at this point.

When they were alone, Ellie grabbed Ryan's arm and asked, "Where did you go?"

Ryan almost blew off her question, and the first thing that he asked Ellie while he began quickly packing his belongings was whether they could move to her room for the night.

Ellie came back with, "Of course, my room is on the 3rd floor, and we can stay there, but…talk to me first." Ellie fumbled with the words and then asked again, "Ryan, did the knight visit you again?"

Ryan only nodded "yes" and then looked at Monty's clothes, which covered the floor. He almost started crying again and said lowly, "What do we do with his...his...things?"

Ellie came over to him, kissed him gingerly, and gently said, "We are going to call the front desk and have them take all his things to my room upstairs. Then we are going to have a large glass of whiskey, followed by you telling me what the fuck is going on. Finally, you tell me what we need to do next."

Ryan looked at her and said, "Of course you are right. You are going to have to have the steady mind tonight. Mine is just going in every direction at a huge amount of speed right now. That is what happens while I am in the middle of having a panic attack, and I am having one hell of a whopper right now."

Ellie only said, "Shh," softly and stroked Ryan's hair until his hands quit shaking. Then she said quietly, "Step one, we get out of this room and go to mine, take my hand and follow me."

Ryan shook his head in a "yes" manner again, gripped her hand tightly, and followed her to the sink.

The last thing that Ryan grabbed from the room was the bottle of Scotch whiskey that Monty had wanted when they first checked in. Before they left, Ellie grabbed two plastic glasses from the bathroom and poured each of them a full glass.

Ryan immediately took a large swallow of the potent liquor and said, "I have never had such a smooth drink out of a plastic cup… not since my high school days, when Monty and I would travel to a party up in the mountains of Montana. It is a wonder that we didn't get into a wreck driving on those horrible gravel roads."

Ryan then started to shake again and sorrowfully continued to say, "We did this just to sit by a cool creek in the mountains that had a large keg of beer sitting in it to keep it cold. Not to mention a blazing campfire that kept us warm. Of course, we weren't alone in doing this; we had these parties all the time, and we called them keggers. Fuck, we never would have thought that anything like this would be going on back then."

Ryan held up his glass as if he were silently toasting Monty. He then took another rather large swallow, which made him grab the bottle and refill his glass.

Ellie looked annoyed and then said, "Okay, Ryan, we really don't have time for a trip down memory lane. What did the knight tell you?"

Ryan then stated, "His name is James, and he looks like an honest to God knight from the medieval ages. This last time that he visited me, he was walking with his horse. He told me why Monty was killed. He also told me when he would be coming to see us next and where to go."

Ellie stood up anxiously and then said, "Well? He needs us when, and why?"

Ryan had her sit back down on the bed next to him, and then he told her, "James said that they killed Monty and tried to kill us, because we have them scared. They tried to strike first and take us out. And before you ask, I don't know who 'they' are. James didn't tell me. However, what he did tell me is that the final battle is tomorrow night at midnight, and he said that he and some other people would pick us up underneath the bridge at 11:00 p.m. He also said that we would leave for the battle by boat."

Ryan then took another drink and finished saying, "The last thing he didn't need to tell me, was that we had better prepare well for tomorrow night's battle. After what happened to Monty tonight and what almost happened to us, I don't have to tell you that our lives are counting on us being as well prepared as possible."

Ellie began biting at her fingernails, and then she said absent-mindedly, "I don't think that it is just our lives that we have got to be worried about. I believe that we will have to be prepared for anything out there tomorrow night. I also think that many lives are now our responsibility."

Ryan pulled her closer, kissed her, and then said, "Tomorrow is going to come very shortly, and I would love to stay with you and not sleep any given night. However, I think that we had better just get some rest and be vigilant tonight, if we can. The whiskey is helping, and it will help us sleep, but I am afraid of what will show up when I close my eyes."

Ellie kissed his eyelids and said, "Don't worry, we will be holding onto each other tonight. I am not going anywhere, and we will watch out for one another."

Ellie took a deep breath, and then continued to say lowly, "But... I may not feel safe all alone in the shower tomorrow morning."

Ryan laid back on her bed and cradled Ellie in his arms. She put her head on his upper chest, and then he said to her, "Well, that will be a bridge to cross when we get to it. I am so glad that you are with me tonight, though. Thank you for not giving me that 'all alone' feeling that I have gotten in the past."

Ellie yawned and simply said, "I am, too."

When Ryan awoke the next morning, uncertainty arose within him as he was the only one laying in the bed. At first, he didn't know where he was, and he yelled out Monty's name. This caused Ellie to look at him from around the main door as if he had startled her.

She cautiously carried two cups of coffee to the bed and handed one of them to Ryan, while saying, "Here you go... I don't know if you want any coffee, but I sure need it."

Ryan took a sip of coffee and then said, "The English don't know shit about making coffee. They drink way too much tea in this country. I am sorry Ellie, but I think that I am going to have to throw away their poor excuse for coffee."

Ellie cringed and then asked, "Is it that bad?"

Ryan looked up at her sleepily, and said jokingly, "Sorry, but that tasted like I was chewing on a day-old coffee filter. Don't worry, I will take you out for some real coffee when this is over. What time is it?"

Ellie looked at the silver watch that she was wearing and said, "A little after 9:00 a.m."

Ryan screwed up his face and said, "That gives us about 14 hours in which to get ourselves ready. First off though, I need a shower, and then I need to find some real caffeine.

Ellie said, "You can buy us brunch since you don't like the coffee that I brought you."

Ryan sat up on the side of the bed and said, "I can do that. I promise that I will try to get used to the coffee that you get for me from now on. That is if we make it through tonight."

Ellie's voice sounded kind of shaky when she thought of this, and Ryan noticed how nervous and anxious she was and said gently, "Don't worry Ellie, I can't tell you what will happen tonight, but I am glad to be here with you, now."

Ellie came over, bent down, and kissed him softly. She then said, "But I just found you. I don't want to lose you right after you came into my life."

To which Ryan replied, "I'm not planning on going anywhere." Ryan arose in order to get into the shower, and then he stopped and said to her, "I never considered myself to be much of a prize, I guess."

Ellie smiled and then said quietly, "I think that you are the cutest Kewpie doll that I could ever win."

Ryan laughed a little and said to her playfully, "A Kewpie doll? You happen to be looking at a big ol' prize buck, darlin'. That is where the saying buck naked should have come from, don't you know? Do you want to take a shower with a trophy buck deer?"

Ellie threw a towel at him, and then she giggled and followed him into the bathroom.

The sun was shining through the windows of The Medieval Experience that morning. The restaurant was not yet open to the public, and there were no employees inside to bother the King of England. He sat at the head of a table drinking a sour, warm black ale, and he was scratching at the hairs on his scraggly neck.

This king was short, skinny, and extremely pale. That morning, he had a very stern and disturbing look on his face. He also had long, brown, stringy hair that hung down under his crown and over his pointy ears. The sun rose further in the sky, and it shone in through the window and lit up one of the king's shoulders.

One shoulder was raised more than the other one, to give him the appearance of having a deformed hump on his back. In between drinks of the sour ale, he wrung his hands together nervously and looked pensively at the person in the corner of the room.

He then finally said to the only other person in the room, "Come here and sit down, my darling. You are making me quite nervous."

Queen Anne Boleyn walked out of the shadows and slowly over to him, fell onto her knees, and kissed the top of his hand. She then raised her head to the king and said reverently, "You don't seem worried at all, my king."

She had a small white bandage covering her eye now, and she looked up at him with one questioning, wide, dark eye. Richard looked down at Anne, and then gently said, "Why should I be? I fear them not. Plus, I have a secret weapon."

Anne looked at him while being confused and asked him, "I know not of what you are speaking of? What secret weapon do you speak of?"

He stroked her cheek softly and then tore the bandage from her eye. He sneered at her and said, "You, my darling. You are my secret weapon. Plus, I have a very powerful magi, from the old religions on my side. I cannot be defeated."

Her eye was completely crimson red and was bulging out now with a yellowish pus. The king then pushed her away from him and said, "Get me more to drink. This time, I think that I will have some wine. This ale tastes like goat piss!"

Ryan and Ellie had found an out of the way cafe in order to eat breakfast and speak quietly at a table that they had found in the corner.

Ellie tried to say with a mouthful of scones, "I absolutely love these scones with honey butter, and the bangers and mash that I had this morning were quite good. I have always been taught that English food is not very good, but I kind of like it."

Ryan had eaten one small scone and was picking at his own bangers as if he couldn't eat, and seemed to be thinking very seriously.

Then he looked at her and said, "Bangers are just large links of sausage, you know. Speaking of bangers, where do you think that we could get some guns in a city where they are banned?"

Ellie made a disapproving noise and then told Ryan, "I have got to tell you, I don't like guns very well. I did not grow up around them, and I have never even touched one, nor do I want to."

Ryan then shook his head and stated, "Well, I grew up around guns. I went to hunter's safety, where I learned how to handle them correctly, when I was 13 years old. All through high school, I had a .223 rifle and a Remington

12-gauge shotgun in my gun rack. Let alone the smaller .38 pistol that I had hidden underneath my seat. A person could never live that way now. However, I believe that it all depends on how guns are used."

Ryan shuffled in his chair and then continued by saying, "This was how I was brought up and how I was trained to use them safely. Would you believe that my high school science teacher was my gun safety instructor. I took his daughter to my high school prom. If a person is in their right mind and not misusing them, they can be incredibly useful tools of protection or for providing food."

Ryan finished his speech by saying, "I would much rather have a gun and not need it, than need a gun and not have one handy. However, without ever touching a gun and having already made up your mind on their uses, you may have to be given a quick lesson on them."

Ellie looked concerned and said back, "What if I don't want to learn how to use them? Please respect how I feel. I don't want to have to use a gun. I believe that we are having our first difference of opinion, and I must put my foot down on this subject."

Ryan looked a little disappointed and then said, "Okay, I won't push anything on you, and I respect your opinion. We are going to have to find a sword or a spear that you can use as a weapon instead. If you don't feel right about using a gun, that is just fine. We each come from different backgrounds. Maybe we can find you a crossbow? Will you use something to protect yourself and that could even hurt other people, like a crossbow?"

Ellie thought about this, and then a smile spread across her face, and she said, "Yes, I think that I could use a knife or a crossbow, but nothing like a gun."

Ryan then looked apprehensive but pleased and said, "Now then, where do we find all of these things?" Ryan stood up, placed money on the table, and said, "Come on, let's go and find someone to help us?"

Ryan and Ellie walked out onto the curb, and Ryan hailed a taxi by whistling loudly at a passing vehicle. After entering the taller car, the cab driver said in a crisp and proper English accent, "Where can I take you and the pretty lady today, sir?"

Ryan then leaned forward in the rear seat and asked quietly, "Do you have any British army surplus stores in London where we might get some... uh...prohibited items?"

The cab driver's name was Basil, and his curt British accent seemed to slip into a more street-used way of speaking. He was sitting with a proper stance in his spine, and when Ryan asked this question, he relaxed his shoulders and slouched as he turned to them.

He then nosily asked, "Aww, you are Americans. What kind of prohibited items are we talking about? Drugs?... prostitutes?... weapons?"

Ryan looked at him with a startled look at that word, and the driver shook his head up and down and said, "I see... weapons. Do you have money? You will need a large amount of cash in order to make this happen."

Ryan then said, "Stop by this bank up here, and I will get all the cash that I can get my hands on."

Ryan entered the bank, leaving Ellie to sit in the taxi outside, and then exited the building a short time later. He gave Basil two fifty-pound bills and said, "Is this enough for your help... and your silence?"

Basil smiled widely and then said, in a rather Cockney accent, "This is a start...I know of a place where we can go, but I hope that you have a huge amount more of this money. You will need it where we are going."

Ryan sat back in silence, even at the prodding of Ellie, who was asking him about how much money he had gotten. He simply looked at her and said quietly, "Not now, and not here."

Basil had driven the two Americans for approximately one hour until they were in the vividly green countryside outside the city limits of London. He pulled up to a smaller house that looked rather scrubby and had chipped white paint on the outside of it.

However, in all actuality, the house was quite comfortable on the inside, with a large kitchen that had newer appliances, as well as a very cozy living room with a 65-inch big screen TV in it.

There were other video displays showing every location of the yard and inside the barn, as well as any approaching vehicles. The barn also had worn, chipped paint on the outside of it, but it housed no livestock of any kind, and had loose hay lying all along the earthen floor.

The black taxi, or 'Lorry,' as this vehicle is called in England, pulled up in front of the house.

Basil looked back over his shoulder and said warningly, "Please exit the vehicle with your hands raised and the money sticking out from one of your fists. I will wait for you here."

Ellie asked where they were, but Basil only ignored her and nodded at Ryan.

Ryan and Ellie stepped out of the vehicle and were swarmed quickly by two armed men, who gave each of them a quick pat-down. They then nodded up at a video camera that was on the eve of the house.

When this was done, a woman who had a slight limp and was walking with a silver cane exited the house and walked up to them.

She had a rather stout body and had strikingly red-colored hair, grayish-green eyes, and a strong, well-formed chin. She was smoking a skinny cigarette that had been placed in a gold holder on one end.

She then smiled with shockingly white teeth, took the cigarette out of her mouth, and said with a strong Irish accent, "And wha can I 'elp ya wit today?"

Ryan tried to stand even taller, pushed out his chest, and then said back to her, "We need some guns, ammunition, and maybe some sharp swords, and a dagger or two. Oh, yeah! We also have got to buy a crossbow with a quiver and bolts."

The red-haired woman dropped her cigarette on the ground and put the flame out with the heel of her black steel-toed boot.

"Follow me. We will do our business en de barn." She said, commanding them all.

She turned on her heel and began to lead them, while limping on the silver cane, to the door of the shabby looking barn.

Then the red-haired woman asked of Ryan, "Dat es quite a strange assortment o' weapons dat ye want ta ave. How much money did ya bring with ya?"

He opened his hand and then stated truthfully, "$9,000 pounds… That is all that I can get right now."

Ellie looked at Ryan in amazement, and he gave her a warning look and finished asking, "What can I get?"

The red-haired woman then looked Ryan up and down and said, "Call me Auntie… just Auntie."

She lit up another skinny cigarette, and then she continued saying, "I will be kindly to ya, as long as ya don't work fer the police… dat is."

Ryan shook his head vigorously, and then she continued saying quickly, "Fer 8,000 pounds, I will sell you a 9 mm Beretta handgun and a 12-gauge shotgun wit plenty of ammunition fer both. I will also sell ya two older iron swords, and a couple o' scabbards fer both. Ye will also get 2 steel daggers, as well as an ol' English longbow, with a quiver and two dozen arrows. Dat will leave ya with 1000 pounds left over…Will dat do?"

Ryan smiled and then said firmly, "We need a shorter crossbow with at least two dozen bolts, instead of a longbow and arrows."

Auntie took another drag off her cigarette and then asked, "Are ya planning on going ta war during da dark ages? What da fuck ya need all of dis' fer?"

Ryan looked her in the eye and then said, "My best friend was murdered by some real bastards last night, and I want them to pay...well...in a very nasty way. It is going to take a lot of firepower to do this. The guns are for me, and the crossbow is for her. She won't be able to use an English longbow with any speed or accuracy. She needs something short, something easier to use and move around with. I just want to be ready for anything."

She glanced at Ellie, and then she stated, "Righto… done. I tink that I ave a crossbow around ere somewhere. We don't get many questions about selling any crossbows."

Ellie then asked about 'Auntie's Cane' and how she had hurt herself. 'Auntie' guffawed and said, "I ave a bad case o' da gout, and I see me cane as I see one o' me weapons. I would rather not need it and have it wit me..."

Then Ellie finished the line for her by saying, "Than needing it and not having it with you. I have heard this saying before."

Auntie looked at Ryan and then said, "I like er, she es a quick study and full o' strong piss n' vinegar... I will bet that she will end da day enjoying the feel of a weapon in er hand… but only if she needs it n' knows how ta use et properly."

With this statement, 'Auntie' laughed heartily, until it broke off into a coughing fit.

She then left Ryan with 1,000 pounds in his hand and took the other 8,000 from him. She then said, as an order to the men working for her, "Get da goods, men!"

Armed men then swept dirt away from the main door and lifted openings in the floor that entered a vaulted room. Below the barn, there were an incredible number of weapons being stored.

As promised, a 9mm pistol was offered and a shotgun was given to Ryan. Two swords that had been sheathed in scabbards were shoved into each of their hands, along with two daggers apiece. Ellie was given her crossbow and bolts last, as they had to find an older one in the corner for her to use.

'Auntie' then shook Ryan's hand and said, "If we ave any uninvited visitors come looking fer us after dis unwanted meeting... we will hunt ya down and kill ya...Is ya okay with dat deal?"

Ryan gave her a stone-faced expression and then simply stated, "Yes."

Auntie then lit up another cigarette and asked, "Do ya need anyting else from us? Or will a good luck be good enough fer ya?"

Ryan had a pistol in his waistband, a sword hanging from his belt, and a shotgun hanging over his shoulder. Along with this weaponry, he also had his arms full of other weapons and ammunition.

This made him look at her and ask for one more thing, "Do you, by chance, have a couple of duffel bags? Carrying these around, could look rather...obvious."

They were given two black duffel bags, and then Ryan and Ellie loaded everything into the taxi. When they were all loaded, they asked for the driver to take them back to the hotel.

Ellie leaned closer and then asked in a whisper, "Ryan, where did you get that much money so quickly?"

Ryan smiled at her solemnly and answered by saying, "I maxed out Monty's credit cards at the bank by pretending that I was him. I used his ID for the withdrawal. We looked a bit different, but we had the same build. I just said that I was hungover when they took my photo back in the States. If we live through this, I will have to owe his estate the money, but we need it terribly right now. I thought that he would maybe understand that."

Ellie then added, "Thank God that he had decent credit. Otherwise, we would have been seriously fucked."

Ryan gave Basil another 50-pound note upon leaving the cab and told him that they *thanked him and that he had really saved their asses.*

Basil's last words were said with utter seriousness, and with his polite British accent, "You may not know of these organizations very much in America, but there are still offshoots of the IRA here. Even today, they are not someone that you want to fuck over. They will also hold me and my family accountable if you screw them over. Please be thinking about how this doesn't just affect you and don't be stupid. Good luck to you, both."

Ryan felt the weight of the duffel bags, and he carried them directly through the lobby with barely a second glance from anyone. A bellhop offered to carry Ryan's bag, but he gently turned him down and climbed aboard the elevator.

Upon entering the room, Ryan called the front desk and ordered a wake-up call at 7:30 p.m. They would have to grab something to eat and then come back to the room for final preparations before nightfall. Ryan and Ellie then laid down on the bed, as they both needed some more rest before their final confrontation with the knights of the past.

After receiving the phone call that woke them up, Ryan and Ellie went down to the restaurant at around 8:00 p.m. Ryan chose another big medium-rare steak, a baked potato with sour cream and bacon, and some nice spears of artichoke. He requested that his vegetables be fried in the delicious honey butter. Ellie ordered a large plate of shrimp Alfredo, and an appetizer of fried calamari, and steamed clams. Seafood would be her choice of delicacy that evening.

They both knew that tonight might be their last time on this earth, and they weren't going to be worried about cholesterol when ordering this meal.

They ordered a bottle of white wine that was offered to them to go with their meals. When the waiter left the table, Ellie looked at Ryan lovingly and said, "If tonight is our last night on earth, I say that we go out eating like royalty."

Ryan nodded his head and then asked her if they could share each other's meals. She looked at him jokingly, and said, "Well, it is only fair, you are sharing a possible gruesome death with me... and I get to share my seafood with you. That sounds fair."

She then winked at Ryan and said, while laughing, "You are such a man."

"When you've been fighting for it all your life
You've been struggling to make things right
That's how a superhero learns to fly
Every day, every hour, turn the pain into power!"
(The Script)

Chapter Eighteen

"Never interrupt your enemy when he is making a mistake." (Napoleon Bonaparte)

After dinner, Ryan and Ellie went back to the room and got dressed for the upcoming battle. Ryan wore blue jeans, a black T-shirt advertising a Canadian rock band underneath, and a red flannel shirt buttoned up over the top. He thought about buying some protective, steel toed work boots, but decided to go with the comfort and speed of his high-top tennis shoes.

Ellie had not packed for a hardened battle, and she wore black leggings, a loose-fitting skirt over them, and a black sleeveless top. She was hoping that she would be camouflaged in the dark and virtually unseen. Ryan then reached into Monty's bag and pulled out a denim jacket that hung off Ellie, but it did offer her a small amount of tough exterior protection.

Ellie wrinkled her nose at this addition to her wardrobe. Not because of the size of the denim jacket, or that it had belonged to Monty, but because Monty had been a smoker and this jacket smelled like old cigarette smoke. Ellie tried to wear this coat but decided to leave it in the room. She just could not handle the constant smell of the jacket, even though it offered her advanced protection.

Ryan's final act was to look at the digital clock, which said it was 10:36 p.m. He looked again inside the duffel bags full of weapons. He then lifted it and asked seriously, "Are you ready for this?"

When Ellie gave him an approving nod, he simply said, "Let's go!"

At exactly 11:00 p.m., Ryan led Ellie down to the water's edge under the bridge. They listened intently, but only heard the sound made by the river rushing by them. A thick fog was also beginning to grow across London, and suddenly they could hear a sloshing sound. They could not see anything yet, as the boat was concealed by the thickening fog coming off the river itself.

A boat then rowed toward them out of the fog, and there were three men sitting aboard it. In the back portion of the boat, sat a dark, hooded fellow who was twirling the hilt of a sword between his hands. The sharpened tip of the sword spun along the bottom of the wooden boat, making scratch marks streak across it.

The medium-sized boat's rower sat in front of this man. He was dressed in a full suit of armor, except he was missing his helmet, which allowed Ryan and Ellie to see the long grayish-brown hair hanging down his head. He also had a strong jawline with thin-set, brown eyes, and a full beard that stood out on his grizzled looking face.

At the head of the boat, stood James, the younger knight. One foot was raised on the bow seat, and the other foot was placed on the bottom of the boat. He threw Ryan a rope to have him pull them in, and then Ryan tied the boat off onto a strut of the bridge. If he did not do this, the boat would float away down river with the fast-moving current.

The knight then looked up at Ryan and said, "You are here. Not all of us thought that you would show up… but I always believed that you would be here. It is good to see both of you."

Ryan bluntly said back to James, "Well, I couldn't have you haunting me for the rest of my cowardly life, could I?"

James smiled slyly, and then asked if he could meet the young woman. Ryan spun on his heels and held out his hand for Ellie to join him.

She moved to his side, and Ryan said proudly, "James… this is Ellie. She will be the crossbow carrying warrioress this evening."

James smiled at her and said, after kissing her hand, "Yes, I know."

Ellie had a look go over her face that said that she was completely confused and perplexed. She then asked him, "How could you possibly know who I am?"

James simply smiled back at her, ignored her question, and said, "All of your questions will be answered later tonight. Right now, we must be going."

Ellie put her foot down and then said loudly, "No! I will not move any further unless you tell us what is going on here, and who these other men are?"

James blushed a little and then said, "Of course… the older knight behind me who is rowing the boat is named Sir William Tyrrell. In the back, is a man quite famous throughout history. Perhaps you have heard of him…"

The man suddenly stood and pushed back his hood, showing a quite handsome face and brown hair that was cut short. He then covered up his head with a blue wide brimmed hat that was curled up on one edge. He looked at them with steely dark eyes that seemed to dance in his skull. He also had a well-trimmed beard that was formed downward into an inverse triangle upon his chin.

Ellie pointed at him and said loudly, "I know him; that is Sir Walter Raleigh, but how could he be here?"

James the Knight then said seriously, "How can any of us be standing in front of you? This truly is Sir Walter Raleigh, and he fights on our side tonight. Magic started many years ago in this country, long before any organized religions. They came into being well back in the annals of time, when it was controlled by the Pagan King's wizards and witches."

James looked at both Ryan and Ellie to make sure that they understood, and then he continued what he was saying. "There is a lot of magic in the air...again...tonight. To tell you the truth, there have always been many centuries of blessed good knights and unjust, evil knights in this world. They have all been battling for control of the land and people's beliefs. Tonight's battle is a way of sorting out the two. History will bleed tonight."

James then stopped and shuffled his feet in impatience. He then continued speaking when Ellie didn't immediately crawl into the boat. "You and Sir Ryan are very much needed tonight; I will promise you that… also, all your questions will be answered tonight, as well. I also promise you that, dear lady. Lest, we do have to go *now*. Otherwise, there won't be a later."

Ellie's brow furrowed, and she asked quietly, "Where are we going?"

James the Knight let his arm protrude outward sideways in frustration, and he stated reverently, "To the Tower of London, young lady."

Ellie bit at her lower lip, stepped into the boat, and took a seat in the back of the craft next to Sir Walter Raleigh. She then pushed at his body with a pointy finger, as if he may be a figment of her imagination.

Ryan then untied the rope holding the boat in place and asked, "Our only problem is how in the hell do we get this boat to go upstream? The current is way too quick in the river."

James the knight closed his eyes and raised one hand at this point. The river continued to flow swiftly out in the main channel, but next to the bank, the river seemed to stop and then started to flow backwards up the river. It was as if the boat were in a backwater channel.

When James opened his eyes, Ryan looked at him with an exasperated expression on his face, and Ryan asked, "How the hell did you do that?"

James only looked at him and said, "I told you, very old magic, my dear boy… there is old magic in the air."

Ryan jumped aboard the boat, and the older knight, William, began easily rowing them up the back-current of the river.

Ellie raised her hand with concerns, and she asked them, "Why and how are we getting into the Tower...by boat...at night?

James looked at Ryan and then asked him, "You didn't show her the gate on your tour?"

Ellie then angrily asked, "What gate are you talking about?"

James gave Ryan a dour look and explained, "The traitor's gate, my lady. When a member of the British royal family, or a well-known, influential person, was transferred as a prisoner into the Tower of London, they were brought in by this gate. They did this to keep their entry private and away from the throngs of poorer people."

Ellie then cleared her throat and stated, "So this is like when a rich, famous person gets thrown in jail and they don't want 'lesser people' to see them.

However, now-a-days, cameras are everywhere, and anybody can get their hands on famous people's mug shots. Nothing seems to be private anymore, not even people's private areas."

James just looked back at Ellie, shook his head, and asked questionably, "You mean their own private living quarters?"

This statement made Ellie giggle, and then she said back to him embarrassingly, "No, I mean their own private areas on their bodies. It would help if influential people would keep from flashing their goodies, but that is the way that it is now. Famous people are well known when they are arrested, but they are never hanged or beheaded in public anymore."

Ryan then shrugged his shoulders and came to her defense when he said, "This is true…unfortunately."

Sir Walter Raleigh finally broke the stunned silence when he stated, "You people live in strange times."

The boat traveled from the river, through the outer gate, where it closed behind them. The boat then had to stop and sat there while water rose upward into a tidepool below them. When this happened, the inner gate opened, and the boat went directly through, slowly.

As the boat entered the Tower of London, Ryan looked upward, and there were medieval soldiers now encircling the embattlements of the tower. They could also be seen on the walking areas around the grounds as if they were on guard duty.

Ryan then looked amazingly at James and asked, "Why couldn't I see the soldiers from the outside, but now I can see them on the inside of the Tower?"

James looked at Ryan and said, "It is like this every night. Our worlds are separated by an invisible barrier that keeps the living out and keeps the people that came before us inside. In most cases, anyway. There have been rare cases of our worlds overlapping, like in your interactions with us. It is like living in a different realm of existence. The living people who stay here can only sense us, but they can never see us."

James then clarified why he and Ellie could experience seeing them by saying, "Of course, this doesn't apply to you, because of your own invitation's. You are supposed to see this. Some soldiers and their families that live within these walls often hear and see what they want, but they have not been invited into our realm."

Ryan then looked at James with astonishment in his eyes, and he stated thoughtfully and with a form of understanding, "It is this place, isn't it? This tower has been here for so long that history practically reverberates with its power. These soldiers are people who have come here from many different locations and different time periods. Mainly, because this place draws them here, or they have a connection with this place, in some way. Am I right?"

James stepped out of the boat and helped Ellie onto solid ground while saying, "Very good, Sir Ryan. Now you understand this situation in the most basic manner of how things work here. That is all that we ask of you, for now."

James then stared into Ryan's eyes and said, "The afterlife is about forgiveness or redemption. Sometimes that redemption takes a rather long time to happen. We first need for you to remember and believe in all of us again and come to the realization that the war between good and evil is still being fought."

Sir Walter Raleigh stepped lastly out of the boat and then said, "May I recommend that we continue this conversation in a safer location. Might I suggest my old home here in the Bloody Tower?"

That suggestion made James stop in his tracks and look intently at Sir Walter. He had turned extremely pale, and he said back to him, "You know that this location is where the boys lived at one time."

Sir Walter walked directly past him and said coldly, "Exactly, that is where the boys once lived and where they died. The location won't change that fact, and your soul needs this, James. You need to forgive yourself."

Sir Walter led the group of people to the upper level of the Bloody Tower. He turned around and said, while bowing, "Welcome, weary travelers, to the place that I once called home, courtesy of King James."

Ellie looked around at the rooms during the dark hours and asked him straight-forwardly, "What did you do in this place for 13 long years?"

Sir Walter smiled slyly and then said, "I wrote about the history of all mankind. It was long and rather boring, but it did pass the time for me. This used to be named the 'Garden Tower' as I provided and grew many plants here. I grew a very nice garden on the side of the tower. I used to walk around the flowers, take in their wonderful bouquets, and enjoy the outdoors. I could even talk to people who were over the walls. I tried to keep myself as busy as possible. However, it did wain on me."

Ryan then opened his first duffel bag, and started to unload his guns, when James wearily said, "You cannot use those weapons here."

He shuffled his feet and then continued by stating, "These forms of weapons were never used by the inhabitants of this place, and it is not allowed to use any explosives against them either. You must use weapons that they were using during their time here, such as broadswords, axes, halberds, and bows and arrows."

Ellie piped up and asked, "How about a crossbow?"

James smiled at her and then said, "Yes. A crossbow is a most fitting weapon for the time period."

Ryan complained by saying, "You could have mentioned this to me earlier, James. Do you know how much money and time was spent getting these items put together?"

Ryan suddenly yelled out in frustration, "Bloody Hell!"

James stood patiently and then said, "It is a rule that I did not remember to tell you about. I did not even think of this, and I am sorry for that. This place has stood for hundreds of years because we don't blow buildings up or make holes in the walls. You believe in protecting true historical places and facts, so why does this bother you so much?"

Ryan looked at the floor in quiet embarrassment and then said toughly, "I guess that I want revenge for the most part. I don't know how to handle medieval weapons as well as modern ones. My best friend was killed because of this fucking place. Ellie and I were almost killed last night, as well. It seems like nobody will tell me why this is happening or the rules of this sick, fucking game that you have recruited me for.

Without saying another word, Ryan put the guns back in the bag. He then took out Ellie's crossbow, the two daggers, and the two older sheathed swords.

James stepped forward and pulled one of Ryan's swords out of its sheath. He stared at the blade of the sword and said plainly, "These swords are also shite! They are dull and have not been taken care of."

Ryan let out a frustrated sigh as another angry expression crossed his face. When James saw it, he raised his hands in defense and said, "I only meant that they were not good for you to use in battle. You are a beginner at this form of fighting, and I want you to be well protected. These weapons will not do that."

James then took the long, beautiful sword from off his hip and kissed the hilt of the sword. He handed Ryan the elaborately emblazoned sword and simply said, "Here, I want you to fight with my personal weapon. I will find a sword to use during the battle. I have spent my whole life and many more years after that practicing sword play."

The hilt of the sword was jewel-encrusted, along with some silver and gold carvings upon it. When Ryan pulled the sword from its sheath, he could feel the weight of the weapon. As well as the well-balanced piece of steel that had been perfectly molded and finely created by an expert blacksmith. He was surprised that a heavier sword would feel so good in his hand.

James then nodded to Ryan and continued, "Now then, the daggers that you brought will be effective in close quarter fighting. You now have a grand sword, as well as Lady Ellie with her crossbow. You both look rather battle ready, except that I think that you may also need a shield, Sir Ryan. Please, use the one with my family's crest upon it, I would be honored."

Ryan then looked at the crest upon the shield and said, "I thought that only a member of your house could use your colors?"

James merely said, "That is true. However, I insist that you use it. Once again, I would rather you be more protected."

Then James quickly changed the subject by giving Ellie a quick lesson in loading and shooting the small arrows from her weapon. At that moment, she was dropping bolts on the floor and didn't know how to carry her crossbow on her back.

After Ellie's quick lesson in using the crossbow, and Ryan sharpening his new sword with a wet stone, James finally raised his hands and asked Ryan and Ellie to sit down. He would finally give them some answers, since they had not begun their missions yet.

The group fell silent, and then James started to tell his heartbreaking tale. While staring at the floor, he said, "Many years ago, two young princes were smothered to death with their own pillows, in this very tower. As a matter of fact, right over there…"

He pointed to an area in the next room where a feather bed had once stood. He then continued by saying, "Only 12 and 9 years had passed for the boys. They were very young."

James wriggled his hands together as if he were going to surprise them with a magic trick. He then continued saying, "Ryan, I believe that you saw these young boys when you were here before. You even came into contact with the spirits of the boys."

Ryan interjected at this moment and said excitedly; "I sure did, they were on the stairs, and they were playing with a torn leather ball. My Beefeater friend, Mel, was showing me the prison and..."

In mid-sentence, James put a hand on Ryan's shoulder, which stopped him from speaking anymore.

Then James continued with his story by saying, "The year was of our lord, 1483...this very month of July. The boys were then buried, unceremoniously, in a small box under some winding stairs that stood in the White Tower. They were just thrown in a crate and put into a shallow grave while they were doing some repairs to the stairs. My God, that sounds and is such a horrible thing to do."

Ryan then looked confused and scared while quietly saying, "How do you know all of these things, James?"

James got a pained expression on his face, and he looked at Ryan and stated pointedly, "Because I killed them!"

Ryan looked horrified and only asked, "What the hell, James? You killed them?"

Ellie had also thrown her hands up to her mouth and uttered something unintelligible. Tears were now welling up in her eyes.

James's eyes grew tears in them as well, and he said, "After 750 years, I still cry about those...boys." Then silence hung in the air, with only the sound of soft sobbing to be heard.

James then sniffled in the tears that had entered his sinuses, and he said, "My full name is Sir James Tyrrell...I was a knight under command of King

Richard III. He gave me the order to have the boys killed. I was just following the will of the king, but it was on my word that it was done. I am the one who is seeking redemption and forgiveness because of the boys who were smothered in their sleep that night. This is why I have needed your help."

James looked away from Ryan, as he was ashamed of the sins that he had been involved in that night.

Ryan asked, "Over 750 years is a long time to feel guilty, and in my opinion, you deserve to feel extremely guilty. But what does this have to do with myself and Ellie?"

James looked at Ryan and then said, "I think that I know, but the only way of explaining it to you is that you interacted with the boys twenty years ago. You can also see and speak with the man who gave the order to have them murdered… me. That is the main connection that I can find between us all. For some reason, the boys are bringing all of us together."

Ryan stood up angrily and then asked James, "Wait, were you the actual killer or not?"

The Knight raised both of his hands and said, "Please calm yourself, Ryan, and sit down... please... let me try to explain all of this to you."

Ryan sat back down, folded his arms, and sat with a brooding silence about him. Everyone else in the room was sitting with anticipation, waiting for the next confession in this dramatic tale.

James was worried about continuing his story, but then he said, "You see, I was given the task of killing the boys by the king, but I didn't carry out the deed myself. I hired the two men who did the deed of killing the boys. Their names were John Dighty and Myles Forrest."

James then said something that gave Ryan chills when he explained, "You met Myles...he was the large man pretending to be a Beefeater named Mel. He was hired to keep an eye on you and find out what you know. He did his job quite well, and he gave you the information that he wanted you to hear. That was, until you now returned, and he was then given the order to have you silenced… permanently. Thank God, he failed to kill you both."

Ellie then asked, "What about me? When Ryan was here the last time, I was only 2 years old."

James looked at her sympathetically and said to her, "You are here because of Ryan...you have a connection to him as well. Even though you are much younger than him, that doesn't mean that you aren't connected in some way."

James then looked uncomfortable and tried to explain by saying, "Time inside of here, really doesn't work the same way that it does on the ethereal plane. You mortals have got to realize this. Everything is connected...our histories, our younger selves, our present, and especially our futures. Even your children are connected to all of this."

Ellie glanced at Ryan and then gave James a confused look, but he only continued by saying, "All of these things are intertwined like a piece of chain mail. Not all people are connected, or they walk about ignorantly and do not realize that all their experiences are happening because of some reason. However, some connections are indeed stubbornly strong, like the one that you all share."

James started to get further upset, because he was still staring at blank faces. He then began saying loudly, "We are all just living in one interconnected bubble that is controlled by the old magic of all of our ancestors, combined with the new religions and sciences."

Ellie looked shyly at him and stated timidly, "Our kids? Mine and Ryan's? I may have fallen for the big idiot, but having children with Ryan?"

Ryan sat there in disbelief, and then he said cautiously, "I agree with Ellie. Me, becoming a father?

Ryan thought about what Ellie just stated, and said, "Wait a minute... Ellie... you have fallen for me?"

Just then, James the Knight broke into the conversation with an irritation in his voice, and he said, "Aww, bloody hell, forget about all the love and children talk right now. This is the reason why we didn't discuss any futures with either of you earlier because emotions can be very powerful and ruin current thinking."

James took a deep breath and continued to say, "Now then, if either of you get killed tonight, there will be no cause for either of you to worry about all this love shite. Can I finish my story now?"

After that last statement, James hit Ryan on the shoulder with the side of a sword to make him listen more intently again.

James took a deep breath and then looked upward and said to no one in particular, "This is why I didn't want to explain all of this, beforehand."

Then James continued with his story by saying, "Ellie is here because I have also been visiting her in her dream state. Also, I recently found out that she was visited by the young boys when she was also a young girl. I was told to ask her to come...and it is important that she fights with us.

James then gave both Ryan and Ellie a stern look and continued by saying, "As you may know, they have a very powerful woman fighting for them. She is the one who killed your friend. Well, we all wanted a very powerful woman fighting for us, as well."

James then became silent, lowered his head, and said, "I am sorry about your friend, Ryan. I truly am."

Ryan thanked him, grabbed Ellie's hand strongly, and then motioned for James to continue. James thought about what he was going to say next, and then he went on, "You have already dispatched John and Myles on the bridge. They were two of their largest men, and thank God that you defeated them. They were meant to kill you both, but you thankfully prevailed."

Ryan looked at Ellie with pride and said, "Don't mess with me, or m' lady."

James looked at Ryan and said pointedly, "You defeated those two men quite easily, but have you ever been faced with hitting or even killing a woman? I would never tell anyone to do this, but some women cannot be trusted, and you may have to fight one. I don't want you to freeze if this occurs."

Ryan thought about his answer and then looked back at James seriously and he said spitefully, "I would never hit a woman on purpose. However, I would sure make an exception for that Bitch that killed Monty last night."

James looked at him dourly and said, "Understood...her name is Anne... Anne Boleyn."

Ryan looked seriously confused and then said, "What?... As in King Henry VIII's treacherous queen?... That Anne Boleyn? The same Queen buried just 100 yards from this place… That Anne Boleyn… why?"

James raised his hands and then tried to explain, "She had two female children and couldn't offer the king a son to take over the crown. That was why she was executed, along with losing the favor of the king because of adultery and treason. That is also why she still haunts this place. You see, she wants the young boys… The boys who are destined to become kings. She is brutal, and she fights for what she thinks she deserves or needs. She is also violently insane and should never be trusted."

Ryan then exclaimed, "Holy Shit! Ghosts have more complicated lives than most living people have."

James bobbed his head up and down and then said, "You are right, Ryan; most people instinctively don't know that they are not even living anymore. They are on a different plane of existence, and for them, the hardships just continue. They are still trudging through the lives that they have always known. They never try anything new or try to better themselves in any way. What do you think hell is? Some of us, though, realize what we have done in the past and want to make amends and find forgiveness."

Ellie was wrapped up in the Knight's story and then asked, "What happens when you make amends and earn what is right?"

James shrugged his shoulders and said hopefully, "Happiness... forgiveness... Serenity? None of us really knows, and we can only guess and hope for the right outcome. However, forgiveness and serenity are a lot better than worry and self-loathing."

Ryan stopped James from telling the story, and he asked, "I have never thought of it that way before; are you fighting for your own redemption, James?"

James quietly said, "I am fighting for what I believe in and for my own forgiveness, yes. But I am also fighting to simply make it better for all of us. We all need help."

Ryan shook his head enthusiastically and said to James, "Well, you definitely have my support, I will fight with you."

Ryan then looked over at Ellie and asked, "Now then, are you also willing to fight and possibly die with us, my princess?"

Ellie looked at Ryan angrily and asked, "I'm with you, aren't I? I am taking the biggest chance that I can for you. Haven't you figured that out yet?"

James looked at them with a knowing look in his eye and said, "She may be our greatest weapon against them. I don't think that they know about her yet. The evil rulers know about you, Ryan...but Ellie may be a mystery to them.

Ellie nudged Ryan's elbow, and then said mockingly, "You see, I am a mystery."

Ryan rolled his eyes and said jokingly, "Yes, I know. You are a mystery wrapped in a conundrum, rolled up in a riddle."

Then Ryan asked James, "What are we looking at for soldier numbers in our armies? How many do we fight?"

James tried to make a joke and make this a lighter moment. He smiled slightly and said, "Counting the two men that you already killed? We will fight approximately 198 more."

Ryan looked sourly at James and then asked, "How many soldiers do we have fighting for us? You told me one time that you were busy building an army."

James replied, "Yes, I have been building soldiers with which to fight. I have built an army of about 160 souls."

James looked down direly and said, "We are outmatched by 40 or so men, and we cannot use any of your explosive armaments. Have I doomed us?"

Ryan then smiled stiffly, and he stated, "Not if we are smart. I like being the underdog."

Ellie then asked for herself and for Ryan, "Since we can't use any explosives, how do we kill them, then?"

James said in a surprisingly upbeat tone, "They can be stabbed, shot with arrows, or hacked to death. They just need to have their hearts stop beating and their minds stop working. Much in how you killed the two assassins on the bridge. Remember, though, that these injuries can also happen to you. You can die!"

Ryan asked next, "Speak honestly to us. Do we have a chance?"

James said, "Yes, there is always a chance, and we have the magic of goodness and what is right on our side."

Ellie then scoffed at him and said sarcastically, "The magic of goodness? That sounds totally made up."

James smiled and said, "You will be surprised by the magic of goodness. It can usually be found when you need it the most."

"Where do we go when we just don't know where?
And how do we relight the flame when it's cold?
Why do we dream when our thoughts mean nothing?
And when will we learn to control..."
(Godsmack)

Chapter Nineteen

"My favorite athletes have always been the bad guys or the underdogs: Either way, I will never be disappointed." (Bo Jackson)

Before the battle officially started, the group was gathered in the living quarters of Sir Walter Raleigh's prison cells in the Bloody Tower. James, the knight, was trying to lighten the mood with the other combatants after telling them such a devastating story of his guilt.

Acceptance has a very cathartic quality that everyone desires and hopes for. That truly showed in the interactions between the different groups of people.

Sir Walter Raleigh was the current topic of attention when James said, "Now then, if any of you have any questions about this Tower layout, please ask Sir Walter Raleigh. He is our innermost expert on this fortress. He did spend the most time here, and he was imprisoned here… twice."

James laughed and then said, "I believe the first time was because of chasing after the wrong woman."

"Not chasing after," Sir Walter said rather embarrassingly, "You mean marrying."

Sir Walter said this sheepishly, and then he continued by saying, "I had my dalliances with the Queen, and I may have led her on in order to get what

I wanted. However, I never intended to fall in love with her Lady in Waiting, Miss Throckmorton, either."

Sir Walter looked sadly at the floor, and he then said, "It ended up that I did not treat either of these women rather well. Neither of them deserved to be messed up with a cad like me."

Ellie cleared her throat and said forwardly, "Maybe that is why you are here. Perhaps you need to make amends to these women, in some way or another."

Sir Walter laughed harshly and said, "I think that my loves have moved on, without having a second thought about me."

Sir Walter then winked at Ellie and said, "Plus, if I am here to make amends to all the women that I have fallen in love with, I would be here for a much longer time than I have been condemned to, already. No… I am fighting here out of a hatred for the royal, sons-of-whores that were in control of Britain for decades of turmoil and civil wars."

Sir Walter spit on the floor and then said, "Throughout my life and even beyond that, both women and men have either loved me or reviled me. Not one person had any middling feelings about me. I have always been one person's villain, or another person's savior."

Sir Walter then looked pensive, and continued by saying, "However, I put myself in that position as well. I always wanted praise. That is why I was so abhorrent in my behavior when I was alive. This is also why I now fight for my own reputation. Not because of God and country, but I fight for my own stories in the history of this world."

William, the older knight, suddenly ran into the room and said, "I believe that this battle is about to commence. There is a lot of activity going on out there in the courtyard, and I think that you all need to see this."

They all ran into the other room and looked out of the narrow windows that were designed for protection from arrows, as well as for archers to shoot projectiles at their enemies.

William pointed out, "Do you see? That round glass memorial on Tower Green that they have been building on. It is now starting to glow red."

Where the glass monument now stood, a red, rippling mist-like liquid began to boil instead. Ellie strained her eyes and asked, "What is that?"

No one answered her, as it had never happened before. Then James came out with a guess and said, "I think that it may be some kind of portal."

Ellie then asked, "A portal to where?"

James then said with a sneer on his face, "Judging by the color, I don't think that it leads anywhere that we want to go."

Suddenly, a red plume of the frothy liquid shot upwards. Several medieval soldiers flew out of the red mist and landed on the grass-covered lawn. They were wearing a red tunic with an emblazoning of white, tusked boars facing one another across their chests.

James was looking at the soldiers intently and said, "I know that coat of arms on their tunics. That is the symbol for Richard III and any soldiers who back him. My soldiers are the men in black tunics with a white shield and seven crosses below it. The men wearing red are the enemies. The men in black tunics follow us."

The soldiers wearing black tunics gaped at the sight of these suddenly appearing red soldiers in shock at first. Slowly, they held up swords or bows and arrows in defense of their positions. The red clad soldiers grabbed swords that hung at their waists. They were also carrying spears and halberds that they had been carrying when they had entered the melee. A loud war cry could be heard coming from across the grounds of the ancient fortress.

Then the soldiers who were wearing red tunics began to rush the walls and any nearby soldier wearing a black tunic. The now-red memorial continued to belch out new soldiers onto the lawn, which caused James's eyes to bulge outward wildly with each one.

Ryan then said out loud, "I get it. The color of their tunic is like opposing uniforms in a football game."

James then looked out at his smaller army and said hastily, "Ryan, you and Ellie are destined to remain here in the tower and be on alert."

Ryan started to dispute this, and James raised a finger to silence him and said angrily, "Ryan, do not argue with me, stay here with Ellie. You are supposed to remain here, and you will know shortly why this is so."

James looked at the other combatants and said, "Sir William, Sir Raleigh, and I have got to get to the highest possible point in this fortress. We must view the battlefield and come up with a fighting plan. We are going to the top of the White Tower in the middle. Ryan and Ellie, we will meet up with you again… later. Until then, you have all our best regards."

An armored James and William clanged out of the room and down the stairs, followed by the noiseless and unarmored form of Sir Walter Raleigh. Ryan looked frustrated and watched the grounds, hoping to see the trio of men rushing to the large tower in the center of the complex. However, he didn't see them move across the grounds, and he never knew if they had even reached their objective.

He leaned back against the stone wall when an arrow came flying through the glassless, narrow window that he had just been looking out of. He and Ellie watched it as it arced across the room, clunked against the opposite wall, and fell to the floor.

He then said with exasperation, "What the hell are we waiting for?"

Ellie looked back at him and then said, patiently but forcefully, "Don't be in such a hurry to run off and get yourself killed. You heard what James said, we were meant to be here for some reason. Please don't be foolhardy and ignore these requests. He has been right so far, so quit being so damn stubborn and in such a fucking hurry."

Ryan then leaned under the window and kissed Ellie softly on the lips and said, "You are right… You are right… and I promise to listen more with my brain and not only with my gut."

After Ryan said this, a soft child's chuckle came from the rock stairwell heading downward. Ellie whispered to Ryan, "I think that we just got our answer on why we should be here."

Sneaking across the grass courtyard was easier than expected for the trio of James, William, and Walter. The three men had a very easy time at first, as they exited the Bloody Tower and ran in the shadows across the main road in front of the main entrance doors. The soldiers fighting on the walls above them were very occupied with their own opponents, and they were not opposed by any soldiers on the grounds below.

The three men slipped down a steeper embankment and hid behind an ancient stone wall that jutted out toward the entrance stairs of the White

Tower. Even though the Tower complex is ancient, the old Roman Wall was built 500 years before the buildings of the tower had even been imagined. The wall ran through the ancient city of Londinium, as it was known during the very early ages of Britain and during the occupation of the country by the Roman Army.

They then each took a turn and individually sprinted across the grassy grounds on the south side of the White Tower. When they arrived, they all met at the bottom of the main staircase that ran up to the entrance of the ancient building. They slowly crept up the outer stairwell and slipped inside the massive doors of the main palace.

James and William led the way into the first floor, which was mainly used for servants and locations for protecting soldiers in the past. They then were running to the small stone staircase that took them up to the second floor. They were running in front of the doors leading into St. John's Cathedral when Sir Walter Raleigh stopped and told them that he would soon catch up with them.

A smirk ran across his face, and he said, "There is something inside this cathedral that I must deal with first."

Sir Walter Raleigh was following behind the two knights when he looked over into the interior of the religious center of the building. At this point, he stopped in his tracks and was flabbergasted by the person standing before him.

Standing against the far alter was a short, skinny, and rather gentile man. He had darker, red-colored hair, shallow eyes, a sharpened nose; and a reddish mustache that grew down into a three-inch-long reddish goatee. The rest of his face was pock-marked with red, brown, and short blond hairs that rose on his cheeks when he drew back his mouth in a sneer. He wore a skinny suit of armor that had a black cape attached to it, and he raised a short, skinny sword up in front of his face. It was as if he were taunting Sir Walter Raleigh to come and fight him.

Sir Walter let out a small laugh and began to walk toward the man from the back of the church.

He smiled shrewdly and said with disdain in his voice, "My dear James… Whose balls did you use to come and confront me with?"

King James I, pointed his sword at him and said, "How dare you still address the King of England, Ireland, and Scotland with such animosity, Sir Raleigh."

Walter only strode closer to him and stated, "You are a commander of cocks...and... You are not my king."

James the 1st, sneered at him and said, "At least I died with my head still attached to the rest of my body."

Sir Raleigh was almost running toward King James now, and he pulled his own skinnier, fencing sword out of its scabbard. As he ran, he continued to berate the king, by saying, "So tell me this, King, why is it that you love being surrounded by men so much and have no desire for any woman's company?"

King James then raised his sword in front of his face, causing Sir Raleigh to stop and face him as an equal. At this point, his sword was trembling in his hand with anger. Sir Raleigh had now been challenged to a fair duel of swords with proper sword-fighting etiquette.

Even though he was now in a proper duel with his old nemesis, he still taunted King James even further by saying, "Tell me, James, have you been fantasizing about my cock?"

King James then venomously cried back at him by saying, "I had three children, including a son who ruled England after my death. How dare you pass any aspersions against me."

Sir Raleigh got into a dueling stance and pointed his sword at King James. He then said, "Let us see how well you can fight when nobody is around to protect you. Come on then, you cavernous, gnash of a man."

Ryan and Ellie slowly walked in a crouching stance on their way across the room, until they were hunched down on the top step of the stairwell. Both Ryan and Ellie could now hear the chittered laughter of young boys. They could also hear two different adult voices talking about the noises that they had heard coming from the second floor above them.

Ellie whispered to Ryan, "They are talking about hearing us, and they are coming up here to check it out."

Ryan motioned for Ellie to stand on the right side of the stairwell, while he occupied and defended the left side. They both knew that they had to protect the children first and foremost. However, now they tried to hide as silently and stealthily as possible.

Two men dressed in black shirts, snug brown pants, and a vest of chainmail armor that ran across each of their chests, slowly climbed toward them. The voices of the two young boys were soon silenced by one of the soldiers climbing the stairs ahead of them and harshly "Shushing" them.

At first, Ryan and Ellie thought that this was a trap and that both soldiers had taken the boys hostage. Ryan held his finger to his lips and then signaled for Ellie to get her crossbow ready. When he did so, the blade of his longsword brushed across the stone walls and made a horrible screeching sound.

Ryan looked at Ellie apologetically and then stood up with his sword drawn in front of the men. Ellie stepped out of the shadows soon after him while holding her aim with the crossbow at the soldier on the right.

Ryan looked at the men and said boldly, "Well, we no longer have the element of surprise on our side. Now then, would you please hand over the protection of the boys to us?"

James and Walter burst through a door and found themselves on the roof of the White Tower, which was overlooking the entire grounds below and all the individual battles that were occurring there.

The roof of the White Tower is formed into two smaller peaked roofs that are slightly slanted upward with two leaden shaped roofs that are 100 feet long. It is surrounded on each corner by overhanging 16-foot stone turrets that stand above the top of the roof and run all the way to the grounds below. Across this leaden roof, was wooden scaffolding that was placed there for remodeling purposes that were being done to the castle keep.

Knights wearing black and red tunics were occupying every section of the outer and inner walls of the tower complex, along with the green courtyards below them. They now fought against other knights that they had once known and traveled with to the Holy Lands during the early religious pilgrimages. From James and William's viewpoint, knights and other soldiers flung swords, halberds, maces, and axes at each other with wild abandon.

They would witness one knight wearing a red tunic, cut across the chest of another knight wearing a black tunic. Then the red knight would slide under the blow delivered by the black knight and stab the soldier in the armpit. This area was underneath the steel armor, causing him to immediately fall to his knees, defeated.

However, whenever a true and valiant knight was killed on this field of battle, a white, gleaming ball of light and smoke would go up into the air. Several small popping sounds could then be heard, and a sparkling white light would explode into the air. It was as if someone had lit off a brilliant piece of white firework.

However, if a knight was untrue, and not worthy of the spoils of a good afterlife, a red smoke would emerge from his body. It would then arc directly back into the red liquid that had appeared atop the new memorial, which was dedicated to the souls that were beheaded at that spot. Each time that one of these souls was sucked into this vortex, the red liquid let out a belching sound of disdain.

James the Knight and Sir William looked down as the ghosts of their dying countrymen, fought against each other for their very souls.

Sir James looked over at Walter and said, "It is as if this is one of the battles of the War of the Roses that is being fought once again tonight. Let us see who wins this one."

On the northeast corner of the White Tower, there is another old, smaller circular wooden staircase where men can rise to the roof without anyone knowing of their whereabouts. While James and William looked down at their fellow knights, there was a red smoke that started to rise under a secret doorway and onto the ceiling. The door in the ceiling was forced open, causing the red smoke to billow out from below, and three men silently climbed out onto the roof.

Sir Walter Raleigh and King James began feeling out the fighting stances of the other man and trying to get inside the other man's head. They would lunge their smaller swords quickly at each other, and then pull back in a defensive position.

King James sneered at his opponent and said, "I thought that I was done with you when I had you beheaded 400 years ago. My God, I celebrated the day when you were finally put to death."

Sir Walter quickly lunged again at the former King, and when his skinny dueling sword was swatted away, he backed up into a defensive posture once again.

He then blew an invisible kiss to King James and said maliciously, "You cut off my head because you still liked having my arse around to look at. Admit it."

King James cried out in anger and then tossed the hilt of his small sword from his right hand into his left appendage. He started to lunge and attack forward with ferocity, causing Sir Raleigh to jump backward.

This caused him to trip on the flowing cape that ran down his back and fall backward with little control of his body. While he was falling and with every bit of the talent that he had, Sir Raleigh switched his own sword in between his hands in order to swat the blade of the lunging sword away.

However, when King James saw him fall, he quickly switched the sword back into his right hand again. He plunged the blade into the right side of Sir Raleigh's stomach, where it protruded his abdomen and was rammed through his body. The worst injury from this stabbing blade was when the blade pierced the edge of Sir Raleigh's liver.

Sir Raleigh's arms fell back onto the floor in pain and exhaustion. King James stood above him with a look of morbid joy on his face. He grabbed the hilt of the sword again and forcefully pushed the sword through Sir Raleigh's stomach until he was hitting the rock floor on the other side of his body.

Blood started to flow out of Sir Walter's mouth, and he let out a harsh cough filled with a black-colored liquid. Even though he was in a vast amount of pain, he managed to give King James a crooked smile, and he said, "I will never regard you as my king."

With these words, Sir Walter Raleigh raised his own sword off the stone floor and flicked the handle of it until it knocked the golden crown off the head where the past king had been wearing it. King James immediately raised his arms to his head, trying to grab the crown, and in doing this, he left an opening on his inner neck for Sir Raleigh to grab the other sharp dagger that he had been wearing on his waist and drive it upward.

The point of the blade pierced the king in the bottom of his chin and was driven upward until it reached the gray matter of his brain. King James immediately began to drool blood out of his mouth, and his body fell limply on an injured Sir Walter Raleigh.

Using most of the strength that Sir Raleigh had, he pushed the once again dead king off his body. After losing the additional weight provided by the king's body, he began to pull himself across the stone floor to the altar at the front of the church.

Sir Walter Raleigh turned his head around and witnessed James I's body turn into a red orbital mist, where it was then pulled out of a small clear window that was at the front of the church. It was then sucked into the unknown red portal that had been opened below the castle.

Ellie shot one bolt out of her crossbow and hit the stone wall far to the right of the soldier that was wearing a black colored tunic under chainmail. The knight on the left side, was also wearing a black tunic, chainmail, and a shining helmet. He then made himself ready by pushing his face shield down on his helmet and raising his sword.

Ryan steadied himself as this man took another aggressive step toward him with a forceful stance. Suddenly, two young blond boys came running from behind the soldiers and began waving their arms in front of them.

Their hair was strikingly blond, and it was rather long, hanging down upon their shoulders and into their eyes. They were each dressed in small black shoes, black leggings, bulging black pantaloons, and a loose-fitting white shirt over the top of them.

They each had large blue eyes that peered up at Ryan and Ellie, and they started shouting out of their small mouths. "No! They mean you no harm. Do not attack one another."

Ryan stopped his approach at the men and then looked at Ellie. She kept her crossbow aimed at the men, even though she had no bolts loaded in it. Then Ellie finally stated, "All right, come up the stairs slowly, tell us who you are and what you are doing with the boys."

Each soldier looked at the other one in confusion and they sheathed their swords and slowly trudged up the stairs.

The men entered the rather large cell, along with the boys, and stood by the stone wall with their hands raised. Ryan entered the room with confusion on his face, and Ellie followed behind him, still holding the empty crossbow ahead of her. Ryan sat down on a red, upholstered couch, in which Ellie followed suit, and he reached over and pushed Ellie's crossbow down.

He then looked at the men and asked, "Who are all of you?"

The knight that seemed to be in charge had raised his facemask and taken off his helmet. He then said, "These two young boys are Edward V, the uncrowned king of England… and this younger boy is his brother Richard of Shrewsbury, Duke of York."

Ryan then motioned toward the men and said, "And exactly who are you? We are more worried about the men who are armed with swords."

The knight smiled gruffly and stated proudly, "This young master that is with me is their uncle on their mother's side, Anthony Woodville. My name is Sir Richard Grey, the boy's half-brother."

Richard Grey then cleared his throat and continued by saying, "I was bringing the new king to London from a castle in Wales called Ludlow. Anthony was bringing young Richard here, to the tower, from Middleham Castle in Yorkshire. We met up at a place called Stony Stratford on the River Ouse, half the way to London. However, Richard III's soldiers met up with us at that point and had us arrested."

Anthony Woodville then took over the conversation and said, "We were the true protectors of these boys, and the king's soldiers stole them from us and took them to London. Richard III had the two of us shipped to a place called Pontefract Castle in Yorkshire and had us both imprisoned."

Anthony then grabbed at his neck and continued saying, "The bastard then went before Parliament and announced that the marriage between King Edward IV and his bride, my sister, Elizabeth Woodville, was invalid. He did this even though they had many children together and had gone through all the protected vows of marriage. Because of this, he claimed that these boys' reigns as kings would be illegitimate, and they had no validity to the crown."

Sir Richard Grey then finished the story by saying, "We vowed to protect these boys, and they will not be taken from us again. King Richard may have had our heads cut off nearly 750 years ago, but we will fight anyone that wishes to harm these boys."

Ellie looked over at Ryan curiously and asked, "Well, what do you think? You are the historian. Do you believe them?"

Ryan looked at them seriously and said, "Well, it is not like I can ask them for their driver's license and check their photographs, but yes, I do believe them. Even though this whole situation seems almost fantastical. I know that the Queen, Elizabeth Woodville, had a brother, and I know that Sir Richard Grey was an actual person who was the boy's stepbrother. However, I would feel better if I heard it from a couple of witnesses who knew them. Boys, can you tell me about these men?"

The elder of the boys stepped forward and said, "How do you do? My name is Edward. My father was the king of England, and my mother was Elizabeth Woodville. This man is her brother, which makes him my uncle. This other knight is of my same blood and should be treated like my own brother."

Ryan leaned closer to him and bowed to the young man while saying, "I am very glad to meet you, Edward. My name is Ryan, and this is Ellie. We are here to help you and your brother as well."

The younger boy stepped up to Ellie and introduced himself as Richard. He then asked something that totally shocked her when he asked, "Hello, Ellie, is your true name Elizabeth, like my mother's?"

Ellie looked as though she might faint at the sight of the young boys that she had been friends with when she was a young girl, and she said, "Yes, my name is Elizabeth. I have been called Ellie for short, ever since I was a little girl. I was given the nickname Ellie by two young, invisible friends when I was just a small girl. I did not even think of this fact before now. After getting the nickname, I demanded that my grandparents start calling me by this name."

Anthony Woodville then coughed quietly and said, "We used to call my sister Ellie when we were young, as well. The two of you have a striking resemblance to each other. She was a very beautiful woman."

Ellie looked extremely shocked, and she turned to Ryan and said, "Do you believe that this whole thing could possibly be true?"

Ryan shrugged and then stated, "I wouldn't discount anything at this point. The universe keeps throwing curve balls at us when all we are expecting is fast balls that are right down the middle of the plate."

Ryan then winked at her and said, "He is right about one thing...you are a very beautiful woman."

Ellie blushed, and then said, "Alright, do any of you know what we are supposed to do next?"

All the adults looked at each other with confusion on their faces. Then the smaller voice of Edward V piped up and said, "I think that we are supposed to find the other soldiers and damsels that will be fighting with us. We also need to eventually find Sir James and help him fight against the 'Mad King and his Evil Queen'!"

Ryan then shrugged and said, "Out of the mouths of babes."

He then looked at Edward and asked him, "James went to the 'White Tower' in the middle of this compound; can you lead us where we need to go?"

Edward smiled up at him slyly and then said, "My brother and I have been here for a very long time; we know of all the secret ways of traveling around this fortress."

Ryan then said one more important thing that he needed to express and that he thought would be extremely prudent. He smiled at the boys kindly and said, "Okay, all of you seem to go by the same names, such as Edward, Richard, and William. This could get very confusing, so I am going to give you all shorter names as well. So just like Ellie's real name is Elizabeth, she shortened it to individualize herself. From now on, the young boy who is named Edward, I am going to call Eddie. Richard, I am going to call you, Young Rich. Will that work for both of you?"

The young boys then nodded their heads at Ryan, who continued by saying, "Sir Richard Grey, I am going to call you either 'Old Rich' or 'Sir Grey'. Make a choice of which name you would like."

Sir Richard Grey looked at Ryan, hesitantly, and then said, "I may have died in 1483, but I would rather be called 'Sir Grey' than called that 'Old Rich' name."

Ryan smiled at him and then said, "I am just going to call King Richard by the name that 'Young Rich' already gave to him, 'The Mad King'. I have always called James by the name that was given to him, and William will now be 'Sir William the Elder'. Are we all clear?"

The young boys looked at Ryan excitedly and then asked, "What about the others like Anthony, Sir Raleigh, and Queen Anne Boleyn?"

Ryan then held out his hands and simply said, "Your uncle will now be called by his given name of Anthony…Sir Walter Raleigh will just be called by the name, 'Sir Raleigh.'…now then, Anne Boleyn, we will call her...?"

Ellie broke into the conversation and then said, "The Bitch!"

All eyes turned to Ellie, and then young Eddie said plainly, "You do not just look like our mother, you sometimes sound exactly like our mother, as well."

Ryan burst out laughing and was soon joined by all the others in the room. He rubbed the long blond hair on Eddie's head, and then asked him and his brother to lead them where they needed to go next.

James and William, the younger and older knights, were looking down from the roof of the White Tower at the carnage that was ensuing below them. They had no idea about the small door in the ceiling that was located on the other end of the roof. Out of this door came three men with blood in their eyes.

The first man was shorter and had a more compact body with a roundish face. He wasn't dressed as if he were a soldier; he was dressed as if he were a bishop or a minister of finances. However, he did have a sword in his hand, as well as a dagger in his belt.

The second man that followed him was dressed more as a commanding officer, maybe even a general of soldiers. He had longer, but thinning, brown hair, sharp blue eyes, a sallow face, and a blondish mustache above his lip.

The last man through the door was much larger than the first two men. He looked as if he might have muscles made of iron. He wore tall boots that came up to his knees, brown pants, and a skin-tight white shirt that showed off the muscles of his chest and his biceps. He also wore a black cape as well as a large, wide brimmed Puritan hat that stood atop a massively large skull.

The last man seemed to be the scariest of all the men. He had thicker reddish hair on his head and a darker brown colored beard was on his face. He stood up at his full height, cracked the muscles and tendons in his neck, and then bashed his fists together. He did not carry a weapon, as his body was an actual weapon, itself. The three men began to stalk toward the two knights who had their backs to them and were looking downward.

The shorter, ministerial looking man was the first to arrive at the knights as the three men had to walk single file on the wooden planks on the roof. None of them were wearing armor, which made them more clandestine and quieter.

The shorter man swung the large sword wildly at Sir William's head, but William saw the blade coming toward him and ducked out of the way. He then spun his body around so that he was facing the shorter, yet stockier fellow who was dressed like a minister of finance. Sir William was not intimidated by this man, and grabbed the man's ministerial tunic and forcibly flung him behind him. The man was then confronted by the younger knight, James.

The young knight quickly put the tip of his sword up to the neck of the shorter man. Sir William, the older knight, regained his balance once again and challenged the superior-looking officer who was walking behind the first man. This left only the strong looking man without any opponents at the time. He was thankfully blocked off on the wooden passageway, with no way around the dueling men.

James looked at all three of the men and asked, "Who might you be?"

The first man to answer him was the shorter, sturdier fellow who stood with the young knight's dagger drawn at his throat. He swallowed hard and said, "My name is Thomas Cromwell. I was chief minister for King Henry VIII during his reign...well...until."

James then finished the sentence for him by saying, "Until the king had you beheaded for not making him very happy."

Thomas cleared his throat and uttered, "Um, yes. However, making him happy was an almost impossible task to perform."

James scoffed at him and then asked, "Then why are you fighting here? The King obviously didn't want you, and you can barely hold onto a sword, so why fight for this group of arseholes?"

Minister Cromwell shuffled his feet and then said, "I wasn't asked to be in any king's army...I was asked by Queen Anne Boleyn. We were allies once, and I fought tooth and nail against Catholicism and the Pope himself to get her to become queen. She owes me...She wouldn't even be a footnote in history if it weren't for me. She has now made me certain promises that would help me… immeasurably."

James looked at him sadly, and he stated angrily, "So you fight here only for what the 'evil queen' has offered you...not because of any penance that you may have or any feelings that you have done anything wrong...at all."

James sheathed his own sword and then said spitefully, "You disgust me, chief minister. I cannot stand a man who blames others for all their mistakes and will not take the blame for any of their own responsibilities. You make me sick."

With these words, James stepped toward Thomas Cromwell, who lifted his own sword with the intent of swinging it at James's skull. James grabbed the elbow of the arm that held the sword and held it firmly in place with his left hand. He suddenly grabbed Minister Cromwell's waist with his open right hand.

James picked up the man and threw him over the barrier of the wood walkway that they were standing on. His body flew down the ceiling and went over the battlements of the ancient keep.

They could hear Chief Minister Cromwell's screams as he tumbled off the roof of the White Tower. When his body hit the ground, it immediately turned into a red ball of mist. This ball seemed to bounce off the green grass and directly into the red circular portal that looked amazingly like an infected eye from above it.

The large man watched James throw the minister off the roof without any difficulties what-so-ever. He looked at the walkway, where he was blocked by the other two dueling men, and then he looked out over the raised roof of the building.

While looking at the roof, the large man suddenly saw it. A solitary rope was tied to one of the wooden beams that made up the bottom portion of the walkway. He pulled upward on this rope until it was taut, and then tested its strength with his hands.

He smiled at James, stepped over the barricade, and launched himself up the rising embankment of the roof. He used the rope as a form of guide wire and to keep his body safe if he fell through the roof of the ancient building. There was not going to be a chance that he would fall from this 100-foot-tall castle, as Minister Cromwell had just done.

James was astounded by both the true bravery and the extreme stupidity of the move. He even forgot that he could simply cut the rope or smash the man's head in when he reached the other side of James's position. The man had just made a run across the unrepaired roof of the building. He had come from one wooden gangplank to another, just so that he could face James on the other side.

James shook his head with astonishment and then said to the much larger man, "I didn't know that they made people this large and coordinated in England? Sir William... would you please quickly dispatch with that other fellow? I think that I may need your help here when you are finished."

Sir William looked at the man that stood before him and then asked, "I will try to defeat this man quickly... but he does look more daunting than the last man. And who might you be, sir?"

The more military looking man stated, "I was unbelievably somewhat of a descendant of the man who was just thrown off the building. My name is Oliver Cromwell, and I was the head of the British armies at one time. I was also a member of Parliament during England's darkest days, the Religious Civil Wars of the 1600s.

Oliver Cromwell bowed and then continued to say, "That large man over there is named Guy Fawkes. He and his miscreant friends tried to blow me up once. However, we captured him, and he was held here in the tower for... questioning."

James then said over his shoulder while keeping an eye on Guy Fawkes, "By holding him for questioning, I would guess that you meant that this man was tortured?"

Oliver sighed and then said, "Call it what you will. In the end, my men got him to tell me all about his plot to murder us in Parliament. Of course, this also included killing the other members of parliament, and the King of

England. They tried to take over the country for the Catholic Church. This was called the Gunpowder Plot."

He spat after saying this, and then he said straight-forwardly, "Mr. Fawkes was once a very devout Roman Catholic. However, after several days of being my guest here, he started to believe in the virtues of Puritanism."

Oliver Cromwell smiled at the older knight and simply stated, "I am here just because I love war...plain and simple. I love the utter taste and smell of people battling each other. I broke this large man so badly once, that I haven't been able to get away from him in this entire abysmal afterlife."

He then pulled a large, broad sword out of its sheath and said to William, "I won't be so easy to deal with as my ancestor laying in a puddle on the ground."

Sir Walter Raleigh still had ten yards of cold marble flooring to pull himself across in order to reach the front alter which was made of a raised wooden table. There was a wooden fence in front of the altar, but Sir Raleigh could easily crawl under these slats of wood. A solitary spectacular golden cross stood upon the altar, and Sir Raleigh transfixed his vision upon it as he crawled across the hard surface.

Each foot of distance seemed to be excruciating, as the hole in his stomach felt like it was opening wider as he slowly inched along. He was breathing harder now, and he took his eyes off the crucifix, just to look back along his path. He could only see a pool of blood where King James had once been, as well as a crimson path trailing behind him. He transfixed his vision back on the crucifix, held his intestines in with one gloved hand, and crawled along the floor with the other.

He finally had one foot left to go, and his brow was like he was wearing a water halo of sweat. He took a deep breath and reached out for one more pull toward his prize. He could only raise his head slightly, but he could feel the base of the altar with his hand. He then let out a sigh of both relief and despair.

He spoke out loudly now and said, "My God, please forgive me for my indiscretions, as I have had too many to think about at this time. However, God! I did have two great loves in my life. A queen who could not love me enough and who pushed me away, and her faithful maiden who loved me too much and pulled me too close to her. I ran away from them both...and there is nothing that I am sorrier for now."

Suddenly, a white light started to swirl around the body of Sir Walter Raleigh. The light swirled around him very quickly at first and then slowed until a tall, willowy raven-haired Queen stood on one side of him, and a shorter, more curvaceous, blond woman stood on the other side.

Queen Elizabeth looked down upon the body of Sir Walter Raleigh and said, "Oh God, please don't forget about this man's overwhelming amount of pride."

The woman who had once been the Queen's Lady in Waiting and Sir Walter Raleigh's wife, Elizabeth Throckmorton then said, "And please God, don't forget about his unruly overconfidence."

They both said in unison, "Please forgive him these transgressions." Then they giggled at each other.

The voice was almost inaudible when Sir Walter said weakly, "My sweet Elizabeth's! I truly did love both of thee for completely different reasons. Please forgive me."

Both women looked sorrowfully down at the body of Sir Walter Raleigh, and they looked at each other with eternal friendship and compassion.

Queen Elizabeth suddenly asked the other woman, "What do you think? Should we take him back with us?"

The wife of Sir Walter then said, "I do believe that it is time to do so now."

The circle of white light began to circle again, only going faster as it encircled his body. Finally, the bright light shot upward through the ceiling of the chapel. The body of Sir Walter Raleigh was last seen lifting into the night sky. Each hand was being held by what any ordinary man would call...angels.

The clouds prepare for battle
In the dark and brooding silence
Bruised and sullen storm clouds
Have the light of day obscured
Looming low and ominous
In twilight premature
Thunderheads are rumbling
In a distant overture
(Rush)

Chapter Twenty

"Be not afraid of greatness. Some are born great, some achieve greatness, and others have greatness thrust upon them." (William Shakespeare)

The young boys huddled together with their hands on each other's shoulders. They were speaking quietly to each other about the best possible way to approach the White Tower in the center of the complex. When they had discussed this, they turned to the group of adults and gave them the best choices that they all had. The oldest boy, Edward, or Eddie (as Ryan called him), gave the group the choices.

He explained, "We believe that James, William, and Sir Raleigh would have followed this path out of the Bloody Tower and into the courtyard. We believe that they would have traveled under the protection of this ancient Roman wall. This would give them a shorter run to the central tower.

However, we would be much closer to the main fight now. Any way that we go to the main tower, we are going to be out in the open ground for quite some time. Anyone will be able to attack us if we go there."

The adults then began to argue back and forth at each other, and Ryan asked the boys, "What are the directions to these specific locations? I tend to visualize places like this, as if I am looking at a map in my head."

Eddie then looked earnestly at Ryan and said, "The Thames River is directly behind us in a southerly direction. Northeast of us is the White Tower, so to travel to this tower, we would have to go east to the main gate and then directly north along the path. We could travel directly across the courtyard and hope that we don't run into any enemy soldiers along the way."

Eddie then looked distraught and said, "However, my brother came up with an alternate plan. It is a different way of looking at our whole situation, but it is a good plan for us to discuss. I will let him tell you about it."

'Young Rich' stepped forward and began by saying shyly, "My brother's plan to get to the White Tower is the safer plan… compared to mine, that is. Hopefully his plan will reunite us with the other brave knights. However, I have gotten to know these knights throughout many years...and... well...I have faith in them that they have reached the White Tower in safety. They are brilliant knights, and they will not need our help there."

'Young Rich' then looked at all their faces and continued, "Alternatively, I do think that they need our help in other ways, just not at the White Tower. I want to go to the Bell Tower in the west, in the corner of the grounds. Then we would travel north along the Queen's Walk to the Beauchamp Tower."

'Young Rich' stopped and looked at the confused looks that were staring back at him. He then continued to say more confidently, "The bad people seem to be located on Tower Green, where the beheadings were said to have taken place. This place lies directly between the White Tower, and the Beauchamp Tower. If we could get there, we would have the bad soldiers surrounded on the east by our fellow knights and on the west by us."

'Young Rich' stopped again and then tried to sell his plan by saying, "It is a much bolder way to go, and we will have to fight additional soldiers in the towers and battlements along the way, but it would be so rewarding. It is a much more treacherous path to go, but if we do hold this ground..."

Sir Grey then finished his sentence by saying, "If we can get there, and if James, Walter, and William are safe, we will have the advantage on them from either side. They will have to split up their armies in order to face all of us. He is right; to get there will be much more perilous and dangerous. However, I think that it is the best idea that we have had. Brilliant thinking, my young brother."

These words were followed by nods of approval, and Ryan finally sighed and stated, "Well then, God hates a coward."

Ellie nodded in agreement, and then also stated, while raising her eyebrows, "Out of the mouths of babes, indeed."

A slight wind started to blow across the men that stood atop the large White Tower. James, the younger knight, and William, the older knight, stood back-to-back and had formidable foes in front of each of them.

William and Oliver Cromwell's battle was a straight-up knights-duel between two sword-wielding opponents. This pair of combatants was equally challenged when it came to their fortitude in sword play.

James's fight with Guy Fawkes was anything but that kind of fight. It was more a battle between one man who had superior intellect and weapons on his side, while the other had size and pure strength.

Right before they began battling, William said one thing to James when he stated, "Whatever happens in this battle, keep our backs to each other so that neither of us gets any sneak attacks handed to us."

James simply grunted out his reply and then swung his broad sword outward to try and stab the larger man in the stomach. Guy hit the sword away with one forearm while smashing James's jaw with the other fist. This made James to fly backward into the back of Sir William. James shook the cobwebs out of his head, and then Sir William pushed him off his own back and pushed him toward the figure of Guy Fawkes.

William was more used to the fighting style that he had to perform against the older Cromwell. They were closer to the same age, but still had the ferocity of a younger man when it came to battle.

Oliver Cromwell would swing his sword upward at William's head and shoulders, and the older knight would easily tarry these advances. He would then try to swing his sword on a lower trajectory, which Oliver would then jump away from. Both men tried to find fault in each other's fighting style as they brazenly threw blows with their own swords and blocked the other's blows with calculated moves of their own.

Both men had just tried to charge at one another, while trying to knock the other man off the wooden platform. They were hanging onto each other as if they were boxers trying to catch their breath.

Sir William then looked at Oliver's feet and oddly asked, "Did you ride your horse here?"

Lord Oliver Cromwell did not answer the older knight, as the question caught him off guard. Sir William pushed Oliver with all his might and spun his body around with a hard hit from the hilt of his sword onto Oliver's cheek. This move knocked Oliver off balance and facing the opposite position from Sir William. The British officer was quickly calculating the next defensive move that he would make with his sword.

Instead, William stomped down hard on the back of Oliver's heel and drove the spikes of one of his spurs into the wooden walkway. Oliver tried to turn around with all the strength left in his legs and his waist, but his foot was stuck facing away from his enemy. Oliver started to panic and began to flail his sword in different directions and behind him. Just then, Sir William stepped in close to Oliver Cromwell, while warily dodging the flailing sword of his enemy.

Sir William grabbed him by the hair and sliced through the neck muscles and eventually the vertebrae of Oliver's neck. Oliver's body fell directly downward, causing Sir William to stand in victory with Oliver Cromwell's head in his fist.

Once again, his body turned into a red mist and drifted off the roof to its destination in the circular red orb on the ground. As the body's red energy sifted off the roof, William nonchalantly tossed his head after it.

On the other side of William, James was trying to find a way of getting the deadly end of his weapon at the body of Guy Fawkes. While William and Oliver were still fighting, James tried to swing the older broadsword at the belly of the much larger man.

This only made Guy Fawkes grab the blade of the sword with one hand and then twist the sword out of James's own hand with the other. Guy looked down and sneered at James as he raised the sword up over his head with his shoulder outstretched and threw it over the edge of the roof with all his might.

The sword landed in the grass that stood next to the red portal of souls and made a clattering noise that the two men could even hear on the roof. Guy then made a grimace with his teeth and put each massive arm around James's body. He did this while enclosing his arms, and basically beginning to crush James to death.

Guy was looking over James' shoulder and watching the fight that ensued behind them. The large man grunted and let James pull one arm upward and almost free from Guy's grasp. This happened when Oliver Cromwell's head was dispatched from his body and thrown off the tower.

At the sight of Oliver's head toppling off the roof, Guy had loosened his grip, but he now began to lift and squeeze him even harder. James started to feel light-headed, and if this kept up, he would soon lose consciousness.

From behind him, James heard Sir William say, "Going low... between your legs."

A dagger was then thrust upward by William into the crotch of Guy Fawkes' body and driven up into his bowels and small intestines. Guy let out a thunderous roar of pain, and when he did this, Guy let go of James's body, which landed hard on the wooden walkway below him.

James breathed in a large amount of air and then stood up and pulled a dagger out of a sheath on the back of his own pants. He drove it into Guy Fawkes' ear and then twisted it, scrambling the brain inside Guy's head immediately.

Guy's hand tried to still grab at James's ankle, but he stepped away from it in surprise. The body of Guy Fawkes fell off the walkway in the other direction, causing it to lifelessly slide downward until it lodged itself against another wooden walkway. He then turned into a red mist and exploded off the ceiling.

James slumped to one knee and grabbed his throat, as if he were trying to guide air into his chest. After he had gotten a full amount of air back into his lungs again, he looked up at Sir William and said earnestly, "Thank you for the warning back there. That was close."

Sir William let out a guffawing laugh and said back to him, "Well, I wasn't going to cut open my own son's nut sack, was I?"

James simply said to Sir William, "Thank you, father."

A door in the upper floor of the Bloody Tower exited onto an upper walkway that had a staircase going down to where the gardens were located. This walkway also runs to the timbered buildings of the Queen's House, which are built directly into the outside wall that runs to the Bell Tower. The Queen's House is mainly apartments where the Lieutenant of the Guard used to live and is now the home of the Resident Governor.

However, at one time in the 16th and 17th centuries, this was also home to many prisoner's cells, a grand council chamber, and many rooms used for torture. Guy Fawkes may have been tortured by being stretched on the rack in the basement of the White Tower, but he did not make his final confession there. He finally made his confession to the treason of trying to blow up the Parliament buildings during the Gunpowder Plot in the Queen's House in 1608.

The group of four adults and two children that were on the second floor of the 'Bloody Tower' decided that this would be the door that they would leave from. Anthony and Sir Grey would take the lead, the young boys would travel in the middle of the pack, and Ryan and Ellie would bring up the rear of the procession.

They arrived at this order when they went to open the door onto the stone walkway outside and were unsure if soldiers might be just outside of it. Anthony volunteered to open the door, and Sir Grey would be the first one through the door with his sword at the ready.

The first part of the plan went anything but splendidly when the first door was opened. Sir Grey ended up jumping right into the middle of a sword match between two knights involved in a battle with each other.

First, both knights were surprised by the sudden intrusion, and secondly, Ryan and Ellie's group of people were not wearing any colors to designate which side they fought for. Ryan and Ellie both saw the immediate confusion and grabbed the boys by the backs of their shirts and drug them back into the tower.

Some black tapestries hung on the cell walls and would work to show their allegiances. Ellie took one boy to the nearest cell, while Ryan took the other boy to the furthest cell. They tore the tapestries from the walls and began cutting them into pieces and handing the black cloth to the boys. They had worked very quickly and rushed back to the door, only to find Sir Grey and Anthony with their swords drawn and standing over both soldiers' bodies.

One body was lying on top of the other, and the bottom soldier's body turned into a red mist and started to dissipate toward the red portal. The upper soldier's body turned into brilliant balls of white mist and shot up into the air. They exploded into several 'sparkle bombs', as the children liked to call them. At one point, the two colors inter-swirled with each other and made for an incredible color formation tumbling together as one.

Anthony looked at the boys and the couple coming back out the door. He frowned and said, "They did not know if we were friends or foes, and they attacked both of us. I took the life of the just knight with a sword in the back as he was trying to attack Sir Grey. I have never killed anyone before. How does anyone ever get used to this?"

Sir Grey sadly looked up at the remnants of the brilliant sparkles. He then put his hand on Anthony's shoulder and said, "Don't think of it as killing him. You just released his soul; that is what you did. Some people are just evil and enjoy killing, but most people justify taking someone's life any way that they can. It is the only way to stay sane."

Anthony smiled a little at these words, and then the boys handed all of them the black cloth for them to tie around their chest like a sash. Ellie had tied another piece of cloth around her neck as well. She may have gone overboard with the black cloth, but she wanted any soldiers to know where her loyalties lay.

Ellie was the first person to see a man that was wearing a red tunic running up the stairs toward them with his sword drawn. She raised the crossbow and shot the man coming toward them directly in the chest. Ellie grabbed another bolt for her crossbow, but could not get it reloaded, as her hands were shaking too badly.

She looked over at Anthony and said, "I know how you feel, Anthony. That was my first time killing someone, also. This is not a good feeling, but we all had to be protected. You are right, this feeling is horrible. I hope that I can justify these feelings soon."

Anthony looked at her with sorrow in his eyes, and he said back to her, "I would hate it if we ever got used to this feeling."

Ryan then looked at the way that they were going to have to travel to the Bell Tower and said lowly, "We are going to need a lot of rope and some grappling hooks to go over the tops of the houses. This looks like it is going to be a lot harder than running across a stone walkway. The Queen's House is built into the southerly inner wall… is there any other way to get to the Bell Tower without going over the roofs?"

Young Eddie then explained to them, "The Queen's House was not always a part of the wall. It used to be a defensive wall that had parapets on top of it, and buildings were built next to it. The main structure of the tower fortress will be as it was in our time periods. We do not walk around the towers and hallways that are in use today. We are not supposed to bother the living individuals that are here."

Ryan looked suspiciously at the young man and said, "Are you not supposed to bother living people, or not able to do so?"

Young Eddie then looked guilty and said, "Well, we can be seen or heard if we really would like to be. Most of us just want to be left alone or can't think about any other realm beyond the one that we have known and continue to live in. I will just confess that this is an extremely rare occurrence. Nights like tonight have never happened before in nearly 1,000 years."

Ellie examined where the stone walkway ended abruptly and noticed the parapets on the top of the wall to her left. They would have to climb to either the roofs of the buildings of the Queen's House or to the top of the slim parapet wall that was directly next to the buildings. On one side of the wall, there would be a fall in between it and these buildings. On the other side would be a tremendous open fall of nearly 90 feet, to the walkway below.

"Can you handle those kinds of heights?" she asked, looked at Ryan intently, who was now sweating profusely.

Ryan swallowed hard and said back to her, "It doesn't look like I have much of a choice in the matter. It would really help to have a couple of swallows of whiskey right about now, but I must have a clear head. I will just have to go on the roof-tops and not be teetering on the top of that wall."

Ellie turned toward Sir Grey and asked, "We are going to need some long ropes and a couple of grappling hooks, can you find some in the Tower? With the Queen's Houses being how they were in the 15th century… the hooks will have to lock onto stone or brick chimneys. We won't have any antennas or lightning rods to grab onto. Am I right?"

Ellie was only met by blank stares, and then young Eddie spoke up by asking, "What are antennas or lightning rods?"

Anthony and Sir Grey both ran down the stairs and out of sight after declaring that Ellie was correct. Hopefully it would have been easier to find grappling hooks and rope in more ancient times because finding them now may take a trip to the hardware store.

When they were gone, Ryan kneeled in front of the boys and asked them, "You will have to know how this works, but people live in these houses. Ellie and I are not ghosts and are from our own time periods. How are we supposed to climb on the roofs of their houses without causing them to be alarmed?"

Eddie answered him, "There are always ghosts wandering in this fortress every night, and they are never seen by the living. You and Ellie have been invited by us into our time periods. You now must abide by our rules."

Eddie then stopped and looked at their faces to make sure that he was being understood correctly. He then continued to say, "They may hear a bump in the night or feel a presence in the shadows, but they are not usually bothered by any of us. You are now part of the way that we live here. These people have loud battles going on outside their doors on many nights, so I don't see how going over their roofs is a problem.

Ellie then asked the boys, "What about the living guards that are on duty?"

Young Rich answered her when he said laughingly, "Just pretend that they are not there. My brother and I have tried to play tricks on them, but they never see us. They may think that they see something, but it all just comes down to a feeling that they may have that scares them the most."

Sir Grey and Anthony soon ran back into the upper rooms of the Bloody Tower. One held a long stretch of rope, and the other carried an old iron hook.

The first person to speak was Anthony Woodville, who was carrying the hook. He said that he and Sir Grey had to travel by foot to the

Wakefield Tower, which was the next tower over and where they found the two items.

Anthony had found the hook in the chapel where King Henry VI had been killed while he was kneeling in prayer. It is said that this murder happened on the orders of Anthony Woodville's brother-in-law, King Edward IV, on his rise to become the supreme leader. He also happened to be the father of the two boys who now needed them.

Sir Grey had found the long length of rope in the stone rampart that runs in between buildings. It had been carefully wound up into a loop that was lying in the corner of the ancient walkway. He grabbed the hook from Anthony and drew the rope through a rounded hole that was on the top of the iron hook. He tied a tight knot and then tested the strength between him and Anthony by pulling on each end of it.

Ryan then tested the rope again and said with a lump in his throat, "With the help of the rope, I am going to throw the hook and lock it onto the first chimney and climb up to the tops of the buildings. Ellie and I will lead the boys across the roofs of the buildings, while Sir Grey and Anthony will climb to the top of the wall and jump from parapet to parapet. This should conceal them from anyone that may see us from the courtyard and allow them to get across the wall."

Anthony then frowned and asked, "Why do I and Sir Grey have to go along the tops of the wall?"

Ryan only looked at them and said, "Mainly because you would make too much noise. You are dressed a hell of a lot more heavily than us, with the chain mail armor that you are wearing. We will be much quieter on the roofs, and this will be a safer solution for the boys, who cannot jump between parapets and will need our help."

Ryan then continued saying embarrassingly, "Plus, I may need help from the boys as well. I really don't like heights and am scared to all hell and back right now. Also, by going over the roofs, we will have to climb onto the roof of the Bell Tower. We will need for you to open the door on the inside of the building going from the top floor onto the roof. Who knows how many men are there or the resistance that you will get inside the tower.

Young Rich shook his head and said, "It is true. The door only opens from the inside of the tower. We cannot all go over the roofs."

Sir Grey said, "He is right, but how do Anthony and I get into the Bell Tower?"

"The boys said that there is a window where Catholic Bishop John Fisher was held captive on the upper floor of the tower," said Ryan with a slight smile. "The boys say that you can probably squeeze through this window and fight off any soldiers that may be inside. There seems to be no other way."

Sir Grey nodded at him and then grabbed Anthony by the neck and said, "I hope that you can keep your balance with that armor on, old boy."

This comment made Anthony strip all the armor off his body. He then said, "I choose to be light and nimble, over this heavy protection that we have."

It took Ryan three tries until he was able to throw the hook up onto the roof of the closest building and get it to lodge around the edge of a stone chimney. He then gave the rope a tug to test the strength of the rope's holding ability.

He glanced at Ellie and said tentatively, "Well, here I go...Wish me luck. I hope that I don't end up laying on my backside down here with you."

Ellie gave Ryan a soft kiss on the lips and said intently, "I have every bit of confidence in you. If you start to get that panicky feeling, just look at me and get your poise back."

Ryan began to climb the side of the wall first, while all the others gave him their silent encouragement, trying not to make much noise. The first few steps were slow, as Ryan was still not sure of the strength or hold of the iron hook.

After the first five steps up the wall, Ryan's heart began to beat faster, and his stomach seemed to be inching up into his throat. His arms began to shake at these feelings, and he tried to control the rising panic by trying to slow his breathing.

The only frantic thought that seemed to repeatedly go through his head was, "I must get up there... I must get up there quickly. Don't fall... I have total control over my body. Just...Move...faster."

Along with these thoughts and feelings, Ryan was energized with a shot of adrenaline. This seemed to help, and he climbed the remaining portion rather quickly. He clambered onto the roof of the building and grabbed onto the chimney with every fiber in his being.

Little Eddie came next up the rope, and he climbed with no trouble, as young boys are often able to do. Similarly, his younger brother followed him with even less trouble, as it seemed as if he were trying to be more brave and more fearless than his older brother. Ryan was very pleased at their overabundance of courage and tried to feed off their enthusiasm.

Ellie was the last to arrive, after climbing up the wall and onto the ceiling. She gave Ryan a gentle hug when she arrived, invoking a much-needed sigh of relief and a smile from Ryan. Ryan gave the rope a tug, signaling to Sir Grey and Anthony that they were all safe.

Ryan could see the rope grow tight as the two men began to climb the rope up to the stone parapets that ran along the tops of the wall. This would begin their arduous journey to the confines of the Bell Tower.

Ellie looked over at a white-faced Ryan, and she asked, "Are you alright?"

Ryan gave her a weak smile and said, "Well, my heart hasn't beat out of my chest yet. My panic attacks are really kind of strange to explain. The dread of thinking about what might happen in a situation is 100% worse than being thrown into that predicament. When I am usefully involved, I am very courageous… I just have a huge problem in getting the courage to be usefully involved. My brain seems to work in exactly the opposite manner than it should. You give me a huge surge of confidence, though…I hope that you realize that."

Ellie leaned over the edge of the roof and looked at the progress of Sir Grey and Anthony on the wall. Then she leaned back, her eyes widening with anxiety, and said, "That flow of positivity goes both ways. I really did not like looking over the edge. I guess we feed off each other's energy."

Ryan would unhook the rope, and then they would slide down the other side on their butts. When they reached the bottom of one roof, Ryan would then hook onto the next chimney and the group would climb again. At least all these roofs were connected, and they would not be dangling over the edge of a tall drop-off, like the pair of heroic men that were jumping across the top of a parapet wall, below them.

Sir Grey was the leader of the two men, and he had left his shield and slung his sword across his back. He wasn't going to get rid of his armor, but he would have better balance and control by doing this. The leap wasn't far in between parapets, but their main issue would be balance and overcoming their fear of falling the 90 feet to the ground below.

Anthony had not only taken off his armor but had also left his weapons back on the walkway. There was not going to be anything that would make him fall.

Slowly, the men jumped from one stone parapet to the next. They were finding success in finding a handhold on the sides of the buildings that were on one perpendicular side. They were much slower at moving compared to the others on the roofs above them, but safety and composure were the most important items on this journey.

Sir Grey looked down at one point, nearly half-way across the wall, when he whispered back to Anthony, "By God, I would much rather be involved in a swordfight compared to this."

Ryan, Ellie, and the boys had just slid down the second to last rooftop, and they had one more roof to climb over. Ryan began to fear the noise that a grappling hook made when it grasped onto the last chimney. Ellie looked downward into the courtyard below them and signaled to Ryan when to throw the hook.

A battle between two knights was going on below them, and when the white sparkle bombs went off, she motioned to Ryan to throw the last hook. Before Ryan or Ellie could react, Eddie grabbed the rope and climbed up the last roof. He had an idea, which was extremely smart as he only climbed to just below the top of the roof and peered over the edge.

He stared intently for several seconds and then slid back down to the others. His face grew serious, and he said quietly, "There are two soldiers on the roof of the Bell Tower, and I saw a light in the top-floor window of the tower. We have got to let my brother and uncle know that they are there, and we all must do this as quietly as we can."

Ryan smiled broadly at the young man and said while being impressed, "Good job, young man. I never thought about doing that. Ellie, can you pass along the message to Sir Grey and Anthony?"

Ellie moved over to the edge and let out a "Psst" sound to get the men's attention. When Sir Grey looked up and saw her, she put up two fingers, and then she rubbed the top of her head. When she saw a nod from Sir Grey, she pointed to herself as if she were saying that they would take care of them.

Then she kept one hand on her head and, with the other hand, made a single finger sign and motioned to her chin. This caused some confusion among the men, but Anthony finally understood what she was trying to say.

He whispered to Sir Grey, "I think that she means that there is one soldier in the room below the roof, where we are going."

Ellie smiled and pointed at the end of her nose before disappearing from their view. Anthony let out a large breath of air, and then the men once again started going toward the small window of the upcoming Bell Tower.

Back on the roof, Eddie lowered his small voice and said to Ryan, "Just don't let any of those men ring out the alarm of our being here."

Ryan didn't quite understand and asked quickly, "How would they ring out an alarm?"

Young Rich answered this not very smart question by saying bluntly, and rolling his eyes, "By ringing the bell that is hanging in the small white cupola on the roof of the tower. The bell rings twice per day at the opening and closing of the Tower Complex. It is used as a form of curfew bell, or as an alarm in our case, if we are discovered. It is named the Bell Tower for that very reason."

Ryan looked at them apologetically and then said, "Sorry, I just wasn't thinking about an actual bell."

Ellie looked at him nonsensically and said to Ryan, "What did you think was in there?"

Ryan took the crossbow off Ellie's back and then put two crossbow bolts into his pockets while strapping the weapon across his own shoulder and handing Ellie his broadsword.

He kissed her lips and said, "Stay with the boys… down here, out of sight. I am going to take care of those men on the roof."

Ellie reached out for Ryan, but he was already using the rope to climb up the roof. When he reached the top, he loaded the crossbow with one of the bolts and then crawled up to the very edge so that his armpits were just over the peak of the building, and he could aim the weapon.

Ryan had shot a lot of hunting rifles and handguns in his lifetime. He had even used a compound bow when he was hunting elk during archery season, but he had never used a crossbow before. Two soldiers were on the roof of the Bell Tower, just as young Eddie had said that there had been.

One soldier was looking away from Ryan and seemed to be talking to someone on the walking path below them. The other soldier was preoccupied by the ravaging battles that were going on down at Tower Green. In both cases, neither soldier noticed Ryan's presence.

There was a very light breeze coming out of the west, which was in Ryan's face, and he shot the first bolt from the crossbow at the soldier that was looking down at Tower Green. The wind seemed to cause the bolt to lose power, and the arrow fell into the side of the tower wall, falling on top of the roof below it.

Ryan had missed the target as he had shot low by approximately two feet. The wooden arrow made a small crackling sound as it hit the wall, and Ryan slid down behind the confines of the roof.

The soldier looked in Ryan's direction but did not see anything. He was more interested in the battles going on before him anyway. Ryan cussed at himself and then said lowly, "Take your time. This is not the time to get 'buck fever' and rush your shot."

Ryan knew that he was shooting at a man, but shooting at this human being seemed more important than any hunting experiences that he had ever been involved in. Accuracy and concentration were still keys, and he could not think any other way. There was too much relying on him, and if he screwed up this opportunity, they would all suffer the consequences.

After years of having a panic disorder, Ryan knew full well how the brain and feelings could sometimes get in the way of a person's own confidence and abilities.

Ryan lifted himself over the peak of the roof again and aimed the crossbow sights with a huge amount of concentration. He took a deep breath and held it in his lungs as he aimed two feet directly above the man's head. Ryan slowly pulled the trigger and let out the breath that he had been holding.

The bolt was catapulted across the darkness with hardly any sound and struck the man on the right side of his neck. The bolt went directly through the man's throat, an unbelievable expression went across his face, and he made a silent turn in Ryan's direction. He then fell forward, off the top of the tower, and down to the walkway below it.

The other soldier heard the commotion of the man falling from the tower, ran over to the edge of the roof, and looked down at his fallen fellow soldier. Ryan had no other weapon, so he quickly grabbed the hook and the rope that were attached to the chimney and slid down the embankment of the last roof. The soldier saw Ryan's movement and drew his sword while he moved across to look down at Ryan's location on the roof below.

The man's last words were, "Hark… Who goe…!"

Then, from below, Ryan flung up the iron hook as hard as he could. The hook flew past the soldier's face by nearly a foot, then it fell back down and lodged in the back of the man's neck. Ryan pulled hard on the rope, which caused the man to be pulled off the roof of the tower and down onto the ceiling at Ryan's feet.

The man had the wind knocked out of him but was still wriggling his body and grabbing at the hook in his neck. Ryan grabbed the first errant bolt that he had shot from his crossbow, put his hand over the man's mouth, and plunged the arrow into the man's heart.

On weak and shaking legs, Ryan stood up and suddenly vomited onto the roof of the building while falling onto his knees. After gaining some strength, he pried the hook from the back of the soldier's neck, which gave him another violent bout of nausea.

He then threw the bloodied hook back up and hooked it onto the chimney. He climbed up to the peak of the roof and lowered the rope down to Ellie and the boys. Ellie started to have the boys climb the rope, but Ryan had them wait until he slid back down and tried to move the body of the soldier that was waiting for them on the other side. Soon he discovered that the body of the soldier had turned into a red mist and had disappeared. There was only a large blood stain where he had once been.

At this point, Ryan could get all of them to the roof of the Bell tower, and they would have to be patient and wait for the arrival of Anthony and Sir Grey.

Two more leaps, and Sir Grey would reach the smallish glass window that led into the top cell of the Bell Tower. Upon looking through the window and inside the building, he saw that he was looking into a small, arched alcove that was part of the upper cell. He could see that the cell was lit by candlelight, and then he noticed a shadow being cast by one soldier. He seemed to be talking and motioning to someone else in the room.

His first thought was to continue with a surprise attack, smash through the window, and start to fight the men wildly. However, on second thought, he began tapping lightly on the pane of glass.

The first soldier that Sir Grey had seen heard the soft tapping and went to the window to find the cause of the noise. He was carrying a candle in a lantern and held it up to his face as he pushed his nose close to the glass.

Sir Grey then punched through the glass, grabbed the man by the top of his red tunic, and pulled him out of the window, shattering the rest of the glass outwards toward the walkway below.

Sir Grey never watched the man hit the ground as he began to pull himself through the now-open window and into the stone alcove of the cell. While pulling himself inward, his shoulder hit a small painting of a man, which fell to the floor and made for more broken glass.

One more young soldier was standing at the far end of the cell. Sir Grey quickly got to his feet and pulled his sword free from his back. The young soldier was taken by total surprise, as he was taking a drink out of a wooden mug when Sir Grey leapt upon him and drove his sword into the belly of the young man. The soldier tried to call out but only spit ale into the face of Sir Grey, who twisted the sword until the young man fell into a pile on the floor.

Anthony then crawled through the window, leaned down, and picked up the broken painting of the man. He looked passionately at the face of the man, while still clutching the painting with both of his hands.

He sadly said, "This is a portrait of Bishop John Fisher… this must have been his cell… before he was beheaded anyway."

Sir Grey looked at the face of the man in the portrait and said, "What did he get killed for?"

Anthony said sorrowfully, "He wouldn't side against the Catholic Church and give the King a divorce from his first wife, Catherine of Aragon. We died nearly 100 years earlier than he did, but I could not even imagine a different religion than the Catholic faith when I was living. He died for his belief in it... I hope that I can have that kind of faith... again... or ever."

Sir Grey looked at the sorrowful man and said, "You are a good man, Anthony. Don't ever think otherwise."

Suddenly the wooden door burst open, and two more soldiers entered the room. The first of the soldiers lunged forward at Sir Grey with a drawn sword. Anthony courageously shoved at the shoulder of Sir Grey, knocking him out of the way, and received the metal tip of the sword being driven into the side of his body.

The first soldier then looked over his shoulder at the second young man behind him and yelled, "Sound the alarm bell. Go now."

The second soldier then ran out the doorway, and when the first soldier turned back toward Sir Grey and Anthony, he was greeted by the blade of Sir Grey slicing through his throat. Both he and Anthony collapsed onto the floor, and Sir Grey looked down at his friend with sorrow on his face. He then ran after the man who was escaping up to the roof top and the bell that was placed there.

Ryan, Ellie, and the boys were sitting and resting themselves on an upper stone parapet of the Bell Tower when they heard the clanging of chains beneath a trap door that was on the floor of the roof.

Suddenly, a young soldier, dressed in a red tunic, came clambering through the door and slammed it behind him. He looked down at the door as if he could expect something or someone to come behind him. He then began to run to the white belfry where the bell was located.

Ryan stood up at the sight of the young soldier and took off on a run after him. Without thinking, he left his sword leaning on the top of the wall, back with Ellie and the boys. He entered the cupola only seconds behind the young soldier, who was reaching for a rope that was hanging below the bell. On instinct, Ryan yelled out, "Stop! Don't touch that."

There was a small wooden table that was sitting in between Ryan and the young soldier, and when the soldier saw him enter, he tugged at the rope hanging below the bell. As if in slow motion, Ryan saw the bell rise toward the sky on one side.

Ryan leaped over the table, catching one of his tennis shoes on it and tumbling it over. This splintered one of the wooden legs of the table and made it stick upward like a wooden stalagmite. He then put his left hand on the inside of the bell and felt the clapper silently smash against his soft hand and the hard metal side.

He stifled a scream as a sharp pain filled his palm and ran up his left arm. Meanwhile, his right hand was stabilizing the outside of the bell and stopping the ringing motion. With his left hand still inside the bell, he lashed out in the incredible anger that only pain can create in a person. After stopping the bell from ringing, he bashed the young soldier directly in the nose with his right elbow.

Ryan pulled his hand free from the bell, making a small tingling sound that could be heard. His injured left hand was immediately pulled close to his body and could not be moved because of the pain. He raised his right fist again and turned around to face the soldier on the floor.

When he had smashed the man's nose with his elbow, he had knocked the soldier unconscious, and the man had fallen onto the splintered leg of the table. It was now sticking out of the young man's stomach, but the man had not become lifeless yet.

Ryan still couldn't use his left hand, so he grabbed the untrue soldier by his collar with his right hand and started to drag him out onto the roof of the Bell Tower. Sir Grey then burst through the trap door and looked down at the unconscious man.

He looked up at Ryan and asked, "What did you leave him alive for?"

Ryan winced at the pain in his left arm and then said, "I stopped him from ringing the alarm bell, but I also didn't want them to be alarmed by a massive amount of red mist pouring out of the belfry windows. He wasn't killed yet, so I dragged him out here. We will have to toss him down the stairs. Just so he doesn't warn anyone when he eventually explodes into a red mist."

Ellie then looked at the clenched hand that Ryan held against his stomach and ran toward him while saying, "Oh my God, you are hurt."

Ellie then tried to open his clenched fist, and Ryan squirmed his whole body at the pain in his palm. She gave Ryan an extremely worried look and started to lead him to a place for him to sit down.

He grimaced and said to Ellie, "Some bones in the top of my hand were pulverized, and I think some of the fingers have been dislocated as well. I can already feel my hand swelling up, and it is soon going to be worthless. Please find something in order to manufacture a sling for it, and I will make sure that I only fight with my right hand from now on, I swear."

Ellie helped Ryan down the stairs and then ripped another coat of arms off the wall. She gingerly put his arm in a makeshift sling to keep him from moving it. She bent down and kissed his swollen hand, trying not to hurt him anymore.

Suddenly, the soldier's body that they had rolled down into the building exploded into a red ball of mist, frightening all of them. The red smoke drifted down the hallway and up a stone chimney.

Ryan looked at the others and said, "We need to keep moving quickly. We may have only saved ourselves a few minutes by bringing that dying soldier down here. Let's get to the Beauchamp Tower and rest then."

The group of people quickly went down the stone staircase to the cell below them. There, they noticed a man who was sitting in a chair behind a table in the cell on the second floor. He cleared his throat, as if he were getting the attention of the people that were coming down the stairs.

When he stood up, he showed that he was a shorter, stockier man who was dressed in a long, black cloak with a white shirt underneath. He had a very strong chin, thin lips, and a sharply pointed face. He also had very intelligent brown eyes, a stern look upon his furrowed forehead, and a black pointed hat on top of his head.

He raised his hands, as if he were surrendering, and he said, "I am not armed at all, and I do believe that we are fighting for the same side. That is judging by your actions above me over the last several minutes. The man is correct; we need to keep moving before they try to outnumber and overpower us."

Eddie and Young Rich then filled in the story by telling them, "To keep us moving quickly, the upper walkway of the wall will take us from here, directly to the Beauchamp Tower. This was named Elizabeth's Walk as the Queen was imprisoned here by her stepsister, Mary, when she was a younger woman. She would walk between these two towers each day. This will take us there quickly and hide us from view."

Sir Grey then said, "I will lead the way, and I will see you all at the Beauchamp Tower. Good luck and stay together, don't get involved in a long, drawn-out battle. Just keep moving quickly. We will take this new ally with us and get some more information from him when we arrive there."

With these words, he went out the door and started to run along the upper wall. A new unarmed stranger was now running along with the children in the middle of their small pack of people. The group met three battles between knights, where Sir Grey cut down each of the red knights by slashing them across the stomachs, chests, or throats without missing a running step.

Three soldiers dressed in black tunics began following them after their combatants were killed by Sir Grey. Two of the soldiers carried halberds as weapons, and one carried an English longsword. Behind them, a trail of three red explosions burst into the air.

The father and son knights, James and William Tyrrell, had finally caught their breath and began looking out over the grounds that were filled with battling knights and soldiers.

Suddenly, William grabbed James's arm and pointed while excitedly saying, "Look on the far wall."

Along the western inner wall, red groups of mists began exploding into the air. This mist began to rise at intermittent intervals along the top of the wall behind the Lieutenant's Houses.

James furrowed his brow, looked harder, and said almost knowingly, "That is Ryan and Ellie, along with some other soldiers and the two boys. They are making their way to the Beauchamp Tower. Do you know what that will mean?"

William looked down at Tower Green and the red glowing portal and said, "They are placing themselves directly on the other side of that red monstrosity that is down there. My god, that is smart. They will soon be in that horrible prison, and we should have those troops trapped between us. Let's pray that they get there before the arrival of the Mad King and the Evil Queen, who will be arriving here soon."

Directly ahead of the small group of a knight, a woman, two small children, a strange religious leader, and a wounded man, was a battle between the final two soldiers on the walking path. The three true soldiers that were now following behind them made their numbers to be nine people.

Sir Grey screamed out a battle cry and tried to slash at the red tunic, wearing knight. The evil soldier saw him coming, grabbed the shoulders of the good soldier, and spun the body of the soldier toward the oncoming sword. Sir Grey's sword found the true soldier's neck by accident, and a plume of white smoke rose into the air.

The white light exploded upward and caused the red knight to step back on one side of the explosion. When he did this, Sir Grey motioned for the small boys, the new stranger, and Ellie to run past him on the opposite side of the walkway.

Ryan was following lastly; he pulled the sword from the sheath on his belt and prepared to use it with his uninjured hand. Ryan dove forward with James's broadsword and stuck the man directly under the left armpit, and then pushed at the hilt of the sword with his right shoulder.

The sword slid into the man's chest, causing him to collapse, and he exploded red mist into the air almost immediately. Thankfully, this was away from Ellie and the boy's location. Ryan choked back at the red mist surrounding his face, and then he was soon gripped firmly by a weeping Ellie. She put her head on Ryan's chest and sobbed intently with exhaustion.

They stood there for a short amount of time, and then Ryan said, "Ellie, we have to keep moving into the next tower; we can't stay out in the open like this."

They opened the door leading into the Beauchamp Tower and found the inside amazingly abandoned by any soldiers. They went up to the upper cell in the tower and ran to the windows facing Tower Green.

Sir Grey looked down and said dourly, "I see four enemy soldiers at the base of the tower, guarding the doors outside. They must have cleared out of the tower before we got here for some reason. I do believe that we are safe if we stay up here."

Suddenly, the sound of loud horns erupted across the din of the battlefield, causing Ryan to say, "What the hell is that?"

Eddie, the older boy, said with fear in his voice, "The Mad King and the Evil Queen are here!"

Hail to the King
Hail to the one
Kneel to the crown
Stand in the sun…
Hail to the King
(Avenged Sevenfold)

Chapter Twenty-One

"And so, I am become a knight of the Kingdom of Dreams and Shadows." (Mark Twain)

The group of warriors and small boys had a little bit of time to try to relax and catch their breath. They accumulated around the windows that overlooked the beheading scaffold site, and they had a very good viewpoint of the arrival of King Richard III and Anne Boleyn. The king and queen appeared through the main entrance gate into the tower complex. They rode on horses, with four soldiers marching in front of them and four soldiers marching behind them.

Ryan looked back at the boys and said, "I am sure glad that we went this way, and we did not try to enter by the front gate. I think that we may have run into even more trouble going that way. Some people have been injured, and you lost your uncle, but it was a great idea that you boys had. Don't blame yourselves in any possible way."

His voice trailed off as he witnessed a young woman that was becoming visible standing directly behind the group of them. He asked the boys about her, and they turned around to look at her.

Young Eddie simply said, "She means us no harm; she is glad that we are here. Don't try to hurt her."

Young Rich looked at her and then said, "We have always known of her as the 'Weeping Girl', as she is very sad. At first, she scared us, but we have sat and spoken with her since then. She says that she was beaten very badly when she was a child, and that is what makes her shy, even in death. She and her young husband were beheaded here."

The small girl whispered in young Rich's ear again, and he said, "The 'Weeping Girl' says that she witnessed her husband, who was imprisoned in this tower, get taken to Tower Hill. A short time later, they brought his headless body back in front of her window while only covering it with a bloody sheet. She was then beheaded soon after him. Just outside of these walls, at the spot where the red portal now stands."

She whispered more into Edward's ear, then he said, "They were buried together in the church yard on these grounds on that day. However, their souls have been kept apart from each other for some reason, and she knows not why."

The strange man that they had rescued in the Bell Tower slapped his hand against a wooden table and then said excitedly, "I know who she is. She and her husband were imprisoned and beheaded in this place soon after me."

The stranger felt the tension rise in the room, and then he continued, "Her name is Lady Jane Grey, and her husband is Sir Guildford Dudley. She was only in her middle to late teenage years, and she was also Queen of England for only nine days. You see, she was used as a pawn by her unscrupulous father-in-law and was made queen only because of her family's own power-hungry political purposes. She and her young husband were executed because of this. I used to hear her sobs all the way at the Bell Tower."

Ryan then stopped the man from talking by asking, "We saved you from the Bell Tower, and we still don't know who you are. So, are you friend or foe?"

The man took off his small, black hat, bowed, and said cordially, "My name is Sir Thomas More. I was Lord High Chancellor for King Henry VIII, as well as a lawyer, historian, author..."

Ellie then interrupted him and asked, "So why are you here, Sir More? What did you do that was so wrong?"

He bowed again and said, "I asked to be here...mum… I wanted to help you in your quest. I was only beheaded by my friend Henry because I would not defy my beliefs in the faith of the Holy Roman Church. Mainly, I was executed because he wanted to marry that...that...horrible demon of a woman. I can help your cause because I have been dedicated as an actual saint. I do have the power of God on my side, and that can always be helpful."

Sir Richard Grey bowed and said, "We are pleased to have you by our side, Lord More."

The ghostly girl then whispered another thing into Edward's ear, and he said with a smile, "With the help of Sir Thomas More… Lady Jane would like to know if it is possible to find her husband's soul. Maybe if he fought by our side, Lord More could get their souls united again, at last."

Sir Thomas More stepped up to her and made the sign of the cross on her forehead. He then said, "I will make this request happen… for both of you, my child. I promise thee."

Mad King Richard and Evil Queen Anne, who wore a bandage over one eye, rode the horses slowly up to the red portal at the memorial. Two soldiers put two rather regal-looking cloth seats onto the grass of the lawn, facing towards the pulsing red orb. They were careful enough to leave enough room between themselves and the surging hole in the ground in front of them. However, they were sure to be close enough to feel its power.

The seats were also situated directly toward the group in the Beauchamp Tower, and their backs were directed toward the White Tower. Four soldiers were lined up in formation on either side of the portal, making eight soldiers in total to guard the red portal and the royal couple. Ryan looked down and could see an additional four soldiers blocking them from exiting the building.

This made Ryan turn toward the small group of people and state, "The King and Queen have 12 soldiers down there that we can see anyway. We have me, Ellie, Sir Grey, as well as three other fighting men here, and we may also have three more knights over at the White Tower. We also have an actual Saint, a shy ghostly woman, and two children to protect." Ryan began to add the numbers and calculate a plan quickly.

Ryan then looked through the window again and noticed a man with a long gray beard. He was dressed only in a long brown robe with a raised hood covering his face. He was now approaching the Evil Royals.

Ryan quickly turned and asked Sir Thomas More to come to the window and asked him, "Okay, Saint More, what can you tell us about this guy?"

The man in the long robe began sprinkling two circular arcs of white powder around each ruler while chanting an incantation three times! "Garantha… exterria… novectu… barantha..."

Thomas More looked back at Ryan and said, "He is an old shaman, also called a Magi, from the ancient days of the Pagans. He is giving each of them a ritualistic protective circle and saying a protection chant. That means no people or human-made objects can harm either of them when they are inside that circle of white powder.

Ryan furrowed his brow and then asked Saint More, "Can God find a way for us to defeat this?"

Saint More looked over at him and said, "Son, I don't like to say this...but that is an extremely nonsensical question. Of course, God can help us. I just need a room in which to prepare for his old magic. My dear Lady Grey, would you please assist me in a room where we will not be disturbed. Then we can also find the location of your husband in order to hasten his return to you."

Lady Jane Grey shook her head vigorously in a "yes'"fashion; she took Saint More's hand and walked with him out of the cell and down the stairs.

Ryan watched them leave the cell and said, "Alright, now we are most certainly fighting against a force that is a lot larger than our own numbers. And now, we are also battling against ancient magic...James told me that there was an ancient magic happening here."

Ryan looked embarrassed and then said, "Don't tell our personal 'Saint', but I haven't been to church in a very long time. I have really favored the belief in myself and the feelings that I get in my own gut. However, my life has been anything but perfect since I started thinking this way. So maybe I need to believe in something bigger than my own feelings."

Ryan looked out of the window again as one of the soldiers brought the pure white horse that 'Evil Anne' had been riding on and the brown bay horse that King Richard had been riding on. They were tied to a railing outside the shelter of the building below them. The brown horse reared up on his hind legs and almost seemed to dance until he was pulled down sharply by the man with the reins.

Ryan then said aloud, "I know that horse. Where do I know him from?"

Ellie looked out of the window and asked, "What are you talking about? How do you know that specific horse?"

Ryan then said excitedly, "That night in the hotel room that Monty was murdered in. Remember when I passed out and had a vision? Well, James was leading that very horse up to me… I saw him in my vision. I gently rubbed his nose and let him smell my hair..."

Ryan trailed off as if he were in thought, and then Ellie broke the silence and asked him, "How can you be sure that this is the same horse?"

Ryan then looked at her seriously and said, "Because of the strong feelings in my gut...Because we need a diversion, and James specifically showed me a horse that looked just like that one in my vision. James wouldn't do that if it didn't mean anything. Ellie, I have got to get to that horse. Otherwise, we are all sitting ducks."

Ellie then stated, "Then I am going with you."

Ryan looked at her seriously but lovingly and said, "No, this is what I must do. I feel it in my bones. You were meant to protect these two young men from any harm that the bitch out there has intended for them. These soldiers must be drawn away from you and the boys."

Ellie almost pleaded with him and said, "Nooo! Don't leave me here again. Why must it be you who is the diversion?"

Ryan stroked her tear-covered cheek and said lowly, "Because I was meant to do this. That is part of why I am here. I can only use one hand to fight with, and I am still not very good at it. But I know horses, and I can handle a horse with one hand far better than another person using both hands. I will be back and find you...This is our best choice...Trust me."

Ellie sobbed and said through flowing tears, "You had better come back...I just found you."

Ryan kissed her softly and then turned to the boys and said, "Eddie, young Rich, I need your help again. How do I get to these horses that are tied up behind those soldiers that are directly below us… without being seen?"

Eddie was the first to speak, when he recommended going back to the Bell Tower and leaving through the front entrance there. The worst thing about this plan was that Ryan would have to travel in front of the buildings of the lieutenant's quarters, and there were not many objects for him to hide behind. This idea was thrown out by the lack of concealment.

Finally, young Rich raised his hand and asked quietly, "What about the 'Little Hell' in the Devil's Tower?"

Ryan looked bewildered and asked, "Where is the Devil's Tower and why is it called the 'Little Hell'?"

Eddie took over the conversation and pointed it out to them by saying, "The Bell Tower is on the corner of one end of this wall, we are directly in the middle, and the Devil's Tower is located on the other corner of this wall. It is called the Devereux Tower now, but it was once called by those other names because of its old, terror-filled, small prison cells."

Eddie gave young Rich a grave look and then said, "We never explored this tower because some of the meanest, most vile criminals were once held in these prison cells. There are rumors of many tortures happening in this tower. Additionally, there are now apartments in that tower for one of the families that work here."

Eddie shuddered at the thought and continued to say, "You will most likely have to deal with the way the old tower was kept in our time, though, rather than come face to face with a family that is there now. This is not a nice place to visit if you are two young boys, so we stayed away from there. However, if you get there unscathed, the Church of St. Peter ad Vincula is just in front of it, and there were rumors of underground passageways going from there to here. If you could find one of these passages, this could possibly be the way that you need to go."

Ryan had a confused look go across his face, and he asked, "Why did they have secret passageways between the buildings?"

The answer that came back was unbelievable, but Eddie said, "The clergy and other spies often went in between the walls in order to listen to conversations held in cells that were supposed to be private. There were often spies who found out who was visiting and what was being said? This is how so many people were arrested for treason or why some families were blackmailed for ransom while they were here."

The boys then explained by saying, "All of the passages were covered up and taken out in today's reality… but I assume not all secrets have been covered up when you are dealing with the past in this place."

Ryan looked at the group and said, "It looks like I am traveling to "The Little Hell" in The Devil's Tower. I would much rather go to the 'Devil's Tower' in Wyoming."

This statement was only met by silence and confused blinks of the eyes. He then continued by saying, "You would all be impressed if you visited the 'Devil's Tower' in the new world. Anyway, fight your way out of this building when you see the soldiers start to chase after me. That is the best plan for right now."

He kissed Ellie softly, and then whispered, "I promise," into her ear. He suddenly left to go over the roofs of the residence buildings of the clergy that stood in between the Beauchamp Tower and the Devereux Tower. Once again, he was going to have to become an acrobat over the buildings, but this time he would have to do it with mainly one good hand.

From the roof of the 'White Tower', James and William watched Ryan climb clumsily over the roof tops of the chaplain's quarters. Then he ran across the battlements that ran into the Devereaux Tower.

William said aloud, "We have to go help them… now."

James shook his head and said, "No, it is not our time to fight yet. We must wait for the signal...We must have faith and patience."

The two knights could move down the stairs of the White Tower and closer to the others, but from this vantage point, they could keep track of everyone and the battlefield below. That is what was needed most at this moment. There is little use in being stubborn and headstrong or just jumping into a battle without first knowing the details and intentions of the armies involved.

Ryan did not run into any enemy soldiers on the way to the Devereux Tower, nor did he see any friendly ones either. Every soldier now seemed to be congregated at the sight of the red portal, and all of them seemed to be fighting for the 'Mad King and Evil Queen.'

Ryan stepped through the door into the Devereux Tower and instantly felt claustrophobic as this tower's walls seemed older, smaller, and even dirtier than the rest. Darkness seemed to hover in the dank air all around him, and he had to use the stone of the walls to help guide him around the interior of the tower. Ryan could hear whispering voices and the clanging of chains against steel bars all around him.

He let out a deep breath and muttered to himself, "How could there be nice apartments here now? How can anyone live here? I have got to get out of this place; I can hear the pain coming from every room in this tower. I do not want to see any of the spirits that have to stay here."

He felt his way down a small stone staircase and then felt at the walls at the bottom floor of the building. He was almost pounding on these stones, only hearing the thudding of hard rock. If he could not find a way to escape, he felt like he was going to go insane. He kept traveling in a semi-circular path until he slammed his fist into a wood-sounding door.

He fumbled for the latch and thought that it was locked, but finally he was able to press down hard enough with his right hand for the door to swing inward. Ryan stepped out into the freshness of the air and put his shaking hands on his knees. He breathed in deeply while also trying to slow his heartbeat.

At first, he had not even noticed the pain in his arm and hand that he had pulled out of the sling across his chest. He had put his hands on his knees, and when he looked at his swollen hand again, the pain responder in his brain came awake, and a massive amount of pain ran from his fingertips up to his elbow.

Ryan stifled a loud scream of pain and instead broke a small branch off a nearby tree. He stuck it in his mouth so that he could grind his teeth down onto the hard wood. After several minutes of this, Ryan carefully stuck his hand back into its sling, wiped his sweating brow with the back of his hand, and walked to the door of The Chapel of St. Peter ad Vincula.

Ryan entered the ancient chapel in the back of the building and even though the room was not lit by any electric lights or torches, the chapel seemed extremely well lit. The moonlight glowed throughout the clear, almost crystalline, windows and lit up the interior of the chapel. Ryan sat down and was resting in a pew at the back of the church, when he suddenly heard a voice.

He was looking down at the tiled floor and tilting his head so that he could hear better. Ryan heard the voice echo weakly toward him once again, and it said, "Welcome, kind sir."

Ryan sprung to his feet and looked toward the front of the church, where the voice seemed to be coming from. He could see the moon's crisp light coming in through the tall arched windows that showed down on the altar. The alter was covered in a crisp, green tablecloth and had two gold candelabras on either side of it. In this candelabra, there were three unlit, tall, skinny, white candles in each one.

In front of the alter, the base of the green and red Victorian marbled tiles, which contained several family coats of arms, could be seen. Peering closer, Ryan could barely make out the form of a shadowed young man laying at the base of these tiles.

Ryan stepped closer to him and could tell that the young man was chained in a spread-eagle fashion to the floor in front of the marble floored altar.

The young man looked up at Ryan and said with excitement in his voice, "Can you see that I am here, sir?"

Ryan looked down at him and said, "Yes. I can." Then Ryan asked him, "Who are you and why are you chained to the floor?"

The young man answered back, "My name is Sir Guildford Dudley, I was chained here, when my body was thrown into the crypt below me. How is it that you can see me when all others that are living have not been able to?"

Ryan looked at him quizzically and said, "That is probably a much better question that you can ask of yourself, because I really don't know the answer. Now then, how are we going to get you unchained?"

Sir Dudley then informed him, "I believe that you may have to find an axe and cut at the chains. Do you know where one is?"

Ryan looked puzzled and answered him by saying, "There may have been an axe in the 'Little Hell-Devil Tower' that I was just in, but I am not going back in there. Sorry, son."

Sir Dudley just shook his head back and forth and begged Ryan, "Please find one; just promise me that you will come back for me. It is so good to talk to someone who doesn't want to confine or control me once again."

Ryan smiled down at him and promised, "I won't. I think that you are part of this destined journey that I am involved in. I will return shortly."

Ryan ran to the back of the Waterloo Block, which now houses the Crown Jewels of England and prominent executive offices. However, when he entered this building now, it looked much older and yet more orderly, as it held the beds and barracks for nearly a thousand soldiers. Unfortunately, no weapons were to be found in this building either.

"Damn, this is hard with the buildings looking like they did in the past. They look completely different than they do today," Ryan said.

He then ran out of the building, looking both ways. He again looked at the Devereux Tower when he ran back, but he shook his head and refused to go back into those dank hallways.

As promised, he went back into the chapel and gave the bad news about not finding an axe to the young man chained to the floor. However, he pulled the heavy, bejeweled broadsword out of its sheath and said hopefully, "Maybe this will do the job."

The young man pulled the chain taut on his right hand and said, "If we were destined to meet, as you say we were, then these chains will be broken by that sword. Just please, don't miss. Over the centuries I have grown quite fond of my arms."

Ryan lifted the sword with his right hand and carefully came down upon the chain but only causing a small spark. It did not even come close to breaking the bonds.

Ryan then said, "I have got to swing a huge amount harder, so...please just look away from me. I think that your frightened and widening eyes may distract me."

Ryan put the tip of the sword on the ground in front of him and then swung it upward, twisting at his waist to make its arc more powerful. The sword came down sharply, and it hit one link of the chain and burst it into four different pieces.

Sir Dudley was holding the chain tight, and when the link of the chain broke apart, his right arm shot forward and hit him in the chest.

Sir Dudley was breathing heavily now, and he said with astonishment, "It broke! Ye Gods, how did you get enough power built up in the blade in order to cause the sword to do that?"

Ryan blinked heavily and then said, "Golf. You don't know the game, but you are lucky that I play a lot of golf during the summer months. All I kept telling myself was to keep my head down and let the sword do the work. Thank God that it worked and happened that way."

Ryan then used the same technique on three more chains. Sir Guildford Dudley was now free and sitting in a pew next to his savior. Ryan was now very much out of breath and in need of a drink of water.

He stood up slowly, making his back crack as he did so. To quench his thirst, he went to the alter and drank out of a bowl that was sitting behind the preacher's pulpit. He drank heavily until the bowl was empty, and then went back gingerly to his seat next to Sir Dudley.

The young knight laughed and tried to say gravely, "You know that what you just drank was holy water, don't you?"

Ryan then tried stretching his back out again and found that his sore muscles had become loosened. He stood up with vigor, twisted at the waist, and then touched his toes. "That truly was holy water. I feel amazing right now. My hand even feels better."

He then tried to open his left hand, but soon the pain started to run up his arm again. He grimaced and said, "Well, mostly amazing anyway. Now then, how are we going to get back to the Beauchamp Tower without being seen?"

Sir Dudley looked solemn and stated, "Through the secret passageways, of course."

Ryan then sat back down and said confusedly, "I heard about them, but I think that we need to have a talk first."

Ryan gave young Dudley a serious look and started the conversation by saying, "I met your wife, Lady Jane Grey, earlier this evening. She appeared before me in the Beauchamp Tower, and... she is fine...but she is extremely sad, scared, and misses you dearly. How is it that you are not together?"

Sir Dudley then told Ryan his sorrowful tale, "The night before we were supposed to be executed, I figured out a way that I could go to her prison cell and spend one last evening with her. I was extremely excited to see her one more time, and I sent a guard to give her the news. However, she denied my visit and said that seeing me would be too painful, knowing that I would be beheaded in the morning. She said that she would wait to see me until we were both in a different place beyond death. Well, that time has never come."

He went on. "My headless body was thrown into a hole in this place, and that very night, my soul was forcibly chained to the floor, where you just found me. The man who placed me here was a large knight who was wearing a tunic with a crowned shield on it. It had a red dragon on one side of it and a white greyhound dog on the other".

Sir Dudley took a deep breath and then continued to say, "As far as I can tell, my soul was held prisoner here while my wife's soul was held in the Beauchamp Tower. There have been so many people over so many centuries that I have tried to speak with, and nobody has heard me speak out until you. Not one person could see me and just walked right through me while I was laying on the floor below them. This place even burned around me, and I couldn't feel any heat. I was left unheard and unfeeling, chained to this floor."

Ryan listened with patience and compassionately asked, "You mentioned using the secret passages in order to get to the Beauchamp Tower. I heard that all these secret passageways had been sealed; could they possibly still be there?"

Sir Dudley then said, "Like I explained, they may have closed off the passageways in your human plane of existence, but not in mine. These are ancient kings and queens that we are fighting against, and nobody on the human plane of your timeline can see any of this except you. These passages may not exist anymore in your time period, but I am sure that they exist in this one."

Ryan thought about this seriously and then asked, "Just like in the 'Devil's Tower'. Those are now nice apartments, but nobody could live where I just had to travel through. Where are these passageways?"

Sir Dudley smiled and said, "Down below us, in the crypt. We are going to have to break into the ancient crypts."

The old crypts and the ancient secret tunnels of the chapel were located beneath the current tiled flooring that is directly next to the Victorian memorial altar.

Ryan cursed out again and asked with trepidation, "We are going to have to break through the floor? Why is this building not built like the rest of the buildings and is not an older version where there are just some stairs leading to the crypts?"

Sir Dudley replied by saying, "Maybe because this is the main religious center of the complex and hasn't changed much over the years. I just know that we will find a stone staircase under these tiles in the current church, but we must break the flooring in order to find it. My bones are buried beneath the raised altar flooring. Please don't disturb this section of the chapel."

Ryan looked concerned and then asked, "I have never heard of these different hidden crypts. Will these broken tiles only appear in your realm, or will they be there also in mine?"

Lord Dudley said, "Unfortunately, this will appear broken in your world as well. We were never here, remember, and this is the only passage that I know of in either of our realms."

Ryan said sarcastically, "Great!" He then grabbed a tall, gold candelabra and dragged it toward the alter of the chapel. He said a small prayer and had Sir Dudley help him lift it and slam it down on the extraordinary, tiled floor. The tile stone cracked but did not break open, and then the two men slammed the candelabra back down upon the cracked floor again. This time, they heard a sharp break of the tiles below them.

Ryan dragged the large candle holder back to its original position, while young Dudley peeled away the broken pieces of tiled floor. When the hole had been cleared, they both realized that they needed a couple of torches so that they would have some light in which to travel the maze of the crypts below them.

Sir Dudley ran to a small room off the nave and came back carrying two powerful flashlights. He smiled and said, "The priests and other workers keep these false instruments of light in a storeroom, just in case there is an emergency."

Ryan chuckled, grabbed the flashlights and turned on the first one, and handed it back to Sir Dudley. The young man seemed amazed by the flashlight, and he then turned the other one on for himself, looked around, and said, "This is probably the saddest chapel that I have ever been in, but I have a feeling that we are about to see a much sadder side of it."

Sir Dudley traveled down the stairs first, followed by a slow-moving, Ryan. At the bottom of the stairs, Ryan shone the light on a large alcove of cement that was hanging down from the ceiling, and he asked, "Is this large cement portion where the alter and the bones lie?"

Sir Dudley laid his hand on the cement and answered him by saying, "Yes, it is. They put down this piece of stone first, placed our bones within this mass tomb, added dirt on top of it, and then laid the tiles on top of it all. Fifteen people were buried in this ground, including the bones of myself and my wife. We will have to go through this walkway on our hands and knees now. Can you do this with your injured hand?"

Ryan grimaced and said, "I will have to… I made a promise."

After leaving the portion of the crypt under the altar, the hardened stone walls became even skinnier. This made the walkway three feet wide, and it was also only three feet tall. Ryan shone his light at the walls and was amazed to see that they were made up of mortar, in between human skulls.

Sir Dudley saw the shock in Ryan's eyes and said dourly, "Not everyone was buried with their removed heads, and there were many beheadings on Tower Green and on Tower Hill throughout the years. They had to put the heads somewhere. Do you need to rest?"

Ryan spat out, "I do need to rest, but I would really rather get out of here as quickly as possible."

The two men crawled for approximately 80 feet, and then the path started to rise upward. Dudley informed Ryan, "We are almost to the secret paths behind the back wall of the Beauchamp Tower. We will shortly come to an old trapdoor in the floor above."

Upon arrival and at first attempts, the trapdoor would not open. Ryan pulled out his sword again and started hammering the crease between the edges of the door in order to loosen them up slightly. Dirt was falling through the cracks onto them, and with a last mighty push, Sir Dudley burst the door outward with the strength of his shoulder and his upper back.

Above them, they found themselves in a passageway between the back wall of the Beauchamp Tower and the cells in front of them. Ryan then looked amazingly at Sir Dudley and asked, "Where are we?"

Sir Dudley shone his light down the length of the passageway and then answered him, "We are in a passageway of the Beauchamp Tower that was used to spy on the prisoners in their cells or to overhear the private conversations that these people had in them. There should be places to look inside of the cells; we need to find one of these places. The stone is much weaker there."

Ryan shook his head as if he understood what they were doing, and then he let Sir Dudley lead the way forward. Ryan had only one question on his mind at this time, but he would rather save it until they had finished exploring the space.

They started to hear a muffled conversation between a man and a woman echoing toward them. Sir Dudley stopped, put his finger to his lips, and then strode quickly forward toward the voices. He came to the spot where they heard the voices the loudest, and he started to rub away dirt and cobwebs with an enthused vigor from the wall to his left.

His fingertips then seemed to disappear into the very rock of the walls, and he quickly slid the ancient dirt and dust out of the small crack in the wall. A narrow slit was revealed in the wall where a person could see into the prison cell behind it.

Sir Dudley looked at Ryan excitedly, put his eyes against the wall, and spied into the cell behind it. He looked for nearly a minute, and then his hands began to shake, his eyes went wide, and he looked at Ryan with fear and desperation in his wild eyes. A sudden look of astonishment seemed to cross his face, and his knees almost buckled beneath him.

He tried to say it loudly, but the words only came out as a whisper, and he said quietly, "My Lady...My Jane...My wife... is just beyond this wall."

Ryan smiled back at him shrewdly and said lowly back, "Congratulations, you finally found her. Why, oh why... are you acting so apprehensively?"

Sir Guildford Dudley looked back at Ryan and said, "She hasn't changed at all. It has been over 500 years since I last saw her, and she hasn't aged a day nor lost any of her beauty since then. I don't even know what to say to her...It is like we are meeting again for the first time."

Ryan put his good hand on Sir Dudley's shoulder and said knowingly, "Just tell her that you are close to her and that you will soon be together. Just be honest with her and tell her where you have been. I told you that I had met her...She has been longing for your voice and especially your touch. Tell her that we are here."

Sir Dudley put his lips to the slight crack in the wall and said shakily, "My dearest Jane...I am hidden behind this wall and can't find how to get to you...but I do see you and am finally near you."

Lady Jane Grey stood up briskly as she was bending over a table and helping Sir Thomas More with a problem. She then shook her head as if she were hearing voices.

Sir Dudley saw this and continued to speak loudly, with hunger in his voice. "It truly is me, my darling. I have made my way back to you. Look for a small space in between the stones of the wall. I am just behind it."

At this point, Sir Thomas More also stood up and stared at the wall behind him. Lady Jane Grey looked at the wall with apprehension on her face, and she said warily, "Guildford? Can this be truly happening?"

Sir Dudley then got excited and said, "I truly am here. Follow my voice...We need your help in getting out of here."

Lady Jane began rubbing at the walls vigorously, and then Sir More joined her in the search for the small crack. Sir Dudley suddenly told them to stop moving because he had just seen a palm go across his vision. Sir Thomas More looked more closely at the center of the wall and then blew into an almost invisible crack that was on his side of it.

He then said excitedly, "Move back, I found the crack and am going to blow into it to clear the additional dirt out of it."

Sir Dudley and Ryan moved to either side of the viewing crack and heard a large blow of wind enter it. A stream of dirt and dust flew into the pathway, which caused both men to start coughing.

Ryan then looked at Sir Dudley and said, "We need to have them find a way to get us out of here. We don't have time to travel back along the long way around and hope that we don't get caught by someone."

Sir Dudley then pressed his lips against the wall and asked them to try to find a way to help them get into the cell. Lady Jane began frantically clawing at the stones, looking for any way to get to her husband. Saint More grabbed her hands in his, and then he placed his hands on either side of her head.

A white light seemed to light up in the palms of his hands, and he asked her to move to the other side of the cell. He also spoke loudly for the men to move as far away from the wall as they could. With the white light still emanating from his hands, he placed them against the stones of the back wall and began to quietly chant out a prayer.

Suddenly the wall began to quake, and dirt fell from the surrounding ceilings and walls, all around them. The quaking became stronger, and slowly, the stones began to crumble down onto the dirty floor below them. After approximately 20 seconds of shaking, a hole large enough for a man to fit through was exposed in the stone wall.

The floor was scattered with stones, but this didn't stop Sir Guildford Dudley from bursting out of the crack in the wall and running to his young bride. He simply held her in his arms for several minutes and then began to kiss her ravenously about the mouth, the neck, and even the ears.

Sir Thomas More cleared his throat, causing Sir Dudley to look back at him squarely and say, "I am truly happy to be with my bride again, and I am very appreciative of your help, but damned your saintly eyes, right now."

Ryan chuckled at this and then said to everyone in the room, "I am sure that the two of you would like to be alone right now, but you are both going to have to wait. The noise of the breaking wall is going to bring some soldiers to investigate. We now must make ourselves ready for them. Lady Jane...you and Saint More go to the other side of the wall and stay quiet. As for me and Sir Dudley, we will take care of whoever may be coming after us."

The outside door was heard creaking open, and Ryan went to the left-hand side of the door that went into the cell. Sir Dudley hid himself behind the wooden door on the right-hand side of the cell. The first soldier who entered the cell was walking gingerly across the entryway.

Behind him, one more soldier was following him and asked, "What was that noise? Do you see anything?"

The first man turned toward him and then said, "Bloody ell, tha wall fell in."

With these words, the soldier saw Ryan and tried to yell out an alarm. This made Ryan stab him in the throat with his dagger. The man only made a low, gurgling sound, and he fell onto his knees.

Sir Dudley stepped from the other side of the door and covered the second soldier's mouth with his hand. He sliced the skin and the veins of his throat with another shortened dagger. He then lowered this man onto the floor and looked to see if there were any more soldiers coming their way. When no enemies were in view, he then called for his wife and Saint More to come out of the broken crack in the wall.

Ryan grabbed a wooden chair and placed it below one of the windows. He stood on the chair while saying, "I really hope that this is a newer and stronger reproduction in this jail cell. All that I need is to have the chair crumble underneath my feet."

Luckily, the chair withstood his weight, and he looked out of the window with calculation and reasoning. Ryan then whistled quietly and said to the others without looking away from the window, "I will be damned; this tower is somewhat sunken and there are stairs rising to Tower Green from the entrance of it. There is a paved wall and shrubs rising above us. This will give me plenty of cover when I leave this building. I can amazingly see the horses tied to a railing, just to the right and above us."

Sir Dudley then said with foreboding in his voice, "We have dispatched two of their soldiers, but they know that the others are still in here and they will be guarding the front door. Additionally, they will be looking for the return of those two soldiers, soon."

Ryan looked at Sir Thomas More and asked him, "You and your God handled the wall fairly well; can you do anything with these windows?"

Saint More looked up at the window and only said, "If God wills it, my son."

Sir Thomas More lifted the cloth of the religious smock that he was wearing and climbed up onto the chair with the help of Sir Dudley.

He let out a "Hmmm" sound, looked back at Ryan, and said, "I am afraid that God is not on our side with this window. The iron bars are on the outside, and the window would have to be broken in order to get at them. I could probably break open the bars, but it would be tremendously noisy. You would also have to crawl over broken glass and exposed iron just to get to the horses."

Sir Thomas More shook his head sorrowfully and said, "I am afraid that you would just get your head through the hole in the bars and then lose it on the other side. God only leads the way in most cases, but we need to find our own way on the paths that are given to us."

Ryan let out a loud curse word by spatting out, "Shit!"

Sir More said, "I do not know of this word, shit...but I can assume that it is a cursed word."

This made Ryan laugh out loud, and he told Sir More, while helping him down off the chair, "The word has an interesting history, but the quick version is that it is just a short way of saying horse or cow manure."

Saint More then smiled and said, "Then let us get the shit out of here."

While the rest of the men were laughing about curse words, Lady Jane was concentrating about the Tower. She then cleared her throat and said in a quiet, almost weak voice, "I... I may have an idea."

The men turned her way, and she continued by saying in a stronger voice, "I have been here for many years, and in the small stone stairwell there is a window with no bars on it. It is on the outer edge of the building, so it would be hidden from view. We could break the glass out and lower a person down to the ground below."

Ryan looked very interested and then asked, "What about the noise that the breaking glass would make?"

Lady Jane then answered him with still more confidence, "We have the other soldiers that are upstairs join us down here, and we have them break out the glass of these windows at the same time. They will come in here to see what is making this noise, and these windows will be broken out. We can then battle them here, where we will be expecting them to be."

Sir Dudley hugged her, kissed her deeply, and said, "That is a brilliant plan, my dear."

Lady Jane sadly looked at Sir Dudley and said, "Also, I and Miss Ellie will take the boys back to the chapel through the tunnel system. So…my love, we were just given a chance to be together again for a short amount of time. This plan is going to tear us apart again."

Lady Jane began to weep at the thought of this. Sir Dudley wiped the tears off her cheeks and said, "We have waited 500 years; one more night is nothing compared to that, and it is the best plan that anyone has come up with. I am so proud of you."

Sir Thomas More then said honestly and compassionately, "That *is* the best plan that I have heard in a long time, as well. I believe that there is a cloth tapestry hanging on the wall up the stairs that we can use as a rope to lower Ryan down to the ground."

With these words, the group began climbing the small stone staircase. They stopped at a small arched window that stood along the stairs, and Lady Jane Grey was correct; there were no bars on this window. However, there was about a twelve-foot drop to the shaded sidewalk below.

They stopped very briefly at the window, and Ryan whispered loudly up the stairwell, "Ellie, it is me. We are coming up to you. Don't let anyone attack any of us at the top of the stairs."

Ryan waited for a reply when suddenly he heard Ellie's voice say, "Ryan? How did you get to the level below us? We have been rather scared up here. We heard several loud noises below us and prepared for the worst. It is so exhilarating to finally hear your voice again."

The first person that met them while going through the doorway on the upper level was Ellie, who threw herself at Ryan with open arms and wet kisses.

Ryan hugged and kissed her back. She then noticed that he was not alone and said, "I knew that Sir Thomas More and Lady Jane Grey were downstairs, and I am so happy to see them unharmed, but who is this young gentleman?"

Ryan looked back at the man and introduced him as "Sir Guildford Dudley...Lady Jane Grey's young husband."

Ellie bowed at him and said, "It is a pleasure to meet you. Is he another part of your destiny, Ryan?"

Ryan chuckled while smiling at Ellie and said back, "Yes, I feel like finding him was rather fate like. Hell...I feel like Hansel, and I am just following the cosmic breadcrumbs out of these crazy woods."

Ellie snuggled into him and said, "Does that make me Gretel?"

Ryan pulled his head away and said emphatically, "I hope not; she was his sister."

Ellie giggled at his reaction and then asked what the plan was. Ryan told the group of people about Lady Jane's idea and that he would be the one to climb out of the window. He said this even though he could feel an angry expression coming off Ellie.

She then said with fury in her voice, "You have an injured hand; how do you expect to climb down a wall?"

Ryan looked at her and stated emphatically, "Hopefully, slowly... I will wrap the tapestry around my left armpit and have total control over it with my right hand. I am not going to climb down this tapestry alone, as I am being lowered to the ground by Sir Dudley and Sir More. We did not have the manpower earlier to do all this."

He continued by adding to the plan by saying, "Now then, you and Lady Jane are going to take the boys and protect them along the hidden path to the Chapel of St. Peter Ad Vincula. These other two soldiers are going to break the glass in the windows of the cell below us at the same time we break the window in the stairwell."

He continued, "Finally, Sir Richard Grey is going to stand in the middle of all this activity and coordinate all of it so that it happens at the same time. Soldiers will undeniably be going to come in here and attack whoever is inside."

Ryan paused to make sure the importance and the danger were made clear to everyone involved.

Then he continued by stating, "Sir Richard, Young Sir Dudley, and the other two soldiers will make four men with which to meet them. The safest place for you and the boys will be in the chapel...and my ever-continuing destiny has got to get to that horse. Please just kiss me and try not to be too angry with me...I will make a promise to you once again."

Ellie looked at him with a pout on her face and said, "You had better come back in one piece. I want to show you something before you go, though."

Ellie led him up the stairs and showed him the graffiti that was inscribed into the wall. Ellie held his hand and then said, "Look at this one."

Ryan tilted his head and said jokingly, "It looks like two naked dogs climbing a tree."

Ellie then showed him another inscription that was nearby and said, "Look, the inscription of Jane's name is carved into the stone wall.

Ryan didn't want to sound uncaring, but he said to Ellie, "That looks like 'Iane' to me.

A voice came from behind them, and standing in the doorway were Lady Jane and Lord Guildford. The young lord then said, "That is the inscription that I made in this prison cell. 'Iane' is the old-English spelling of the name Jane. My brother, 'John Dudley' made the other inscription. This is my family coat of arms, with a lion on one side and a bear on the other climbing up a ragged staff. I and my brothers were held in this cell. That 'gillyflower' on our family insignia is meant to describe me.

Ellie looked sadly over at Sir Dudley and asked, "What became of your brothers?"

Guildford made a painful expression and said more happily, "My brothers were released from this prison. I was the only one to lose his head. However, my brother 'John,' who did this carving, died soon after being released. He was never the same after being incarcerated here."

Ellie then grabbed Ryan by the hand and led him to one more inscription and said proudly, "Look at the name who wrote this one, William Tyrrill. There is a different spelling of the last name, but do you think…?"

"Old William may have written this?" Ryan said with amazement. Then he continued to ask Lord Dudley, "Guildford, can you tell us what he wrote here. It is written in that old-English style of writing, and I can't read it."

Sir Dudley looked at the wall and then started to translate the writing:

"Since fortune has chosen that my hope should go to the wind to complain,
I wish the time were destroyed; My planet being ever sad and ungracious."

Ryan then whistled and said, "I guess that is why old William has become a time-traveler. It sounds as if he were predestined to become one.

Ellie then grabbed Ryan's hand and led him down the stairs again to the window on the stairwell where they found Sir More. Ryan was then taken by surprise again when Ellie continued by asking, "Saint More...will you please bless Ryan and what he must do?"

Ryan looked at the massively religious Roman Catholic saint and then said, "Are you sure that you want to do this Saint More? I must admit that I am not Catholic, nor was I baptized as a Catholic."

Saint Thomas More smiled kindly at Ryan and then said, "I will always be a devout follower of Catholic principles, but that is just my belief. One of the first things you learn after death is that God is whoever you believe in. God is love, and in everything all around each of us. God is one meaning of a 'divine being' to one person, and another meaning of a 'divine being' to someone different."

Every one of the people was hanging on Saint More's words, and he continued, "When human beings lived in more ancient times, men could not handle the thought that one God could control all things. Therefore, they created a multitude of powerful Gods that were needed for their religious needs. They had Gods for everything."

Saint More continued to give more understanding, saying, "The divine being that guides the universe and all the energies surrounding us is God...in whatever form you choose for them to be, or no matter how many of them there are...Mother Nature is God...the air, the earth, and the skies are God. We are all surrounded by God!"

Saint More looked at them all to make sure everyone understood before completing, "All a person must do is look for their own personal clues along their own path. They do this to find his wisdom. It is what you do with these clues and this knowledge that makes you into what you will become. Have faith in yourself, and this is how to praise God the most. You pray with your actions...not your words."

He made the sign of the cross on Ryan's forehead and said a prayer in Latin. Saint Thomas More then looked at Ellie and said, "Is this a good enough blessing for the hero of your story, Ellie?"

Ellie didn't say a word and only nodded and kissed Ryan. She then ran down the stairs, following the young boys. Ryan only looked at Saint More and said quietly, "She probably wasn't expecting a sermon, but thank you very much."

Thomas More smiled and said back to him, "I didn't think that just telling you to do the right thing would appease her dour feelings at this time. Just come back for her. That is what she wants most of all."

Ryan smiled and stated, "You just worry about not dropping me on my head, right now."

"Did the promise of day, turn cold in the night
You are the light
All you have is your name, but the air is alive
You are the light…
…I believe in you."
(Vertical Horizon)

Chapter Twenty-two

"Lightning does all the work; but thunder takes all of the credit." (Ken Alstad)

Sir Richard Grey was standing at the base of the stone stairwell, just above the soldiers in the lower prison cell. He yelled and asked the groups of men, "Are you ready to break the windows on each side?"

A resounding "Aye" came from both sides of him, and he signaled by just saying, "Now."

In the prison cells below him, the two soldiers broke the glass out of the windows with metal-tipped spears… while in the stairwell, Sir Dudley used his sword to break out the full glass of an arched window.

He was smiling as he did so, and he exclaimed, "That felt so good. I was in the mood to destroy something in this damned place."

Ryan had wrapped the tapestry around his shoulder and looked down at the ground from the window. He took in a large breath and closed his eyes before stepping out of the window and onto the brick outside wall of the Beauchamp Tower. Glass was still heard breaking in the cells below them. Ellie and the boys were safely going underground to the chapel of St. Peter. Finally, Thomas More and Sir Dudley were lowering Ryan to the ground as gently as possible.

Ryan was still approximately 9 feet off the ground below them when they began to hear the main entrance door of the tower being kicked in.

Sir Dudley then yelled excitedly to Ryan, "We are going to have to lower you faster...they need my sword downstairs."

Ryan braced himself and said, "Go ahead."

The final 9 feet lowered rapidly, and Ryan had to unwrap himself from the tapestry and jump the remaining 3 feet to the ground below. He tugged at the tapestry to show them that he was on the ground, even though he saw Sir More looked down to make sure.

Saint More mouthed the words, "Go with God." toward Ryan.

Ryan knelt into a crouched position and looked upward, where the horses should be tied to the post.

Lady Jane was leading the two boys on hands and knees throughout the tunnels leading to the safety of the Chapel. Ellie took up the rear of the group and could hear the distinct sound of breaking glass behind her. Both she and Lady Jane had the flashlights, and they illuminated the path forward.

A loud scream came from the front of the line when Lady Jane discovered the walls that were made of human skulls. She said back to the boys, "Don't look to the side; just keep staring at the floor as you crawl along."

Of course, this suggestion didn't work, as curiosity got the better of the two boys and Ellie heard exclamations of fright coming from in front of her. As an anthropologist, Ellie was amazed by the bones and skulls of this secret passage, and this slowed her journey through the ancient bones by several minutes.

She told Lady Jane to keep trudging forward and get the boys to the safety of the chapel. She felt intrigued enough by the bones that surrounded her and felt like she had to study them. If only for a limited time and given this opportunity that she would never have again.

At least, she had to examine them quickly and with as much detail as she could. However, intrigue can sometimes cause time to slow down to a snail's pace. Ellie soon found herself all alone in the caverns below, while Lady Jane and the two boys climbed the stone staircase that led into the darkness of the Chapel of St. Peter Ad Vincula.

The soldiers that broke down the entrance door of the Beauchamp Tower came into the room with blood in their eyes. There were four enemy soldiers in total, and the closest allied soldier that had broken out a window was brought down quickly by the slashing sword of one of the first invaders. The four intruders then started to stalk the remaining soldier backwards into the recesses of the cell.

The soldier was holding out his spear at them in fear when Sir Richard Grey burst into the room from behind them. With one long swoop of his broadsword, he sliced along the backs of the two soldiers that were facing the other way. They both let out a curdled scream and then fell to the floor in heaps of quivering bodies.

One of the two remaining intruding soldiers spun around and raised a sword at Sir Grey. The other man didn't turn, and he faced the spear-carrying soldier in front of him.

An even-handed sword battle broke out against Sir Grey and the larger, impending enemy soldier. Back and forth, they blocked each sword swing that was thrown by the other man. This was until the enemy soldier hit Sir Grey's sword with such force that it threw the sword from his hand.

The man let out a devious laugh and gave Sir Grey a dirty, toothless smile. Sir Grey then screamed out a war cry and ran at the man in order to tackle him. He took the soldier by surprise and barely bypassed the blade of the sword. He then punched the man in the eye while stepping on his foot and tripping him onto the cell's floor. Sir Grey sat on the bigger man's chest while slamming his fists down upon the soldier's face.

The allied soldier with the spear thrust it at the midsection of the enemy soldier's stomach. He barely missed the enemy soldier, who grabbed the wooden handle of the spear and pulled him close enough in order to hit the allied soldier's chin with the hilt of his sword. The allied soldier fell backwards at this hit, and the invading soldier pushed the blade of his sword into the man's chest.

The enemy soldier's hands lifted to the hilt of the sword, and then he twisted the piece of deadly metal. The enemy soldier then pushed the other man off the blade of his sword with his foot and spun around to the back of Sir Grey, who continued to beat his fellow enemy soldier on the floor.

He raised both his arms with the hilt of his sword, meaning to thrust it downward into the back of Sir Grey. As the enemy soldier hulked over the undefended back of Sir Grey... Sir Dudley broke into the room with a scream on his lips and his sword held out in front of him.

He drove his sword deeply into the lower stomach of the enemy soldier, who was about to cowardly kill a man with his back facing him. Sir Dudley stepped over the two bodies on the floor and continued to push the man backward with his sword. He did this until he felt the steel hit the hard stones on the far wall. The enemy soldier was impaled by the blade of the sword until Sir Dudley pulled it free. The man slid to the bloody floor and immediately burst out into a red mist.

Sir Grey smashed the other man in the face with one more mighty blow and broke the cartilage of his nose for the third time. This time, the soldier fell limp, and the cell was filled with both red and white colors of mist streaming out of the windows. If a person looked at the broken-out window from the outside, he would not be able to differentiate who was slain and who was still surviving inside the tower.

One man was looking at these windows at this very moment, and his heart sank at the vision of two white explosions leaving the cell of the Beauchamp Tower. Ryan could only feel sorrow at the sight of one of his new friends losing the battle.

Ryan slowly climbed the stairs in a crouched position, and at the top of them, he slid sideways behind the shrubs. He did this to make sure that he was concealed by the greenery that had been growing outside of the building. He was still hidden behind a shrub when he reached through the scratching branches and untied the reins of the horses.

The female white mare, which Anne the Queen had been riding on, whinnied out in fear at the sight of a strange man. However, the brown stallion looked deeply into Ryan's eyes, as if Ryan had already gained the confidence of the horse.

Ryan slapped the ass of the white horse, making her run to the left and through a line of soldiers. He then grabbed the reins of the bay pony and pulled himself into the English riding saddle.

He felt the difference between an American range saddle and the narrower English riding saddle as soon as he sat down on the horse. The first thought to come into his head, even before any dangerous situations, was that the saddle would probably cause him to get a wedgie or a hemorrhoid.

The horse made a circling pirouette underneath Ryan, and then Ryan kicked his sides so that he would run out to the right and away from the soldiers. He rode the horse at a trotting pace along the inside buildings of the tower grounds. He then turned the horse to the left and rode up to the main gate that allowed tourists to venture back into the days of Old English history.

He stopped in front of the gate and turned the horse to look in the direction of the 'Mad King and the Evil Queen.' His plan had worked because almost half of the remaining soldiers were running after Queen Anne's horse, which was now eating grass in front of the Chapel of St. Peter ad Vincula. The other half of the soldiers had broken away and were now running after him. He then looked up at the White Tower and nodded his head. He could only hope that his head gesture had been noticed.

James and William looked down at Tower Green and the movement of the soldiers in front of the Beauchamp Tower. They heard the glass shattering first, and soon they saw a mixture of white and red mist-like spheres escape from those openings in the buildings. James looked at the main entrance door, as he was sure to see that a group of warriors would soon be leaving there.

However, out of the corner of his eye, he witnessed Anne Boleyn's horse run through the group of soldiers standing at attention in front of the king and queen. As this happened, he shifted his gaze and saw Ryan mount the brown horse. He was leading another group of soldiers in the opposite direction.

James poked William with his elbow and stated excitedly, "That is what we have been waiting for. My God, he figured out how to split up the remaining soldiers. Let's get down to the entrance as fast as we can."

James smiled and said, "We have just been invited to a battle."

In all the confusion, 'Evil Queen Anne' wanted her precious horse to be under control and unharmed. Her horse had been a present from King Henry VIII himself, and there is no way that she would risk his safety. King Richard III and she were now only being guarded by two soldiers and that ancient magic shaman that Richard insisted on always bringing along. She stepped out of the protective circle and walked toward her horse and the Chapel of St. Peter.

The soldiers were just now trying to surround and corral her horse with their arms raised up over their heads or held out at their sides. They were trying to hush and calm the horse, only to see her neigh loudly and rear back on her hind legs.

There was a pot of flowers standing on a rock wall outside the chapel. Queen Anne ripped the blooming flowers out of the pot and then struggled in between two soldiers while screaming at them, "Get your filthy hands away from my horse."

The horse calmed at the sight of her and reached out with her nose in order to have it gently nuzzled. She fed the horse the yellow flowers and spoke softly, "Shh, my baby. None of these bad men are going to hurt you. Mommy is here for you now."

Her voice trailed off when she looked through a window and saw a woman lead the two small boys out of a hole in the floor. A greedy grin came across her face as she thought about finally getting her grips on the young male princes. They were innocence without corruption, and they would finally be her way of getting out of this blasted prison and having her soul move into paradise.

Sir Grey and Sir Dudley threw open the door of the Beauchamp Tower and climbed out in the fresh air while trying to brush both white and red mists out of their faces. They were both having spasms of coughing fits while they tried to climb the pavement stairs leading up to Tower Green.

At the top of the stairs, they were met by the two soldiers that were still left there to guard the king and queen. One large soldier had a sword in one hand and a shield in the other, while the other, skinnier soldier fought with only a longer, spear-tipped halberd. Sir Dudley began fighting the skinnier soldier with the halberd, when the ax blade of this ancient, speared weapon was thrown down at his head in an arc from above.

Lord Dudley jumped to his left, and the ax head that had been thrown at him thudded into the grassy ground where Sir Dudley's right foot had just been. The wet grass became entangled in the ax blade, and it stuck in the ground. This allowed Sir Dudley to step forward and plunge the blade of his sword into the flesh of the armpit of the skinnier soldier. With a heaving grunt, he pushed at the hilt of the sword and drove it deeply into the man's chest.

The larger soldier swung his sword at the neck of Sir Grey, who ducked below the blow and swung his own sword at the man's legs, who blocked it easily with the shield that he was holding in his left hand. This happened several times as each man was feeling out the other man's strengths and weaknesses.

The heavier soldier glanced a blow of his sword off the chain mail armor that was across Sir Grey's chest. This blow didn't severely wound Sir Grey, but it did weaken and puncture the armor enough that a bleeding gash was left across Sir Grey's chest. This made small droplets of blood go through the holes in the chain mail and a stinging pain emanate across the muscles on his chest.

The sharp pain of this wound made Sir Grey drop to one knee, and when he did, he kicked out at the larger man's leg. His foot slammed into the man's kneecap, causing him to collapse onto the ground in pain. Sir Grey stood up and hovered over the soldier while holding the blade of his sword directly above his heart.

The man on the ground started to spit out an insult about Sir Grey making love to a pig. As a result, the blade of Sir Grey's sword was driven through the chest of the man and into the muscled tissue of the heart.

Sir Dudley looked over at his fellow knight and pointed with the blade of his sword while saying, "Our battle is not finished here, yet. There are four more soldiers running at us from the direction of The Chapel in the north."

Ryan trotted on the horse toward the stairway leading upward to the entrance doors of the White Tower above him. His attention was now focused on the four oncoming soldiers running toward him. He lowered himself from the uncomfortable saddle, pulled the seat of his pants out of his butt crack, and lowered his legs into a stronger stance.

He rubbed the neck of the horse and whispered, "We might as well not both die today."

He then slapped the horse on the backside and sent him running in the opposite direction of the oncoming soldiers. He pulled the heavy sword out of its sheath and prepared for the onslaught of overpowering professional soldiers.

The soldiers were now eight feet away from Ryan when two large metal objects fell on the bodies of the soldiers. The first soldier's head was crushed under the weight of Sir William's armor-clad body falling onto him.

The oncoming soldiers stopped running toward Ryan when another armor-clad form of James leapt upon them and tackled them to the ground. Ryan let out a sigh of relief and strode forward with confidence at the sight of his knightly friends.

One soldier had not been killed or tackled to the ground, and Ryan stepped toward this man while swinging the sword at the man's stomach. The man stepped out of the way of the blow and dropped down onto one knee. He slashed forward with his own sword, cutting the flesh on the side of Ryan's left thigh.

Blood began to flow down Ryan's left leg and into the tops of his white, high-top tennis shoes, as the sword had cut through the denim of his jeans. Ryan let out a cry of pain, fell onto his side, and prepared for the sharp pain of the cold metal to enter his body with the death blow.

James had quickly stepped up behind the soldier and had cut the man's throat with a sharpened, smaller dagger. He then quickly turned around and drove this same dagger into the stomach of another soldier's lower gullet.

Sir William had dispatched the last soldier with a blow from his own sword, and then the grounds around the White Tower had grown silent. James lowered his arm in order to lift Ryan up onto his feet. He held him there while Ryan pulled the leather belt from his waist and tightened it onto his upper thigh with a grimace and a grunt of pain.

James asked with concern, "Are you well enough to fight with us?"

Ryan tried to put any weight on his left leg and then said, "No, I cannot even stand up on this thing."

Ryan and the two knights then huddled together, trying to figure out their next move. That is when the brown horse lowered his nose into the circle of men.

Ryan scratched his nose and then said hopefully, "I can't walk on my leg, but his are just fine. Help me get back up on top of the horse. But first, let me get this god-awful saddle off his back."

The 'Evil Queen Anne' tied her horse to a branch of a small tree. She then opened the back door quietly, and it barely made a clicking noise when it closed. She even took off her white shoes so that she could sneak across the floor silently without being noticed.

She was hiding behind a stone sarcophagus with a carved stone knight praying on top of it that happened to be raised in the center of the chapel. A thin rope was surrounding the ancient tomb so that tourists would not touch the ancient object with their dirty and greasy hands. She untied one end of the rope and pulled at it slowly and silently toward herself until she had a long, coiled rope in her hands.

The only sound that made any noise was the squeaking of one of the metal rings that she pulled the rope through as it swung back and forth in a kind of rocking alarm. The sound echoed around the old chapel as if a slight breeze had blown the golden metal ring, but Lady Jane and the boys heard the squeaking noise and had to investigate where it was coming from. Lady Jane held each of the boy's hands and slowly walked to the carved coffin in the center of the chapel.

'Young Rich' stopped the rotating motion of the metal ring with his finger, and the noise abruptly stopped. A loud breath was heard being exhaled, and then the flashlight was knocked out of Lady Jane's hand. She bent down to pick it up, and a very hard object came down on the back of her head.

Lady Jane dropped the boy's hands and slumped to the floor with a loud thud. The boys saw the light lift off the ground, and then it shone up to the ashen white face of the "Evil Queen."

She gave them a hungry smile and said, "Hello, my darlings!"

Sir Richard Grey turned his body around, only to be greeted by the sight of four more soldiers running in his direction. Shortly, he felt the shoulder of young Sir Dudley standing beside him, and he said, "It has been an honor fighting with you, Sir Grey."

Sir Grey, a little bit older and much more cynical, said back to him, "The only honor today, lad, is when all these bastards are killed and sent back to where they belong."

With these words, neither of the heroic men could move their arms, legs, or even swivel their necks. It was as if every signal from their brains to control their muscles had been severed, and they acted as if they were now stone statues.

The 'Mad King Richard' yelled, "Halt," stopping his advancing soldiers.

He then said like a childish sociopath, "It feels like forever since I have had archery practice. Necromancer... place these two men up in the air as if they were archery targets."

With a wave of his hands, the shaman with the long gray beard, made a pulling motion, and Sir Grey and Dudley were pulled backward as if they had a giant magnet wrapped around them. The heels on their feet were being dragged across the ground, and their hands had dropped their swords.

Their arms and their legs were spread outward in a spread-eagle shape, and it was as if they had been nailed to an invisible X. In this moment, they could not move their bodies far enough to even make any sounds.

'Mad King Richard' then yelled at one of the last four soldiers left to guard him for a bow and a quiver full of arrows.

Ellie was captivated by the skulls and bones located in the crypt underneath the Chapel of St. Peter ad Vincula. She held her light over the construction of the concrete poured over and in between each skull in order to make it a structurally sound tunnel.

She then looked at her illuminated watch and cried out, "Shit!"

She scrambled through the short tunnels and below the alter graves themselves, wishing that she had more time to investigate. When she was about to climb up the stairs leading into the chapel, she could hear the banging sound of a door being closed.

She cocked her head, trying to hear other noises, and when she heard none, she called out the name "Jane....Lady Jane?"

She then listened again and thought that she heard the neighing of a horse in the distance. By then, she was yelling out for the children with a panicked tone in her voice. There was no reply...So Ellie shut off her flashlight and climbed out from the crypt silently.

Moonlight was shining through the clear windows, and Ellie tried calling out for 'Lady Jane' again. She bruised herself and was making herself sore by crawling around the stone aisles on her hands and knees. She raised her head up above the pews and noticed a dark lump next to a stone sarcophagus in the very middle of the chapel.

She turned on her flashlight and stood up slowly while shining the light in that direction. She then yelled out, "Lady Jane," and ran in that direction.

When she arrived, Lady Jane was groaning wildly while holding a painful knot on the back of her head. She spoke in a slow, slurred tone of voice, saying, "Someone hit me...Took the children."

Ellie stood up straight, looked in all directions, and then ran to the window, where she saw 'The Evil Bitch Queen' leading the boys away from her.

She had them tied together at the waists with one end of the rope. She was leading them, as if they were on a leash, toward the 'Mad King', who was shooting arrows at Sir Grey and Sir Dudley's bodies. It looked as if the men were suspended directly across from him and as if they had been nailed to invisible targets.

"No," Ellie said tiredly, and then a mean, violent look came across her face.

She checked to make sure that she had her crossbow's drawstring pulled back and that her weapon was at the ready. She also had eight additional shooting bolts still in her arrow quiver, and she was not afraid to use them.

Ryan needed William to hold the reins of the horse as he gingerly and painfully raised his wounded left leg into the hand of the young knight. James had to push his leg and butt for him to swing his right leg over the back of the horse.

Pain shot through his leg as he was being lifted, and he could hardly stand sitting on the horse until he became more comfortable, and the pain subsided into a dull roar, in his leg.

He led the way, a little ahead of Sir James and William who walked on either side of them. They could see Sir Grey and Dudley being used as target practice by the king directly ahead of them, and this made them all trot at a faster pace. While they were faster in getting there, the metal of the suits of armor was quite noisy, and the clopping hooves of the horse did not help either.

'The Mad King' fired an arrow at Sir Grey and smiled coldly when he struck the man in the outstretched bicep of his arm. As the arrow pierced through Sir Grey's upper arm, the king looked to his rear at the approaching men. He said something in Old English to the ancient Shaman, who then raised his other outstretched hand at Ryan and his oncoming companions.

The group of three men were within ten yards of the king when their arms became incredibly heavy, and then their legs began to move in slow motion.

Even the powerful legs of the horse were slowed down as if the group of men and the steed were moving through a thick quicksand of mud and guck.

Before the next shot of his bow, which would plunge an arrow into Sir Grey's opposite leg, 'The Mad King' told the remaining four soldiers to take care of the intruders. The group of soldiers looked at the slowly moving bodies and then began marching toward Ryan, James, and William's location.

Sir Thomas More had been in deep meditation and praying inside the Beauchamp Tower. At the end of his deep invocation, he strode out of the entrance door and up the steps to Tower Green. When he first entered the courtyard of green grasses above him, he noticed the statuesque figures of Sir Grey, with two arrows sticking out of his limbs, and that of Sir Dudley, who was fighting against his invisible bonds, to no avail.

He then looked over at Ryan on the brown horse and the two knights on either side of him, moving at an incredibly slow rate of speed.

The 'Mad King' looked at him with venom in his eyes and said, "So, this is your Holy Man."

King Richard III drew back the string of his bow and shot out an arrow, which went through the small rip in the chain mail and pierced the breastbone of Sir Richard Grey. Sir Grey's body lurched upward and then his head fell to one side and his body fell limp.

Saint Thomas More lowered his head in reverence and sorrow at the sight of his severely wounded compatriot.

He closed his eyes and lowered his head when he heard the king say, "I believe that target is of no use to me anymore. I wonder how badly the other man will squeal out in pain when the arrows pierce his skin."

At these words, Saint More's eyes flew open as he stared up into the night sky. Both arms reached upward, like he was reaching out for the stars. As he did this, storm clouds began to gather above the invisible dome covering the Tower of London.

These storm clouds swirled and boiled in a counterclockwise direction and violently looked as if they were an almost dark green and gold color. He quickly lowered his arms and pointed directly at the ancient shaman standing opposite him. Two sharp, spear-like bursts of bright lightning came down from these clouds and entered either side of the neck of 'The Mad King's' magical shaman.

These bolts of brilliant light stayed on the old man's neck until his arms dropped to his sides and his legs gave out beneath him. His body fell downward, almost as if the dirt of the earth had swallowed him whole.

The smile on the king's face disappeared, and instead, his lips seemed to curl back into an evil sneer. Sir Dudley and Sir Grey's bodies fell onto the grass, where the younger knight immediately crawled over to Sir Grey's side.

Ryan's steed kicked back onto his back legs as if he had just emerged from a drowning pool of mud, and James and William's motions became normal once again.

Ellie checked on Lady Jane one more time and found her confused and slightly light-headed but otherwise in good spirits.

Ellie said to her, "Stay here and hide. Don't come out until the battle is over and your senses have come back to you."

Lady Jane asked about the children, and Ellie said back to her with anger in her voice, "I will get the children back...and... I really want to tear that bitch's eyes out of her head."

The 'Evil Queen' was dragging the tied-up boys at a slow pace and with a great deal of difficulty. They kept whimpering and struggling against the confines of the ropes that they were bound in, causing Anne to constantly stop her progress and give a hard pull on the rope.

She was horribly startled by the two amazing lightning bolts that had struck the ancient magical shaman. Also, she was amazed to see him fall downward and disappear into the earth. Finally, she began to panic when she saw the two knights fall to the ground and the other men regain their normal fighting force.

She had to yell at the King and ask loudly, "Is the circle of protection still working without the magician here?"

The King called back, "Yes, I am still being protected by the potion...no person's or human made weapon can penetrate it. You, however, that is a different story...unless you get those horrid brats over here and return to my side."

This gave the 'Evil Queen' an extra incentive to reach his side, and she gave the rope a massive tug, which almost knocked the boys onto the ground.

After Ryan and the others could move normally, they still had four soldiers to deal with. James yelled out, "William, take the two men on the left, and I will take on the other two soldiers."

Ryan saw the knight duck under the first soldier's mighty swing with an axe. With a quick motion, James then stepped forward and slashed the man's Achilles tendon in the back of his right ankle. The soldier screamed out in pain, and James quickly stuck the dagger in his neck. His screams immediately stopped, and James pulled the older weapon free and turned toward the next soldier.

As if by instinct, he threw the dagger at the next oncoming soldier, who saw it coming and knocked it easily away from him. James was standing there with no weapon, and the soldier would soon be right on top of him. Ryan grabbed the jewel-encrusted sword that James had given to him and threw the original ornate blade up in the air toward James.

Expertly, James grabbed the hilt of the sword and blocked the blow of the second soldier that was coming after him. Using the heavy hilt of the sword, he quickly spun around the soldier and hit him in the back of the head. He then looked back at this fallen man and plunged his broadsword into the back of the neck of the prone man lying on the ground.

Looking on the other side of the horse, Ryan witnessed William avoid a sword blade that came at him low and from the left. He jumped over the blow, and countered with a high arcing blade that came down on the left collarbone of the charging enemy soldier. Blood and bone fragments flew into the air around the man's face, transforming it into a blood-covered, grotesque mask of what is used to be.

The last charging soldier stopped in his tracks, threw his lead tipped spear on the ground, and quickly ran up the steps of the White Tower, never to be seen again.

James smiled at William and said proudly, "I killed both of my assailants; how did you fare, Father?"

William said back, "Son, I would have killed both of mine if the second man hadn't run like a fearful little rabbit."

Ryan then said in admiration, "Father and son knights. It would be so admirable to have such accomplished knights in my own family. You work so well together."

James gave him a knowing little grin and said, "Yes, it is a wonderful feeling. We trust each other. You may admire us, but only one of us was guilty, and that was me. However, we were both beheaded on Tower Hill for treason against the crown in the early 1500s. He taught me how to be a knight. I owe everything to him and so much more."

William then replied to him, "He did turn out to be a fine knight, but his choices in who to fight for in the past...were utter shite. His trust in the lies that people have said to him has been horribly skewed. I must admit he did make a few good choices, and you were one of them, Ryan. Now then, let's go kill this bloody Madman."

Ellie burst through the door of the chapel and began angrily stomping on the ground after Queen Anne. She saw Ellie coming after her with a furious look on her face, and she tried to pull the boys along even faster.

Ellie yelled to the young boys, "Edward... Richard...Slow her down. Push on the ropes in my direction."

The boys did as they were told, and the 'Evil Queen' was severely slowed by the boys' resistance. Ellie kept marching in their direction, and then she stopped abruptly and lifted her crossbow. She took careful aim between the shoulders of the queen with the sights of her crossbow. However, she didn't allow for the breeze that was blowing in her face. This breeze caused the bolt to descend sharply and pierce the muscles of Queen Anne's right butt cheek.

The queen fell forward onto her face with a loud grunting noise. Ellie ran to the tied-up boys, laid down her crossbow, and began working at the knots in the rope. Her hands were shaking with anger as well as fear, which made it incredibly hard to untie the knots in the rope.

Suddenly, she noticed the darkness of a shadow that stood up in front of the glow of the red portal and was coming after her. Queen Anne was limping noticeably harder on her right leg, but she had gotten to her feet, and began staggering back toward Ellie and the boys.

When she had stood up, Queen Anne had reached up to her face and ripped the bandage from her grotesque eye. The redness in her eye had grown worse, and it was now a bright red, pus-filled, tumor on her face. It looked as if there was a smaller version of the red portal placed on her face.

She screeched out a high-pitched scream and ran quicker than expected back at Ellie. Her arms were held out in front of her, and her palms and fingers seemed to drive toward Ellie's throat.

Queen Anne tackled Ellie away from the boys and then sat on top of her while her long, alabaster fingers were gripped tightly around Ellie's windpipe. Ellie was grabbing at the queen's grip, but the 'Evil Queen' continued to shut off any air from reaching Ellie's lungs.

Then a small voice from behind the Queen let out a bellowing order: "Stop, you are killing her. I will strike you down."

Queen Anne turned toward the boys, and pointing directly at her face was Ellie's crossbow. The queen tried to swing her arm at the crossbow, but when she did, young Edward let a bolt fly from a small distance of only a few inches. The point of the arrow was driven into the swollen, bloody eye that was on her face.

She screamed, and her hands came off Ellie's throat and up to her own eye socket. She fell off Ellie sideways and started violently wriggling and thrashing on the grass-filled ground.

Her hands fell away from her face, and the red liquid in her eye started to spray upward in a funnel-like arc. At one point, the thick red liquid shot up to about 5 feet in height. From a distance, her face looked like a cone-shaped piece of fireworks that was shooting out red sparkles.

Ellie looked away from the body of the queen and covered the faces and bodies of the two young children. When the body finally fell silent, Ellie looked at 'The Evil Queen's' last location. Only a large red blob of pus was pooling in the grass and starting to drain toward the red, bubbly portal in the earth. It was as if what had remained was being sucked into it.

Ellie looked at the boys in relief, and she said, "Nice shot, Eddie!"

Young Rich then said sarcastically, "He was only two inches away from her face. I don't think that he could have missed if he tried."

Ellie rubbed Edward's hair and then exclaimed, "To me, that was the best shot that I have ever seen."

Ryan rode up to the "Mad King' with James on one side of him and William on the other. King Richard looked at the trio of men, especially William, and said as if he were unimpressed, "I do not know of this old man...Who be ye?"

With these words, Sir William took offense and said, "I will show you 'old' ye daft prick!"

Sir William had picked up the spear left on the ground by the fleeing soldier and threw it at the king with all his strength. The spear hit the invisible barrier and veered off it to the right nearly 20 yards. Ryan heard Sir William let out the expression, "Bloody Hell!" when it did this.

James, on the other side, started swinging his sword from the left-hand side of his body. He chopped at the invisible force field with the full exertion that his strength and motion could provide.

The impact of the blow knocked James's body backward approximately 10 feet, where he collapsed onto his backside. The sword was reverberating so badly in his hands that he had to drop the weapon onto the ground. William ran back and kneeled at his son's side, leaving only Ryan to face the 'Madman, King Richard III'.

'Mad King Richard' looked up into Ryan's eyes and said, "All that is left is the fearful human. You can't hurt me boy. There is no way that you can do me any harm and there is nothing that you can attack me with. I am invincible to any human weapons."

He then continued saying spitefully, "You know, I am very good at judging people, and you...you have been plagued by fear. I can see it now in your eyes. You are nearly mesmerized by the fear that surrounds you. Run away, human...ride away on the horse, and I will spare your miserable life. If you want the woman who killed Anne...take her and ride out of here. If you do not, I promise you that your fear will be your undoing."

Ryan turned the reins of the horse to the right and faced away from King Richard III. He looked down at James and William and said with a quake in his voice, "I am sorry...He is right. I am afraid."

The two knights looked at Ryan and started to disagree when he raised his hand to quiet them. He looked sorrowful and said forcefully, "I am not the man that I was 20 years ago...I have had so much pain and fear in my life since that time. I am almost struck numb with panic and fear right now. I do know one thing though...."

With a great amount of pain traveling down his gashed bleeding thigh, he pushed out with his feet and pointed his legs in a forward position. He then pulled backward on the reins, causing the horse to start to retreat backwards toward the king.

He stopped the horse and said angrily, "There is a fine line between the look of fear and the anger in another person's eyes. This can also be the look of strength and incredible energy in their eyes."

With these words, his heels kicked back with tremendous force. The pain in his thigh was immense, but the heels of his shoes dug into the stomach of the horse. The horse's eyes went wild, he neighed out a loud, painful cry, and then the horse kicked out with his hind legs.

The horse's back hooves passed through the invisible barrier and contacted the 'Mad King' directly in the face.

The king's nose and mouth were struck by one horse hoof, and the other hammered him in the forehead. This caused his head to almost explode from the force of the blow. It also threw his body backward and into the red, bubbling portal behind him. The red portal seemed to burp out a loud, gushing funnel of liquid ooze when his body entered it.

Ryan smiled down at James and William while saying in a mocking British tone, "No human or man-made object can harm me. How about a pair of horse hooves…you, Royal Dick Bag!"

Ellie finished untying the boys and ran to Ryan, who was trying to painfully dismount off the horse. The horse looked back at Ryan, who scratched his nose and said, "I am really sorry about the kick into your belly."

The horse huffed softly and nuzzled at Ryan's hair. James and William joined Ryan, and with their help, they all walked to the other side of the red portal. Sir Grey was lying on the ground, still badly injured, with Sir Dudley kneeling on one side of him, and Sir Thomas More on the other.

Ryan then said sorrowfully, "Is he going to make it?"

Sir More raised his head and shook it vigorously. The saint then said, "Not in this world anyway."

The boys had been holding onto Ellie's hands when they let go and hugged the limp body of Sir Richard Grey. He looked at them, forced a smile onto his face, and said weakly, "I was put in charge of looking after you boys, and I will always continue to look after you. I made a promise to your mother...and a good knight never breaks his promise."

This utterance was Sir Richard Grey's last words as a bright light encircled him. His body then shot into the air, as if he became one of the stars in the sky looking down on them all.

A female voice then rang out, and they heard it say, "Guildford... Where are you? Please answer me."

Sir Dudley stood up and yelled back, "Jane, I am here, my love."

Lady Jane ran very quickly to them and plunged herself into Sir Dudley's arms. They began kissing madly at each other, until it became quite awkward for the rest of the group.

Sir William cried out, "Oy...We don't need to see you bed her."

Lady Jane pulled herself away from Young Dudley's lips and said with a matter-of-fact tone in her voice, "Well then, if this is all over, why have we not gone anywhere?"

Sir Dudley asked her, without thinking it through, "What do you mean? We are the victors of this battle, aren't we?"

Lady Jane then replied by saying, "If we are the victors, then why is that awful red portal still here? Plus, I do not feel like we are on the winning side of anything yet...Something feels very off."

With these words, the ground below them started to quake, and two more forms started to lift out of the red oozing mist.

"If there is one thing, that's true
It's not what I say, it's what I do
And I say too much, yeah, that's true
So just listen to what I do
A thousand years go by...
But love don't die."
(The Fray)

Chapter Twenty-three

> *"A horse! A horse! My kingdom for a horse!"* (The last words of King Richard III according to the play by William Shakespeare)

The forms of a man and a woman slowly emerged out of the red ooze of the portal. She was loosely holding onto his forearm in a rather formal manner. The forms shimmered, as if throwing off a red coating of paint. Standing before the group of people were two very pale and skinny figures.

The man was extraordinarily thin and tall. He was wearing a long red cloak with a white ermine fur collar on it. He was also wearing a large gold chain around his neck and a golden, bejeweled crown on his head.

The woman was wearing a long, black dress, and she also wore a pure white headdress. This almost looked like an early version of a nun's habit, and it was tightly worn below her skinny chin and then grew wider above the crown of her head.

Her look reminded Ryan and Ellie of an extremely spiritual woman who liked to pretend that she was extremely pious...but in all actuality, had been ostracized by anything that was pure and spiritual in nature. They both had elongated, sharp-looking features, including a thin nose and a slender, weak chin.

They were obviously mother and son, but the mother looked stronger and far more irritated, as if she could bite the head off a puppy. The son looked bored, and his dull, blue eyes looked down at them with contempt. He looked to be far too skinny and sickly, as if he could be tossed about by a stiff wind.

James, the younger knight, looked up at them and said distastefully, "I could go for another 500 years without seeing these two bloody sons-of-whores!"

Ellie looked at him and asked, "Do you know who they are, James?"

James nudged his father's side with his elbow and said spitefully, "My father and I know exactly who they are..."

Sir William squinted his eyes and said loudly, "Is that bleeding King Henry VII and his gash of a mother, Margaret Beaufort?"

He then grabbed James's arm and stated, "Those are the two arseholes that had us publicly beheaded."

Henry Tudor looked at him and said in a snooty sort of way, "Ah, the Tyrrell father and son...Why do you have your heads again and are able to find your mouths with a spoon."

Sir William stepped forward and said, "Finally, someone that I really have a thirst to get rid of."

He was then grabbed by the back of the armor, which held him back from attacking wildly. James let out an audible sigh and said, "Now then, father, I want their bodies thrown to wild pigs, as well. However, I am curious about why they are standing before us."

Henry VII then asked proudly, "You mean, you still haven't figured this out yet, Young Tyrrell? You still do not know who has been pulling the strings all along? Do you even know why you are here in the tower in the first place?"

James looked sorrowfully at the ground and said softly, "Because King Richard III ordered me to foolishly kill these two young boys so that he could become the new King of England. This has been the penance for all my wrongdoings in life...I am here to protect their souls."

James stood taller and then continued by saying, "My soul is probably already lost forever, but it is my intention to make things right by protecting these innocent boys. Richard thought that he could defeat us, but they are going to be cleaning his teeth out of that horse's hooves for quite some time."

King Henry laughed harshly and said, "Do you think that the death of the boys was that dolt's idea? No, not in the least."

He then motioned towards Lady Margaret and said, "He was simply a puppet under the influence of my mother. She came up with the idea of killing the future king and his brother. My mother does not like to take 'no' for an answer. She has even been compared to a ravenous dog who has been thrown a bone...she will not stop speaking about a situation until the other person relents and gives in to her."

Henry gave his mother a rueful smile and then continued to say, "She is quite good at politics and in judging the influence of other people's actions. She just had to dangle the prize of the golden crown in front of Richard's eyes, and he hired you to carry out the crime. I was still in exile in France, so she worked the puppet strings in my absence. When it was time, I then invaded England, and my troops tore poor Richard apart in the Battle of Bosworth Fields."

Henry then looked at his mother, and they both laughed with a petty cackle. She finished the story by saying, "I always knew that my son was going to become king...his destiny just needed a simple push from God. The boys were now out of the way, and after a small tip about Richard's forces, my son could then dispatch him and take over the crown."

Sir Thomas More spoke up then and said confidently, "God does not work in that manner, ma'am. I was your grandson's high advisor, and he wouldn't listen to me about the will of God any more than you will. His only thought was about finding the next home for his hungry pecker, not in the grace of God's blessings. You are nothing but a false priestess who hides behind the power of the Catholic Church. Damn you to hell, woman!"

Margaret turned her head toward Sir More and said, "Ah, God's saint. Forgive me if I do not bow. God spoke directly to me...he told me what I must do."

Saint More spat at her angrily, saying, "The devil also speaks to people. He also enjoys working through these people's actions whenever he can. He was once an angel in God's graces at one time; do not forget that. Your self-pious attitude could very easily have been influenced by God's fallen angel. The God of Love does not speak of killing for one's own gain. Men and women have free will in which to understand these issues spoken to them...But they should also be able to recognize the differences in the messages given to them."

King Henry VII looked bored again and pointedly said, "All right, mother, you will soon get to show Saint More who God likes more between the two of you. Now, may I please finish my story?"

His mother bowed to him and then he continued by saying, "My main reason for being here is to exact my own revenge upon these two boys."

Ryan yelled out the words that all of them were thinking: "Revenge? You bastard, you had them killed."

Henry Tudor raised his hand and pointedly said, "Yes, I had the boys' mortal bodies extinguished, but not their vengeful souls. My oldest and dearest son, Arthur, died suddenly at Ludlow Castle on the English/Welsh border. This is the same castle where the older boy, young Edward, was living when he heard of his father's death. This is also where he discovered that he was to become the new King of England."

Henry then became sorrowful and full of vengeance as he spoke again, saying, "My son died at an early age of fifteen years in 1502, and the physicians said that he died of the sweating disease, but I don't believe that to be true."

Henry looked down at the boys and spitefully said, "One of the last priests who saw my son, on his deathbed, said that he had died because of the fright caused by two young ghostly spirits. These two ruthless boys standing before me were killed in 1483 and tried to invade my dreams before my son was killed by them in 1502. However, I escaped their ire. They couldn't get to me, so they got to him."

Henry wiped away a tear and finished by saying, "My dearest Tyrrell's, I thought that you would have figured this out. I was the first ruler who refused to live in the Royal Apartments at this place where the boys were killed. Then I had you and your father executed. With your deaths, no one else knew how the boys had died. Nobody could ever figure out any of my actions or my mother's intentions."

Ryan spoke to James and said, "In my place and time, that is what is meant by taking care of any loose ends that can come back to incriminate you. Or as I like to call it…Getting rid of any truths that can come back and bite you in the ass!"

James looked at the boys and asked, "Is any of this true? Did you play a part in his son's death, and did you try to attack him from beyond the grave?"

Young Eddie looked guilt-ridden and then said, "Well…Yes...We only made our presence known to King Henry and showed him how displeased we were with him and his actions. When he did not appear to have any soul in which to haunt, we visited his more… believing son."

Young Eddie grabbed his younger brother's hand and then continued to say, "His son, Arthur, believed me when I told him what had happened to us. He also believed in the person who had killed us, and he became weaker each day after that. I personally believe that he did not die because of anything that my brother and I did. He became ill and died out of shame at what his father had done. He could not follow in the footsteps of the man who would ever do these horrid things."

Ryan then asked the boy's, "Did you then try to haunt his brother, King Henry VIII? He took over the throne after this Royal Prick had died."

Young Eddie then said, "We tried to, but he was so consumed in himself and his own pleasures. He simply ignored our very existence. I found his arrogance quite sad, really."

Henry Tudor then said amusingly, "Mother, I do believe Sir Thomas thinks that he is a better Catholic than you. He has been ordained a saint, but you lived a lot of your life like a nun. Even though you were married, you kept yourself chaste and would not even sleep with your own husband in the later years. I am curious: Who does God love more? The Mother of God's Anointed King...or...the Saint?"

Saint More pulled a large gold crucifix from under his long red priestlike cloak, kissed it, and stated calmly, "I have no ill will with which to fight you, madam. You have performed horrid acts of selfishness in the name of the Lord. You can yell out that you have been performing God's will all that you would like, but this is probably your worst sin of all. Your hubris has given you undeserved self-worth."

Saint More stared at her intently and said, "You have only given birth to a man...a man for whom you have sold your very soul. Just so he and you could obtain power and greed, nothing more."

Lady Margaret Beaufort looked at Saint More as if vipers might come out of her eyes. Then she screamed angrily at him, "Do not lecture me on the will of God. If it had not been for God, Henry and the Tudors would never have been crowned kings and queens of Britain. God stands by our side to this day."

With these words, Lady Margaret Beaufort seemed out of control in her anger. She reached to her son's side, pulled his kingly sword out, and charged at Sir Thomas More. The Saint only stood there and opened his arms as if he were going to embrace her. She drove the sword directly into the softness of his sternum, where it traveled through his body and emerged out his back.

A spittle of blood came out of the corner of his mouth, and his last words on this earth were, "Now I see where your grandson's temperament came from."

Lady Margaret then jumped back from the body of the man that her grandson had once executed and raised her bony, long-fingered hands to her face, as if she were ashamed. Saint More then fell to his knees and raised his arms and eyes toward the heavens. Many men had found their final calling that night. Some men were sucked downward in a red, swirling portal, while others had a bright light raise upward and explode into the sky.

However, nobody who ever witnessed Saint More's exit from the courtyard of the Tower of London could ever try to explain what happened next. It was as if the kneeling body of Saint More exploded outward in a brilliant flash of blinding white light.

That brilliant light rose from Sir Thomas More's body well beyond the invisible dome above the Tower buildings. It even traveled through the darkened sky and beyond the stars that were above them. His body slowly rose behind the white light and seemed to disappear into the heavens. All while never dropping his arms or lowering his eyes off the realm above him.

The group of people were still looking up at the vanishing body of Sir Thomas More and shielding their eyes from the spectacular light, when they heard a bow string snapping forward with a reverberating sound.

Suddenly, they heard the voice of Lady Margaret yell out, "No, not my son! You cannot take my son from me again."

Ryan looked at King Henry VII, who was still standing erectly on the red portal. His cold blue eyes still seemed to stare at the group of fighters, only he now had a stream of crimson blood running down the bridge of his slender nose. An arrow was now sticking out of the middle of his forehead.

Lady Margaret ran back up to him again and grasped him around the waist while wailing out, "No... no...no!"

His body turned into the red mist and slowly slipped downward through her grasp and into the portal below. Lady Margaret was left kneeling on the portal while heavily crying into her hands.

At this point, she desperately looked at the ground in all directions. When she saw a dagger lying there, she scrambled toward it and stabbed herself six times in the chest and the stomach. After stabbing herself for the seventh time, she stopped her actions and started clawing at the red portal to gain entry.

From behind the group of people, a strong female voice was heard saying, "Stabbing yourself is considered a mortal sin in your religious beliefs. I don't think that God will have you serve him...nor do I think that Hell wants to deal with you either. Margaret, you will have no home except for this prison from now on."

The person with the female voice seemed pleased with herself, and she continued to say, "I think that you may be trapped in this realm forever, Lady Margaret. You will be left without your beloved son to keep you company. Plus, besides being left behind, I think that you will be left with a huge amount of pain in your chest. This was done by your own hand, and you have nobody else to blame this on. Go now; you will never be wanted or needed again."

With these mysterious words, Lady Margaret Beaufort's body simply shimmered and disappeared from view.

Standing behind them was a radiantly beautiful woman with long blond hair pulled back in a ponytail hairdo. She looked strong and defiant, even though she was dressed in a demure white summer dress that was clasped at the waist by a pure white belt.

The only thing that she wore that wasn't white was a bright pink sweater that she wore loosely over her shoulders. She also had a bow in one hand and a quiver of arrows hanging on her back. In all actuality, she looked like a true warrior princess.

She gave them all a magnificent smile and was greeted by one name spoken at the same time by both Sir James and Ryan, "Karen!"

Ryan immediately looked at James in confusion and then looked back at the vision of Karen, demanding an answer with his eyes. Ellie was only looking at the ground while supporting Ryan with his arm around her shoulder and biting at her lip in dismay.

Karen then waved nervously at them and said, "Hello, everyone. I know that I have a lot of hard questions to answer, and I will try to get to all of them. However, first, could we all move away from that ominous, red portal...I think that it should now be destroyed."

The small group of people that were left included Ryan, Ellie, the young boys, Sir Dudley, Lady Jane, James the Knight, and his father Sir William. They moved a safe distance further into the courtyard and sat on the cool grass.

Karen then raised her hands into the air, much like Sir More had done earlier, and she seemed to call upon the storms in the sky and the electricity in the atmosphere. This time, however, four lightning bolts came crashing down from every direction on the globe.

The lightning bolts came down from the north, south, east, and west. Additionally, a strong wind blew directly downward in between the bolts of electricity. This caused such a supreme force of air that it shattered the glass memorial into a thousand pieces across the surrounding area.

This violent wind also broke out more glass windows in the Beauchamp Tower, as well as on the west side of the White Tower. The hair on people's arms stood up with the electricity that was in the air and the wind blew wildly around the people's heads.

Karen then turned back to the very interested members of the group that were staring up at her with their jaws laying open in astonishment.

She slapped her hands together, as if she had just finished doing an extremely hard job. Then she cleared her throat and said, "First, this may be awkward for several of us, so I am just going to be direct with each of you... Ryan, I am going to start with you."

Karen then shuffled her feet as if she were nervous and continued to say to Ryan, "You truly were the first love of my life, and I tried to be as truthful with you as I could be. As it turned out, I was probably too truthful with you. I just didn't want to let you go, and I caused you a massive amount of pain and sorrow when I did this. I am sorry. You see, I knew that I was going to die young. I was told by my...well... I can only call them 'My Special Angels'.

She then continued to say, "I was shocked and amazed when I found out that you could see them as well. I didn't think that this was possible, but miraculously you could. Additionally, you believed in me...and leaving you is still the second-sorriest thing that I have ever done."

Karen furrowed her brow and then continued, "You see, my 'Special Angels' in this strange metaphysical world... the ones that you could see... were in fact past members of my family. It is mostly parents or grandparents that come to us when we need the most help, but instead, I was helped by an aunt and a cousin who were both killed in WWII."

Karen had to stop suddenly, as she had started to sob silently. She then rubbed the tears from her eyes and said, "This still sounds kind of crazy when I say it out loud."

She then took a deep breath and asked Ryan brutally honestly, "There is quite a bit more that I have got to explain to you that you may not like to know. Do you want to truly hear all of this?"

Ryan looked confused, but smiled and replied, "You are asking me if I want to finally know the truth that intertwines all of us...especially with what we all just went through? This whole situation is like a Shakespearean tragedy that is unfolding right before me. Damn straight, I want to know."

Karen smiled at him warmly and said, "Maybe a tragedy, maybe a comedy...Just hold on to something; this is going to be a really topsy-turvy, rollercoaster of a ride."

Karen took another deep breath and then continued by saying, "Ryan, I was not always honest when we first met. I tried to tell you these things 20 years ago, but you always looked at me with those doe-like eyes. You believed that I could do no wrong, so I always chickened out."

Karen then smiled down at him and truthfully said, "When I first met you, I had given birth to a daughter two years before then. I was 15 when I had her, and my parents tried to raise a teenager and a newborn at the same time. She was two years old when I went on the musical tour and first met you."

Karen's eyes began to glisten with tears, and Ryan tried to go to her, but his leg would not allow it. He collapsed back into the grass and knew that he would need help getting to his feet.

Karen saw this, gave Ryan a worried look, and bravely continued, "I said that losing you was the second most sorrowful thing that ever happened to me. Unfortunately, she is absolutely the most excruciating thing that I have ever lost. No offense, but she was the best thing to ever come into my life."

Karen looked very concerned, but continued by stating, "After the tour, I had five more wonderful years with my daughter...and… every single day of being with her was a blessing to me. However, it ended way too soon, like some of the best things often do. She unfortunately witnessed me get run down by a car driven by a teenage girl who was playing with her new phone. My last thoughts while lying on the pavement were of you...and of my sweet daughter, Elizabeth."

Ryan's eyes flew open widely and he heard Ellie say in a quaking voice, "Hi, Mommy!"

Karen looked at Ryan and then asked him, "Are you going to be all right? You look rather pale."

Ryan thought quietly about his answer and then said slowly, "I... truly...don't know. I mean, you and I were never intimate, so I know that she is not my daughter...But I still feel like I am living in an almost backwards, Oedipus-like situation."

Karen walked up to Ryan and said, "Do not worry; I am very pleased by you being together. That is why I have been leading my daughter's pathway toward you."

Ellie jumped into the conversation and then cried out in a shocked voice, "Mother, what the hell? Ryan, I swear, I am in as much non-understanding of this as you are. I had no idea that any of this was happening."

Ellie let out a discouraged sigh and then said, "Mom...I love you dearly, and I have always felt like you were guiding me in some way, but this all seems like it is too much. You were leading me to Ryan? Forgive me for being so angry, but what else have you done to try and control my life?"

Karen looked affectionately at her daughter and said, "I haven't tried to control your life. I only showed you a path that led you to a man that I knew would treat you extremely well and would love you dearly. It was your choice to go down this path with Ryan."

Karen kneeled in front of her daughter, ran her fingers through Ellie's hair, and said, "What I do know is that I left a deep scar in you. I knew that my time with you was short, but I did not know when it would happen. You must know that my dying violently in front of you was never known to me."

Karen continued to tenderly speak to her daughter by saying, "With you being a witness to all this violence, it had to be just terrible on you. I watched you go through many changes throughout the years. I wasn't proud of all your choices, but I can't blame you for any of them. I have only wanted what is best for you, and I am also extremely proud of the person that you have become."

Karen glanced nervously at James and then continued, "I knew Ryan...and I knew what a good man he is. I couldn't wish your or his happiness on any other person. I found out about the reunion coming up, and when an invitation arrived for me to attend in London, I nudged you to travel to it."

Karen then grew very nervous and said, "Now then, I have one more big surprise for the two of you. Ryan was also nudged into coming here by one of his great-grandfathers from his own family history. This is a person who could hopefully convince Ryan to fight with us. He just happened to be a 15th century knight named, James Tyrrell."

Ryan then blurted out, "James? I am a descendant of James the Knight?"

James placed a hand on his shoulder and stated truthfully, "Yes, William and I are both your great-grandfathers from hundreds of years ago. Karen made it known to us that we could make physical contact with you. She had witnessed this unusual power that you have of being able to connect with spirits. We can usually help one of our ancestors throughout life. That is if we choose to become involved."

James stopped speaking to try and find the right words, and then said, "However, it is very rare for a deceased person to be seen. It is extremely uncommon for this to happen. Through Karen and me, we were successful in bringing you and Ellie together in order to find each other…and to also help us."

Ryan then stopped him and said to James, "Wait...Wait...Wait! You and Karen worked together on all of this? How in the world did you get to be near one another?"

James gripped his shoulder with a tighter squeeze of his hand, and then he explained, "My father, William, and I died at nearly the same time, and we found ourselves away from the city of London.

William burst into the conversation by saying, "We were not even in the English countryside for that matter. We discovered a small stone house next to a stream in some random forested mountains, somehow.

James gave his father a stern look and continued, "There was a tranquil stream flowing below our house, and in this stream, there was a pool of fresh water below a small waterfall. Food was plentiful in the forests that surrounded us, and we had fresh water and a good place to fish in the stream. It was as if we had been transported to an idyllic place of peace."

James then looked at Karen and continued to tell the story: "One day, a woman showed up next to the pond by our home. We began speaking, and she taught us to speak the way that you do today. When a person is surrounded by it, they tend to learn the language that is spoken around them the most."

James then looked nervously at Ryan and stated, "After several years, Karen and I fell in love with each other but never touched one another. When we first tried to embrace and kiss, we were denied by an invisible shield around each of us. This was maddening to us, but we learned that each of us had to make amends for mistakes that we made in our earthly lives. The largest misdeed that I ever made is in what happened to the boys, Young Edward and Richard, and I had to try and help them.

Karen then broke into the conversation and said, "My reason, as it turned out, was to help you and Ellie. I could not get past the pain I had caused both of you. I could see that both of your lives could use some guidance, and I knew what my mission would be."

Ryan then said aloud, "Funny... my dream of a place in heaven is just how you described it... a small stone house next to a stream with a pond below a small waterfall. Except in my perfect place, this pond is heated as if fed by warm springs."

Karen looked at him lovingly and said, "It is a rather warm pond. You told me about this place when we were in Europe together, twenty years ago. I loved how you explained its beauty, tranquility, and how serene this place would be. I thought of it often and was transported there, as well."

Karen raised her shoulders with a shrug and said, "I never thought that two mid-century knights would already occupy this place, but they made for good company. Yes, all of us are trespassing in your special heavenly place. Do not worry, though; the home expands if any other person ever joins us. You created a place of utter perfection where anyone who wants to join us has ample room. There is one problem that we have had, though...James, could you join me and see if we can now feel each other's touch?"

James stood and walked toward Karen slowly. Karen looked into his eyes and tentatively held up her right hand. He lovingly smiled down at her and reached up with his left hand. They touched their palms at that instant and then intertwined their fingers together. Karen let out a sobbing cry and kissed the back of his hand.

She continued crying joyful tears, and she simply said, "It really worked!"

James then took her head in his hands, kissed her passionately on the lips, and cradled her in his arms that were wrapped tenderly around her.

James looked over at Ryan while still holding onto the love of his life, and he mouthed quietly, "Thank you, Grandson."

At this point, Ryan reached over and took Ellie's hand in his uninjured palm and curled her fingers in his. He looked over at her and saw a solitary tear roll down her cheek.

James let Karen out of his embrace and kissed her gently one more time before Lady Jane Grey broke the silence by asking, "We now know why you are all here, but what about Lord Guildford, myself, and the boys?"

Karen let out a relieved laugh and said, "Edward and Richard… Boys, we did most of this not only to help you find peace but possibly for you to find a family as well. Would you like to come back and live with us?"

The boys both smiled widely, and they ran to James and Karen, where they had arms immediately wrapped around both of their shoulders.

Karen then looked at the two married teens, Lady Jane and Sir Dudley, and she said, "To be quite honest with you, Jane, saving you and Sir Dudley was just a happy little miracle that happened to all of us. We didn't intend to meet either of you, but we must have been destined to do so. I guess that we are now part of one big interdimensional family. Like I said, the house where we all live expands to fit all our needs, and you are more than welcome to live there as well. Would you like to join us?"

Lady Jane and Sir Dudley jumped up quickly and joined the others in the small circle. Ryan and Ellie suddenly seemed horribly alone, as they were the only two people left sitting on the grass.

Karen looked at them and said with passion and honesty in her voice, "One of the best people on the planet... along with my daughter, the best thing that I ever produced and the greatest love of all time... Together!"

Karen gave them a warm smile and finished by saying, "Now then, enjoy your lives together, and if you ever have any differences, remember that we will always be watching.... but, most importantly.... you will never be alone."

Karen blew a kiss at them, and the boys waved with renewed happiness. All their bodies began to shimmer slowly, and then the vibrating grew at a faster pace until they all disappeared. Ellie looked over at Ryan with love and tiredness in her eyes.

She then leaned closer and gave Ryan a deep kiss on the lips and then on the neck. They both grew increasingly weary and fell back onto the grass inside the Tower of London. Both of their eyes felt as if they suddenly weighed a ton, and they both fell fast asleep.

When they awakened and could open their eyes again, the sun was rising under the spans of Tower Bridge to the east of them. They were still lying in the grass, only outside the walls of the Tower of London. A huge amount of noise could be heard, and there seemed to be a lot of commotion happening inside the grounds.

Ellie then turned to Ryan and asked solemnly, "Did last night truly happen, or did we just dream all of this?"

Ryan sat up and tried to open his left hand, only to be met by a hand that he could not open and a tremendous pain running up his arm. He then felt at his thigh with his right hand, and it came away with a bloody stain on it.

After seeing the blood on his hand, Ryan gasped out in pain and said, "Either it really happened just the way that we remember it, or you are one hell of a restless sleeper."

That evening, Ryan was lying in a hospital bed in one of London's many hospitals. Ellie sat in a chair, holding onto his unbroken right hand and they were very interested in what was coming across the television screen.

The doctor then asked again, "How did this happen, Mr. Maxwell?"

Ryan and Ellie only continued to watch the television, which was talking about an unprecedented occurrence of a rare weather condition called a 'microburst' that had happened. This weather phenomenon came down directly onto the glass memorial inside the Tower of London, which knocked out several windows and caused other damages to several towers. Ryan then looked over at Ellie and gave her a small grin and a slight wink.

"First thing: we make you feel better
Next stop: we pull it all together
I'll keep you warm like a sweater
Take my hand, hold on forever..."
(Rob Thomas)

Epilogue

"If you don't know history, you don't know anything. You are a leaf that doesn't know it is part of a tree." (Michael Crichton)

The car pulled up in front of the Church of the Austin Friars, which is in a neighborhood of northern London. The black door of the car opened, and the first thing to touch the sidewalk was the tip of a silver-handled, highly ordained cane. Ryan now had to use this cane in order to help him walk with any steadiness.

The surgeon had found a cut tendon in Ryan's left thigh, which had caused damage to the strength of the muscles. He would need several weeks or even years of physical therapy in order to make it strong again. In any case, Ryan would always have a limp in his left leg from now on.

He also had a cast covering his left hand, which had been surgically repaired. It would eventually heal with the help of several small metal pins and synthetic tissues and tendons placed inside of it.

He liked to now call it 'His Bionic Cyborg Claw.' Ryan had been finally cleared to leave the hospital, and after some research, he and Ellie hailed a lorry and made one stop before coming to the Chapel of the Austin Friars.

The church reminded both Ryan and Ellie of a building that should be in the Tower of London. Mainly because it was a large building that was made of ancient white stones that exuded the history of the British country. There was a dim glow throughout the chapel, as most of the light in the building was caused by candlelight and the sun's rays coming through the stained-glass windows.

They both gasped at the number of the tombs located in this place, as it was a favored location as a burial place for many knights, ministers, and other important members of English history. Most of whom had been executed by beheading at Tower Hill, just outside the walls of the famous prison.

Ryan looked around for nearly 10 minutes, and then he had to sit down in the back of the chapel. At this time, that was about the limit for Ryan to be able to stand on his leg, but Ellie kept searching around the inside of the chapel. There were very few people in the chapel that day, and Ryan could keep track of Ellie by the sounds of her footsteps on the hard tile floor.

Suddenly, the sounds of her footsteps stopped, and Ryan heard a small sob, followed by Ellie's voice saying, "I found it. It's over here."

Ryan stood up with the help of his silver-handled cane and walked toward Ellie's voice. She was sitting on a pew that was in front of a memorial dedicated to many men whose bones were buried nearby.

The one place where they had to stop on the way to the chapel was a florist so that Ellie could buy a bouquet of daisies, her favorite flower. When Ryan arrived at the tombs, she stepped forward and placed the daisies on the memorial, and then sat back into the pew. Ryan laid down next to her and placed his head in her lap.

She began brushing her fingers through his hair and read aloud the engraving on the memorial stone:

"Sir James Tyrrell—B: ca 1455-—-D: 6 May 1502—Knt,
Beheaded for Treason Against King Henry VII"

Ellie shook her head and then continued by saying, "Do you think that this is the way that history will always remember him?"

Ryan answered her quickly and said, "Unfortunately, yes. However, he started out with very few people believing in him. Now, he has a beautiful new bride, two very good friends, and two children who also believe in him.

Ellie emphatically said, "Don't forget about Sir William; he has never left his side or stopped believing in him."

Ryan grabbed her hand, kissed it, and continued to say, "Time can be incredibly fickle. Great men were often cocky assholes, or great women were often hard-natured bitches… but they are still remembered to this day. Most of the god-fearing, more passive, and caring individuals seem to get lost in time. James was lucky enough to find out how to perform in the most pious way possible and do the right thing. He was eventually rewarded for it. Most people are never so lucky."

Ellie then asked, "How do you know that what you are doing is the right thing?"

Ryan pulled her head down to his, kissed her gently on the mouth, and then said, "Follow your gut... and… make other people proud of your actions!"

Ellie leaned back in the pew again, chuckled softly, and then said, "I hope that we can work together from now on. You know, historian and anthropologist working on the same projects. It sounds lovely to me."

Ryan looked up at her and said, "You mean I find 'em and you study 'em. It sounds like a great idea. What should our first project be about?"

She smiled and said, "Right now, whatever would pay the bills and pay back Monty's estate. However, now that you mention it, I noticed a lot of these knights' tombs are unstudied and forgotten. I think that many of them were even Templar Knights...isn't that what a red cross on their shields and their tunics is supposed to mean?"

Ryan looked very surprised and said, "Very good. You know, there is a lot of interest just starting that the Templar Knights had a lot to do with the organization of the Masonic Temple. Maybe we should work together on this subject...After some time off. of course."

Ellie thought about his response and then asked Ryan curiously, "How are your panic attacks? We are taking off for America tomorrow. Do you want to go out on the town tonight and then bring home a bottle tonight? It may help you with your fears."

Ryan shook his head in a 'no' motion and then answered her by saying, "I don't think that I need to have any drinks anymore. I have found something else to calm my nerves. How about you? Do you want to have some wine or anything?"

Ellie also shook her head and then stated, "You talked about taking some time off; I think nine months to a year ought to do the trick for me. I am not sure...but...I have a strong feeling that I shouldn't have any alcohol."

Ryan sat up from lying on her lap, looked her in the eyes, and asked excitedly, "Really?"

Ellie bit her lip and shook her head up and down while saying, "I think so. I don't know for a fact, but I feel positive about it."

Ryan smiled broadly and joyfully replied, "I think that I will start writing about history again and be there to cater for your every need. What do we name her if she is a girl?"

Ellie smiled and said, "I thought about it; I would name a daughter KJ...Karen Jane. What do we name him if it is a boy?"

Ryan smiled back at her and answered quickly, "I would name him Monty James, or MJ, for short."

Ryan then raised his good arm and wiped a single tear from her cheek. She smiled and said to him, "I think that those names sound just perfect."

"*...You are the strength,*
That keeps me walking.
You are the hope,
That keeps me trusting.
You are the light, to my soul.
You are my purpose,
You're everything!"
(Lifehouse)

Printed in the USA
CPSIA information can be obtained
at www.ICGtesting.com
CBHW072122120724
11509CB00025B/706

9 798887 291543

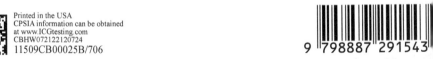